KEYS FROM THE GOLDEN VAULT™

CREDITS

Project Leads: Amanda Hamon, Christopher Perkins

Art Director: Kate Irwin

Project Concept: Dan Barrett

Writers: Justice Ramin Arman, Kate Baker, Makenzie De Armas, Dan Dillon, Brooks Donohue, Amanda Hamon, Tim Hitchcock, Sadie Lowry, Jeffrey Ludwig, Sarah Madsen, Mario Ortegón, Christopher Perkins, Ben Petrisor, T. Alexander Stangroom

Rules Developers: Jeremy Crawford, Dan Dillon, Ben Petrisor

Editors: Judy Bauer, Eytan Bernstein, Janica Carter, Laura Hirsbrunner, Gregg Luben, Kim Mohan, Adrian Ng

Lead Graphic Designer: Bob Jordan

Graphic Designers: Trystan Falcone, Paolo Vacala, Trish Yochum

Cover Illustrators: Simen Meyer, Anna Podedworna

Interior Illustrators: Olivier Bernard, Bruce Brenneise, Kai Carpenter, Sidharth Chaturvedi, Conceptopolis, CoupleOfKooks, Daarken, Alayna Danner, Kent Davis, Nikki Dawes, Axel Defois, Evyn Fong, Alexandre Honoré, Julian Kok, Katerina Ladon, Andrew Mar, Robson Michel, Scott Murphy, David Auden Nash, Irina Nordsol, Svetlin Velinov, Zuzanna Wuzyk, Kieran Yanner

Cartographers: Francesca Baerald, Mike Schley

Consultants: Ma'at Crook, James Mendez Hodes

Concept Illustrator: Shawn Wood

Project Engineer: Cynda Callaway

Imaging Technicians: Daniel Corona, Kevin Yee

Prepress Specialist: Jefferson Dunlap

D&D STUDIO

Executive Producer: Kyle Brink

Game Architects: Jeremy Crawford, Christopher Perkins

Studio Art Director: Josh Herman

Art Department: Matt Cole, Trystan Falcone, Bree Heiss, Kate Irwin, Bob Jordan, Emi Tanji, Trish Yochum

Design Department: Justice Ramin Arman, Makenzie De Armas, Dan Dillon, Amanda Hamon, Ron Lundeen, Ben Petrisor, Patrick Renie, F. Wesley Schneider, Carl Sibley, Jason Tondro, James Wyatt

Managing Editor: Judy Bauer

Editorial Department: Eytan Bernstein, Janica Carter, Adrian Ng

Senior Producer: Dan Tovar

Producers: Bill Benham, Robert Hawkey, Andy Smith, Gabe Waluconis

Director of Product Management: Liz Schuh

Product Managers: Natalie Egan, Chris Lindsay, Hilary Ross, Chris Tulach

ON THE COVER

Daring thieves infiltrate a conservatory to steal a magical instrument, unaware of the evil that awaits them. Illustrator Anna Podedworna gives us a glimpse of the danger.

ON THE ALT-COVER

The Golden Vault is your gateway to adventure. Simen Meyer shows us the door to this vault, but not the treasure within. That you must discover for yourself!

620D2429000001 EN
ISBN: 978-0-7869-6896-1
First Printing: February 2023

987654321

Tell us what you think of *Keys from the Golden Vault.* Take our survey here!

Printed in the USA. ©2023 Wizards of the Coast LLC, PO Box 707, Renton, WA 98057-0707, USA. Manufactured by: Hasbro SA, Rue Emile-Boéchat 31, 2800 Delémont. CH. Represented by: Hasbro, De Entree 240, 1101 EE Amsterdam, NL. Hasbro UK Ltd., P.O. Box 43 Newport, NP19 4YH, UK.
Jeu en anglais. Contenu: 1. FABRIQUÉ EN USA

CONTENTS

A rogue rappels down the icy walls of Revel's End, a prison in the frozen north.

A COLLECTION OF HEISTS

KEYS FROM THE GOLDEN VAULT PRESENTS thirteen DUNGEONS & DRAGONS adventures that feature heists. In each adventure, the characters receive a mission, plan the job, execute their plan, and try to escape the scene. You can run each heist as a standalone adventure or as part of a larger campaign (see "A Campaign of Heists" later in this introduction). Each adventure can be adapted to take place in any campaign setting you wish.

USING THE ADVENTURES

The Heist Adventures table summarizes the adventures in this anthology. Each adventure is designed for four to six characters of a particular level and adheres to the following narrative structure:

Mission Briefing. The characters are recruited to undertake a specific job. In most cases, this involves procuring an object.

Plan the Heist. The characters investigate the heist location, learn about the obstacles they need to overcome, and strategize about completing the job. Each adventure includes a way for the characters to create or obtain a map of the target location.

Execute the Heist. The characters enact their plans. Unforeseen complications often arise during this stage.

Conclude the Heist. The characters' success determines their reward and how the story might progress beyond the main adventure.

These short adventures work best with players who enjoy the heist genre. In addition to thrills, drama, strategizing, and twists, each adventure includes opportunities for exploration, roleplaying, and combat.

RUNNING THE ADVENTURES

To run these adventures, you need the fifth edition core rulebooks (*Player's Handbook*, *Dungeon Master's Guide*, and *Monster Manual*).

> Text that appears in a box like this is meant to be read aloud or paraphrased for the players when their characters first arrive at a location or under a specific circumstance, as described in the text.

When a creature's name appears in **bold** type, that's a visual cue pointing you to its stat block as a way of saying, "Hey, DM, get this creature's stat block ready. You're going to need it." If the stat block appears elsewhere, the text tells you so; otherwise, you can find the stat block in the *Monster Manual*.

Spells and equipment mentioned in the adventure are described in the *Player's Handbook*. Magic items are described in the *Dungeon Master's Guide* unless the adventure's text directs you to an item's description elsewhere.

CREATING A HEIST CREW

This book's adventures require the characters to practice teamwork. Encourage your players to think of their characters as longtime associates or perhaps relatives so they feel tight-knit from the start.

Similarly, ask your players to consider creating characters suited to undertaking heists. Combat prowess is less important when sneaking through a guarded complex, for example, whereas stealth, skill with locks, social skills, clever problem-solving, and versatile character abilities will shine.

Well-outfitted characters are also more likely to succeed at these adventures. Equipment such as thieves' tools, rope, and a grappling hook might mean the difference between taking a shortcut to the objective and getting caught.

Characters can accomplish these adventures' missions in multiple ways. As the Dungeon Master, reward creative thinking!

A CAMPAIGN OF HEISTS

You can combine the adventures in this book to form a campaign. Each adventure would be an episode in the campaign, with you filling in the details of the characters' stories between jobs.

If you go this route, encourage the players to create a crack team and a base of operations, a supporting cast of allies, and other hallmarks of a heist crew. Have your group decide on these details before play begins so the adventures progress seamlessly.

To ensure the characters are always prepared for their next heist, make sure their level matches the heist's level, as shown in the Heist Adventures table. For example, the characters should be 2nd level before undertaking "The Stygian Gambit."

Adventure	Level	Description
The Murkmire Malevolence	1	Retrieve a mysterious egg ensconced in a museum to avert disaster.
The Stygian Gambit	2	Rob a Nine Hells–themed casino built with stolen money.
Reach for the Stars	3	Search for *The Celestial Codex* in a mansion warped by the Far Realm.
Prisoner 13	4	Obtain the key to a vault from a spymaster imprisoned in Revel's End.
Tockworth's Clockworks	5	Liberate a svirfneblin town besieged by clockwork automatons.
Masterpiece Imbroglio	5	Infiltrate a thieves' guild to retrieve a stolen painting.
Axe from the Grave	6	Recover a stolen mandolin to lay a dead bard's spirit to rest.
Vidorant's Vault	7	Retrieve a stolen diadem from the vault of a notorious thief.
Shard of the Accursed	8	Use a magical shard to mend a giant's broken heart and save a town from destruction.
Heart of Ashes	8	Retrieve a king's heart to save his kingdom from a terrible fate.
Affair on the Concordant Express	9	Obtain information from a stranger traveling aboard an interplanar train.
Party at Paliset Hall	10	Snatch a diamond from an archmage in the Feywild.
Fire and Darkness	11	Wrest the *Book of Vile Darkness* from an efreeti and his lackeys.

THE GOLDEN VAULT

A heist crew might have a patron organization that hires the characters to undertake these adventures. If you wish to use such an organization, consider the Golden Vault.

Rumored to be associated with metallic dragons, the Golden Vault is a secretive organization that has its base on one of the good-aligned Outer Planes. Its membership and activities are almost impossible for outsiders to track, but those in the know are aware that the organization rights moral wrongs, supports virtuous underdogs, and handles delicate situations local authorities won't touch. The Golden Vault's motto reflects its primary motivation: "Do good, no matter the cost." Missions from the Golden Vault are often illegal, but they always support a just, moral cause.

The Golden Vault's undercover operatives monitor adventuring groups from major cities on the Material Plane. An operative might be a priest, a scholar, a charity worker, a government liaison, a philanthropist, or any other upstanding local.

Once an adventuring group proves itself effective and virtuous, an operative approaches the characters to offer Golden Vault membership. Should the group accept, its members join the ranks of the Golden Vault, and the person who invited them becomes their handler for future missions. For an example of a handler, see the "Meera Raheer" section.

If the characters get stuck, the Golden Vault can provide unexpected help. For instance, if the characters lack vital information needed for a heist, their handler might share a recent discovery. If the characters need special equipment, their handler might be able to obtain it for them, provided the equipment is readily available and not too expensive.

If you decide to use the Golden Vault as the characters' patron organization, work with the players to determine what heroic or impressive deeds their characters performed in their backstories to gain the attention of the Golden Vault. Then improvise a roleplaying scene in which the characters meet their Golden Vault handler.

KEYS FROM THE GOLDEN VAULT

If the characters become Golden Vault operatives, they receive an ornate, key-operated music box from their handler. Each adventure in this book includes a "Using the Golden Vault" section, in which the Golden Vault dispatches a golden key to the group, usually via a hired courier. When the golden key is inserted into the characters' music box and turned, the box pops open and plays a message that assigns them a heist, provides basic details, and sets them on the right path. After the message plays, the box closes and the key vanishes.

HEROES IN THE SHADOWS

Secrecy is paramount for the Golden Vault. To protect the organization, the characters' handler never provides more information than is absolutely necessary. Similarly, Golden Vault operatives are aware of only a handful of their fellow members. This compartmentalization ensures no one individual knows enough to jeopardize the organization at large.

MEERA RAHEER

fighting against government corruption, and Meera has followed in her parents' footsteps, continuing their anti-corruption work by becoming a city's clerk and a member of the Golden Vault.

Meera lives and breathes city protocols, procedures, and statutes. She also understands that sometimes doing the right thing means operating outside the law.

HEIST COMPLICATIONS

Unforeseen complications are an iconic aspect of heist narratives. Whether they take the form of a rival crew appearing out of nowhere or a treasure that turns out to be fake, complications ratchet up the tension and require the characters to think on their feet.

If you want to challenge your players, consider adding one of the complications below to any of this book's adventures.

THE MOVING MACGUFFIN

Many of this book's heists involve procuring a MacGuffin. Part of preparing for these heists is determining where the MacGuffin in question is located.

If the characters are having too easy of a time finding the MacGuffin, consider shifting its location to another place that makes sense. Or consider revealing that the MacGuffin is a fake, and the real prize is still nearby. The characters should still be able to determine where it's really located.

For example, in "The Murkmire Malevolence," perhaps the MacGuffin is no longer in the Gemstone Wing and is being stored in the museum's attic overnight. The characters could learn this detail by reading notes they discover in the curator's office or by questioning one of the museum guards.

If you use the moving MacGuffin complication, be careful of moving the MacGuffin more than once. Having trouble locating the object of the heist could unduly frustrate your players.

RIVAL CREW

A rival crew vying for the same goal can increase the pressure on the characters. Regardless of your players' goal, once another crew appears, the adventure becomes a race to accomplish the objective first.

You can add a rival crew to an adventure at any time. When you do, make it clear to the characters that they have competition. The characters might see evidence of their rivals, such as an alarm that has already been disabled or an incapacitated guard. At some point, the characters might even catch their rivals trying to steal the adventure's MacGuffin from right under their noses!

Should operatives be caught breaking the law while serving the Golden Vault, the organization does its best to protect them. It may pull strings to ensure members aren't incarcerated—or worse—depending on the organization's resources in the area.

MEERA RAHEER

Meera Raheer (lawful good, human **commoner**) is a Golden Vault handler you can assign to oversee your players' heist crew.

When Meera was young, her kindhearted and upstanding mothers served as city clerks. But when they began investigating financial irregularities, the unscrupulous mayor framed them for embezzlement to cover his own corruption. The only evidence of the Raheers' innocence was a packet of letters between the mayor and his conspirators. The letters were locked in the mayor's office.

Luckily for the Raheers, a crew of Golden Vault operatives infiltrated city hall, retrieved the letters, and revealed the mayor's crimes. The Raheers kept

The rival crew could include some or all of the following members:

Arlo Kettletoe (neutral halfling) is abrupt and direct with their compatriots. Arlo loves puns and wordplay.

Enna "The Silence" Galakiir (neutral elf) is an intimidating, stealthy woman who rarely speaks; when she does, her voice is a quiet hiss.

Gregir Fendelsohn (lawful neutral human) is loyal and passionate. He insists on the crew getting paid no matter what.

Sabrina "Kill More" Kilgore (chaotic neutral human) is a brash, violent woman who loves thrills and sweets.

Torgja Stonecrusher (chaotic neutral dwarf) has a jovial, happy-go-lucky nature that belies her ruthlessness.

Tosh Starling (neutral orc) is loquacious but always focused on his objective. He takes pride in his meticulously groomed appearance.

If a fight breaks out between the characters and a rival crew, use stat blocks for the rivals that are appropriate for the adventure's level, as indicated in the Rival Crew Statistics table. The stat blocks can be found in the *Monster Manual*.

RIVAL CREW STATISTICS

Rival	Levels 1–4 Stat Blocks	Levels 5–8 Stat Blocks	Levels 9–11 Stat Blocks
Arlo	Bandit captain	Knight	Mage
Enna	Bandit	Spy	Assassin
Gregir	Bandit	Thug	Veteran
Sabrina	Bandit	Thug	Veteran
Torgja	Bandit	Thug	Veteran
Tosh	Scout	Spy	Veteran

RIVAL CREW IN PLAY

Decide whether the rival crew is ahead of or behind the characters in pursuit of the objective. If either would make sense for your game, roll a d20. On an even result, the rivals are closer to achieving the objective than the characters. On an odd result, the rivals are nipping at the characters' heels.

Pay attention to how the characters respond to their rivals' presence. If the characters take pains to thwart trailing rivals or catch leading rivals, the characters should achieve their objective without further complication. If the characters ignore the rival crew, the rivals should achieve the objective first. Then it's up to the characters to chase their rivals and try to salvage the mission.

Always give the characters the opportunity to confront rivals who have achieved the objective first. This might lead to a negotiation scene or a fight.

RIVAL CREW MOTIVATIONS

A rival crew might pursue the characters' objective for a variety of reasons. Greed might motivate rivals to steal a valuable objective, or they might have deep emotional involvement in the story.

A rival crew might be working at the behest of a patron. Perhaps an evil guild leader has hired the rivals to steal the MacGuffin. If the characters aren't working for the Golden Vault, perhaps the rivals are—and they might try to recruit the characters to their cause.

The Rival Crew Motivations table provides hooks for how a rival crew might become involved in each of this book's adventures.

GOLDEN VAULT SEAL

RIVAL CREW MOTIVATIONS

Adventure	Rival Crew's Motivation
The Murkmire Malevolence	Museum curator Alda Arkin hires the rivals to steal the Murkmire Stone, a curiosity she knows would fetch a high price on the black market.
The Stygian Gambit	Regor Falsain (neutral evil, human **noble**), a gambler who wasn't invited to participate in the three-dragon ante tournament, hires the rivals to steal the erinyes statuette.
Reach for the Stars	Yexanthal (chaotic evil, elf **cult fanatic**) was one of Markos Delphi's researchers until he was caught trying to steal *The Celestial Codex*. Eager to commune with Far Realm entities, Yexanthal hires the rivals to steal the book from Delphi Mansion.
Prisoner 13	Horath Axebreaker (lawful evil, dwarf **veteran**) hires the rivals to retrieve a copy of Prisoner 13's keystone tattoo so he can steal Clan Axebreaker's treasure for himself.
Tockworth's Clockworks	Tockworth's security key is a copy of a key that opens a vault containing vast wealth in another svirfneblin stronghold. Waltabeth Brambleroot (neutral evil, deep gnome **mage**) hires the rivals to retrieve the key for her so she can claim the treasure.
Masterpiece Imbroglio	The rivals are members of a thieves' guild from a neighboring city. They seek *Constantori's Portrait* for Skandor Torreth (neutral, human **assassin**), a guildmaster who needs information only the portrait knows.
Axe from the Grave	Zarthine Delthion (neutral, human **noble**), the daughter of the wizard who gave Frody the Canaith mandolin, believes the instrument is rightfully hers. She hires the rivals to retrieve it.
Vidorant's Vault	The rivals are members of the Silver Fingers Society and wish to impress Samphith Goldenbeard by stealing the diadem. They are unaware Goldenbeard has hired the characters.
Shard of the Accursed	Everett Stillwater (neutral evil, human **mage**) hires the rivals to steal the shard the characters seek to return to the tomb. He believes he can break the shard's curse and sell it on the black market for a high price.
Heart of Ashes	Barolophine (neutral evil, elf **archmage**) hires the rivals to recover the heart of Jhaeros, a focus item the archmage needs to fuel her journey to become a lich.
Affair on the Concordant Express	The rivals are members of the Stranger's former outlaw gang. They are determined to free the Stranger before the Concordant Express reaches Mechanus.
Party at Paliset Hall	The **adult black dragon** Inkscale, one of Zorhanna's oldest and bitterest enemies, hires the rivals to steal the *shard solitaire* out of spite.
Fire and Darkness	Vrakir's jilted lover Zaltima, an **efreeti**, hires the rivals to steal the *Book of Vile Darkness* for her.

ADVENTURERS NAVIGATE AROUND ONE OF
THE MORE FEARSOME EXHIBITS IN THE
VARKENBLUFF MUSEUM OF NATURAL HISTORY.

THE MURKMIRE MALEVOLENCE

U NBEKNOWNST TO ANYONE BUT A DISGRACED academic, the Varkenbluff Museum of Natural History is in grave danger. Archaeologists at a nearby dig site recently unearthed a curiosity: the Murkmire Stone. This object is actually an eldritch creature's egg, and it's about to hatch. The characters must infiltrate the museum, steal the egg, and return it to Dr. Cassee Dannell to be neutralized before it releases an eldritch horror.

ADVENTURE BACKGROUND

Dr. Cassee Dannell, a brilliant academic, long ago learned to hide her interest in the occult. She instead built a career gaining expertise in the peoples and cultures of the region surrounding Varkenbluff, continuing her occult research in secret. By age twenty-four, Dr. Dannell had earned her doctorate in anthropology from Varkenbluff University, a prestigious institution in her home city. Her ability to connect local archaeological objects with their cultural context was unrivaled, so after her graduation, Dr. Dannell became a Varkenbluff faculty member and field scientist, accompanying the university's archaeology crews on digs in the area.

On a recent expedition into the nearby Murkmire, the archaeologists unearthed a strange object. Light green, opaque, and with a gemstone-like sheen, this ovoid stone was covered in strange furrows. The stone seemed ritualistic in nature, but it matched no recorded historical practices, and no one could identify its composition. The more Dr. Dannell studied it, the more she became convinced this object, which the archaeologists dubbed the Murkmire Stone, was not created by any known civilization—and might be dangerous.

Dr. Dannell tried to convince the dig's archaeologists to isolate the Murkmire Stone until she could learn more about it, but word of the discovery spread quickly. When the Varkenbluff Museum of Natural History offered a generous price for the stone, it was soon whisked from the dig site to the museum.

Dr. Dannell continued to research the strange stone. Her concern turned to dread when she found descriptions of similar objects in her occult tomes. These objects were, in fact, the eggs of eldritch creatures. She learned that such eggs lay dormant for generations, but once the eggs are unearthed, the creatures within rapidly develop and hatch. The resulting creatures are ravenous for raw meat and grow exponentially as they feed, eventually overwhelming entire villages. The eggs are nearly indestructible, but the tomes claim encasing them in crystal can neutralize them.

According to Dr. Dannell's research, the Murkmire Stone is due to hatch in a matter of days. She frantically presented her findings to the university's administrators, who deemed her work pseudoscience and refused to interfere with the museum's upcoming exhibition of the Murkmire Stone. Desperate, Dr. Dannell snuck into the museum after hours and tried to steal the stone, but she was caught. The university disavowed her actions and fired her. With mere hours left in the Murkmire Stone's gestation period, Dr. Dannell is nearly out of options.

USING THE GOLDEN VAULT

If you're using the Golden Vault as a patron, a golden key is delivered to the characters in whatever manner you deem fit. When the characters use this key to open their music box, the lid pops open and a soothing voice says the following:

"Greetings, operatives. The Golden Vault has learned that the egg of an eldritch horror has been mistaken for a historical object and is about to go on display at the Varkenbluff Museum of Natural History. The anthropologist Dr. Cassee Dannell tried to warn officials about this egg, known as the Murkmire Stone, but none believed her. We do, and we know that if this egg hatches, many will die—or worse. This quest, should you choose to undertake it, requires you to infiltrate the museum, steal the egg, and return it to Dr. Dannell, who will neutralize it. There's no time to waste; the egg could hatch at any moment. Start by meeting with Dr. Dannell. Good luck, operatives."

Closing the music box causes the golden key to vanish.

A Cry for Help

Time is short, and Dr. Dannell is desperate for help. She has exhausted all official channels and has turned to the characters.

The characters should have some connection to Dr. Dannell to explain why she reaches out to them. Have your players determine this connection before the adventure begins. Here are some possibilities:

Dannell Family Friend. Dr. Dannell hails from a family of professors and scientists who have interacted significantly with Varkenbluff's intellectuals and nobility. One or more characters have rubbed shoulders with members of the Dannell clan, including Cassee.

Museum Enthusiast. Dr. Dannell's research is cited liberally in the Varkenbluff Museum of Natural History's exhibits, and she regularly corresponds with fans of her work, including one or more characters who have earned her respect.

Varkenbluff University Student. Dr. Dannell has taught numerous anthropology and history classes attended by one or more characters and is impressed with their occult acumen.

Once the characters have determined their connection to Dr. Dannell, read the following out loud to get this adventure started:

No matter your business this morning, a grave halfling messenger finds you and hands you a sealed parchment.

"Meet me at the Sage's Quill today as soon as you can," the missive reads. "I beg your help in a delicate matter whose importance cannot be overstated. I shall await you in a purple hooded robe."

The note is signed, "Dr. Cassee Dannell."

When you look up, the halfling has wandered off.

THE CLOCK IS TICKING

The Sage's Quill is a quiet, plush tavern that caters to the city's academics and intellectuals. It is located next to the Varkenbluff Museum of Natural History, less than a mile from Varkenbluff University.

Once the characters arrive at the tavern, read the following out loud:

As you enter the Sage's Quill, soft light reveals mahogany furniture and luxurious carpets. A few genteel patrons murmur in the lounge. You soon notice a purple-hooded figure tucked into a corner booth.

Dr. Dannell gestures for you to sit. You notice lines of worry etched into her normally cheerful face.

Dr. Dannell (neutral good, human **commoner**) has an Intelligence score of 18. She anxiously addresses the characters:

"Thank you for coming so quickly," she says. "A few weeks ago, I attended a dig in the Murkmire that unearthed a furrowed, light-green stone. I'll give you all the details, but the bottom line is that it isn't a stone at all—it's the egg of an eldritch horror. Moreover, my research indicates it'll hatch at midnight tonight.

"Trouble is, no one will listen to me. The university ignored me, and I was caught trying to steal the egg from the museum so I could contain it. Now I've been fired, the Murkmire Stone display at the museum opens tomorrow, and the egg is about to hatch.

"You've got to steal the Murkmire Stone and bring it back so I can save the city!"

WHAT DR. DANNELL KNOWS

If the characters talk with Dr. Dannell further, she gives more information about their mission and what she has learned about the stone:

Getting the Egg. The characters need to reconnoiter the museum in search of security measures, steal the Murkmire Stone at an opportune time (see "Stealing the Murkmire Stone" below), and deliver it to Dr. Dannell. She'll wait for them in an alley between the museum and the Sage's Quill.

Traits of the Egg. The Murkmire Stone can't be damaged or destroyed. Unearthing the egg triggered the rapid development of the creature within, which will soon be ready to hatch.

Containing the Egg. At this point, the only way to keep the egg from hatching is to encase it in a specially prepared crystal container. Dr. Dannell created a crystal box for this purpose. She still needs to seal cracks in the crystal, so the characters can't take the box with them on the heist.

What's in the Egg. Dr. Dannell's occult sources indicate an extremely dangerous creature will hatch from the egg unless it can be safely contained.

STEALING THE MURKMIRE STONE

The Murkmire Stone is going on public display tomorrow at the Varkenbluff Museum of Natural History, Dr. Dannell explains. A private gala celebrating the new exhibition will occur tonight in the museum's second-floor Gemstone Wing.

The characters aren't required to attend the gala, but doing so is the only way to glimpse the stone—and the security measures around it—before their heist. Dr. Dannell has secured a gala ticket for each character, and she gives them the tickets now.

The characters must wear formal dress to the gala. Dr. Dannell has an appropriate outfit for each character in her heirloom *bag of holding*. Dr. Dannell lends the bag to the characters to store their adventuring gear, which they'll need while sneaking about the museum after hours.

DR. DANNELL'S TOOLS

Before her unsuccessful attempt to steal the Murkmire Stone, Dr. Dannell scouted the Varkenbluff Museum of Natural History. She pretended to be a patron and recorded the museum's layout, filling in what she knows about nonpublic areas, such as the basement.

Dannell's Map. Dr. Dannell gives the characters her sketch of the museum (see map 1.1) before they leave for the gala. Although she's a brilliant academic, Dr. Dannell is neither an architect nor a burglar. Her map is based on the public map of the museum's exhibits, so it is incomplete and lacks information about the museum's security measures.

DR. CASSEE DANNELL

For instance, Dr. Dannell knows the museum is outfitted with alarms after it closes to the public, but she doesn't know where those alarms are located or how to bypass them.

MUSEUM STAFF

Dr. Dannell knows that the museum has twelve guards and that the museum curator—the elf Alda Arkin—likely has a record of the areas the guards patrol at night. Dr. Dannell suspects this information is in Arkin's office, located somewhere in the eastern wing on the first floor. Arkin herself will attend the gala.

THE REWARD

For bringing the Murkmire Stone back to Dr. Dannell, she offers her *bag of holding* plus 20 gp per character. If a character succeeds on a DC 13 Charisma (Persuasion) check, Dr. Dannell increases her offer to 30 gp per character.

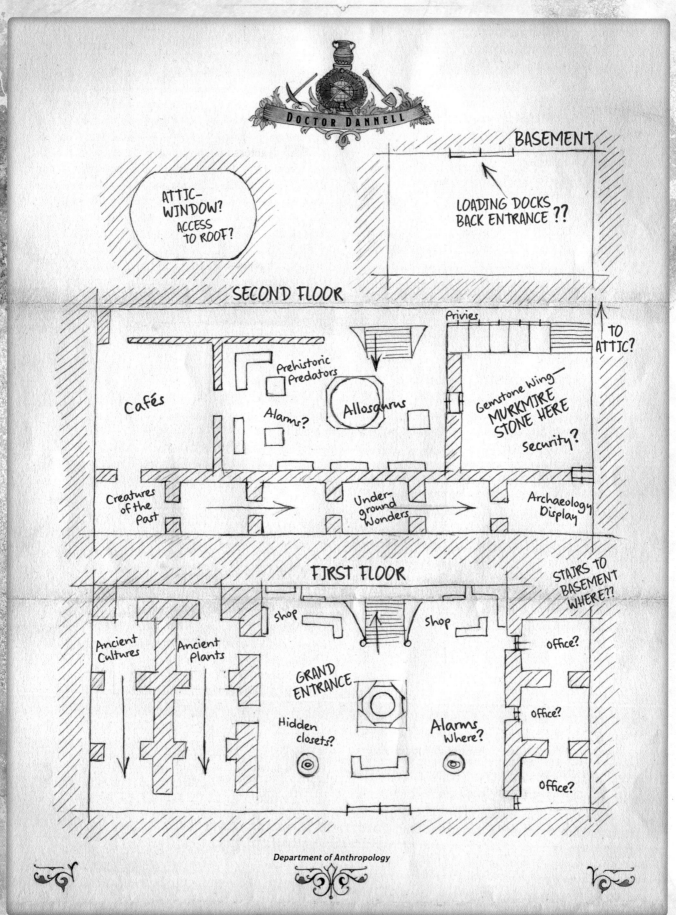

The Opening Gala

The private gala celebrating the opening of the Murkmire Stone exhibition begins at 6 p.m., and the museum closes at 8 p.m. There's enough time for characters to prepare before attending, including retrieving or procuring formal attire if they don't wish to wear the clothes Dr. Dannell provided. Weapons and visible armor are not permitted inside the museum and must be stashed in Dr. Dannell's *bag of holding* or elsewhere.

Once the characters are ready to enter the museum, keep track of which character has the *bag of holding* that contains the group's adventuring gear. Then read the following aloud:

> The facade of the Varkenbluff Museum of Natural History boasts enormous columns and elegant archways hewn from marble. Cosmopolitan visitors bustle about the entrance, including some clad in sleek formalwear.

The museum is open to the public today; only the Gemstone Wing on the second floor is closed for the ticketed gala. The Murkmire Stone is ensconced in the Gemstone Wing.

Scouting the Museum

The characters can explore the public areas of the museum while it's open. The entire museum is public except for its offices (areas V5–V7), basement (area V16), and attic (area V17).

The characters have about two hours to prepare for their heist before the museum closes. If the characters don't immediately go to the Gemstone Wing (area V13), museum guards notice their formal attire and periodically suggest they do so.

Information relevant to the characters' heist plan is below. More information about specific areas of the museum is included in the "Museum Locations" section later.

Entering Nonpublic Areas

The doors to the museum's offices (areas V5–V7) and basement (area V16) are locked at all hours, as described in the "Interior Doors" subsection of the "General Features" section. Curator Alda Arkin, whom the characters might meet at the gala, carries a master key, while the museum's guards have keys that grant access to specific areas (see "Circumventing Security" and "Curator Alda Arkin").

Encountering Museum Guards

As long as the characters aren't caught entering a restricted area or causing a public incident, the museum's guards ignore them during the gala.

If one or more characters are spotted in a restricted area or cause a public incident, a **guard** approaches them. Roll on the Museum Guards table to determine which guard arrives. Characters in formal dress are escorted to the Gemstone Wing, while characters who are improperly dressed for the occasion are told to leave the museum at once. If the characters protest, the guard becomes hostile and shouts for backup. At the end of each of the guard's turns, an additional 1d4 **guards** arrive until all the museum guards are accounted for.

Provided a guard hasn't shouted for backup, a character can take an action and use trickery or intimidation to convince a guard to leave. The character must make a DC 10 Charisma (Deception, Intimidation, or Persuasion) check. If the check succeeds, the character convinces the guard to look for trouble elsewhere. If the check fails, the guard becomes hostile and behaves as described above, and the character can't repeat the check on that particular guard.

Museum Guards

d12	Guard Description
1	Darrison Blackwaters (neutral human), a former soldier who takes everything literally
2	Franceena Van Lictor (neutral good elf), a sarcastic newbie who respects history
3	Billie Quartermile (lawful neutral halfling), who loves policy and procedure
4	Milanova Wumplestocking (lawful good gnome), who is very serious but loves a good pun
5	Garent Millaneff (neutral evil human), a bully who loves money and bragging rights
6	Violet Pendergilt (neutral good human), a wistful dreamer who plans to quit soon
7	Sureth Dhanvhal (neutral human), a reserve soldier who is always pressed for time
8	Brendara Valindril (lawful neutral elf), a graduate student in history at the university
9	Grendor Battleaxe (neutral good dwarf), a wanderer paying off a debt to the museum
10	Clark Jonathan Vanth (lawful good human), a young and naive individual
11	Sareena Shu (chaotic neutral tiefling), an overeager lover of history and learning
12	Maryam Bikram (lawful neutral human), a city watch veteran who rigidly enforces the rules

INVESTIGATING SECURITY MEASURES

The museum is protected by several security measures after it closes at 8 p.m.

Alarms. Audible *alarm* spells have been cast in areas marked (A) on map 1.2. The museum's guards and the curator have pass cards that allow them to bypass these alarms, and spare pass cards are kept in area V7 (see "Bypassing Alarms" below for more information). The alarms are located as follows:

- The front doors to area V1
- At the bottom of the stairs in area V1
- In each hallway leading from area V1 to area V3
- On the doors leading from area V1 to areas V5, V6, and V7
- In the hall leading from area V11 to area V12
- On the door leading from area V12 to the hallway to area V13

If an alarm is on a door, touching the door sets off the alarm. If an alarm is on a 5-foot square, entering that square sets it off. The alarm on the front doors in area V1 extends 10 feet, covering the entire width of the doorway. When an alarm sounds, any guards in the area plus 1d3 other guards from that floor hear it and investigate.

The characters can find a record of the museum's payment for these spells, including their specific locations, by searching the records room (area V6); the alarms can also be detected using *detect magic*. The alarms aren't armed while the museum is open to the public.

Animated Statues. The statues that flank the front desk in area V1 and the statue next to the stairs in area V12 can animate after hours to attack intruders. These statues use the **animated armor** stat block. Causing a statue to animate alerts any guards in that area.

A *detect magic* spell reveals an aura of transmutation magic around each statue. A character who becomes aware of the statues' magical nature can make a DC 10 Intelligence (Arcana) check. If the check is successful, the character realizes the statues can animate.

Gemstone Wing. If the characters don't carefully remove the Murkmire Stone from its pedestal in area V13, *arcane lock* spells cause all doors leading to the room (including secret doors) to close and lock. As an action, a character can either try to unlock a door using thieves' tools, doing so with a successful DC 20 Dexterity check, or force open the door by succeeding on a DC 20 Strength (Athletics) check. The characters can learn about this security measure by attending the gala (see the "Attending the Gala" section).

Guards. After hours, Maryam Bikram is stationed at the entrance to the gala. Eleven other museum guards watch the areas indicated in the Guard Locations After Hours table. Guards have keys to certain areas. Guards also have pass cards that allow them to bypass the museum's alarms (see "Bypassing Alarms" below).

If the characters get into a noisy fight with one or more guards, an additional 1d4 **guards** arrive each round until all the remaining museum guards are accounted for.

If the guards incapacitate a character or a character surrenders, the guards haul that character to the nearby city watch headquarters. If all the characters are caught, their mission is unsuccessful and the adventure ends.

GUARD LOCATIONS AFTER HOURS

Guards	Area	Guards	Area
2	V1	2	V9–V10
1	V3	1	V11
1	V4	2	V12
1	V8	2	V13

CIRCUMVENTING SECURITY

Characters who discover the museum's security measures can find ways to circumvent them. A few suggestions are provided below:

Avoiding Statues. Characters can keep the statues from animating by staying more than 5 feet away from them.

Bypassing Alarms. The curator and guards each carry a palm-sized pass card embossed with the museum's logo. A *detect magic* spell reveals an aura of divination magic around each pass card, which allows the bearer to bypass any of the museum's alarms. The characters can find a stash of extra pass cards in area V7. A character who is hidden and within reach of a guard can try to steal that guard's pass card without the guard's knowledge, doing so with a successful DC 14 Dexterity (Sleight of Hand) check.

Sneaking Past Guards. The characters can find a document in the curator's office (area V5) that outlines the guards' stations after hours. During the gala, the curator keeps this document on her person (see the "Curator Alda Arkin" section). Characters who spend at least 1 minute studying the document have advantage on Dexterity (Stealth) checks made to sneak past guards after hours.

Stealing Keys. The curator carries a master key, while each guard carries a key that unlocks all doors to the area in which the guard is stationed. Guards in area V1 also have a key to the break room (area V7). A character can steal a guard's key in the same way as they can steal a pass card, described in "Bypassing Alarms" above.

HIDING IN THE MUSEUM

The characters can hide in numerous locations while the museum closes. Below are good options, which are detailed in the "Museum Locations" section:

Cleaning Supply Storage. Short hallways that hold cleaning supplies are concealed behind secret doors in areas V3, V4, V8, V9, V12, and V13.

Privies. The guards nominally check area V15 before closing, but anyone who hides here avoids detection.

Attic or Basement. The guards don't enter areas V16 or V17 before the museum closes.

REENTERING THE MUSEUM

The characters might decide to leave the museum when it closes and sneak back inside after hours. Below are some strategies they might use:

Front Doors. The characters could pick the lock on the front doors to area V1, use pass cards to bypass the alarm (see "Bypassing Alarms"), and contend with the falling net trap just inside the doors while remaining a safe distance from the animated statues.

Attic Skylight. The characters could pick the lock on the skylight to enter the building. Grappling hooks and ropes are required to scale the building. By the end of the gala, it is dark enough to allow characters to enter through the attic skylight without being seen.

Basement Doors. The characters could pry open the loading dock doors or prop open the secret door if they find it.

ATTENDING THE GALA

If the characters approach the private gala in the Gemstone Wing (area V13), they encounter Maryam Bikram (lawful neutral, human **guard**). The captain of the museum's security force, Maryam is a serious woman and a veteran of the city's watch. She admits any character who is dressed for the occasion and has a ticket. Others are turned away.

When the characters enter the gala, read the following aloud:

> The Gemstone Wing's oak doors open into a luxuriously appointed ballroom. Crimson tablecloths and fine china adorn dining tables, and chandeliers sparkle overhead. Cabinets with glittering gemstones surround the space. At the wing's center is a marble pedestal bearing a peculiar, light-green stone.

Twenty other gala attendees (unarmed and unarmored **nobles**) mill around the event. All are dressed in elaborate finery, and most are long-time donors to the museum.

When a character interacts with an attendee, roll on the Gala Attendees table to determine whom they meet. The attendees know nothing about the Murkmire Stone beyond basic details about its discovery. However, if the characters fish for information about the stone or the museum and succeed on a DC 12 Charisma (Persuasion) check, an attendee reveals one random piece of information from the Museum Gossip table.

Gala Attendees

d4	Attendee
1	Captain Frankheim Walters (chaotic neutral human), who never served in the military but implies he did
2	Georgina Lucina Vandylarahal (neutral evil elf), a sneering heir to a mining fortune
3	Countess Helene Danforth (neutral good human), a member of an ancient, titled family with little actual wealth
4	Dr. Horthnar Stonecrusher (lawful good dwarf), a surgeon who loves natural history and gemstones

Museum Gossip

d4	Juicy Tidbit
1	The curator has been fidgeting with her clutch all night. Has she gotten some sort of bad news? Maybe she's about to fire someone!
2	Sometimes the museum keeps displays hidden in the basement at night. The curator must think her own guards might steal something!
3	It's unfortunate that the museum has fallen on hard financial times. If only they sold all those ore and gem samples they keep in the basement. I've heard there's a fortune down there!
4	The curator adores oversized vintage dolls. I've heard she keeps one in her office that's as big as a grown human!

Curator Alda Arkin

Mingling with the gala's attendees is Alda Arkin (neutral evil, elf **noble**), the museum's curator. During the gala, the curator is unarmed and unarmored. A retired university professor, Alda is responsible for the museum's close ties to Varkenbluff University's anthropology and archaeology departments.

When she notices the characters, she assumes they're wealthy museum donors, welcomes them, and engages in chitchat. Alda is familiar with Dr. Dannell. She deeply dislikes the anthropologist due to Dr. Dannell's interest in the occult. If the characters mention Dr. Dannell's fears about the Murkmire Stone, Alda snorts, dismisses their concerns, and leaves to mingle with other attendees.

Alda's Clutch. Characters who watch Alda closely notice a fancy clutch she holds behind her back. Inside the clutch is a map of the museum guards' after-hours stations, a master key to the museum's locked doors, and a pass card that allows Alda to bypass the museum's alarms (see "Investigating Security Measures" earlier in the adventure for details).

Examining the Murkmire Stone

The Murkmire Stone sits atop a pedestal in area V13, flanked by informational placards about the stone's discovery and theories about its use—though Dr. Dannell's occult theory is missing.

Gemstone Wing Security Measures. A character who spends at least 1 minute studying the pedestal during the gala realizes it has an elaborate defense mechanism (see area V13).

Varkenbluff Museum of Natural History

Once the Murkmire Stone exhibition gala ends, the museum closes. Its staff members activate the protections listed in the "Museum Security Measures" section.

General Features

The Varkenbluff Museum of Natural History has stone walls and tiled floors. The building's other features are described below:

Ceilings. The museum's ceilings are 30 feet high.

Interior Doors. The interior doors are closed and locked, with the exception of the privies in area V15. A character can use an action to try to unlock a door using thieves' tools, doing so with a successful DC 12 Dexterity check unless otherwise noted. Attempting to use thieves' tools to unlock a door with an enabled *alarm* spell triggers that alarm.

Lighting. On the first two floors, most areas are lit with *continual flame* spells placed on sconces. The grand entrance (area V1), Prehistoric Predators exhibit (area V12), basement (area V16), and attic (area V17) are areas of dim light. Guards in areas V1 and V12 carry hooded lanterns.

Secret Doors. A secret door can be found by any character who takes an action to examine the surrounding wall and succeeds on a DC 12 Wisdom (Perception) check.

MUSEUM LOCATIONS

The following locations are keyed to map 1.2. The descriptions assume the characters are exploring the museum after it's closed to the public.

V1: GRAND ENTRANCE

> Statues depicting robed human women flank the sides of this public mingling space, which boasts a marble column in the center. The museum's information desk is situated just inside the front doors. To the north is a grand staircase draped in rich carpet.

Two **guards** patrol this area. The two statues flanking the information desk animate if a character comes within 5 feet of either of them. The statues use the **animated armor** stat block and fight until destroyed.

Alarms. An *alarm* spell has been cast on the bottom of the grand staircase. Another such spell has been cast on the front doors.

Front Doors. The museum's front doors are locked from the inside. As an action, a character can try to pick the lock using thieves' tools, doing so with a successful DC 16 Dexterity check.

Trap. The 5-foot-by-10-foot section of floor immediately north of the museum's front doors (marked T on map 1.2) contains a pressure plate hidden under a rug. Lifting the rug or pushing it aside reveals the pressure plate, which is activated and deactivated by a toggle switch hidden under the nearby information desk. The trap is normally activated while the museum is closed to the public and deactivated while the museum is open to the public.

The first time a creature steps on the pressure plate while the trap is activated, a weighted net drops from a secret compartment in the ceiling, covering the 10-foot-square area between the front doors and the information desk. Creatures in that area are restrained by the net, and those that fail a DC 10 Strength saving throw are also knocked prone.

A creature can use its action to make a DC 10 Strength check, freeing itself or another creature within its reach on a success. The net has AC 10 and 12 hit points. Creatures are no longer restrained by the net once it drops to 0 hit points.

V2: MUSEUM SHOPS

> Display racks here are filled with tunics, bandannas, books, and bric-a-brac, most emblazoned with the museum's logo. Plush benches serve as seating areas.

The eastern shop sells cheap souvenirs and bears a sign that reads, "The Historian's Gifts." The western shop sells books and artifact replicas and is labeled "The Archaeologist's Spade."

Treasure. Each shop includes a small back room with a locked door. As an action, a character can try to unlock either door using thieves' tools, doing so with a successful DC 16 Dexterity check. Inside each shop's back room is a till containing 1d6 gp, 2d6 sp, and 3d6 cp. Additionally, one set of thieves' tools can be cobbled together from the supplies in the back rooms.

V3: ANCIENT PLANTS EXHIBIT

> Artificial plants made of wood, silk, and other materials sprout from artfully arranged planters. Tall ferns, bushes with strange berries, and slender trees are represented alongside placards about ancient plant life.

One **guard** patrols this area. Hallways to the north and south connect to area V4.

Alarms. The short hallways that connect this area to the grand entrance (area V1) have *alarm* spells cast on them.

Secret Doors. The northern and central exhibit rooms each have a secret door in the west wall that opens into a short hallway containing cleaning supplies. At the opposite end of the hallway is another secret door that doesn't require an ability check to spot from inside the hall. This secret door pulls open to reveal a similarly sized exhibit room in area V4.

V4: ANCIENT CULTURES EXHIBIT

> Glass display cases boast objects related to life in ancient Varkenbluff. Clay pots, stone tools, and scraps of leather clothes are interspersed with informational placards about their historical use.

One **guard** patrols this area. Hallways to the north and south connect to area V3.

Secret Doors. The northern and central exhibit rooms each have a secret door in the east wall that opens into a short hallway containing cleaning supplies. At the opposite end of the hallway is another secret door that doesn't require an ability check to spot from inside the hall. This secret door pulls open to reveal a similarly sized exhibit room in area V3.

V5: Curator's Office

A solid oak desk stands on a plush carpet in the center of this office. In the southeast corner, a strange, human-sized doll is posed in an elaborate silk dress.

Alarm. An *alarm* spell has been cast on the door that connects this room to area V1.

Deadly Doll. After hours, the curator enables her office's defense mechanism: a five-foot-tall doll with the name "Marigold" sewn onto its vintage dress. When a creature other than Alda enters the room, the doll animates and attacks. Marigold uses the **scarecrow** stat block and fights until destroyed.

At your discretion, a noisy fight might attract the attention of the guards patrolling area V1.

Guards' Patrol Routes. If the characters didn't snatch Alda's clutch during the gala, they can find a copy of the guards' after-hours patrol routes on the desk under some other loose paperwork (see the "Curator Alda Arkin" section).

V6: Records Room

Filing cabinets stand in this records room.

Alarm. An *alarm* spell has been cast on the door that connects this room to area V1.

Records. This room contains records about past and current exhibits as well as the museum's financial records. A character who searches this area also finds information about the placement of the building's *alarm* spells (see "Investigating Security Measures" earlier in the adventure).

V7: Break Room and Storage

Boxes of display supplies are stacked into this room's corners. Chairs surround a circular table in the middle.

Alarm. An *alarm* spell has been cast on the door that connects this room to area V1.

Pass Card Stash. Characters who take a minute to search the boxes find a small, partially open box in the southwest corner. Inside are three palm-sized pass cards, each stamped with the museum's logo. A scrap of paper inside the box reads "spare alarm pass cards." Each pass card allows its bearer to bypass the museum's alarms, as described in the "Bypassing Alarms" section earlier in this adventure.

Treasure. Tucked between supply boxes in the northwest corner is a vial containing a *potion of vitality*.

V8: Creatures of the Past Exhibit

Fossils of small prehistoric creatures are arranged here, some as fully reconstructed skeletons. The exhibit includes microraptors, ornithopods, dwarf elephants, and an ancestor of the cockatrice. Informational placards tell the stories of these creatures and their bones' discovery.

One **guard** patrols this area.

Secret Door. Between two of the 15-foot-square exhibit rooms is a secret door that opens into a short hallway heading north. At the opposite end of the hallway, which holds cleaning supplies, is another secret door that doesn't require an ability check to spot from inside the hall. This secret door opens to reveal area V12.

V9: Underground Wonders Exhibit

Glittering ore and gemstones are arranged in velvet-backed display cases. Informational placards explain local geologic history.

Two **guards** patrol this exhibit and area V10, moving from one room to the other every 5 minutes.

The gems on display here hold little value; precious stones are reserved for display in the Gemstone Wing (area V13).

Fake Murkmire Stone. A character who examines the stones on display in the easternmost room realizes the central display cabinet includes a chunk of jade similar in size and weight to the Murkmire Stone. The display case is locked, but a character can take an action to try to open it using thieves' tools, doing so with a successful DC 10 Dexterity check. Smashing the display case's glass attracts the guards patrolling this area.

Secret Door. Between this exhibit and area V10 is a secret door that opens into a short hallway heading north. At the opposite end of the hallway, which holds cleaning supplies, is another secret door that doesn't require an ability check to spot from inside the hall. This secret door pulls open to reveal area V13.

V10: Archaeology Display

Picks, trowels, brushes, and other archaeological tools are on display here. Informational placards label them as tools famous local experts used to dig up the wonders found in the museum. Murals along the south wall depict famous digs.

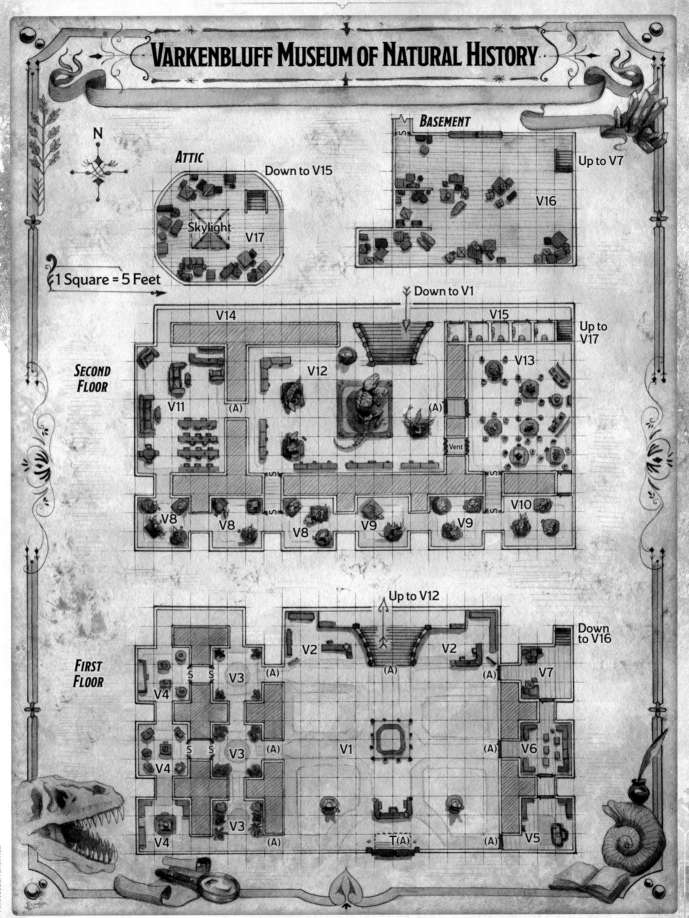

Varkenbluff Museum of Natural History

N

Basement

Attic

Down to V15

Up to V7

V16

Skylight

V17

1 Square = 5 Feet

Down to V1

V14

V15

Up to V17

Second Floor

V13

V12

V11

(A)

(A)

Vent

V8

V8

V8

V9

V9

V10

Up to V12

Down to V16

First Floor

V2

V2

(A)

V3

(A)

V7

(A)

V4

S S

V1

V3

(A)

(A)

V6

V4

V3

T (A)

(A)

V5

V4

FRANCESCA BAERALD

Two **guards** patrol both this exhibit and area V9, moving from one room to the other every 5 minutes.

This exhibit tells the story of the infamous Rogerson dig, where most of the creatures in the Prehistoric Predators exhibit were found. The placards dismiss local legends that claim the excavators were subsequently cursed.

Treasure. A character who studies the exhibit and succeeds on a DC 10 Wisdom (Perception) check realizes the items on display include two flawless weapons: a *+1 dagger* and a *+1 handaxe*. The weapons are inside a glass case with a jammed lock, so the characters must break or cut through the glass to access the weapons. Breaking the glass attracts the guards patrolling this area.

V11: Unearthed Café

> This space holds a mix of cafeteria-style tables and lounge furniture. A counter in the northeast corner sits underneath a sign that reads, "Unearthed Café."

One **guard** patrols this area.

Treasure. A small lockbox is stashed under the counter. As an action, a character can try to open the lockbox using thieves' tools, doing so with a successful DC 14 Dexterity check. The lockbox contains 15 gp, 7 sp, and 24 cp.

V12: Prehistoric Predators Exhibit

> The intact skeletons of several large prehistoric monsters are on display here, including the museum's most famous display: the beautifully preserved body of an allosaurus, its leathery skin appearing supple to the touch. An informational placard next to the dinosaur explains it died in the Murkmire millennia ago and was naturally preserved. Display cases along the room's walls hold fossils of other ancient local predators.

Two **guards** patrol this area.

The statue west of the stairs depicts a winged satyr. If a character comes within 5 feet of the statue, it springs to life. The statue uses the **animated armor** stat block and fights until destroyed.

Alarms. An *alarm* spell has been cast in the hallway leading to the Unearthed Café (area V11). Another *alarm* spell has been cast on the door in the middle of the east wall (which leads to area V13).

Allosaurus. The allosaurus looks like a preserved specimen, but the museum hired rock gnomes to transform it into a harmless animatronic display. A character who examines the display's base notices a small hatch covering a panel of buttons. A character can use these controls to turn on the animatronic display, which alerts not only the guards in this area but also the guards in areas V11 and V13.

As an action, a character can use tinker's tools or thieves' tools to try to overload the magic that powers the controls, doing so with a successful DC 10 Intelligence (Arcana) check. This causes the animatronic creature to break free from its display base and rampage for 10 minutes before becoming inert again. The creature stomps through the area, then heads down the grand staircase, causing mayhem in area V1. While it rampages, the creature uses the **allosaurus** stat block, with these changes:

- The animatronic allosaurus is a Construct.
- It is immune to poison and psychic damage, as well as the charmed, frightened, paralyzed, and poisoned conditions.

Vent. The east wall has a 3-foot-high, 3-foot-wide, 5-foot-deep air vent leading to area V13. The vent is 10 feet above the floor. Reaching it requires a successful DC 10 Strength (Athletics) check. Safely returning to the floor doesn't require an ability check.

V13: Gemstone Wing

> Chairs surround several tables cluttered with crystal and silver tableware. Against the east wall, a light-green stone rests atop a marble pedestal.

Two **guards** patrol this area.

Staff members plan to remove the tables and restore the normal gemstone exhibits in the morning before the museum opens. For now, the contents of those exhibits are in the basement (area V16).

Light-Green Stone. The light-green stone on the pedestal is the Murkmire Stone, which is described at the end of this adventure. As Dr. Dannell fears, the stone is indeed an eldritch creature's egg. At 10:30 p.m., the effects described in "The Murkmire Stone" begin, and at midnight, the egg hatches. See "Museum Feeding Frenzy" to learn what happens when the egg hatches.

Rigged Pedestal. A *detect magic* spell reveals an aura of transmutation magic around the pedestal, which is attached to the floor and can't be moved. A character who examines the pedestal notices tiny glyphs carved into its base and can make a DC 12 Intelligence (Arcana) check. On a success, the character realizes that all doors leading to the room will lock if the stone is removed from the pedestal.

If the Murkmire Stone is removed from the pedestal, *arcane lock* spells activate on all doors leading to the room (including secret doors), causing them to close and lock. As an action, a character can try to open a locked door using thieves' tools, doing so with a successful DC 20 Dexterity check, or force open a locked door by succeeding on a DC 20 Strength (Athletics) check. The *arcane lock* spells don't prevent the curator or the museum guards from opening the doors.

Replacing the Murkmire Stone with a fake can prevent the trap from triggering. A suitable fake can be found in area V9. Swapping it for the real Murkmire Stone without activating the *arcane lock* spells requires a successful DC 10 Dexterity (Sleight of Hand) check.

Vent. The west wall has a 3-foot-high, 3-foot-wide, 5-foot-deep air vent leading to area V12. The vent is 10 feet above the floor. Reaching it requires a successful DC 10 Strength (Athletics) check. Safely returning to the floor doesn't require an ability check.

Secret Door. The south wall contains a secret door that opens into a short hallway containing cleaning supplies. At the far end of the hallway is another secret door that doesn't require an ability check to spot from inside the hall. This secret door pulls open to reveal the hallway between areas V9 and V10.

V14: Access Hallway

This hallway connects the Unearthed Café (area V11) to the Prehistoric Predators exhibit (area V12) and the privies (area V15).

V15: Privies

This area holds five stalls. A simple latch allows the door of each privy to be locked from the inside. East of the privies is a staircase to the attic (area V17).

V16: Basement

> Boxes and crates are piled here in groups. Enormous warehouse doors take up much of the basement's northern wall.

Objects formerly on display or not yet prepped for display are stored here. The area is infrequently visited, and a **mimic** recently took up residence in the centermost pile of boxes. The mimic waits to attack until a character moves within 5 feet; it then fights until destroyed.

Loading Docks. The warehouse doors open onto an underground ramp that leads to street level. A character who has observed the whole building from the outside can easily find where the ramp exits at ground level. The doors are locked, and their hinges are stiff. Unlocking them requires a successful DC 14 Dexterity check with thieves' tools; after that, shoving the doors open requires a successful DC 15 Strength (Athletics) check. This is noisy and attracts the attention of one guard patrolling the grand entrance above (area V1).

Secret Door. In the basement's northwest corner, a secret door opens into a 50-foot-long tunnel that emerges in a copse of trees near the museum.

Treasure. Most of the items in the boxes would be nearly impossible to sell, as they would quickly be identified as stolen museum property. However, the boxes in the southeastern corner contain the items from the Gemstone Wing that were stored to make room for the Murkmire Stone gala: gemstones and chunks of raw silver ore, all found locally. The 20 pounds of gems and ore are worth 150 gp total.

V17: Attic

> A winding staircase leads up to this cramped space filled with haphazardly stacked boxes. Starlight pours into the space through a large skylight.

Supplies for events—such as lecterns, linens, and tableware—are stored here.

Skylight. The skylight overhead is locked. A character can use an action to try to unlock the skylight using thieves' tools, doing so with a successful DC 14 Dexterity check. Lifting the skylight to open it then requires a successful DC 12 Strength (Athletics) check.

Loose bricks are scattered on the roof near the skylight. A character could use a brick to prop the skylight open.

Conclusion

If the characters escape the museum with the Murkmire Stone, they can deliver it safely to Dr. Dannell. The anthropologist locks it in a box made of crystal, whereupon the stone becomes inert and its effects stop immediately. Dr. Dannell assures the characters that the egg will be safe in her care for the time being. The characters receive their rewards, and Dr. Dannell tries to regain her position at the university while making provisions to ensure the Murkmire Stone remains in its crystal box. At your discretion, Dr. Dannell might ask the characters to help (see "Reinstate Dr. Dannell" below).

If the characters don't bring the Murkmire Stone to Dr. Dannell by midnight, it hatches into a nascent eldritch horror. Additionally, Alda Arkin might be revealed as a syndicate head. These outcomes are discussed in the "Further Adventures" section.

FOR THE GOLDEN VAULT

If the characters are working for the Golden Vault, they must deliver the Murkmire Stone to Dr. Dannell by midnight. Once they do, the organization rewards the characters with an uncommon magic item of their choice (subject to your approval) as payment. The item is delivered to the characters the next day.

FURTHER ADVENTURES

Once the heist ends, the adventure's story might continue. Use the following hooks for a successful or an unsuccessful mission.

MISSION IS SUCCESSFUL

If the characters bring the Murkmire Stone to Dr. Dannell before it hatches, use the following adventure hooks to continue their story.

Another Stone. After the Murkmire Stone is neutralized, Dr. Dannell hears from a colleague that another expedition in the Murkmire has unearthed a similar object. This time, however, the egg is closer to hatching, and strange happenings are befalling the excavation crew. With Dr. Dannell still discredited, it's up to the characters to venture into the dangerous Murkmire, locate the crew, and contain the egg. But when the characters arrive at the dig site, the egg has hatched—and now the characters must defeat the hatchling before it causes more harm. The hatchling uses the **ankheg** stat block, except its bite deals poison damage instead of acid damage.

Investigate the Hatchling. A strange creature has appeared in the crocodile enclosure at the Varkenbluff Zoo. The creature hatched from an egg similar to the Murkmire Stone and is now nearly 8 feet long. The zoo's baby crocodiles have disappeared, and animals near the crocodile enclosure have become violent. Headaches plague zookeepers who have tried to capture the creature. While Dr. Dannell tries to convince the zookeepers of the creature's nature, it's up to the characters to stop the hatchling. It's growing bigger by the hour as more animals disappear or act erratically. The hatchling uses the **ankheg** stat block, except its bite deals poison damage instead of acid damage.

Reinstate Dr. Dannell. Now that she knows her theories about the Murkmire Stone were correct, Dr. Dannell seeks to regain her position at Varkenbluff University. She has assembled proof that the Murkmire Stone is an eldritch creature's egg. But the museum's curator blocks her reinstatement bid—and then goes missing, casting further suspicion on Dr. Dannell. Dr. Dannell offers the characters a share of her future earnings for their help tracking down the curator and convincing her to reverse her vote against Dr. Dannell. The characters follow Alda's trail through Varkenbluff's high society and discover the curator is the head of an illegal syndicate fencing stolen objects. The characters must confront her and her minions to save Dr. Dannell's reputation and prevent stolen historical objects from being sold illegally.

MISSION IS UNSUCCESSFUL

If the characters don't retrieve the Murkmire Stone in time, use the following adventure hooks to continue their story.

A Stolen Stone. Shortly after the characters' unsuccessful heist, Alda Arkin steals the stone herself. The secret leader of an illegal syndicate that fences stolen historical objects, the curator believes she can get a high price for this strange piece. Using an arcane ritual, the curator renders the egg unable to hatch, but its dire effects persist. When the egg's eldritch energy transforms the curator into a Monstrosity, she holes up in her manor with the egg, unable to think straight. The characters must confront the warped creatures within Alda's manor—including the curator—before the stone can cause more mayhem.

Museum Feeding Frenzy. The Murkmire Stone hatches into an eight-foot-long, nascent eldritch horror, and the stone's effects cease. At first, the museum's staff assumes someone stole the stone and closes the building. But the hatchling terrorizes and eats the guards one by one. Curator Alda Arkin admits Dr. Dannell's theory might be correct and hires the characters to stop the eldritch creature. The wily monster is now the size of a pony and uses the **ankheg** stat block, except its bite deals poison damage instead of acid damage. It has set traps using the slime it secretes while metabolizing its food, and the entire museum is its nightmarish habitat. The characters must stop this creature before it outgrows the museum.

If the eldritch horror isn't defeated within a few days, it rampages through the museum's front doors, bolting toward Varkenbluff University. Now grown to enormous proportions, the juvenile eldritch horror uses the **behir** stat block but speaks no languages and has an Intelligence score of 18. It also has the following additional action option:

Spellcasting. The eldritch horror casts one of the following spells, requiring no components and using Intelligence as the spellcasting ability (save DC 14):

2/day each: *blindness/deafness, blur*
1/day: *project image*

The city needs heroes to track down the horror and incapacitate it before it causes even more carnage.

THE MURKMIRE STONE

Recently unearthed from the Murkmire outside the city of Varkenbluff, the nonmagical object called the Murkmire Stone is the egg of an eldritch creature. The opaque, light-green stone weighs 10 pounds and has abstract furrows on its surface.

The egg's removal from the Murkmire rapidly accelerated the development of the creature inside it. Starting at 10:30 p.m., the egg's stony shell becomes translucent, revealing the horror inside, and it begins to emit a pulse of magical energy every 10 minutes. Whenever a pulse occurs, each creature within 20 feet of the egg must make a DC 10 Wisdom saving throw, and a creature holding the egg has disadvantage on the roll. If the egg is placed in a *bag of holding* or some other portable extradimensional space, the effect radiates from the container instead. Any creature that fails the saving throw is subjected to an effect determined by rolling on the Murkmire Stone Effects table. When a creature rolls for a new effect, the previous one ends. The effects end when the egg hatches or when the egg is encased in the crystal box Dr. Dannell provides.

THE MURKMIRE STONE

MURKMIRE STONE EFFECTS

d12	Effect
1	Harsh whispers in an unknown language assault your consciousness. You gain vulnerability to psychic damage and can't maintain concentration on spells.
2	Adrenaline courses through your veins. You have advantage on Strength checks and Strength saving throws.
3	Your limbs feel leaden, and your body responds sluggishly. You have disadvantage on Dexterity checks and Dexterity saving throws.
4	Your skin takes on a weird sheen. You gain resistance to piercing and slashing damage.
5	Your walking speed increases by 5 feet.
6	Your mind is pulled in a thousand directions, making it difficult to focus. You have disadvantage on attack rolls.
7	Ripples pulse underneath your skin like vermin are skittering inside your flesh. You have disadvantage on Charisma checks and Charisma saving throws.
8	Your joints stiffen. You have disadvantage on Dexterity checks and Dexterity saving throws.
9	You receive premonitions of attacks made against you. Attack rolls against you have disadvantage.
10	Your thought processes are sluggish, as if you just awoke from terrible nightmares. You have disadvantage on Intelligence checks and Intelligence saving throws.
11	Your senses are dulled, as if an invisible barrier sits between you and reality. You have disadvantage on Wisdom (Perception) checks.
12	A shimmery film covers you. You gain a +2 bonus to AC.

THE AFTERLIFE CASINO, WHERE FORTUNES
ARE WON AND LOST, IS BUILT INSIDE A
MASSIVE CAVERN.

THE STYGIAN GAMBIT

AT THE AFTERLIFE CASINO, A THREE-DRAGON ante tournament called the Grand Minauros Invitational awards one winner with a sizable purse and a golden erinyes statuette. A former gambler with a score to settle hires the characters to steal the statuette as well as gold from the casino's vault before the tournament ends and the winner is declared. The characters must case the casino, steal what they came for, and escape.

ADVENTURE BACKGROUND

A skilled three-dragon ante player and a shrewd tiefling entrepreneur, Verity Kye toured the gambling circuit for years, making a name for herself and winning numerous large tournaments.

While on the circuit, Verity met a gnome gambler named Quentin Togglepocket. The two hit it off, and they formed a plan to save enough winnings to open their own casino. Just as they seemed poised to put their plan in action, Quentin disappeared, taking all their money with him—only to resurface years later, having built the Afterlife Casino using the stolen money.

Now, Verity needs the characters to break into the vault at the Afterlife Casino, steal the erinyes statuette meant to be the prize for the casino's three-dragon ante tournament, and retrieve her share of the money from the vault. For Verity, it's not the money or the statuette that matters—it's ensuring that Quentin's betrayal comes back to haunt him, and that he knows the person he betrayed made him pay.

USING THE GOLDEN VAULT

If you're using the Golden Vault as a patron, a golden key is delivered to the characters in whatever manner you deem fit. When the characters use this key to open their music box, the lid pops open and a soothing voice says the following:

> "Greetings, operatives. An ally of the Golden Vault named Verity Kye had her life's savings stolen from her by a devious gambling partner. We've found an opportunity to right this wrong. This quest, should you choose to undertake it, requires you to infiltrate the Afterlife Casino and steal a statuette and a sum of money. Meet with Verity at the Brine Widow tavern to learn more details. Good luck, operatives."

Closing the music box causes the golden key to vanish.

STARTING THE ADVENTURE

The characters start this adventure at the Brine Widow, a local pub near the water, having received directions from the Golden Vault (see above) or a mysterious invitation to discuss an "advantageous opportunity" with someone named Verity Kye, who waits for them in the Brine Widow's back room.

> ### ROLEPLAYING VERITY KYE
> Verity Kye is bold, confident, and genuinely kind—though not always nice. Quentin's betrayal cut her two ways—the deception from a potential business partner hurt, but such treachery from someone she called a friend was unforgivable.
>
> Verity has little patience for cheats and liars (card-table deception notwithstanding). Though she has no expectation of total honesty from the characters, blatant deception or an attempt to double-cross her quickly earns her ire.

AT THE BRINE WIDOW

Verity Kye (neutral good, tiefling **spy**) sits patiently at a table in the back room and makes small talk with the characters if they arrive in ones and twos. Once all the characters have arrived, Verity asks the last to enter to close the door.

To begin this scene, read the following text:

> The back room in the Brine Widow is well appointed, with a polished wood table, paintings of local landscapes, and wrought-iron lanterns. Platters on the table are piled with food, and a pot of tea steams in the center of the table.
>
> The tiefling before you has red skin, cobalt-blue eyes, and curly white hair she wears in long twists. Black horns rise from her forehead in tight spirals.
>
> "Thank you for accepting my invitation. I'm Verity Kye, and what I'm about to discuss with you requires the utmost secrecy. I can't stress to you enough how important it is that you speak nothing of what you hear within these four walls."

Once Verity gets assurances from the characters that they will keep quiet about her mission, she tells them about the job:

> "The Afterlife Casino is a new Nine Hells–themed attraction just outside town. The owner, Quentin Togglepocket, built it using prize money he stole from me, and I'd like you to give him hell. He's hosting a tournament there. I want you to steal the erinyes statuette he plans to award as a prize, embarrassing him in front of the big names at the tournament. I also want you to steal back the five thousand gold pieces he stole from me. Bring the statuette and the gold here, where I'll be waiting for you."

Verity can provide the characters with transportation, a rough map of the casino (see "Verity's Map" below), and a *bag of holding* for transporting the loot. She offers to pay the characters 100 gp apiece and cedes any claim on additional coin or items they acquire within the casino. A character who negotiates the reward and succeeds on a DC 15 Charisma (Intimidation or Persuasion) check gets her to raise the payment to 150 gp apiece.

The characters have just over 48 hours to steal the erinyes statuette, as the tournament ends two nights from now and the statuette will depart with the winner. While the characters could try to take the statuette from the winner on their way out, Verity wants to limit the heist's impact to Quentin as much as possible to shame him publicly.

VERITY'S BAG OF HOLDING

Made of purple fabric with red stitching, Verity's *bag of holding* functions the same as a standard *bag of holding* in every way but one: to remove any items from the bag, the holder must say the command word, "hyacinth." Verity's custom bag was given to her by a friend after Verity won her first professional tournament (ironically enough, the tournament where she defeated Quentin).

When Verity gives the party the *bag of holding*, she doesn't provide them with the command word.

VERITY'S MAP

The map Verity gives to the characters is a hand-drawn floor plan of the casino and the employee-only areas, as shown in map 2.1. Verity paid Gildur Draak, a dwarf who worked for the construction company that built the casino, to provide her with information about the building's nonpublic areas. However, Verity is no artist, so the map's accuracy is questionable.

WHAT VERITY KNOWS ABOUT THE CASINO

Verity can give the characters a few ideas about what to expect, but she hasn't been to the casino herself, so she can't provide details. She tells the characters the following information:

Arrival. Wooden boats shuttle visitors and personnel to and from the casino, which is built inside a cavern. The boats ply the river that leads to the cavern. (Verity knows no other way to enter the casino.)

Employees. The casino employs tieflings only.

Employee-Only Areas. Doors to employee-only areas have bright-green trim and are magically locked. Getting into them might require the characters to obtain an employee pass card, which bypasses the magical locks.

Security Mirrors. Magical security mirrors throughout the casino (marked on Verity's map with red icons) project what they reflect onto twin mirrors in the security office (area A16).

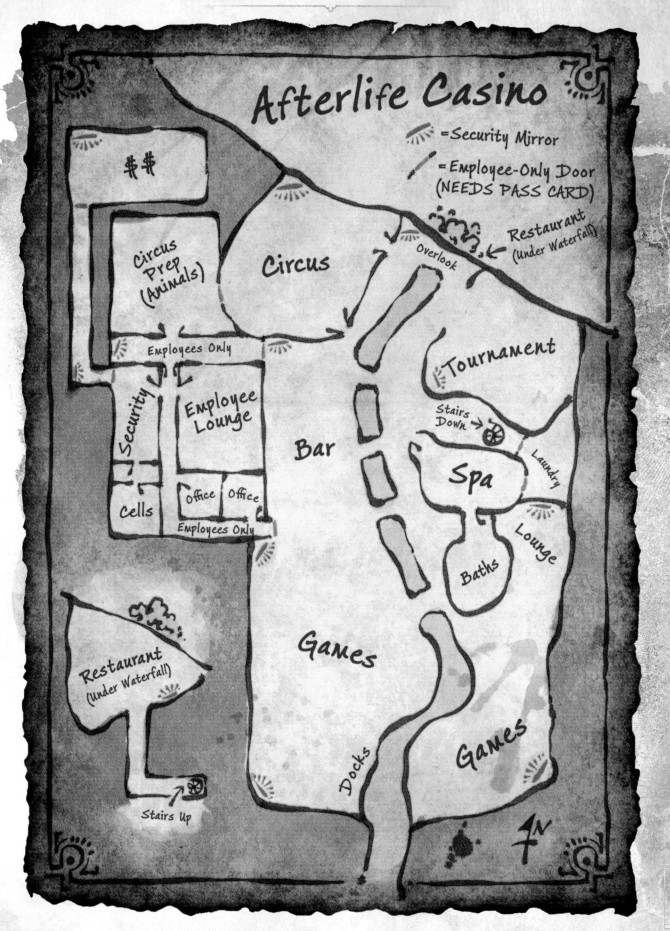

Afterlife Casino

= Security Mirror

= Employee-Only Door
(NEEDS PASS CARD)

Restaurant
(Under Waterfall)

Overlook

Circus Prep
(Animals)

Circus

Employees Only

Tournament

Security

Employee
Lounge

Bar

Stairs
Down

Spa

Laundry

Cells

Office   Office

Lounge

Employees Only

Baths

Games

Docks

Games

Restaurant
(Under Waterfall)

Stairs Up

N

The Prize. The gold coins and the erinyes statuette are kept in the vault. (Verity is not entirely correct. The coins are in the vault, but the statuette is on display in area A9, where the tournament takes place.)

PLANNING THE HEIST

How the characters execute the heist is up to them. Allow your players to flex their creativity.

The characters would be smart to scout the casino and learn as much as they can about the layout, personnel, and security arrangements before perpetrating the heist. They can also try to acquire employee uniforms and pass cards.

DISGUISES

Dealers, bartenders, and other floor employees wear sleek uniforms that consist of black tuxedo pants and red jackets with thin lapels. The characters might try to steal the uniforms to disguise themselves as new hires. The easiest approach would be to snatch uniforms from the laundry (area A7).

Since all casino employees are tieflings, non-tiefling characters who wish to disguise themselves as employees will need disguise kits or appropriate magic to perpetrate the deception.

Whenever a disguised character enters a situation where the disguise might be detected by an onlooker who takes more than a passing interest in the character, have the character make a Charisma (Deception) check. If the check's total is higher than the passive Wisdom (Perception) score of the onlooker, the disguise does its job. If the check fails, the onlooker sees through the disguise and either alerts security or demands a small bribe (5 gp) to keep silent.

EMPLOYEE PASS CARDS

Every casino employee carries a pass card made of green metal and embossed with a devil's smiling, winking visage. A *detect magic* spell reveals a faint aura of abjuration magic around the card.

Anyone in possession of a pass card can open any locked door in the casino, bypassing the *arcane lock* spell on the door.

As an action, a character within reach of an employee can attempt to steal that employee's pass card, doing so with a successful DC 15 Dexterity (Sleight of Hand) check. If the check fails by 5 or more, the employee notices the botched theft and cries for help. Otherwise, a failed check goes unnoticed.

THE AFTERLIFE CASINO

The Afterlife Casino lies three miles north of the nearest town. It's an architectural marvel built into a natural cavern carved by a river nicknamed the River Styx. Since the real River Styx is a route to the afterlife, Quentin Togglepocket named his establishment the Afterlife Casino.

After passing through the casino, the river pours over a waterfall into a larger body of water (which could be a lake or an ocean, depending on where you set the adventure). The waterfall isn't a safe way to enter or leave the casino.

ARRIVING AT THE CASINO

The characters can take the carriage offered to them by Verity or find their own way to the casino. At a branch in the road, they see a freshly painted and lacquered sign declaring, "This way to the Afterlife!" in gaudy, gold lettering, with an arrow pointing down the narrower branch. Characters who follow this route for a short distance come to a cobbled turnaround and lot where carriage drivers can wait while their patrons gamble.

As the characters step from the carriage, they are greeted by a red-robed tiefling **commoner** who welcomes them to the Afterlife Casino. This tiefling directs them down a brightly lit row of docks, where boats wait to take the characters downriver. The casino's entrance is visible a short distance away, where the river enters a wide-mouthed cave.

BOAT RIDE

A tiefling ferrier (**commoner**) in a heavy, hooded robe waits silently to convey characters to the casino.

The ferrier plays the part of Charon on the real River Styx. The tiefling keeps their hood up at all times and doesn't speak to passengers. If the characters touch the ferrier or attempt to pull back the ferrier's hood, the ferrier breaks character and asks the characters to stop—the tiefling is just trying to do their job.

When the characters enter the casino for the first time, read the following:

> The ferrier ably navigates your boat downriver and into an underground channel. As the cave mouth swallows you, you hear music over the echo of a distant waterfall.
>
> The cave's ceiling rises high above your heads, and dancing lights bob around hanging stalactites. The river winds through the casino floor, splitting the cavernous chamber in two and passing under arched stone bridges at various points. Card tables and other gaming stations surrounded by chattering patrons fill the open space. A cheer rises from deeper in the cavern, which is decorated to suggest excitement, opportunity, and excess.
>
> The ferrier steers your boat toward the left bank, and your boat rocks as it bumps up against a wooden dock. The ferrier then raises one hand, gesturing at the glittering sights before you, and intones in a deep, raspy voice: "Welcome to the Afterlife. Temptation awaits."

The characters can leave the boat and freely explore what the casino has to offer. Any character who tips the ferrier with two coins gains inspiration.

CASINO FEATURES

The Afterlife Casino is built within a natural cavern. Its common features are described in the following sections.

CASHIER STATIONS

The casino has four cashier's stations (in areas A2 and A4), where tiefling cashiers (**commoners**) in smiling devil masks make change or trade out cash for chips. The casino's chips are thin, painted wooden disks. Stamped on both sides of every chip is the casino's emblem: a golden pitchfork.

A cashier has no cash on hand but is attuned to a magical sigil on the station's countertop. The cashier places coinage on the sigil, sending it directly to the vault, or pulls coins from the vault through the same sigil. Withdrawals of more than 250 gp require a second cashier to confirm the transaction. Transactions occurring through the sigils are automatically recorded in the magical ledger in the clerk's office (area A15).

CEILINGS

The ceiling in the public parts of the casino is 50 feet high and festooned with hanging stalactites. The ceilings in the employee-only areas are 20 feet high and smooth.

DOORS

The casino's interior doors are made of wood. *Arcane lock* spells have been cast on the doors that lead to the employee-only areas, the vault hallway, and the vault itself. These doors have bright-green trim, making them obvious to visitors. (On map 5.2, these doors are marked with dots to indicate they are locked.)

Casino personnel use pass cards (see "Employee Pass Cards" earlier in the adventure) to bypass the *arcane lock* spells on the doors, which can be shouldered open with a DC 25 Strength (Athletics) check.

EMPLOYEE-ONLY AREAS

Entering an employee-only area requires a pass card (see "Employee Pass Cards" earlier in the adventure).

Security guards who encounter unauthorized individuals in employee-only areas immediately try to usher them out. If those individuals resist, the guards attempt to apprehend the intruders and take them to the holding cells (area A17).

LIGHTS AND MUSIC

The casino is lit by programmed *dancing lights* spells that create flames of a hellish hue. These lights float and bob at varying heights. The employee tunnels contain *continual flame* spells cast on sconces.

The music that plays throughout the casino is illusory and sounds a lot like cowboy country music. The music plays more softly in employee-only areas.

SECURITY GUARDS

Five tiefling security guards (use the **thug** stat block) patrol the casino floor, and a sixth stands next to the display case containing the erinyes statuette (in area A9). If the characters cause a ruckus, the nearest guard moves toward them and tries to quell the disturbance without resorting to violence. If attacked, the guard reacts in kind and shouts for reinforcements. All other guards arrive in 3 rounds.

SECURITY MIRRORS

Throughout the casino are security mirrors, each one anchored to a wall at a downward angle twelve feet off the floor. A *detect magic* spell reveals an aura of divination magic around each mirror, which is a Large object with AC 13, 5 hit points, and immunity to poison and psychic damage. In addition to functioning as a normal mirror, each security mirror acts as a magical scrying device, allowing guards in the security office (area A16) to see through it like a window. Casting *dispel magic* on a security mirror suppresses its scrying property for 10 minutes.

Breaking a mirror or suppressing its magic leads two guards from area A16 to investigate and report what they learn to Quentin.

WALLS AND FLOORS

The casino's perimeter walls are made of rough, naturally carved stone. Interior walls are made of 2-foot-thick stone; these walls look natural but were sculpted using *stone shape* spells. The floors are made of smooth worked stone and are covered with garish rugs.

GAMES OF CHANCE

The casino has many diversions for its patrons to enjoy, the most popular being games of chance.

THREE-DRAGON ANTE

Three-dragon ante is a card game. If you own an actual three-dragon ante deck, you can play the card game for real. Otherwise, adjudicate the outcome of a three-dragon ante game using d12s and the following rules:

Step 1. Randomly determine which participant is the dealer.

Step 2. Each participant (including the dealer) places their opening bet, then rolls five d12s to determine their hand, keeping these die rolls hidden from the other participants.

Step 3. Starting to the left of the dealer and continuing clockwise, each participant reveals one of their die rolls. This step is repeated twice more; on the second and third round, each participant can raise their bet before revealing their next die roll. The other participants each have three options: match the bet, raise their bet (in which case all participants must match that bet in turn), or fold, forfeiting any bet they've placed and dropping out of the game.

Step 4. Each participant who hasn't folded totals their die rolls. The one with the highest total wins. The winner becomes the dealer for the next game (assuming the participant wants to keep playing).

LIFE AND DEATH

Life and death is a dice game played between the house (represented by a dealer) and a player. While up to five players can sit at a table, their only opponent is the house.

To play, each player places a bet; once bets have been placed, the house and the players each roll a d20. If a player rolls lower than the dealer, the house wins. A player who rolls higher than the dealer reclaims the money they bet and wins that same amount from the house.

War. A player who ties with the house has two options: the player can surrender and lose half their bet, or the player can "go to war," in which case the player must double their bet, and then the player and dealer both roll again.

Push Your Luck. When a player wins a roll of life and death, they can opt to push their luck on their next bet. In this case, they bet everything they won on the last roll (their ante plus the winnings from the house). If they win, the house pays double their bet.

COPPER SLOTS

These machines, referred to by some casino patrons as "tricky devils," are simple clockwork devices that accept copper coins. Each machine has a spring-loaded lever and five identical spinning cylinders called reels. Six golden, Infernal runes are painted on each reel. A player inserts between 1 and 9 copper coins into the machine's slot and pulls the lever, which causes the reels to spin, stop, and display a row of five runes. The player wins by matching three or more runes.

To determine the result of a pull, have the player roll 5d6 (the dice represent the five reels of Infernal runes). The player's goal is to roll as many of the same number on the dice as possible. The payout, if any, varies according to the results, as shown in the Copper Slots Payouts table.

COPPER SLOTS PAYOUTS

5d6 Result	Payout
Three of a kind	2-to-1
Four of a kind	4-to-1
Five of a kind	10-to-1

QUENTIN TOGGLEPOCKET

Quentin Togglepocket (lawful evil, gnome **noble**) has a Mephistophelian aspect to his appearance. He dresses garishly, slicks back his wavy hair, curls his mustache, and cultivates a long, pointy beard. Only the freckles across his nose undermine his devilish countenance.

Quentin used to be a professional three-dragon ante player, but his rise to prominence was cut short ten years ago when, in a major tournament, he lost the final gambit (and the entire prize) to a relative newcomer: a young tiefling named Verity Kye.

Quentin never forgave Verity for what he felt was a stunning humiliation and vowed to take his revenge. He spent the next several years building up a false friendship with her, traveling the gambling circuit with her and cultivating a mutual dream: owning and operating their own casino. Then, three years ago, he saw his opportunity, stole all the money they had pooled together, and vanished from Verity's life.

ADVENTURERS KILL TIME PLAYING THREE-DRAGON
ANTE WHILE SCOPING OUT THE AFTERLIFE CASINO.

Opening the Afterlife Casino was the final coup de grace in Quentin's vengeance against Verity, and he is riding high on the grand-opening weekend. He secretly hopes Verity arrives to confront him herself so he can laugh in her face.

Quentin couldn't have accomplished his goals alone. To make his casino a reality, he sold his soul to Mammon, the archdevil of Minauros (the third layer of the Nine Hells). In turn, one of Mammon's subordinates put Quentin in touch with wizards who could help him build and decorate the casino.

Roleplaying Quentin

Quentin sees himself as Verity's victim and portrays himself as a martyr for losing to her. He sees the theft and his new casino as his rightful chance to even the scales and reclaim his dignity.

Quentin is a classic villain, happy to monologue if given the chance—how will the characters know how brilliant he is otherwise?

Quentin's Location

You decide where Quentin is at any given time. If he's not chatting with patrons or boosting staff morale on the casino floor, he's usually in his office (area A14). He also visits the holding cells (area A17) to question patrons who have been detained by security.

Casino Patrons

The Afterlife Casino is bustling with patrons from all parts of the world. Roll or pick randomly from the Casino Patrons table when you need a patron.

Casino Patrons

d6	Patron
1	Lysa Silvertongue (neutral, tiefling **noble**) is eager to break the monotony of her life of leisure.
2	Georgie Simmons (neutral good, human **commoner**) is a down-and-out loser who is determined to have a good time.
3	Karlton Keyes (lawful neutral, human **commoner**), a merchant, hopes to open his own casino and is here doing research.
4	Lowell Brassborn (neutral good, dwarf **commoner**) thinks gambling is a waste of money but is here with his sister, Lorna.
5	Lorna Brassborn (lawful neutral, dwarf **commoner**) is a hard-nosed copper slots player who thinks she has the machines' algorithms figured out.
6	Rythil Ire (chaotic neutral, elf **noble**) aims to enjoy the cocktails at Bar Malbolge and soak away his stress in the spa.

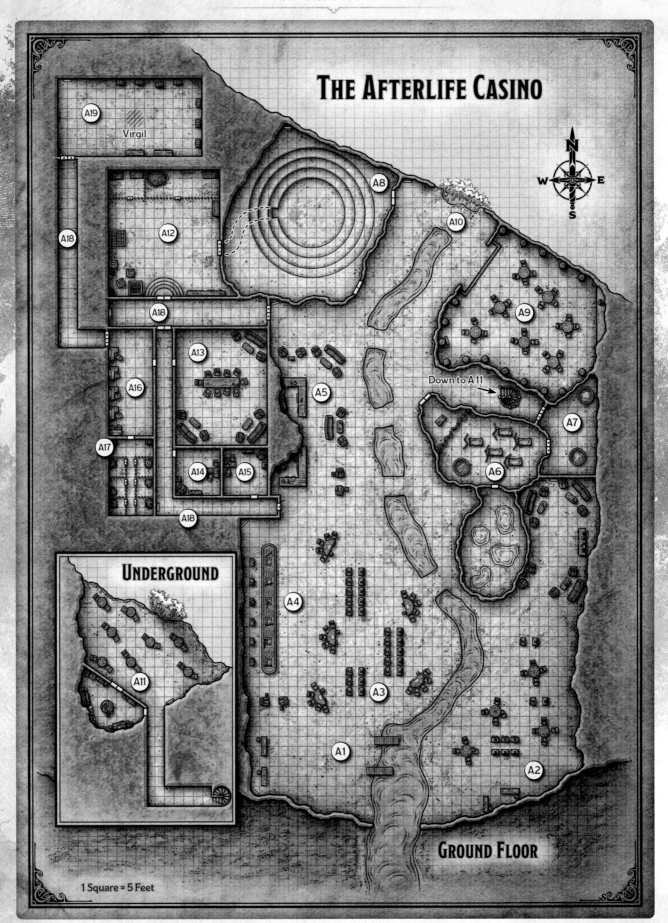

THE AFTERLIFE CASINO

A19

Virgil

A8

A10

A18

A12

A18

A9

A13

Down to A11

A5

A16

A7

A17

A6

A14

A15

A18

UNDERGROUND

A4

A11

A3

A1

A2

GROUND FLOOR

1 Square = 5 Feet

MIKE SCHLEY

AFTERLIFE CASINO LOCATIONS

The casino is divided into nine areas of gaming and entertainment. The north end of the casino ends in an 80-foot rocky cliff face. The river that runs through the casino pours over the cliff at the overlook (area A10) and empties into a larger body of water below.

The following locations are keyed to map 2.2.

A1: DOCKING AREA

The casino's boats load and unload passengers at a pair of wooden docks. Two tiefling attendants (**commoners**) help patrons into and out of the boats.

Patrons are expected to abide by the casino's rules, which are posted on placards near the docks. The placards read as follows:

> **RULES IN THE AFTERLIFE:**
> Stay out of the River Styx.
> Don't cheat. (Cheaters never prosper.)
> Don't accost or threaten other patrons or the staff.
> Keep your weapons hidden or sheathed at all times.
> Only employees may pass through
> green-trimmed doors.
> WIN, WIN, WIN!

A2: AVERNUS

This area holds three-dragon ante tables and copper slot machines. Just south of the game tables are two cashier booths. Just north of the games area is a secluded lounge that holds a small bar as well as chairs and couches.

Security Mirrors. A security mirror hangs in the southeast corner overlooking the games area. Another security mirror hangs on the north wall, above the chairs in the lounge area.

A3: DIS

This section contains rows of copper slot machines and five life and death tables, each with a different bet value: 1 cp, 5 cp, 1 sp, 1 gp, and 10 gp.

A4: MINAUROS

> A narrow racing track dominates the center of this section, with shouting and cheering patrons clustered around it. Numbered rats scurry along their respective lanes. As the rats cross the finish line, cries of victory and groans of defeat erupt from the patrons. Just south of the track are a pair of lounge chairs and two cashier booths staffed by tieflings wearing devil masks.

Security Mirrors. A security mirror overlooks the cashier booths in the southwest corner. Another security mirror hangs in the northwest corner of this area, overlooking the track.

A5: BAR MALBOLGE

Bar Malbolge features two bars and plenty of plush, comfortable chairs and cushions. The tiefling bartenders (**commoners**) serve spirits and a bitter ale called Brimstone Gulp. This ale is served in copper flagons embossed with prancing imps. Patrons can also buy cigars here for 1 cp each.

Security Mirror. A security mirror in the northwest corner of this area faces the northernmost bar and seating area.

A6: PHLEGETHOSIAN SPA & STYGIAN BATHS

> The air in here is warmer and more humid than in the casino proper and bears a sulfurous fragrance. A tiefling seated behind a desk gives you a warm smile. Chintz curtains are drawn behind her.
>
> "Dear souls," says the tiefling. "Care to enjoy a massage, relax in our sauna, or take a warm bath?"

The tiefling attendant (**commoner**) is happy to schedule massages or time in the sauna or baths. Patrons are allowed to explore the areas beyond the curtain:

Phlegethosian Spa. The northernmost chamber is where patrons receive therapeutic massages (10 gp for an hour) or relax in the wood-sided sauna for free. A locked double door in the east wall leads to the laundry (area A7).

Stygian Baths. The southernmost room contains four steaming pools of water. Patrons can pay 2 gp for two hours in the pools or 5 gp for an all-day pass.

A7: LAUNDRY
Employee-Only Area

This area holds two large washtubs, as well as a clothesline hung with towels and employee uniforms. Characters who want to disguise themselves as employees can find plenty of uniforms here.

A8: CIRQUE MALADOMINI

Cirque Maladomini performs here for the enjoyment of all. Hour-long performances occur here once every four hours. Each show presents a mix of tiefling acrobats and trained animals, all performing to the music of a tiefling banjo player. The star of the show is a trained lion named Emrys, which leaps through flaming hoops on command. See area A12 for more information about these creatures.

Casino patrons come and go through two sets of double doors in the east wall. Descending rings of seats encircle a 35-foot-wide, 10-foot-deep depression in the floor. When the circus is in full swing, performers and trained animals enter and leave through an open tunnel in the west wall of the depression. This tunnel leads to a staging area (area A12) behind a locked double door.

Security Mirror. A security mirror hangs in the northwest corner, overlooking the seating area.

A9: Cania

> Steps lead to the sunken floor of a gambling haven ringed with pillars of black basalt. Seven three-dragon ante tables take up the floorspace. A three-foot-high shelf carved into the far wall bears a glass case, displayed in which is a gold statuette of a winged devil. Standing next to the display case is a tiefling security guard.

The five tables closest to the entrance are high-stakes tables (50 gp buy-in) open to anyone, while the easternmost two tables are reserved for the final rounds of the Grand Minauros Invitational tournament.

Grand Minauros Invitational. When the characters first arrive here, the tournament is in full swing. Its eight remaining participants (see the "Tournament Participants" sidebar) are arranged as shown in the Tournament Seating table. Between rounds of the tournament, characters are free to mingle and chat with the tournament participants.

Tournament Seating

Table 1	Table 2
Anaïs Bellefleur	Jetta Moore
Karn Ironpebble	Nightshade
Lahdia Mizreem	Ruthie Swifford
Whipp Walsh	Wumpus Thistledown

Security Guard and Display Case. A tiefling security guard (use the **thug** stat block) stands next to the display case and allows guests to examine the statuette without touching the case.

The display case is 2 feet wide, 2 feet deep, and 3 feet tall, and it weighs 25 pounds. It is a Small object that has AC 13, 3 hit points, and immunity to poison and psychic damage. The erinyes statuette is a Tiny object that weighs 9 pounds.

A character who examines the display case and succeeds on a DC 18 Intelligence (Investigation) check spots a line of barely visible runes inscribed around the perimeter of each pane of glass. A *detect magic* spell reveals an aura of abjuration magic emanating from these runes. Damaging the case triggers a magical trap that forces each creature in a 15-foot-radius sphere centered on the case to succeed on a DC 17 Wisdom saving throw or be paralyzed for 1 minute.

The front of the display case is a hinged door with a locked latch. The door can be unlocked and opened using the key found in Quentin's office (area A14). As an action, a character using thieves' tools can try to pick the lock, doing so with a successful DC 15 Dexterity check.

Security Mirror. A security mirror hangs on a pillar in the southwest corner, overlooking the room.

A10: Waterfall Overlook

> The casino floor ends where the river spills over the edge of a cliff and into a much larger body of water. The waterfall is thunderous, drowning out the noise from the casino. Above the waterfall is a stone overlook bounded by three-foot-high railings.

The waterfall is 100 feet tall and plunges into water that is 30 feet deep.

Security Mirror. A security mirror is mounted in the northeast corner, overlooking the area.

A11: Nessus

Nessus is a restaurant located 20 feet below the casino. It can be reached by descending a spiral staircase in the hallway between areas A6 and A9.

The restaurant's dining area sits on a ledge behind the waterfall (area A10). The ceiling here is uneven but is roughly 12 feet high. A smooth wall separates the dining area from the kitchen, which contains two large stoves.

The restaurant is open all day and offers the following menu of options:

> **NESSUS—MENU**
> Appetizers
> Seasonal pan-fried fungi with garlic butter • 2 cp
> Spicy shredded stirge sliders • 3 cp
> Main Dishes
> Abyssal chicken egg omelet • 1 sp
> Otto's irresistible noodles • 5 cp
> Otyugh steak, well done • 3 sp
> Desserts & Drinks
> Night hag's delight (blackberry tart) • 2 cp
> Stench kow cheese plate • 2 cp
> Nessian liqueur • 2 cp
> Coffee/tea • 1 cp (first cup is complimentary!)

Security Mirror. A security mirror hangs on the southeast wall, just north of the entry tunnel, overlooking the dining room.

A12: Staging Area and Animal Cages
Employee-Only Area

Cirque Maladomini uses this room as a holding pen for animals and a staging area for performers. Characters entering from the south must descend a flight of steps to reach the chamber's sunken floor.

When the characters enter this room for the first time, read the following:

> This room smells like hay and musk. Three crates rest on the floor in one corner, and a portable cage on rollers sits beside them. Floor-to-ceiling bars form two larger cages against the north wall. A wooden chest sits against the east wall near the biggest cage. Resting on the lid of the chest is a ring of keys.

A locked double door in the middle of the east wall conceals a curvy tunnel that leads to area A8.

When Cirque Maladomini isn't performing in area A8, the northwest cage holds three trained **baboons** that shriek whenever someone new enters the room, and the northeast cage contains a quiet trained **lion** named Emrys. Three tiefling acrobats (**commoners** with Acrobatics +4 and Performance +4) are also rehearsing together in the middle of the room. One tiefling performs a one-handed handstand, while another twirls a flaming hoop, and the third plucks a banjo. During performances, the tieflings and the animals are all absent.

Wooden Chest. The wooden chest next to the lion's cage is unlocked. The keys on the chest unlock the doors to the animal cages. The chest itself contains juggling pins, rubber balls, colorful streamers, and other circus doodads. A *potion of animal friendship* can be found here as well.

A13: Employee Lounge
Employee-Only Area

> This room is sixty feet long by fifty feet wide. A long table surrounded by ten chairs takes up the center of the room, and the far corners each hold a couch, two cushioned chairs, and a coffee table.

At any time during casino hours, three tiefling employees (**commoners**) are here on a break.

The off-duty employees are chatty and not overly fond of their employer. Characters who question the tieflings can learn the following information:

Minotaur Skeleton. Quentin recently added a new security measure to the casino's vault: an animated minotaur skeleton. Quentin refers to it as "Virgil." It can be controlled using a magic rod that Quentin keeps in his office (area A14).

Security Office Personnel. Three guards staff the security office across the hall.

A14: QUENTIN'S OFFICE
Employee-Only Area

> This roomy office contains an L-shaped desk sized for a gnome, cushioned chairs, and knickknacks on shelves. A painted bas-relief spans the entire north wall and depicts a host of winged devils catching mortals as they plunge into the depths of hell.

If Quentin Togglepocket is in his office and notices one or more of the characters, add the following:

> A garishly dressed gnome with a devilish countenance to rival Mephistopheles sits behind the desk, stroking his pointy beard. When he notices you, he curls his lips in a lopsided smile. "Well, now," he says. "What can I do for you?"

Quentin (lawful evil, gnome **noble**) shrewdly shuns combat, but he draws his rapier and defends himself if threatened and cornered. As an action, he can utter a prayer to Mammon, which causes two **spined devils** to magically emerge from the bas-relief on the north wall. Each devil appears in an unoccupied space next to the north wall, acts as Quentin's ally, and sticks around for 1 minute before returning to the Minauros, the third layer of the Nine Hells. If the devils are defeated, Quentin shouts for help, attracting the three security guards from area A16 if they haven't already been dealt with.

Ain't Foolin' No One. Quentin personally hires all casino staff and knows all their names. Consequently, he isn't fooled by characters pretending to be employees he doesn't know.

Quentin's Counteroffer. If the characters come clean to Quentin, he is amused to hear that Verity hired them to rob his casino. He refuses to give the characters what they came for, instead offering to pay them 150 gp each to forgo the heist and return to Verity with a letter from him.

If the characters agree to his terms, Quentin writes a quick letter, slides it into an envelope, and hands it to them with their payment before leading them back to the casino floor. In addition, he gives each of them a handful of casino chips equivalent to 15 gp.

Quentin's letter to Verity reads as follows:

> It is such a disappointment when one attempts to conceal their lack of skill by sending others to do their dirty work. Nevertheless, after all this time, it appears I am, in fact, better than you.—Q.

Desk Drawers. The top drawer of Quentin's desk holds a red candle, a quill, a jar of ink, a few sheets of parchment, a few envelopes, a tiny glass key that unlocks the display case in area A9, a copper ring bearing Quentin's wax seal, and a velvet pouch containing 25 gp.

The bottom drawer of Quentin's desk contains an unlocked wooden case that contains a 12-inch-long rod made of bone with a stylized copper minotaur head mounted at each end of it. A *detect magic* spell reveals an aura of enchantment magic emanating from the rod. As an action, the holder of the rod can use it to telepathically command the minotaur skeleton in area A19, provided the rod is within 30 feet of it. The minotaur skeleton follows such commands to the best of its ability. If the minotaur skeleton ever leaves the casino, it goes berserk and can't be controlled by anyone, and the rod turns to dust.

Treasure. Quentin wears nine gem-inlaid gold rings (100 gp each) on his fingers and keeps an employee pass card in his waistcoat pocket (see "Employee Pass Cards" earlier in the adventure).

A15: CLERK'S OFFICE
Employee-Only Area

> This office contains an L-shaped desk, atop which sits a candlestick and a thick, open ledger. Other furnishings include cushioned chairs and two bare bookshelves.

The ledger on the desk magically tracks all money moving in and out of the casino. Every coin and chip that passes through the cashier booths is recorded here in the appropriate column, scrawled in ink as if by some invisible hand. Any character who spends 1 minute reading the ledger can verify that the casino's vault contains roughly 5,000 gp in coinage.

A16: SECURITY OFFICE
Employee-Only Area

Five desks face the west wall, which is covered with mirrors. Each mirror on the wall corresponds to a security mirror elsewhere in the casino, and whatever is happening within line of sight of the mirrors is displayed here. Three tiefling security guards (**thugs**) monitor the mirrors.

Ring of Keys. A ring of eight keys dangles from a hook next to the south door. Each cell and chest in area A17 has a corresponding key that unlocks it.

A17: Holding Cells
Employee-Only Area

This area holds six jail cells and two padlocked wooden chests (see "Wooden Chests" below). The keys in the security office (area A16) unlock the cells and the chests. As an action, a character using thieves' tools can try to pick a lock, doing so with a successful DC 17 Dexterity check. If the character tries to pick the lock of a cell door from inside the cell, the check is made with disadvantage.

Wooden Chests. Both chests are unlocked and empty. If one or more characters are detained here, their weapons are locked in the chests for safekeeping.

A18: Back Hallways
Employee-Only Area

These three hallways are used frequently by casino employees. At your discretion, characters who linger here might encounter one or more of these employees heading to or from the casino floor.

Security Mirrors. Each hallway has a security mirror on its west wall that faces a single or double door to the east.

A19: Vault
Employee-Only Area

The double door leading to the vault has cast-iron devil faces mounted on its south side. If a creature without an employee pass card comes within 10 feet of the double door, the devil faces open their mouths and breathe a 10-foot-wide, 30-foot-long line of fire down the hallway. Each creature in the line must make a DC 14 Dexterity saving throw, taking 10 (3d6) fire damage on a failed save, or half as much damage on a successful one. This trap resets at the next dawn.

When the characters peer into the vault for the first time, read the following:

> The vault is forty feet deep and almost twice as wide. A security mirror stares back at you from the far wall. Seven treasure chests rest on low tables positioned against the north and east walls, and two tall wardrobes stand against the south wall.
>
> Standing in the middle of the room is the animated skeleton of a minotaur.

Virgil the **minotaur skeleton** stands guard in the center of the room. Virgil attacks any intruders who aren't escorted by Quentin. A character who has Quentin's magic rod (see area A14) can use it to telepathically command Virgil.

Iron Chests. A *detect magic* spell reveals an aura of transmutation magic around each iron chest. All seven chests are magically linked to the cashier stations in the casino. The interior of each chest's lid is scribed with a rune that enables the cashiers to remotely deposit coins into and withdraw coins from the chests. The chests must be closed for their magic to function, and the chests become nonmagical if removed from the vault.

At any given time, the seven chests contain mixed coinage worth a total of 2d4 × 1,000 gp.

If all the coins are removed from the chests, the cashiers quickly discover they are unable to withdraw money from the vault and alert the guards immediately. It's only a matter of time until someone investigates.

Security Mirror. A security mirror hangs on the north wall of the vault, facing the double door.

Wardrobes. The wardrobes hold items of value given by rich patrons for collateral against the house: a gold and ruby necklace (250 gp), a jade rabbit figurine (75 gp), and a *+1 rapier*.

Conclusion

The adventure ends when the characters return to Verity Kye with the fruits of their heist, Quentin's letter, or nothing:

Returning with the Loot. If the characters obtained the statuette and the money and return both to Verity Kye, she is pleased. She pays the characters and thanks them for their service.

Returning Empty-Handed. If the characters return empty-handed, Verity is disappointed but open to the possibility of giving them more opportunities to prove themselves, if they're game for it.

Returning with Quentin's Letter. If the characters return without the loot but give Quentin's letter to Verity, she reads it in furious silence. She then tells the characters to leave and offers them no recompense.

For the Golden Vault

If the characters accomplish the heist for the Golden Vault, Verity ensures that the Golden Vault learns about the characters' success. She also informs the characters that they are entitled to an uncommon magic item of their choice (subject to your approval) as payment for the statuette. The item is delivered to the characters the next day.

A FRIENDLY SPIRIT APPEARS AS A
DISEMBODIED HEAD, WARNING HEROES
ABOUT THE DANGERS THAT AWAIT THEM IN
DELPHI MANSION.

REACH FOR THE STARS

MARKOS DELPHI'S CURIOSITY HAS TAKEN a tragic turn. A Far Realm entity called Krokulmar has taken control of Markos, compelling him to commit evil acts. At Krokulmar's command, Markos is using a book called *The Celestial Codex* to bring part of Krokulmar into the world. The book's rightful owner hired adventurers to retrieve *The Celestial Codex* and prevent Markos from using it, but these adventurers fell prey to the horrors of Delphi Mansion. A new group of adventurers—the player characters—must now complete the task. Meanwhile, Markos is close to accomplishing Krokulmar's goal.

Acquiring *The Celestial Codex* is the primary goal of this adventure, but the characters also have a chance to free Markos from the Far Realm entity's control. Body horror is a recurring theme in this adventure; before running it, discuss with your players their level of comfort with these elements.

ADVENTURE BACKGROUND

Markos Delphi grew up with an insatiable curiosity. Eventually, he had his fill of worldly knowledge and began delving into the arcane, eager to understand the secrets of the planes of existence. Raised in a family of scholars and academics, Markos wished to make a breakthrough discovery that would propel himself and his family to new heights.

This quest for understanding became Markos's obsession. He sequestered himself and his fellow researchers in the remote Delphi Mansion. Markos used astrology-based magic to attempt to contact other planes, and something finally answered him: an entity that called itself Krokulmar. This entity made a pact with Markos, granting insight into the multiverse in exchange for influence on the Material Plane. Markos assumed Krokulmar's intentions were benign.

Krokulmar hails from the Far Realm. In making its pact with Markos, Krokulmar corrupted the mansion and its residents, then eroded Markos's sense of self until he became eager to commit evil acts in Krokulmar's service.

Acting under Krokulmar's control, Markos visited one of his peers, a sage named Vasil Talistrome. Markos incapacitated Vasil and stole *The Celestial Codex* from the sage's library. In addition to containing lore about stars and the planes of existence, the book describes rituals that can be used to summon extraplanar entities. Krokulmar needs Markos to perform one of these rituals to bind a fragment of Krokulmar to the Material Plane.

Without any knowledge of the profane entity influencing Markos, Vasil Talistrome hired a warrior named Elra Lionheart to retrieve *The Celestial Codex*. Elra and three other adventurers traveled to Markos's mansion, where they witnessed a number of peculiar magical effects caused by Krokulmar's growing influence. One by one, they fell prey to the mansion's sinister occupants.

USING THE GOLDEN VAULT

If you're using the Golden Vault as a patron, a golden key is delivered to the characters in whatever manner you deem fit. When the characters use this key to open their music box, the lid pops open and a soothing voice says the following:

> "Greetings, operatives. Vasil Talistrome, a sage who works with the Golden Vault, has reported the theft of *The Celestial Codex*. This book contains rituals that, in the wrong hands, could be used to summon dangerous extraplanar entities. The book was stolen by a nobleman named Markos Delphi, who might be under the influence of some profane entity. Four adventurers hired to retrieve the book from Delphi Mansion have disappeared without a trace. We have good reason to believe they're dead. This quest, should you choose to undertake it, requires you to travel to Delphi Mansion and retrieve The Celestial Codex. May you fare better than the last group. Good luck, operatives."

Closing the music box causes the golden key to vanish.

Adventure Hooks

If you're not using the Golden Vault as the characters' patron, choose one of the following adventure hooks instead.

Hired by Vasil

Vasil Talistrome, a human sage who lives in a city of your choice, hires the characters to retrieve *The Celestial Codex* from Delphi Mansion. Vasil doesn't want any harm to befall Markos, whom he still regards as a friend. Vasil is worried about what might've prompted Markos to steal the book and what he might do with the book's information.

The characters aren't the first group to receive this quest, as Vasil is quick to mention. The last group he hired was led by a human warrior named Elra Lionheart. Elra and her companions perished in Delphi Mansion. (Vasil paid for the casting of a *divination* spell that confirmed as much.)

Vasil's Reward

Vasil is prepared to pay 250 gp to each character if *The Celestial Codex* is safely delivered to him.

Hired by Markos's Family

Shortly after Markos stole *The Celestial Codex* from the library of Vasil Talistrome, the incident was reported to Markos's wealthy family. Several family members are concerned about Markos and fear his recent studies have led him down a troubled path. One of Markos's family members hires the characters to travel to Delphi Mansion and stop Markos from doing anything that might hurt himself or others. The family member asks the characters to return *The Celestial Codex* to its rightful owner, preferably without harming Markos.

Reward

Markos's family is prepared to pay 100 gp to each character for delivering *The Celestial Codex* safely to Vasil Talistrome, plus an extra 150 gp each if the characters bring Markos home. (The family strongly prefers him to be alive but pays to have him raised from the dead if necessary.)

Meeting Elra

The journey to Delphi Mansion can be as eventful as you wish. When the characters get within 1 mile of the mansion, they encounter a manifestation of the late Elra Lionheart.

Elra's spirit manifests as a disembodied head. In this form, Elra reaches out to the characters and provides some helpful information:

A ray of sunlight shines down on a tree stump by the side of road, and the disembodied head of a human woman appears above the stump.

"My name is Elra Lionheart," says the head. "My companions and I died trying to retrieve *The Celestial Codex*. Heed my words, lest you too fall prey to the dangers of Delphi Mansion. Markos is using the book to conjure an otherworldly being not meant to exist in this world. Meanwhile, his purple-robed cultists busy themselves with eldritch experiments. Beware creatures that look like puddles of eyes and mouths. Beware the thing that has hooks for hands. And beware the mansion itself, for it transforms weirdly. Most of all, stop Markos before it's too late!

"My companions and I had a camp on a bluff due south of the mansion. If you go there first, you'll find a backpack containing a map of the mansion and some notes we acquired from a dubious source. These might help you plan your approach. Best of luck!"

The characters have a choice: go to Elra's camp or to the mansion.

At your discretion, Elra's spectral head can float alongside the characters as they explore Delphi Mansion. In this form, Elra can't be harmed, nor can she physically interact with her surroundings in any way. Moreover, Elra can't stray more than a few feet from the characters. But she can provide helpful advice if the characters get stuck and don't know what to do.

If you choose not to have Elra accompany the characters, her head fades away.

Elra's Camp

Elra and her companions camped on a bluff that has an unobstructed view of the south wall of Delphi Mansion. The characters can locate the camp without difficulty.

A quick search of the camp yields a backpack containing a rolled-up map of Delphi Mansion. Give your players a copy of map 3.1 at this time.

Accompanying the map are some scraps of paper with notes written on them in Common. Elra and her companions obtained the map and notes from one of Markos's cultists, whom they caught leaving the mansion. The notes are as follows:

- "Markos has a room on the third floor where he performs rituals."
- "A cavernous room underneath the basement contains four large crystals—purpose unknown."
- "Mansion windows can be unlocked using the password 'Krokulmar.'"

DELPHI MANSION.

1st Floor

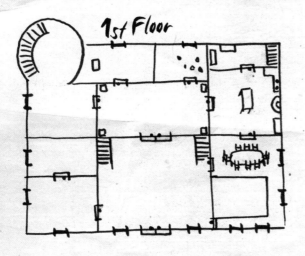

2nd Floor

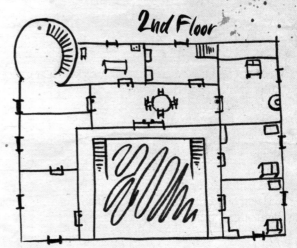

3rd Floor

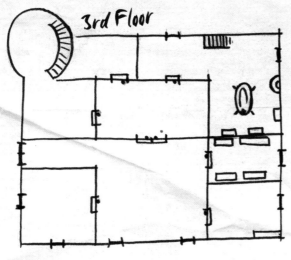

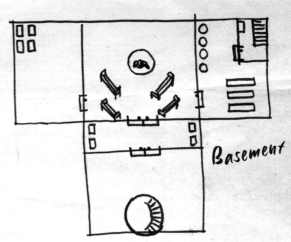

Basement

Beneath the House

= Door

= Window

= Chimney

N

DELPHI MANSION

Members of the Delphi family are nobles known for their academic studies of the multiverse. Markos's ancestors built Delphi Mansion in a forest away from civilization so they could study in peace.

ARRIVING AT THE MANSION

Once the characters are within sight of the mansion, read or paraphrase the following:

> A three-story mansion stands alone in a clearing. It has alabaster walls, windows on all three levels, and a closed double door on the ground floor. The area around the mansion seems unnaturally quiet.

DELPHI MANSION FEATURES

The mansion has the following features:

Ceilings. The ceilings throughout the mansion are 20 feet high.

Doors. The mansion's doors and secret doors are unlocked unless the text states otherwise.

Lighting. The mansion is illuminated by *continual flame* spells cast on candles that are mounted to the walls.

Windows. Each window is under the effect of an *arcane lock* spell. The password to circumvent the magical locks is "Krokulmar."

ELDRITCH SURGES

Since the day Markos contacted Krokulmar, its presence has slowly warped Delphi Mansion and its residents. Krokulmar's influence is strongest in certain rooms. When a room's description calls for it, or whenever a creature casts a spell in Delphi Mansion, roll on the Eldritch Surges table to see how Krokulmar's influence manifests in that location. The surge lasts for 1 hour. Rolling on the Eldritch Surges table while a surge is already in effect causes the current surge to end.

> ### THE ENTITY
> Krokulmar, the entity at the center of this adventure, is an enigmatic being from the Far Realm. Krokulmar can serve any campaign, or you can replace it with a more suitable otherworldly being.

ELDRITCH SURGES

d4	Surge Effect
1	The air becomes heavy and malleable. The space in the room becomes difficult terrain. While in the room, creatures have a flying speed equal to their walking speed.
2	Doors and windows in the room grow biting teeth. A creature that passes through a door or window in the room must succeed on a DC 13 Dexterity saving throw or take 5 (2d4) piercing damage. A creature can take this damage only once per turn.
3	Illusory magic causes one to perceive objects and creatures a short distance from their actual locations. While in the room, a creature has disadvantage on attack rolls.
4	An animated shadow of the creature that caused the surge appears in its space while it is in the room. Until the creature leaves the room, immediately after it makes an ability check, an attack roll, or casts a spell on its turn, the shadow makes a melee spell attack (+4 to hit) against a random creature within 5 feet of it, dealing 5 (2d4) necrotic damage on a hit.

DELPHI MANSION LOCATIONS

Locations in Delphi Mansion are keyed to map 3.2.

D1: FOYER

> A sickly sweet scent hangs in the air of this dusty foyer. Two staircases rise from the hardwood floor to a balcony, and a glass chandelier hangs above the center of the room. Below the chandelier, the pelt of an owlbear has been made into a fine rug, its head staring at the entrance.

The stairs climb to a balcony (area D10). The ceiling here rises 30 feet from the floor. The owlbear rug weighs 50 pounds.

D2: DINING HALLWAY

> This L-shaped hall is lined with large paintings of members of House Delphi. The ones that feature knights in silvery suits of armor have their faces scratched off.

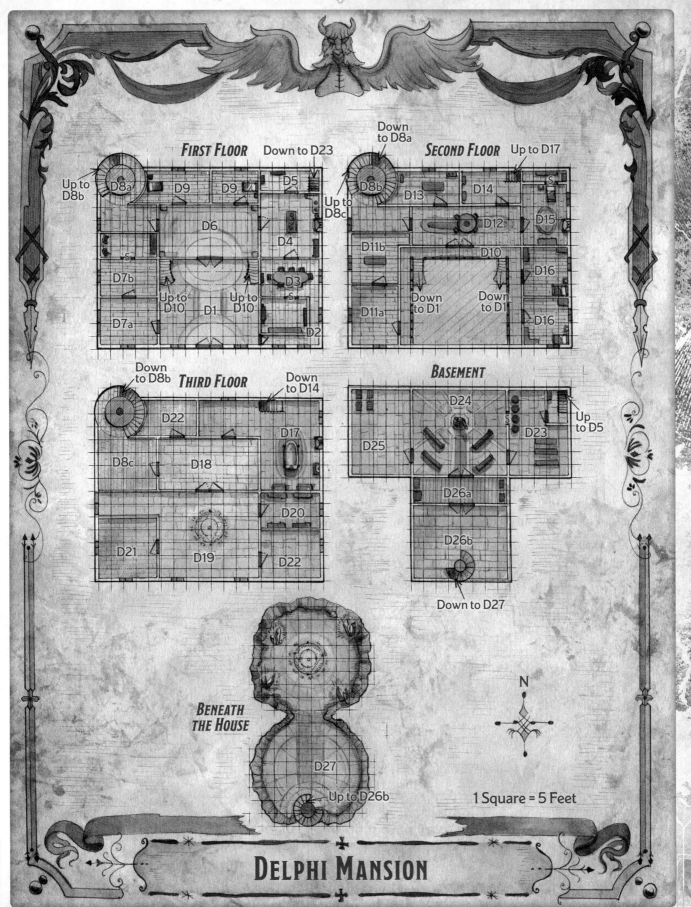

First Floor

Up to D8b
D8a
D9
D9
D5
Down to D23
D6
D4
S
D7b
D3
S
Up to D10
D1
Up to D10
D7a
D2

Second Floor

Down to D8a
Up to D17
D8b
D13
D14
S
D11b
D12
D15
D10
D16
Up to D8c
D11a
Down to D1
Down to D1
D16

Third Floor

Down to D8b
Down to D14
D22
D17
D8c
D18
D20
D21
D19
D22

Basement

D24
S
Up to D5
D25
D23
D26a
D26b
Down to D27

Beneath the House

D27
Up to D26b

N

1 Square = 5 Feet

Delphi Mansion

FRANCESCA BAERALD

A character who examines the armor in the paintings and succeeds on a DC 10 Intelligence (History) check recalls that the knights belong to an order of paladins that battles extraplanar threats.

D3: Dining Room

> Chairs and candelabras accompany a large dining table. The heads of several deer are mounted on the walls.

A **mimic** disguised as a stuffed deer head has attached itself to a blank wooden plaque mounted on a secret door in the south wall. Markos trained the mimic to guard the secret door, which leads to a hidden room (described below). The mimic attacks if a character comes within 5 feet of it.

Hidden Room. The wooden plaque behind the mimic is a lever of sorts. A character who inspects the wall and succeeds on a DC 11 Wisdom (Perception) check spots scratches around the plaque that suggest the plaque can be rotated in either direction. Doing so causes the secret door to swing inward, revealing a dusty room with several shelves. Lining the shelves are jars, most of which contain harmless liquids. Among these are six specimen jars, each containing one **slaad tadpole**.

Hiding in the dark corners of the hidden room are two **crawling claws**. If one or more characters enter the hidden room, the claws start pushing the jars with slaad tadpoles off the shelves and onto the ground, releasing the tadpoles. On its turn, a crawling claw can move to a specimen jar and take an action to release the slaad tadpole trapped within.

Treasure. On the shelf along the dining room's west wall is a small box with the Delphi family crest (a purple eye) engraved on the lid. The box is unlocked. Inside is a bag that contains 150 gp and three *potions of healing*.

D4: Kitchen

> This large kitchen is in poor condition. Flies cover foul-smelling messes of several meals stacked on a worktable in the middle of the room.

The kitchen is in shambles. The half-eaten food on the cookery and plates has begun to rot.

Chimney. A fireplace in the middle of the east wall contains a black iron pot hung on a hook. The chimney is too narrow for Medium or Small characters to climb, but a Tiny creature could fit.

D5: Pantry

The pantry is well stocked, and the foodstuffs here haven't spoiled yet. A sack of potatoes rests against the east wall next to stairs that lead to the wine cellar (area D23).

D6: Parlor

> Small circular pedestals dot the room, each one large enough to hold a couple of drinking cups. In the corners of the room stand four suits of armor. The two on the west side of the room are noticeably cleaner than the others.

The two suits of **animated armor** on the west side of the room attack if a character comes within 5 feet of either of them. They fight until destroyed.

D7a: Empty Sitting Room

All furnishings and decorations have been removed from this room, leaving nothing but dust and cobwebs.

D7b: Room with a Secret

> The walls of this sitting room are decorated with grim paintings, but all furnishings have been removed except a ten-foot-square rug in the middle of the floor and a sword mounted on the middle of the north wall.

The rug is a **rug of smothering**, and the sword is a **flying sword**. They both attack if a character comes within 5 feet of either.

Hidden Room. A secret door in the north wall (where the flying sword hangs when it isn't attacking) leads to a hidden room. A character who examines the north wall and succeeds on a DC 10 Intelligence (Investigation) check finds the secret door, which pushes inward easily enough.

The hidden room has a pair of cobwebbed chairs at one end and a dusty table at the opposite end. Tucked under the table is a small wooden chest with handles.

Treasure. The wooden chest is unlocked and holds three *spell scrolls* (*arms of Hadar*, *bane*, and *dimension door*) and a bag containing six pieces of jewelry worth 100 gp each.

D8a: Tower Ground Floor

> A cold wind descends this tower staircase.

The stairs here climb 20 feet to area D8b.

D8b: Tower Stairs

The stairs here descend 20 feet to area D8a and climb 20 feet to area D8c.

D8c: Stargazer's Roost

> Rubble lies scattered across the floor where part of the roof has collapsed, revealing the sky. Perched atop the rubble is a hunched figure wrapped in a cloak. It gazes at the sky, unaware of you.

ZALA MORPHUS

The cloaked figure is Zala Morphus, a human mage who has been transformed into a **nothic**. Zala helped Markos contact Krokulmar and blames this Far Realm entity for her transformation. Now she anxiously turns to the stars, hoping to find a way to return to her human form. Zala has no interest in Markos's current activities and little knowledge about them.

Zala speaks Common, Deep Speech, and Elvish. If the characters attack her, Zala responds in kind. If they claim to be looking for *The Celestial Codex*, Zala advises them to search Markos's office (area D11b) or his bedroom (area D15).

Zala wants a map of the Great Snake constellation from the star-map room (area D21). If the characters retrieve the map for her, Zala tells characters about the locked secret door in the wine cellar (area D23) along with the password ("farrl'v hrak").

Treasure. Zala carries two *spell scrolls* (*crown of madness* and *sleep*) and a spellbook that contains the following spells: *arcane lock, detect magic, detect thoughts, knock, mage armor, magic missile, phantasmal force, shield,* and *suggestion.*

D9: Guest Bedrooms

These two adjacent rooms are furnished identically:

> This dusty room contains a bed, a wardrobe, and a writing desk.

The first character to enter the westernmost bedroom triggers a roll on the Eldritch Surges table.

The easternmost bedroom contains a **gibbering mouther**. It attacks any character who opens the door and fights to the death.

D10: Balcony

This balcony overlooks the foyer (area D1), the floor of which is 20 feet below.

D11a: Empty Office

All furnishings have been removed from this room, leaving nothing but dust and cobwebs.

D11b: Markos's Office

> This room contains a black wooden desk with a cushioned, high-backed chair behind it. Two smaller chairs face the desk with their backs to the door. A niche in the northeast corner contains a wooden file cabinet.

The first character to enter the office triggers a roll on the Eldritch Surges table.

Correspondence. The file cabinet in the northeast niche is unlocked and contains correspondence between Markos and other nobles. You can decide if these letters are addressed to or written by anyone of significance to the characters.

Desk. The desk contains a complete set of calligrapher's supplies.

D12: Gallery

> Framed portraits and alabaster busts of members of the Delphi family decorate the walls and corners of the room, with facial expressions ranging from proud to downright haughty. Four cushioned chairs surround a table in the center of the room, on which is displayed an ivory dragonchess set.

Treasure. Two of the busts and five of the framed paintings are well made and in good condition, and each could fetch 50 gp from a collector. Each bust weighs 30 pounds, and each framed painting weighs 15 pounds. The ivory dragonchess set is worth 150 gp.

D13: Alchemy Lab

> This room reeks of chemicals. A long table with various vials and compounds occupies the center of the room. At the table, two cloaked figures oversee various alchemical experiments.

One of the cloaked figures is Markos's head researcher, Xander (lawful evil, human **cult fanatic**). The other figure is an apprentice named Kura (lawful evil, human **cultist**). Both have embraced the Far Realm entity and the power it offers. Xander and Kura are indifferent toward intruders and don't attack unless the intruders aim to harm them or hinder their research.

Xander and Kura don't keep track of Markos's movements, but they know he has been spending a lot of time in the caves below the basement (area D27). They assume *The Celestial Codex* is with Markos or in his bedroom (area D15).

Treasure. Characters can assemble two sets of alchemist's supplies (50 gp each) from the contents of this lab. Among the various concoctions found throughout the room are four *potions of healing*, a *potion of gaseous form*, a vial containing *oil of slipperiness*, and a vial with one dose of assassin's blood poison (see the *Dungeon Master's Guide*).

D14: Meditation Room

> A fetid stench permeates this room, which is empty save for two small, bare tables standing against the west wall and an ornate rug in front of the window. Resting next to the rug is a wooden candlestick holding the melted stump of a red candle. A long pull-rope hangs from a wooden trapdoor in the ceiling.

There's no obvious source for the horrible smell that lingers here. The first character who enters the room triggers a roll on the Eldritch Surges table.

Markos used to sit on the rug and meditate while pondering the forces of the multiverse, but he hasn't used this room in a while.

Trapdoor. The trapdoor in the ceiling leads to the master bath (area D17). An unfolding wooden ladder allows easy access.

D15: Markos's Bedroom

> This room contains a bed with an ornately carved frame, a wardrobe, a writing desk, and a leather chair. A fireplace stands along the east wall.

Behind the headboard of the bed is a secret door to a hidden walk-in closet. A character who examines the wall and succeeds on a DC 15 Intelligence (Investigation) check discovers not only the secret door but also a secret button on the headboard. Pushing the button causes the bed to slide eastward, allowing easy access to the hidden closet.

Hidden Closet. This closet contains clothing on hooks and shelves, plus an assortment of footwear. On a small table against the east wall sits an iron lockbox. A character using thieves' tools can try to pick the lock, which requires 1 minute and a successful DC 14 Dexterity check.

Treasure. The lockbox contains an amethyst cloak pin shaped like an eye (125 gp) and a *ring of jumping*.

D16: Student Quarters

These rooms were set aside for Markos's pupils, who shared his drive for knowledge but didn't share in their master's reward for contacting Krokulmar. The pupils fled the mansion after Markos made his pact. Each room now contains two psychic **gray oozes** (see the "Variant: Psychic Gray Ooze" sidebar in the *Monster Manual*) that mill about. They attack intruders on sight.

Treasure. Characters who search the northernmost room find a spellbook that contains the following spells: *comprehend languages*, *detect magic*, *detect thoughts*, *identify*, *mage armor*, *misty step*, *Tasha's hideous laughter*, and *unseen servant*.

D17: Bathroom

> A raised marble tub occupies this room. Near it are two marble sinks with oval mirrors mounted above them, a fireplace, and a small table against the east wall that has a colorful collection of bottles atop it.

The tub and sinks have pipes that draw rainwater from cisterns on the roof. Further, each basin is equipped with a plugged drainpipe and two faucets: one that magically heats water and one that magically cools it.

Treasure. Four bottles of perfumes and scented oils (25 gp each) sit on the small table.

Alchemy is afoot in Delphi Mansion.

D18: Third-Floor Hall

This hallway has become a lair for **stirges**—two per character. The stirges entered the mansion through the hole in the roof above area D8c. They attack anyone who tries to cross the hall.

D19: Eldritch Observation Room

> This room is empty except for a circle of vile symbols on the floor. Standing in the circle is an eight-foot-tall, bipedal creature with two long arms, each one ending in a sharp hook. The creature wears the tattered remnants of a butler's uniform.

The first character who enters the room triggers a roll on the Eldritch Surges table.

Circle of Symbols. A *detect magic* spell reveals an aura of divination magic around the circle on the floor. A creature standing fully inside the circle feels the unsettling presence of a Far Realm entity and can choose to receive an omen from that entity, as if the creature had cast an *augury* spell. After receiving such an omen, the creature can't receive another one for 24 hours but still feels the otherworldly presence while inside the circle.

Esquire. The hook-handed figure is Markos's former butler, Esquire (use the **hook horror** stat block). Esquire isn't bound inside the circle and attacks intruders on sight. He doesn't know the cause of his transformation. If the characters explain that an evil entity is responsible for Esquire's transformation or that Markos might be in danger from this entity, Esquire lets them live if they vow to save Markos.

Esquire's tattered butler uniform has a pocket containing a locket and a note. The locket is under the effects of a *magic mouth* spell; when opened, it speaks the password to the temple (area D24), "farrl'v hrak," which is Deep Speech for "forever changing." The note contains a sketch of a wine bottle and a row of four circles. The second circle from the left is crossed out. (The circles represent the casks in area D23, the crossed-out one representing the cask blocking a secret door.)

D20: Component Storage

This walk-in closet contains four cabinets, each one filled with carefully organized material components.

Treasure. Characters who search the cabinets can find a material component for any 1st- or 2nd-level spell, provided the component has a value less than 1 gp. Characters also find a potion, its bubbling green liquid stained by a drop of some dark substance (octopus ink).

A BUBBLING GREEN POTION CONTAINS A FAR REALM SURPRISE.

The alchemists in area D13 concocted the potion, which functions as a *potion of poison* but has an additional property. When the poison effect ends, the imbiber sprouts a tentacle made of inky shadow. This shadowy tentacle lasts for 1 hour. As a bonus action, the potion's imbiber can use the tentacle to make a melee weapon attack (+4 to hit) against a creature the imbiber can see within 5 feet of itself. On a hit, the target takes 4 (1d8) necrotic damage.

D21: Star-Map Room

The walls and floor of this room are covered with star maps. The **ghost** of an elf researcher named Farenhel wanders the room, looking through the maps and searching for an answer the ghost will never find. The ghost is harmless and attacks only in self-defense or if a character tries to steal a star map. The ghost stops attacking as soon as the stolen map is returned.

Characters who examine the maps closely find one that depicts a constellation called the Great Snake. This is the map sought by the nothic Zala Morphus (see area D8c).

D22: Storage Rooms

Each of these unfurnished rooms contains two **ghouls** that were attracted to the mansion by Far Realm energies. The ghouls are hostile.

D23: Wine Cellar

> The faint aroma of grapes fills the air in this cellar. Four large wine casks stand against the west wall, a fine layer of dust covering each of them. The three wine racks to the south are empty.

Three of the wine casks contain varying amounts of wine. The fourth cask is empty and positioned in front of a secret door in the west wall. Characters who examine the empty cask see handprints on it, suggesting it has been moved multiple times. The characters also feel cold air coming from the wall, suggesting the presence of a secret door. The wine cask must be moved aside to access the secret door.

Secret Door. An *arcane lock* spell has been cast on the secret door. The password to bypass the spell is "farrl'v hrak," which is Deep Speech for "forever changing." Esquire's locket (see area D19) speaks the password when opened.

Alternatively, a character can use an action to try to force open the locked secret door, doing so with a successful DC 20 Strength (Athletics) check.

D24: Temple

> Four wooden pews face a stone statue in the middle of this torchlit chamber. The statue has a roughly bipedal shape and is carved to look like it's coming undone, like a frayed rope. Its form is covered with mouths and outstretched tongues.
>
> Standing before the statue are four purple-cloaked figures, their faces hidden by cowls. They are writing on pieces of paper and muttering to each other, oblivious to your presence.

The arcane energies in this room are particularly volatile. The first character who enters the room triggers a roll on the Eldritch Surges table. After the surge begins, on initiative count 20 (losing initiative ties), roll again on the Eldritch Surges table.

Cloaked Figures. The cloaked figures are four neutral, human **cultists** who are taking notes on the eldritch surges that occur in this area. These cultists defend themselves if attacked but otherwise pose no threat. They know Markos is performing a ritual in area D27 but won't share this information until the statue is destroyed.

Statue. The statue depicts Krokulmar and was created with the aid of a *spell scroll* of *stone shape*. Any creature that touches the statue for the first time on a turn must succeed on a DC 11 Wisdom saving throw or take 3 (1d6) psychic damage.

The statue amplifies the eldritch surges, which a character can ascertain by examining the statue and then succeeding on a DC 15 Intelligence (Arcana) check. If the statue is destroyed, the eldritch surges stop occurring throughout the mansion. The statue is a Medium object with AC 17, 36 hit points, and immunity to poison and psychic damage.

D25: Storage

> Four severed heads and three headless bodies lie on the floor of this room, which also contains four small crates in the far corner.

The severed heads and decapitated bodies belong to Elra Lionheart and her three human adventuring companions. The body of one of Elra's companions is missing (and can be found in area D27).

If Elra is with the characters (see "Meeting Elra" earlier in this adventure), she mourns her dead companions and hopes there might be a way to bring her and her friends back from the dead.

Treasure. Four small crates rest in the northwest corner. One contains a set of gold-plated cups and plates worth 200 gp total. Another contains a *wand of magic missiles* hidden in a pile of straw. The third contains 20 days' worth of edible rations. The final crate contains a dozen torches and three flasks of alchemist's fire.

D26a: Vestry

This dusty chamber contains four unlocked wooden trunks, each of which contains four dark-purple silk robes.

D26b: Ceremony Room

> Iron brackets bolted to the walls hold four sputtering torches that cast this otherwise empty room in dim light. On the far side of the room, a spiral staircase descends into darkness. From below, you hear a human voice chanting in a blasphemous tongue.

The spiral staircase descends 20 feet to area D27. The voice rising up the stairs is chanting in Deep Speech, calling to an entity named Krokulmar.

D27: Ritual Room

This location consists of two roughly circular caves joined by an opening. The staircase from area D26b leads to the southern cave, which is empty. From the stairs, characters can see activity in the northern cave:

> The staircase leads to a roughly circular cave that is empty and unlit. Opposite the stairs, though a twelve-foot-wide archway, you see a similar cavern lit by purple light emanating from four large crystals jutting from the floor. All crystals flicker in concert with the chanting that echoes through the caves.
>
> The chants come from a sallow, dark-robed figure who stands near the edge of a circle of arcane runes inscribed on the floor. The figure recites an eldritch passage from a book, then carefully sets the book atop a wooden crate near the back wall. The figure turns toward the circle, wherein kneels a headless body in plate armor. A sluglike creature has attached itself to the body's neck, almost like a makeshift head. The slug's form is covered with mouths and eyes that open and close in and out of existence.

Markos Delphi is performing a ritual that will allow a **fragment of Krokulmar** (see their stat blocks at the end of the adventure) to attach to the headless body of one of Elra's adventuring companions, thus enabling a piece of Krokulmar to exist outside the Far Realm. The headless body is stunned and remains so until the ritual is complete. It is possible to attack the fragment without harming the headless body.

On each of his turns in combat, Markos defends himself while taking a bonus action to continue the ritual. If he's able to take this bonus action three more times, the fragment of Krokulmar takes control of the headless body, at which point the body is no longer stunned.

The fragment of Krokulmar and the body to which it is attached are considered two creatures occupying the same space. Neither can be separated from the other until one or both of them drop to 0 hit points, at which point the fragment of Krokulmar returns to the Far Realm. While under the fragment's control, the body uses the **knight** stat block, has blindsight within a range of 30 feet, is blind beyond this radius, and acts immediately after the fragment in the initiative order. The fragment determines what the body does on the body's turn.

The fragment uses the body to protect itself from harm and to destroy the characters.

Helping Markos. As an action, a character can make a DC 14 Charisma (Persuasion) check to try to convince Markos he's being controlled. If the check fails, nothing happens and the action is wasted. If the check succeeds, Markos has disadvantage on attack rolls and ability checks until the end of his next turn as he wrestles with the possibility that he's not in control of his actions.

THE CELESTIAL CODEX

Crystals. As a bonus action, a character can make a DC 15 Intelligence (Arcana) to ascertain the purpose of the large crystals sprouting from the floor. These crystals focus the ritual's extraplanar energy, allowing the fragment of Krokulmar to remain on the Material Plane long enough for it to bond with the headless body. A character who succeeds on the check also knows that destroying all four crystals stops the ritual. Each crystal is a Large object with AC 13, 10 hit points, vulnerability to bludgeoning and thunder damage, and immunity to poison and psychic damage.

Each time a crystal is destroyed, Markos has disadvantage on attack rolls and ability checks until the end of his next turn as he confronts the possibility that he might not be in control of his actions.

Ending the Threat. If all four crystals are destroyed, if Krokulmar or the body it's attached to drops to 0 hit points, or if Markos drops to 0 hit points before the ritual is completed, the fragment of Krokulmar returns to the Far Realm. Sending the fragment back to the Far Realm ends the eldritch surges in Delphi Mansion, frees Markos from Krokulmar's influence (see "Conclusion" below), restores Zala Morphus and Esquire to their former human selves, and causes the cultists in area D24 to flee.

Treasure. The book resting on the crate is *The Celestial Codex*. A *mage hand* spell can easily lift the book. An invisible character can sneak across the room and try to steal the book without Markos

noticing, doing so with a successful DC 14 Dexterity (Stealth) check. On a failed check, Markos detects the theft. Although he no longer needs the book to complete the ritual, Markos won't give it up without a fight while he's under Krokulmar's influence. Once free of that influence, Markos is horrified by his actions and gladly gives up the book (see "Markos Lives").

The Celestial Codex is filled with arcane lore about the stars and the planes of existence. Nestled among its benign descriptions are eldritch incantations written in Celestial, and tucked between the book's pages are two *spell scrolls* (*armor of Agathys* and *arms of Hadar*).

CONCLUSION

If the characters obtain *The Celestial Codex*, they can return the book to its rightful owner and claim their reward.

MARKOS DIES

If Markos dies, the characters can return his body to his family. The Delphi family gives each character 150 gp for bringing Markos home and pays to have Markos raised from the dead.

MARKOS LIVES

Defeating the fragment of Krokulmar frees Markos from the evil entity's influence, at which point Markos is eager to make amends for the trouble he has caused. He allows the characters to keep whatever treasure they found in the mansion.

If Markos is reunited with his family, the family gives 150 gp to each character as a reward.

DEAD ADVENTURERS

If the characters recount the horrors of Delphi Mansion to Markos's family, the family makes arrangements to rid the mansion of any remaining monsters. The bodies of adventurers who were killed in the mansion (including Elra and her companions) are brought to a temple, where they are raised or resurrected at the Delphi family's expense. If the characters are present when Elra's life is restored, she congratulates them on their heroism and looks forward to one day repaying the favor.

FOR THE GOLDEN VAULT

If the characters are working for the Golden Vault, the organization's representative approaches them after their harrowing experience at Delphi Mansion. For returning *The Celestial Codex* to its rightful owner, the characters are promised an uncommon magic item of their choice (subject to your approval) as payment. The item is delivered to the characters the next day.

MARKOS DELPHI STANDS OVER A NIGHTMARE
CREATION THAT COMBINES THE BODY OF AN
ADVENTURER WITH A FRAGMENT OF KROKULMAR.

MARKOS DELPHI

Medium Humanoid (Human, Warlock), Chaotic Neutral

Armor Class 12 (15 with *mage armor*)
Hit Points 44 (8d8 + 8)
Speed 30 ft.

STR	DEX	CON	INT	WIS	CHA
8 (−1)	15 (+2)	12 (+1)	17 (+3)	13 (+1)	16 (+3)

Saving Throws Wis +3, Cha +5
Skills Arcana +7, History +7, Perception +3
Damage Immunities psychic
Senses darkvision 60 ft., passive Perception 13
Languages Common, Celestial, Deep Speech
Challenge 3 (700 XP)   **Proficiency Bonus** +2

ACTIONS

Multiattack. Markos makes two Ceremonial Blade attacks, two Psychic Orb attacks, or one of each.

Ceremonial Blade. *Melee Weapon Attack:* +4 to hit, reach 5 ft., one target. *Hit:* 5 (1d6 + 2) piercing damage plus 3 (1d6) poison damage. If the target is a creature, it must succeed on a DC 13 Constitution saving throw or become poisoned for 1 minute. The creature can repeat the saving throw at the end of each of its turns, ending the effect on itself on a success.

Psychic Orb. *Ranged Spell Attack:* +5 to hit, range 60 ft., one creature. *Hit:* 10 (2d6 + 3) psychic damage.

Spellcasting. Markos casts one of the following spells, requiring no material components and using Charisma as the spellcasting ability (spell save DC 13):

1/day each: *arms of Hadar, charm person, mage armor*

BONUS ACTIONS

Swap Space. Markos targets one Medium or Small creature he can see within 30 feet of himself. The target must succeed on a DC 13 Constitution saving throw or it teleports, along with any equipment it is wearing or carrying, exchanging positions with Markos.

FRAGMENT OF KROKULMAR

Tiny Aberration, Chaotic Evil

Armor Class 13
Hit Points 10 (3d4 + 3)
Speed 0 ft.

STR	DEX	CON	INT	WIS	CHA
4 (−3)	16 (+3)	12 (+1)	16 (+3)	16 (+3)	16 (+3)

Skills Arcana +7, History +7, Persuasion +7, Stealth +7
Damage Immunities psychic
Senses darkvision 60 ft., passive Perception 13
Languages Deep Speech, telepathy 60 ft.
Challenge 0 (10 XP)   **Proficiency Bonus** +2

ACTIONS

Psionic Revitalization. The fragment touches one creature that has 0 hit points in the fragment's space. The target regains 10 hit points, and each creature within 10 feet of the healed creature takes 3 (1d6) psychic damage.

Squirming Dodge. Until the start of the fragment's next turn, any attack roll made against the fragment has disadvantage, and the fragment makes saving throws with advantage.

OLIVIER BERNARD

PERCHED ON A WINDSWEPT BLUFF IS THE PRISON OF
REVEL'S END, WHEREIN WAITS PRISONER 13.

PRISONER 13

N THE WORLD OF TORIL, IN THE FROZEN reaches north of the Sword Coast, lies an impenetrable fortress built to house the region's most dangerous criminals. One of this prison's earliest inmates, a dwarf known as Prisoner 13, spends her days in seeming quiet and solitude while secretly pulling the strings of a spy network that spans much of the continent. She holds the key to a treasure she stole from a dwarf clan. In this heist, the characters must infiltrate the prison, retrieve the key from Prisoner 13 (found in a tattoo on her hand), and return the key to Varrin Axebreaker, the dwarf who hired them.

ADVENTURE BACKGROUND

Prisoner 13 is a dwarf named Korda Glintstone. Prior to her incarceration years ago, Korda was an ally and agent of Clan Axebreaker, a moderately influential dwarf clan in a stronghold called Gauntlgrym. Korda built a network of informants and agents, ostensibly all to the benefit of Clan Axebreaker. With each success, she paid tattooists to inscribe a memorial of her triumph onto her skin. Using ancient rituals, Korda infused many of these artful etchings with the magic of Gauntlgrym's forges, granting her wondrous gifts.

Korda grew too ambitious for her role as an agent, so she devised a plan to take power for herself. Over five years she took careful stock of Clan Axebreaker's wealth and, in one fell swoop, used her network of lieutenants to steal away most of the clan's gold, leaving only a pittance.

The Axebreaker dwarves discovered her almost immediately. They rounded up her agents, who either fought to the death or were executed. They captured Korda and interrogated her, but she never revealed the location of the stolen fortune, even under magical compulsion. The Axebreaker dwarves used their influence to have her sentenced to life in prison at Revel's End. There, Clan Axebreaker was hopeful Korda would eventually break and reveal the location of the stolen wealth. This played right into Korda's hands, since she had made copious enemies who can't move against her while she's incarcerated.

Korda, now known as Prisoner 13, prepared for her imprisonment by laying the groundwork for a new spy and criminal network, which cost her much of her stolen fortune. She now runs her operations from the prison. Using her magical tattoos, she telepathically coordinates agents throughout Faerûn and beyond, none of whom know the identity of their employer. As for what remains of the stolen Axebreaker wealth, it rests in an unmarked vault in the depths of Gauntlgrym, sealed by a magical lock that only the runic sequence tattooed on Korda's right hand can open.

ADVENTURE HOOKS

After years of financial hardship due to their stolen fortune, the mountain dwarves of Clan Axebreaker have located the lost treasure but have been unable to access it. A representative of the clan, Varrin Axebreaker, wishes to hire the characters to learn how to access the treasure. If you're not using the Golden Vault as a patron (see "Using the Golden Vault" below), here are some possible ways Varrin learned about the characters:

By Reputation. Varrin learned of the characters in the aftermath of a previous adventure, especially one that involved retrieving a person or treasure from a dangerous location.

Mutual Acquaintance. One of the characters' patrons is an old acquaintance of Varrin's and arranged the meeting. If the characters are involved with the Golden Vault, use this option.

Trial Run. Varrin was responsible for a previous adventure the characters completed successfully. It was a test to see if they were worthy of this mission.

USING THE GOLDEN VAULT

If you're using the Golden Vault as a patron, a golden key is delivered to the characters in whatever manner you deem fit. When the characters use this key to open their music box, the lid pops open and a soothing voice says the following:

"Greetings, operatives. We have discovered the location of a great dwarven treasure, but only a prisoner incarcerated within the prison Revel's End knows how to access the vault. This quest, should you choose to undertake it, requires you travel to the prison, infiltrate it, and learn how to access the treasure from the prisoner. Return this information to the dwarf known as Varrin Axebreaker, who will brief you on the details of the mission. Good luck, operatives."

Closing the music box causes the golden key to vanish.

VARRIN'S PROPOSITION

Varrin Axebreaker (lawful good, dwarf **noble**) contacts the characters to enlist their aid in retrieving the key. Varrin's braided hair and beard are black with streaks of gray. He wears a loose, comfortable robe over a steel breastplate. Whether Varrin approaches the characters or invites them to a meeting, read the following text:

"Thank you for hearing me out. My name is Varrin Axebreaker, and I have a proposition for you. My clan has located wealth stolen from us many years ago, but it's sealed in a vault that's magically locked. If you can recover the key—whatever it is—you'll gain the undying gratitude of Clan Axebreaker. And I'll cut you in for a percentage of the recovered treasure, of course.

"The catch here is the person who knows how to open the vault is rotting away in the prison of Revel's End. She's proved uncooperative with my people in the past, but I recently discovered the vault where she hid what she stole from us. I need you to question her and learn how to open the vault. How you do that is up to you; if you need to spring her from the prison in exchange for this information, please do so. I can provide you with a way in, as well as the layout of Revel's End and a few useful tricks."

Give the players a copy of map 4.1 (see "The Breaker's Map" below), and read the following text:

Varrin retrieves a faceted sapphire the size of a small orange and places it on the table. He waves his hand over the gem, and a glowing blue image of a building floor plan appears in the air above it. He taps the gem, and the image vanishes. The sapphire splits into sections, and he passes one fragment to each of you. The fragment grows warm in your hand, melts, then vanishes, leaving a warm, tingling sensation behind. "Think about the map of Revel's End, and you'll be able to see it."

The gem's magic lasts until five days after the characters reach Revel's End.

THE BREAKER'S MAP

Each character can now cause a magical image of map 4.1 to appear in the air before them while they aren't incapacitated (no action required). A breaker's map isn't visible to others while a character is viewing it. Varrin explains each of the features the characters can see on their maps:

Cells. The cells, highlighted in red, are blanketed in permanent antimagic. Prisoner 13's cell is clearly marked.

Doors and Hatches. The doors and hatches are sealed with *arcane lock* spells that only prison staff can bypass. However, while the characters are within 100 feet of Revel's End, the map allows them to use an action to touch the image of a door or hatch and suppress the lock on that portal. While a lock is suppressed, its image turns green. The lock remains suppressed for 1 minute or until another lock is suppressed.

Patrol Route. The yellow path marked on the map is the regular patrol route guards take. The usual patrol rotation is once every 20 minutes, but if the guards are suspicious, patrols will likely become more frequent.

THE DEVIL IN THE DETAILS

In the likely event that the characters want more information, Varrin answers their questions succinctly and honestly. He has spent the last of his personal fortune gathering information on the prison and making the arrangements for a team to confront Korda. These are the details he can provide:

Entering the Prison. The prison staff rotate out periodically. Varrin knows the schedule of the next rotation, and his agents are standing by to capture a number of guards and cooks so the characters can take their place (see "Approaching the Prison").

REVEL'S END

Dock

Elevator   +160 Feet

Guards   Hospital

Guard Tower   Guard Tower

Storage   Privy   Courtyard

Prisoner 13's Cell

Meeting   Armory

Surveillance

Kitchen

Cells

Mess Hall

Guard Tower   Guard Tower

Stables   Guards

Councilors

– – Guard Patrol Route
■   Permanent Antimagic Field

Barracks   Warden
                Trial   Office

TOWER LEVEL 1   TOWER LEVEL 2   TOWER ROOF

1 Square = 5 Feet

PRISONER 13

Prisoner 13. Prisoner 13 was a trusted agent of Clan Axebreaker until she betrayed the clan and stole its fortune. If pressed, Varrin reluctantly tells the characters her name (Korda Glintstone), but he stresses that they shouldn't reveal they know it. No one in the prison except perhaps the warden knows Prisoner 13 by her real name, so using it would only raise suspicion. Her cell is marked on the map.

Key. Prisoner 13 must have the vault key or know where it is, but every magical method Clan Axebreaker has tried to locate the key has failed. Varrin presumes Prisoner 13 would give up the key only in exchange for freedom, but if the characters can find the key or convince her to give it up any other way, he'll be just as pleased. Clan Axebreaker tried to arrange her release, but the Absolution Council at Revel's End denied the request.

Meeting Prisoner 13. Visitors can request meetings with prisoners, but those meetings are always supervised by the warden (to learn about the warden, see "R21: Warden's Quarters"). If the characters want to talk to Prisoner 13, their best bet is to try when she's not in her cell, hopefully out of sight of the guards. Prisoners do chores

such as emptying latrine buckets and cleaning up after meals, and they exercise in the courtyard daily. When prisoners are injured or fall ill, they are taken to the prison hospital.

Revel's End Details. Varrin can give a general overview of Revel's End, the security features on doors and hatches, and the prison's high-alert procedure (see below). Varrin also knows the armory has a dangerous guardian, but he doesn't know the details.

Treasure. The treasure is locked in a vault deep beneath the dwarf stronghold of Gauntlgrym. Varrin promises the characters 2 percent of whatever treasure they recover if they make it possible for him to open the vault. If the characters press for more, Varrin is irritated, but he agrees to 3 percent if the characters succeed on a DC 20 Charisma (Persuasion) check. Varrin notes that the warden likely has some funds hidden in her office or quarters, if the characters are inclined to seek these out.

Escape Route. Varrin will have a small ship within sight of the prison but at a safe distance. When the characters are ready to leave the prison with their target, they can shine a light from the dock after dark, and the ship will pick them up.

When the characters are ready to depart from their meeting with Varrin, he provides them each with the choice to pose as a guard or a cook. Guards must wear splint armor, and kitchen staff must wear simple uniforms. Cooks can hide light armor under their uniforms. Small characters also have the option to stow away inside a crate of supplies.

TREK TO THE PRISON

Varrin has sent word to his agents, and Bethra (chaotic good, dwarf **spy**) meets the characters when they arrive in Luskan. She provides the uniforms for their chosen cover and directs them to report to a ship called the *Jolly Pelican* the following dawn. The ship regularly delivers a fresh rotation of prison staff to Revel's End and returns the relieved shift to the Sword Coast. The journey to Revel's End by sea is 350 miles, which a sailing ship can cover in three days under normal conditions.

Twenty-five guards and six cooks are bound for the prison, including any characters taking their places. If the characters express concern over the fate of staff they're replacing, Bethra assures them that none of the people were killed, and they'll be released safely when the job is over.

The players can make up whatever names they like for their cover. Those are the names of the guards or cooks they've replaced.

Revel's End

Revel's End is a panopticon, a prison configured in such a way that the activities of the prisoners can be closely monitored from a central location. Situated on the frigid, misty coast of the Sea of Moving Ice, the prison is a single-story structure topped with battlements. Rising from the core of the panopticon is a tower that holds the prison's administrative offices and guard barracks. Both the prison and the tower are carved from a tall, blade-shaped rock that rises high above the sea cliffs. This rock, called the Windbreak, shields the tower against the brutal winds that sweep down from the Reghed Glacier.

One can approach Revel's End by land, sea, or air. A pier allows prisoners to be taken from ships up an elevator to the prison, and a mooring dock at the top of the tower allows prisoners to be delivered by airship.

Revel's End is controlled by the Lords' Alliance, a loose confederation of settlements whose current members include the cities of Baldur's Gate, Mirabar, Neverwinter, Silverymoon, Waterdeep, and Yartar; the towns of Amphail, Daggerford, and Longsaddle; and the dwarven stronghold of Mithral Hall. To be imprisoned in Revel's End, one must have committed a serious crime against one or more of the member cities and been sentenced to a lengthy period of incarceration (typically a year or more).

Each member of the Lords' Alliance assigns one representative to Revel's End, and together the representatives form a parole committee called the Absolution Council. Rarely are all ten council members present, since Revel's End offers little in the way of comfort and amenities. If the council needs a tiebreaking vote to determine whether to commute a prisoner's sentence, the prison warden—a neutral arbiter with no ties to any Lords' Alliance member—casts the deciding vote.

Prison Features

The prison, hewn from stone, has 20-foot-high outer walls and flat, 20-foot-high ceilings throughout. Additional information about the prison is summarized below:

Doors and Hatches. Each door and rooftop hatch is made of reinforced iron held shut by an *arcane lock* spell. Prison personnel can open these doors and hatches normally. A locked door or hatch is too strong to be shouldered or kicked open, but it can be destroyed if it takes enough damage. A door or hatch has AC 19, a damage threshold of 10, 30 hit points, and immunity to poison and psychic damage.

Heating. Interior spaces are magically heated. The temperature in these areas is a constant 68 degrees Fahrenheit (20 degrees Celsius). The exterior of the prison, including the guard towers, is 0 degrees Fahrenheit (–18 degrees Celsius) or colder. Creatures outside the prison are exposed to extreme cold (see below).

Lighting. Unless a location states otherwise, the courtyard, corridors, rooms, and staircases are brightly lit with *continual flame* spells cast on wall sconces. (The unlit cells in area R17 are exceptions.) In some locations, the magical lights can be dimmed or suppressed, as noted in the text.

Prison Guards. The prison has a garrison of 75 guards (use the **veteran** stat block) who work eight-hour shifts. Two-thirds of the garrison is off duty and resting in area R19 at any given time. While on duty, each guard wears a tunic that bears the Lords' Alliance emblem: a gold crown on a red field.

Prisoners. All prisoners in Revel's End are identified by a number. This simple protocol keeps prisoners on an equal footing. Prison personnel commit these numbers to memory, and the records of all prisoners—past and present—are stored in area R22. Each inmate wears a uniform that consists of a hoodless robe without pockets, leather slippers without laces, and cloth undergarments. While outside their cells, prisoners wear manacles on their wrists and ankles. While manacled, a prisoner's walking speed can't exceed 10 feet.

Approaching the Prison

When the characters approach the prison, read the following text:

> Perched on a high cliff overlooking the Sea of Moving Ice is a bleak stone fortress carved from a gigantic, blade-shaped rock. A central tower looms above the rest of the fortress, and light leaks from its arrow slits. Four smaller towers rise from the outermost corners of the fortress, and guards can be seen atop them.

Characters might approach the prison via the *Jolly Pelican*, or they might choose to approach on their own (see "Getting Inside" below).

Characters approaching from the north can also see the prison's northern entrance at the top of a 160-foot-high cliff with a pier protruding from its base. A giant wooden crane stands nearby, and a wooden scaffold clings to the cliff face.

Characters approaching from the south can see the prison's south entrance and the trail that leads up to it.

Extreme Cold

The temperature outside is at or below 0 degrees Fahrenheit (–18 degrees Celsius) while the characters are at the prison. A creature exposed to the cold must succeed on a DC 10 Constitution saving throw at the end of each hour or gain 1 level of exhaustion. Creatures with resistance or immunity to cold damage automatically succeed on the saving throw, as do creatures wearing cold-weather gear (thick coats, gloves, and the like) and creatures naturally adapted to cold climates.

Guards on Watch

The prison has four guard towers (see area R9), and three guards in cold-weather clothing are stationed atop each one. If you need to make Wisdom (Perception) checks for the guards to determine if they notice something, make only one roll with advantage.

If the guards on a tower see or hear something out of the ordinary—such as an approaching ship, a group of visitors, or a monster flying overhead—one guard descends into the tower to alert the rest of the prison while the others stay at their posts.

Getting Inside

If the characters use the cover Varrin provided, their ship arrives at Revel's End just before dawn, three days after leaving Luskan. The characters are directed off the ship, ride the elevator to the cliff top, and are admitted through the front doors. Characters posing as guards are taken to the barracks (area R19), where they meet with head guard Yula Dargeria, a no-nonsense stickler for the prison's rules. Characters posing as cooks are delivered to the kitchen (area R8), where they report to Chef Tiny Toulaine, a hulking, jovial man who carries an enormous saucepan instead of a heavy crossbow. Small characters who stowed away in supply crates are taken to either the storeroom (area R13), the kitchen's cold storage room (the middle room off area R8), or the pantry (the northernmost room off area R8). If more than one Small character stows away, pick one location where they're all delivered.

Characters who bang on the prison's north or south door are admitted into a 30-foot-long corridor, where they are greeted by the three guards from a nearby guard room (area R3). These guards insist on confiscating the characters' weapons and storing them in a nearby lockbox. In addition, one guard searches each character for concealed weapons. A character can conceal a dagger or similarly sized weapon from a guard's notice with a successful DC 13 Dexterity (Sleight of Hand) check.

If the characters have sled dogs or pack animals, a guard grants the party access to the stables (area R5), where the animals can be kept safe. Animals aren't allowed in the prison otherwise.

After relinquishing their weapons and securing their animals, the characters are escorted by one of the guards to the meeting room (area R12), where they must wait one hour for the warden to greet them. During this time, the characters are unattended and can attempt to sneak into the prison at large. Doing so without alerting the guards requires a successful DC 13 Dexterity (Stealth) check. Recovering the characters' weapons from the lockbox requires a successful DC 16 Dexterity check with thieves' tools. If the characters are caught attempting either of these tasks, the guards return them to the meeting room and wait with them for the warden, who throws them out unless they provide a satisfactory reason for their visit and subterfuge.

The warden only accepts the characters' presence if they are seeking shelter. In that case, she grants them temporary accommodations (in area R7) for up to two days and two nights, and the characters receive three meals a day during their stay. If the characters fail to provide a satisfactory reason for their visit, the warden has their weapons and animals returned to them before throwing them out.

Suspicion

Activities outside the daily routine of the prison draw attention from the guards and what few other staff members there are. Suspicion is measured in levels from 1 to 6. When the characters arrive at the prison, the suspicion level is 1.

Suspicion can increase when prison staff members witness or find evidence of behavior outside the norm. Circumstances that increase the suspicion level include the following:

- Using a prisoner's real name while in the guise of prison staff
- Getting caught by a patrol (see Patrol Routes)
- Casting a spell that has perceptible components or effects in sight of a guard
- Conversing with a prisoner about anything other than prison business (such as giving them instructions for tasks)

For suspicion to increase, prison staff members must witness the characters performing unusual activity, and any witnesses must report their observations. If the characters can convince the witness what they saw was justified, the suspicion level doesn't increase.

Distractions

A character can create a distraction, giving themself or an ally time to undertake a suspicious activity without being witnessed. If the distracting character succeeds on a Charisma (Deception) check against a DC set by the current suspicion level (see the Suspicion table), the suspicious activity goes unnoticed. Use your discretion to decide if any given activity is subtle enough to be covered by a distraction. For example, a glib conversation can't cover up an explosion.

EFFECTS OF SUSPICION

As the suspicion level increases, patrols become more frequent, and the prison staff become increasingly vigilant. At suspicion level 6, the warden puts the prison on high alert.

SUSPICION

Level	Patrol Die	DC	Level	Patrol Die	DC
1	d20	10	4	d8	16
2	d12	12	5	d6	18
3	d10	14	6	d4	20

Level. The current suspicion level is reduced by 1 (to a minimum of 1) every 8 hours if the prison staff detects no suspicious activity during that time.

Patrol Die. Roll a die based on the current suspicion level when characters enter the patrol route to see if they encounter a guard patrol (see "Patrol Routes").

DC. The DC of Charisma checks made against prison staff and of ability checks made to avoid patrols is set by the current suspicion level.

HIGH ALERT

When a matter of concern is brought to her attention, the warden (see area R21) decides whether to place the prison on high alert. Circumstances that warrant taking such action include a prisoner revolt, an escape, the approach of an unfamiliar ship, a dragon sighting, an attack, discovering a dead body, or suspicious activity (see "Suspicion" above).

By speaking the command word, "maristo," the warden—and only the warden—can place the prison on high alert (or speak it again to end the high alert), with the following effects:

High-Alert Signals. For 1 minute, a warning horn blares throughout the prison, and all light created by *continual flame* spells in the prison takes on a reddish hue.

Prison Deployment. The guards in area R19 don their armor, arm themselves, and move to area R18. The warden does the same and commands the garrison from there. Members of the Absolution Council retreat to area R20.

See Invisibility. The warden and all prison guards gain the benefit of a *see invisibility* spell.

PATROL ROUTES

Guards regularly patrol in pairs from the guard rooms (area R3, alternating which room for each patrol) around the hexagon (area R15), with short checks into the courtyard (area R11) and the armory (area R10). The route is marked in yellow on the players' map of Revel's End. It normally takes 4 minutes for a patrol to make its round and return to its post.

When one or more characters enter an area marked on the patrol route, roll a die. The size of the die rolled is determined by the current suspicion level of the prison, as indicated on the Suspicion table. On a 1, the characters encounter a patrol. Ask the players how their characters react, and give them 1 round of actions. The characters can try to slip away if there is a nearby exit or corner to duck around by making a group Dexterity (Stealth) check or try to blend in by making a group Charisma (Deception) check. Each check is made against a DC set by the current suspicion level. On a failure, the patrol notices the characters, who must account for their presence.

If the characters try to talk their way past a patrol, have one of the characters make a Charisma check using Deception, Intimidation, or Persuasion, depending on their story, against a DC set by the suspicion level. If other characters support the story, the check is made with advantage. On a success, the patrol lets them go. On a failure, the patrol escorts the characters to a guard room (area R3), where the guard interrogates the characters about the characters' presence in a prohibited area. If the characters have a cover story for being in the prison, the guards escort them to where they should be: the kitchen staff's quarters (the largest side room off area R8) or the barracks (area R19) in the case of off-duty guards. The suspicion level then increases by 1.

Once the characters encounter a patrol, don't check for another patrol when the characters enter the route until 20 minutes have passed.

REVEL'S END LOCATIONS

The following locations are keyed to Revel's End, as shown on map 4.2.

R1: DOCK

Ships dock here to offload prisoners and supplies.

R2: ELEVATOR

A sturdy wooden scaffold clings to the 160-foot-high cliff separating the prison from the dock. Looming above the scaffolding is a wooden crane that is controlled from area R3. The crane raises and lowers an elevator car that has a retractable wooden gate on the side opposite the crane. The elevator car is a hollow wooden cube measuring 10 feet on each side. It takes 1 minute for the car to travel all the way up or down the scaffold.

R3: Guard Rooms

> This room contains a table with four chairs, and a cabinet holding whetstones and other simple supplies for repairing armor and weapons.

Three guards (**veterans**) are stationed in each of these two rooms. The guards pass the time by playing cards, sharpening their weapons, and complaining about the weather.

Embedded in the north wall of the northern guard room is an iron lever that raises and lowers the elevator in area R2. During a patrol, two of the guards leave the room to make their rounds for 4 minutes.

R4: Hospital

> This chamber contains a dozen simple beds. Cabinets along the north wall hold medical supplies.

The cabinets hold enough supplies to assemble twenty healer's kits, five vials of antitoxin, and various other medicines and tinctures.

Some of these substances are poisonous if ingested in the wrong proportion. A character proficient with alchemist's supplies, a poisoner's kit, an herbalist's kit, or the Medicine skill can identify the tinctures and combine them into an ingested poison. A creature that ingests the poison must make a DC 13 Constitution saving throw. On a failed saving throw, it takes 10 (3d6) poison damage and becomes poisoned for 1 hour. On a successful saving throw, it takes half as much damage and isn't poisoned. In either case, the creature has painful stomach cramps until it finishes a short rest, drinks a vial of antitoxin, or is targeted by an effect that ends the poisoned condition. If a prisoner suffers these cramps, the guards bring the prisoner to the hospital to be examined and treated. Characters disguised as guards can volunteer for or be assigned that duty.

R5: Stables

Visitors who bring mounts, sled dogs, pack animals, or pets to Revel's End can keep their animals here. The prison doesn't supply food for animals, however.

R6: Mess Hall

Prison personnel dine here. Tables and benches fill the room, and dishes and dulled cutlery are stored in cabinets along the south wall. The mess hall serves breakfast, lunch, and dinner. The characters can meet here without arousing any suspicion.

R7: Councilors' Quarters

These ten rooms are furnished identically. Each contains a bed, a desk with matching chair, a claw-footed chest, and wall hooks for hanging clothes. The *continual flame* spell that illuminates each room can be suppressed or returned to its normal light level by uttering the command word, "lights."

These rooms are set aside for the ten members of the Absolution Council, though only three rooms are currently in use. The other seven members of the council are absent, so the warden lets visitors use the spare rooms.

Council Members. These three members of the Absolution Council are at Revel's End:

Councilor Voss Anderton. Voss represents the city of Neverwinter. He is a lawful neutral, human noncombatant who has a precise, lawyerly way of speaking. He never misses a council meeting or parole hearing. He votes with his head, not his heart, and he always weighs the ramifications of commuting a prisoner's sentence.

Councilor Jil Torbo. Jil represents the city of Baldur's Gate. She is a neutral, halfling noncombatant who loathes her job. She has no sense of humor and sighs deeply when her patience is tested. She likes giving others the benefit of the doubt, however—perhaps as an act of dissent—and votes yes on commutations more often than not.

Councilor Kriv Norixius. Kriv represents the town of Daggerford. He is a lawful good, dragonborn noncombatant of silver dragon ancestry. He hopes to impress the Duchess of Daggerford by doing a good job. He has no tolerance for unrepentant criminals and often votes no on commutations.

R8: Kitchen and Side Rooms

Six cooks (neutral, human **commoners**) take shifts here, working in pairs to produce meals for the prisoners and staff. The kitchen contains everything one would expect to see, as well as an iron stove and a pump that draws water from a magically heated cistern on the roof.

Off-duty cooks sleep in the largest of the three rooms west of the kitchen. This side room is lit by *continual flame* spells that can be suppressed or activated by uttering the command word, "lights."

The middle side room—not heated, unlike the rest of the prison—is used for cold storage.

The smallest side room is a well-stocked pantry.

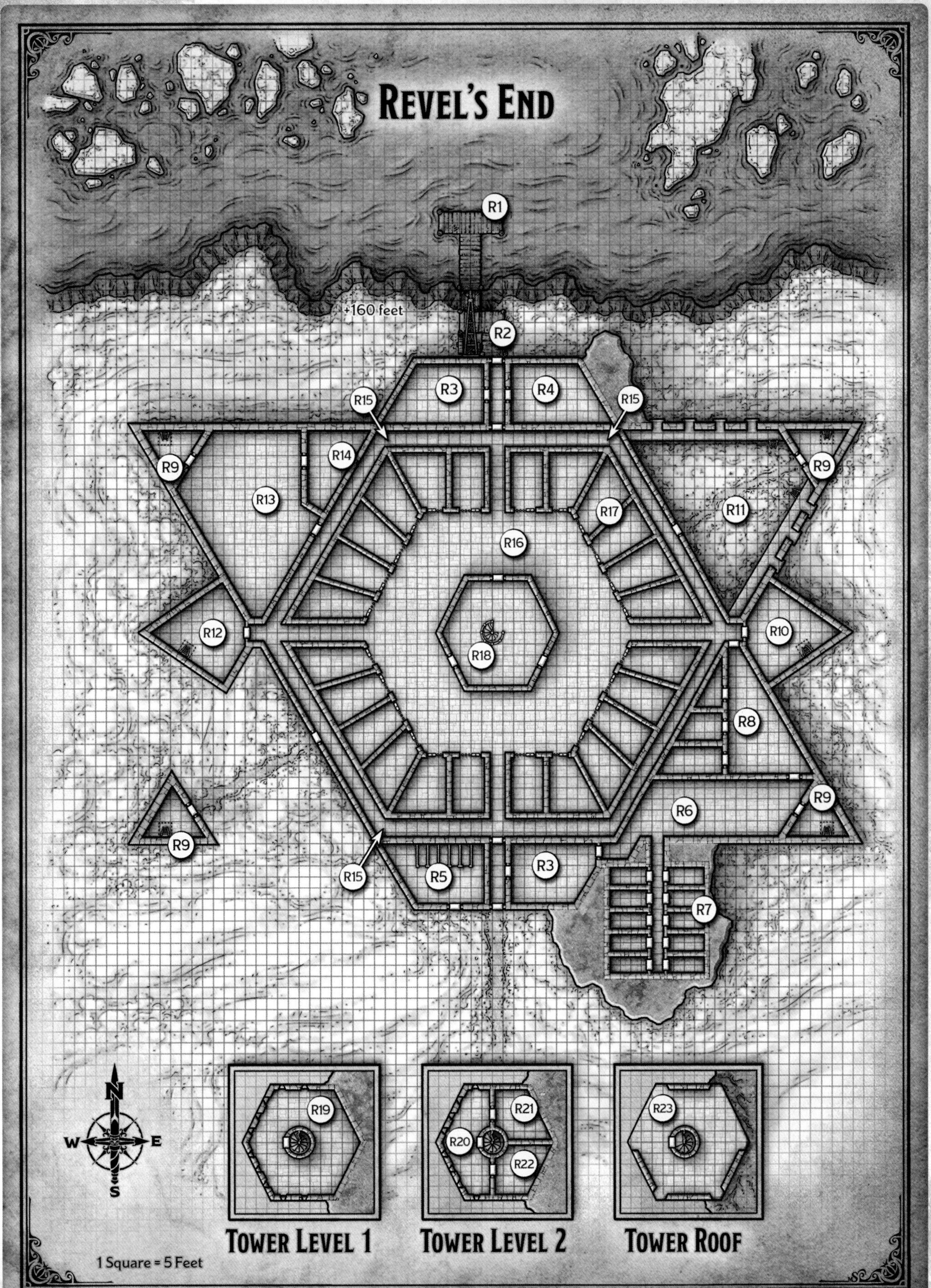
Revel's End
R1
+160 feet
R2
R3
R4
R15
R15
R14
R9
R13
R9
R11
R17
R16
R12
R18
R10
R8
R9
R6
R9
R15
R5
R3
R7
R19
R21
R20
R22
R23
Tower Level 1
Tower Level 2
Tower Roof
N
W
E
S
1 Square = 5 Feet

MIKE SCHLEY

R9: Guard Towers

Each of these four triangular towers is two stories tall. A tower's interior chamber is empty except for a wooden ladder that climbs to an iron hatch held shut by an *arcane lock* spell (see the "Prison Features" section for more details). This hatch leads to the tower's flat rooftop, which is lined with battlements. Three Lords' Alliance guards (**veterans**) in cold-weather clothing are stationed on the roof of each tower.

R10: Armory

> This room contains wooden racks and chests filled with weaponry. Floating in the middle of the room is a spherical creature with a large central eye and four writhing eyestalks.

The inventory is nonmagical and includes twenty halberds, fifteen longswords, fifteen shortswords, ten pikes, ten heavy crossbows, five light crossbows, and hundreds of crossbow bolts.

The armory is guarded by a **spectator** that treats the weapons as treasure. It knows every member of the prison staff on sight. It won't leave the room and attacks anyone it doesn't recognize.

Hatch. A wooden ladder leads to an iron hatch in the ceiling. An *arcane lock* spell seals the hatch (see the "Prison Features" section for more details), which opens onto the roof.

R11: Courtyard

This courtyard is paved with flagstones, which are covered with drifting snow.

When the weather allows, prisoners are brought here—individually or in small groups—for fresh air and exercise. They are watched closely by guards on the ground as well as the guards on the corner tower. Characters can speak quietly with a prisoner without being noticed from the tower.

R12: Meeting Room

This room holds a large, rectangular table with a single chair on one long side and three similar chairs on the opposite side. The room is used for meetings with prisoners or the warden.

Hatch. A wooden ladder leads to an iron hatch in the ceiling that opens onto the roof. An *arcane lock* spell seals the hatch (see the "Prison Features" section for more details).

R13: Storeroom

Supplies are stored here in crates and other containers. At present, the prison has stockpiled enough necessities to continue operations for six months.

R14: Privy

This room contains a dozen wooden waste buckets. Once per day, usually in the morning, manacled prisoners carry the buckets outside the prison and dispose of the waste while watched by guards.

R15: Hexagon

This corridor allows guards and visitors to access the outermost rooms of the prison while avoiding the panopticon (area R16) and its prison cells (area R17). The guards refer to this corridor as "the hexagon" because of its shape.

R16: Panopticon

> This hexagonal chamber is a large open space at the center of the prison. Cells line the chamber walls, and a smaller hexagonal room occupies the center of the space.

The *continual flame* spells that light this area can be dimmed from the surveillance hub (area R18). The hall is dimly lit at night.

R17: Cells

> Each cell is enclosed by formidable steel bars. Bolted to the back wall are iron bunk beds, each with a thin mattress. A waste bucket sits near the beds.

The prisoners are kept in these unlit cells (effectively illuminated by the lights in R16) behind barred gates that can be opened only from area R18. The gates are too secure to be forced open using brute strength or weapons, and magical attempts to open or bypass them are thwarted by permanent antimagic fields. Each field encompasses one cell and its gate. Spells and other magical effects, except those created by an artifact or a deity, are suppressed in an antimagic field and can't protrude into it. While an effect is suppressed, it doesn't function, but the time it spends suppressed counts against its duration.

Bolted to the back wall of each cell is an iron bunk bed with thin mattresses and a waste bucket nearby. Prisoners take their meals in their cells.

Prisoners. Each of the twenty-four cells can hold one or two prisoners. Roll 4d10 to determine the number of prisoners currently incarcerated at Revel's End, give each one an identification number, and distribute them in the cells as you see fit. Numbers are assigned in the order in which the prisoners arrive and are never reused. The longest-serving prisoner currently incarcerated at Revel's End is Prisoner 6, and the newest one is Prisoner 299.

Prisoner 13 (see the "Roleplaying Prisoner 13" section later in this adventure for more details) has no cellmate. Her cell is marked on map 4.1.

To add detail to other inmates, roll on the Prisoners table or choose entries you like. If a prisoner's game statistics become necessary, choose an appropriate stat block from the *Monster Manual*, and remove armor, weapons, and other gear.

PRISONERS

d6	Prisoner
1	Gallia Strand (neutral evil human), convicted of smuggling contraband luxuries, has served 1d6 years of a 10-year sentence.
2	Barlo Rageblade (chaotic good human), a famous adventurer convicted of reckless endangerment, has served 1d4 years of a 5-year sentence.
3	Quillion Sardo (lawful neutral halfling), convicted of using magic to influence others, has served 1d4 years of a 5-year sentence.
4	Pirouette (chaotic evil tiefling), a thieves' guild leader convicted of multiple crimes, has served 1d20 years of a life sentence.
5	Ishar (chaotic evil elf), convicted of conspiracy to murder members of a noble family, has served 1d20 years of a life sentence.
6	Grix (neutral goblin), convicted of espionage, has served 1d6 years of a 10-year sentence.

R18: SURVEILLANCE HUB

This hexagonal room is the base of the prison's central tower. A spiral staircase rises to the tower's upper levels. Several guards watch through the arrow slits, observing the cells, while one sits at a metal desk and console with a myriad of switches and dials and a brass tube with a funnel-like flare.

The stairs lead to areas R19 through R23. Seven guards (**veterans**) are stationed in this surveillance hub. One sits at a console south of the staircase. The other guards watch the prisoners through 4-foot-tall, 1-foot-wide arrow slits in the walls.

AN ADVENTURER MAKES CONTACT WITH THE ENIGMATIC PRISONER 13.

Hanging on the walls between the arrow slits are fifty sets of iron manacles guards use to bind prisoners' wrists and ankles.

Console. The console is a magical device that resembles a desk with a slanted top and is bolted to the floor. It is a Large object with AC 15, 18 hit points, and immunity to poison and psychic damage. The console has the following magical properties, which are disabled if it is reduced to 0 hit points:

Gate Control. Twenty-four switches on the console open and close the gates to the prison cells. A master switch opens or closes all the gates at once. Flipping one or more switches on the console requires an action.

Light Control. A brass dial on the console controls the light level in area R16. Turning the dial requires an action or a bonus action.

Loudspeaker. As an action, a creature can use this device, which resembles the bell of a trumpet, to broadcast its voice throughout the prison.

R19: BARRACKS

> A door in the spiral staircase leads into a large room filled with wooden bunk beds. There are arrow slits in the north, west, and south walls. Footlockers and armor racks accompany each bed. The spiral stairs continue up past the door.

Characters who climb the spiral staircase come to a door 100 feet above the prison roof. The staircase continues beyond this door to the tower's higher levels.

The door opens into a room filled with wooden bunk beds. Areas to the north, west, and south can be viewed through 4-foot-tall, 1-foot-wide arrow slits. The *continual flame* spells that light the room can be dimmed or brightened by uttering the command word, "lights."

When the prison isn't on high alert, fifty guards (**veterans** without armor or weapons) sleep in the bunks. The guards keep their armor and weapons within easy reach. They keep other belongings in unlocked footlockers tucked under their bunk beds.

The guards need 10 minutes to don their armor. If the prison is put on high alert, the guards take the time to put on their armor before making their way down to area R18.

R20: HALL OF ABSOLUTION

The floor of this room is 120 feet above the prison roof. A spiral staircase connects the room to the other levels of the tower (area R18 is 140 feet down, area R19 is 20 feet down, and area R23 is 20 feet up). Narrow windows line the outer walls.

A long, slightly curved table with eleven chairs takes up much of the room. The middle chair has no special adornments, while the others have banners hanging over their high backs, each one emblazoned with the crest of a Lords' Alliance member. Banners hanging on the walls display the alliance's emblem: a golden crown on a red field.

Absolution Council Meetings. Members of the Absolution Council gather here to weigh the merits of releasing prisoners whom one or more council members have recommended for parole. No prisoner can receive such consideration more than once a year. Prisoners up for parole are brought to this room in manacles and given a chance to sway the council members before votes are cast. The warden (see area R21), who always attends such meetings, sits in the middle chair and casts the tiebreaking vote, if necessary.

R21: WARDEN'S QUARTERS

The *arcane lock* on this door can be opened only by the warden. Beyond the door is a comfortable bedchamber lit by a *continual flame* spell that can be dimmed or brightened by uttering the command word, "vaudra."

Prison Warden. The calm and unflappable warden of Revel's End is Marta Marthannis, a lawful good, human **mage** who speaks Common, Draconic, Dwarvish, and Orc. She wears a red robe with gold trim and keeps a ring with seven tiny keys hanging from it in one pocket. One key unlocks the warden's chest (see "Treasure" below); the others unlock the desk drawer and the cabinets in the warden's office (area R22).

Warden Marthannis is secretly a member of the Harpers, a faction that works behind the scenes to keep power out of the hands of evildoers. In her current position, she works to keep some of the Sword Coast's worst malefactors behind bars. So far, the warden has managed to conceal her Harper affiliation from everyone else in the prison.

Marthannis's Possession. Unlike her membership in the Harpers, Marthannis hasn't concealed the fact that she is periodically possessed. Lodged inside her is the spirit of a deceased adventuring companion: a lawful good, shield dwarf fighter named Vlax Brawnanvil. The spirit of Vlax takes control of Warden Marthannis once or twice a day, each time for an hour or two—though never while she's performing important duties, such as supervising prisoner meetings with visitors.

While under Vlax's control, the warden can't cast her prepared spells or use the command word for high alert (see the "High Alert" section), speaks only Dwarvish, and occasionally indulges Vlax's vice for ale and spirits.

Warden Marthannis knows that to rid herself of Vlax's spirit, she must visit the Brawnanvil crypts in Gauntlgrym, a dwarven fortress under Mount Hotenow (near Neverwinter), where the spirits of Vlax's kin can persuade Vlax to join them in the afterlife. The warden refuses to make the journey, however, because she can't bear to lose all contact with Vlax. The warden has made her state known to the prison guards and Absolution Council members, and they have grown accustomed to her personality changes and bouts of revelry. The possession hasn't affected the warden's ability to carry out her duties, and so far, no one has questioned her fitness for her job.

Treasure. Among the chamber's furnishings is a locked wooden chest, for which the warden carries the only key. A character using thieves' tools can use an action to try to pick the lock, doing so with a successful DC 20 Dexterity check.

The chest holds a set of calligrapher's supplies, a sack containing 750 gp (money that's used mainly to pay ship captains who drop off prisoners and cargo), and a silver cloak pin (25 gp) bearing the symbol of the Harpers: a tiny harp nestled between the horns of a crescent moon.

Any character who searches the chest for secret compartments finds one in the lid. It holds a *wand of binding* that the warden keeps for emergencies.

R22: Office

> A heavy desk stands in the middle of the room with parchment, quills, and ink at the ready. Five heavy wood cabinets line the east wall.

Prison records are stored here in the locked cabinets. The cabinets also contain ship cargo manifests and records of past deliveries, as well as prisoner transfer orders and a ledger documenting the names, crimes, sentences, and commutations of every prisoner who has been incarcerated at Revel's End. The records include death certificates for prisoners who died while incarcerated. The cause of death is always given as "natural," "accidental," or "unnatural," with no details.

A desk in the middle of the room has ten financial ledgers packed into a locked side drawer. The keys for the desk and the cabinets are in the warden's possession. A character with thieves' tools can use an action to try to pick the lock on the desk drawer or one of the cabinets, doing so with a successful DC 12 Dexterity check.

R23: Tower Roof

This flat rooftop is 140 feet above the prison roof and 300 feet above sea level. Three 6-foot-high walls to the north, southwest, and southeast provide limited cover, but much of the rooftop is exposed to the elements.

A wooden drawbridge can be lowered on one side to create an airship dock. An action is required to raise or lower the drawbridge.

No guards are stationed here. If the guards in the prison watchtowers (area R9) see an airship or an airborne threat approaching Revel's End, they alert the rest of the prison. The warden then dons cold-weather clothing and heads to the roof to greet the airship crew or deal with the airborne threat herself.

Roleplaying Prisoner 13

The first time the characters encounter Prisoner 13, read the following:

> This tightly muscled dwarven woman keeps her red hair cut short. Her bronze skin is covered in tattoos that stretch from her collarbone to her ankles. She surveys you with unimpressed eyes.

Prisoner 13 is a cunning schemer, ruthless and patient. She listens and watches, absorbing every detail she can, and shares as little as she can get away with.

Prisoner 13 is comfortable with her lot in life, enjoying the anonymity and ironic protection of Revel's End like a warm blanket on a winter night. While confined to her antimagic cell, she is cautious since she can't rely on her magic tattoos to defend herself. Outside her cell, she grows overly confident and even banters if she's able to do so without being caught by guards. In battle she poses a potent threat, creating blasts of flame and striking with magical force in both melee and ranged combat.

She spends her time contemplating the web of schemes she learns through the eyes, ears, and hands of her agents outside the prison. While outside her cell during daily exercise in the courtyard or during chores, she contacts her agents for updates and makes arrangements that keep her network running.

Prisoner 13's Tattoos

Most of Prisoner 13's inkwork is covered by her uniform. Her tattoos include the following:

Dwarven Poetry. An excerpt from a poem in Dwarvish script on her neck and across her shoulder blades reads, "Endless dreams entombed in stone."

Flames. A roiling storm of brilliant flames covers her back and ribs.

Shroud. Black and gray smoke and shadows coil down her left arm, ending in runes on the fingers of her left hand.

Knotwork. Purple and blue knotwork and runes run down her right arm, across the back of her right hand, and down the length of each finger. The runes on her fingers, known as the keystone tattoo, form the key to the vault in Gauntlgrym. The characters must acquire this key to complete their mission (see "Acquiring the Key" below).

Mountain. Silver and brown mountain peaks cover her chest, the tips following the angles of her collarbones.

River. Swirling green and blue waters form a cascading river across her stomach, with scaly creatures leering from the water.

Power and Plunder. Dwarvish script on her hips reads "Power" and "Plunder."

Traced among Prisoner 13's tattoos are tiny magical sigils, each one matching a twin tattooed on one of her agents. A character who examines any visible tattoos and succeeds on a DC 15 Intelligence (Investigation) check notices some of the hidden marks. A character who succeeds on a DC 15 Intelligence (Arcana) check determines that the sigils have something to do with minds or telepathy.

ACQUIRING THE KEY

If she's approached with the possibility of freedom, Prisoner 13 looks genuinely surprised but quickly

---

PRISONER 13

Medium Humanoid (Dwarf, Monk), Neutral Evil

Armor Class 17 (Mountain Tattoo)
Hit Points 102 (12d8 + 48)
Speed 30 ft.

STR	DEX	CON	INT	WIS	CHA
15 (+2)	17 (+3)	18 (+4)	16 (+3)	14 (+2)	16 (+3)

Saving Throws Con +7, Wis +5
Skills Athletics +5, Deception +9, Insight +5, Perception +5, Stealth +6
Damage Resistances poison
Damage Immunities psychic
Condition Immunities charmed
Senses darkvision 60 ft., passive Perception 15
Languages Common, Dwarvish, Elvish, thieves' cant, Undercommon
Challenge 5 (1,800 XP)   **Proficiency Bonus** +3

Antimagic Susceptibility. In an area of antimagic, Prisoner 13's tattoos and reactions don't function, and she suffers the following modifications to her statistics: her AC becomes 13, she loses her immunity to psychic damage and the charmed condition, and her Tattooed Strike becomes a melee attack that deals 7 (1d8 + 3) bludgeoning damage on a hit.

Mindlink Tattoos. Prisoner 13 has telepathic links with dozens of agents operating throughout the land. The links allow Prisoner 13 to communicate telepathically with each of these agents while they are both on the same plane of existence.

Mountain Tattoo. Prisoner 13's AC includes her Constitution modifier.

Shroud Tattoo. Prisoner 13 can't be targeted by divination spells or any feature that would read her thoughts, and she can't be perceived through magical scrying sensors. She can't be contacted telepathically unless she allows such contact.

ACTIONS

Multiattack. Prisoner 13 makes two Tattooed Strike attacks.

Tattooed Strike. *Melee or Ranged Weapon Attack:* +6 to hit, reach 5 ft. or range 60 ft., one target. *Hit:* 12 (2d8 + 3) force damage.

Firestorm Tattoo (Recharge 5–6). Prisoner 13 magically unleashes flame from the tattoo across her back, filling a 20-foot-radius sphere centered on her. Each other creature in that area must make a DC 15 Dexterity saving throw. On a failed save, the creature takes 13 (3d8) fire damage and is knocked prone. On a successful save, it takes half as much damage and isn't knocked prone.

River Tattoo. Prisoner 13 magically ends any effects causing the grappled or restrained conditions on herself. If she is bound with nonmagical restraints, she slips out of them.

REACTIONS

Readiness. When a creature Prisoner 13 can see within 60 feet of herself ends its turn, Prisoner 13 makes one Tattooed Strike attack or uses River Tattoo. She can then move up to her speed without provoking opportunity attacks.

assumes her usual neutral mask. Here's how she responds to some likely questions:

What do you know about the vault and key? She plays coy: "I don't know what you mean." If pressed further, she shrugs. "I've been asked about this vault and key before. Assuming I did know where the key might be, what would be in it for me to tell you?"

Do you want to be set free? "As flattered as I am that you care, I'm afraid I must decline. I'm fine where I am, thanks."

What do you want for the key? She ponders for a moment before answering: "The warden has a ledger, probably in her office. It contains all the names, crimes, and prisoner numbers of everyone ever incarcerated at Revel's End. Bring me that list, and I'll see to it that you get your key."

In response to a verbal threat, Prisoner 13 shakes her head and says, "I could make quite a scene and bring the guards down on you. Maybe even the warden herself. You really don't have anything to threaten me with."

Finding the Key. When Prisoner 13 talks about the key, each character present can make a DC 19 Wisdom (Insight) check. If the check is successful, the character notices Prisoner 13 flexing her right hand and tracing a fingertip across the tattoo there when she mentions the key. The character deduces that the tattoo is the key.

Forcible Jailbreak. Taking Prisoner 13 alive and delivering her to Varrin is difficult but possible. She won't go willingly and fights back if the characters try to force her. In that case, they'll be hard-pressed to knock her unconscious and make their escape without alarming the guards and placing the prison on high alert. If a fight breaks out with closed doors between the battle and the nearest guards, on initiative count 0, make a DC 15 Wisdom (Perception) check for the guards to see if they notice the commotion. If they succeed, roll initiative for the guards. They investigate on the following round.

Trade for the Key. If the characters acquire the prisoner files from the warden's office (area R22), Prisoner 13 demands to read them somewhere outside her cell. She takes 20 minutes to read through the documents and telepathically relay the information to her agents for later use. Following that, she reveals that the tattoo on her right hand is the key to the vault. She allows the characters to study it so they can replicate its image using magic such as *disguise self* or *minor illusion*, or even copy it with pen and ink. In any case, a character must succeed

on a DC 15 Intelligence (Arcana) check to correctly re-create the tattoo, which requires 10 minutes of study or drawing. The characters can retry if they fail, at the cost of more time and more risk of discovery.

Last Resort. A gruesome but effective option is killing Prisoner 13 and taking her body back, or just her right hand. If the characters are working for the Golden Vault, they know the organization would not approve of this method. The characters receive no reward from the organization if they kill or mutilate Prisoner 13.

Conclusion

When the characters successfully deliver the key (Prisoner 13's keystone tattoo), Varrin's joy and relief crack his usually reserved exterior, and he sends his agents to open the vault and reveal the lost Axebreaker treasure (he won't allow the characters to be present for the vault opening). While much of the clan's stolen wealth has been spent, there's still a great fortune remaining. As a result of their success, the characters have advantage whenever one of them attempts a Charisma check that would influence Axebreaker dwarves. Varrin makes good on his bargain and gives a fair share to the characters as promised. The reward includes the following coins and gems (use the amounts in brackets if the characters negotiated a 3 percent fee):

- 2,100 cp (3,150 cp)
- 1,100 sp (1,650 sp)
- 100 gp (150 gp)
- 12 (18) bloodstones worth 50 gp each

The characters can also choose three magic items from the following list, or four items if they successfully negotiated for a bigger reward from Varrin:

- *Cap of water breathing*
- *Dust of disappearance*
- *Gem of brightness*
- *Mithral armor*
- *Potion of resistance* (lightning)
- *Slippers of spider climbing*

For the Golden Vault

If the characters are working for the Golden Vault, they must deliver the key to Varrin Axebreaker. Once they do, the organization rewards the characters with a rare magic item of their choice (subject to your approval) as payment. The item is delivered to the characters the next day.

The svirfneblin town of Little Lockford holds many wonders—and many hidden dangers.

TOCKWORTH'S CLOCKWORKS

T HE CLOCKWORK AUTOMATONS THAT GUARD the svirfneblin town of Little Lockford have attacked the very residents they were meant to keep safe, forcing a town-wide evacuation. At the heart of the matter is Security Overseer Tixie Tockworth, a tinkerer who has turned malicious.

In this adventure, the characters must enter Little Lockford, recover a security key, and use it to activate a fail-safe device that shuts off the automatons.

ADVENTURE BACKGROUND

The clockwork automatons that protect Little Lockford are the creations of a gnome tinkerer named Tixie Tockworth, who recently decided to become a mechanical being herself. She began with a series of procedures whereby she replaced parts of her body with machinery created in her workshop. At some point, Tockworth lost all compassion and empathy for her fellow townspeople. Her fellow tinkerers urged her to stop what she was doing, but she refused. When the militia tried to shut down her workshop, Tockworth unleashed her automatons on the citizens of Little Lockford, many of whom were killed. The survivors fled and regrouped outside the settlement in a nearby network of Underdark tunnels and caverns. The survivors then magically sealed the doors to Little Lockford to keep Tockworth's automatons from escaping.

Tockworth's painstaking transformation into a machine has occupied her for the past few weeks, during which time the other residents of Little Lockford have been searching for adventurers to help them reclaim their settlement.

Little Lockford's mayor, Braith Broadfoot, asks the adventurers to infiltrate the town and retrieve a security key last seen in Tockworth's possession. When used to activate a fail-safe device in Tockworth's workshop, the key permanently shuts down the automatons, rendering them harmless. How the characters deal with Tockworth is left up to them.

USING THE GOLDEN VAULT

If you're using the Golden Vault as a patron, a golden key is delivered to the characters in whatever manner you deem fit. When the characters use this key to open their music box, the lid pops open and a soothing voice says the following:

> "Greetings, operatives. We have learned the svirfneblin town of Little Lockford needs your help. Tixie Tockworth, once entrusted with the town's security, has turned the town's clockwork automatons against the populace. This quest, should you choose to undertake it, requires you to infiltrate Little Lockford, retrieve a security key, and use it to power down the automatons. You are also empowered to stop Tixie Tockworth from doing further harm to the town. Start by meeting with the town's mayor, Braith Broadfoot. She's waiting for you in the caves outside the gates of Little Lockford. Good luck, operatives."

Closing the music box causes the golden key to vanish.

INTO THE UNDERDARK

Little Lockford is situated in the Underdark, but the tunnels leading to the settlement are well traveled and relatively easy to navigate. Stone signs illuminated by *continual flame* spells can be found at every junction, pointing the way to the settlement.

If you want to make the journey to Little Lockford more interesting, you can insert a random encounter or two as the characters make their way through dark tunnels. To determine what the characters encounter, roll on the Underdark Encounters table.

d12	Encounter
1	Two **grells** drop on the characters from above.
2	The characters hear the clicks and clacks of three **hook horrors** several minutes before these predators appear and attack.
3	A **galeb duhr** reveals itself and tries to converse with the characters in Terran. The creature is bored and eager to strike up a conversation, if only to ask about the weather.
4	A **black pudding** oozes from a hole in the wall and attacks.
5	The characters find a Tiny clockwork device that was left behind by a svirfneblin miner. The device produces a miniature flame that can be used to light a candle, torch, or campfire. Using the device requires an action.
6	The characters enter a small cave containing a stone throne fit for a gnome. The throne, which looks like it was carved from a stalagmite, is a **mimic** that attacks anyone who sits on it.
7–12	A **deep gnome** named Nyx Riddlestone is on the lookout for adventurers heading to Little Lockford. Nyx speaks Common, Gnomish, Terran, and Undercommon. She greets the characters curtly and offers to escort them to Mayor Broadfoot without delay.

MEETING THE MAYOR

Mayor Braith Broadfoot (neutral good, deep gnome **commoner**) speaks Common in addition to Gnomish, Terran, and Undercommon. She and her fellow gnome exiles are gathered in a cavern not too far from the front gates of the Little Lockford. If the characters say they've come to help, the mayor eagerly gives them an overview of the situation:

"I can't tell you how pleased we are that you're here to help us! We've sealed the gates of Little Lockford to contain the threat that has claimed so many innocent lives.

"Some weeks ago, Tockworth, our security overseer, ordered her clockwork automatons to attack her fellow citizens. Not knowing what else to do, I ordered an evacuation. But Little Lockford is our home, and I am determined to reclaim it.

"Tockworth built a fail-safe device to shut down the automatons in the event of malfunction. The device is in her workshop, protected by a magic symbol on the floor that messes with the mind of any creature that sets foot on it. To activate the fail-safe, you need a security key that Tockworth keeps in a safe in her workshop. We need you to retrieve the security key and use it to shut down the clockwork automatons. How you deal with Tockworth is up to you."

Mayor Broadfoot provides a hand-drawn map of the town (give your players a copy of map 5.1). In her haste, the flustered mayor has flip-flopped the locations of the infirmary (area L4) and the jail (area L5) on her map.

Mayor Broadfoot also tells the characters about some useful items hidden under her desk in the town hall (area L2). The characters are free to claim the items for themselves. If asked why the items were left behind, Mayor Broadfoot admits she forgot about them in her rush to evacuate Little Lockford. The items are as follows:

- Four *potions of healing*
- A packet of *dust of disappearance*
- Two flasks of alchemist's fire

PLANNING THE HEIST

Armed with Mayor Broadfoot's map, the characters can begin planning their heist. If they do so in the company of Mayor Broadfoot and her advisers, these deep gnomes share the following useful information:

Features. The gnomes can share the information in the "General Features" section. The "Bridges" and "Slagline" sections are especially important when it comes to planning the heist.

Tockworth's Automatons. If the characters request more information about Tockworth's automatons, use the information in the "Security Forces" section to describe them.

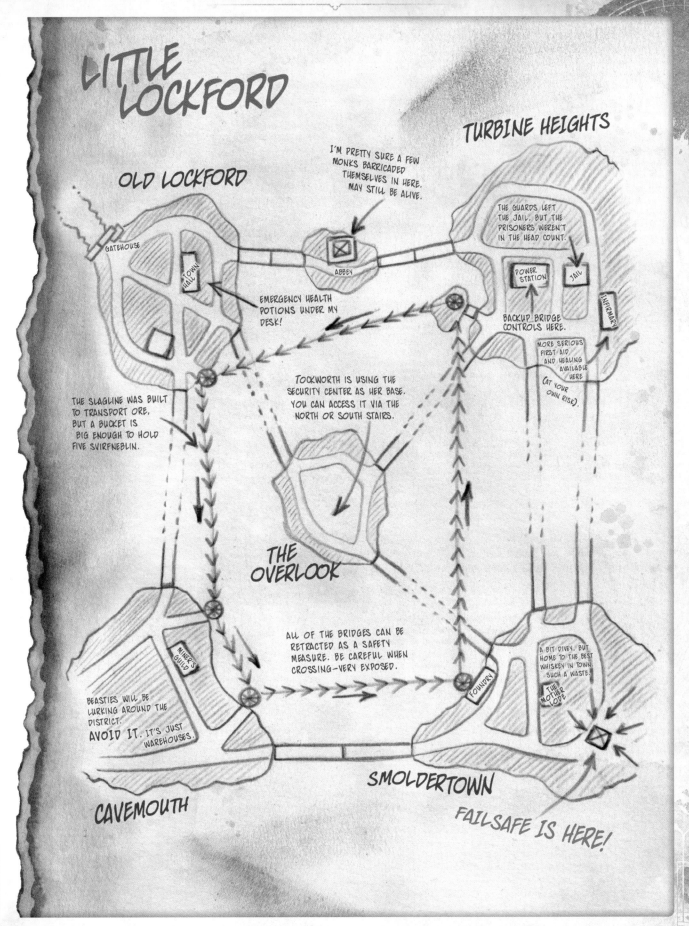

LITTLE LOCKFORD

TURBINE HEIGHTS

OLD LOCKFORD

I'M PRETTY SURE A FEW MONKS BARRICADED THEMSELVES IN HERE. MAY STILL BE ALIVE.

THE GUARDS LEFT THE JAIL, BUT THE PRISONERS WEREN'T IN THE HEAD COUNT.

GATEHOUSE

TOWN HALL

ABBEY

POWER STATION

JAIL

INFIRMARY

EMERGENCY HEALTH POTIONS UNDER MY DESK!

BACKUP BRIDGE CONTROLS HERE.

MORE SERIOUS FIRST AID AND HEALING AVAILABLE HERE

(AT YOUR OWN RISK).

THE SLAGLINE WAS BUILT TO TRANSPORT ORE, BUT A BUCKET IS BIG ENOUGH TO HOLD FIVE SVIRFNEBLIN.

TOCKWORTH IS USING THE SECURITY CENTER AS HER BASE. YOU CAN ACCESS IT VIA THE NORTH OR SOUTH STAIRS.

THE OVERLOOK

MINER'S GUILD

ALL OF THE BRIDGES CAN BE RETRACTED AS A SAFETY MEASURE. BE CAREFUL WHEN CROSSING—VERY EXPOSED.

A BIT DIVEY, BUT HOME TO THE BEST WHISKEY IN TOWN. SUCH A WASTE.

FOUNDRY

THE MOTHER LODE

BEASTIES WILL BE LURKING AROUND THE DISTRICT. AVOID IT. IT'S JUST WAREHOUSES.

SMOLDERTOWN

CAVEMOUTH

FAILSAFE IS HERE!

TIXIE TOCKWORTH

Tixie Tockworth. The trouble began when Tockworth began performing magical procedures on herself, replacing parts of her body with machine parts. Her fellow tinkerers urged her to stop these procedures, but she refused. The mayor ordered the militia to shut down Tockworth's workshop, but the militia was unable to get past the shield guardian stationed outside the workshop. After the militia was rebuffed, Tockworth instructed her automatons to attack everyone else in Little Lockford.

Warehouse Contraption. Warehouse 6, in the Cavemouth district, contains a magical drilling machine big enough to hold two characters (see area L11 for details). The svirfneblin have no clue what the characters might use it for, but it could come in handy.

REWARDS

If the characters retrieve the security key and shut down Tockworth's automatons, Mayor Broadfoot promises to award the characters the following treasure:

- Ruby ring worth 5,000 gp
- *Boots of striding and springing*
- *Driftglobe*
- *Stone of good luck*

If the characters make the case that one or more of the magic items might help them accomplish their mission, Mayor Broadfoot agrees to give them one magic item as a down payment—though if the characters abandon the mission, she expects them to return the item.

SHOWN THE DOOR

When the characters are ready to enter Little Lockford, they're led to the town's fortified entrance by Sergeant Yombad Cragknuckle (neutral good **deep gnome**), the highest ranked of the surviving militia members. Stern and scowling, he walks with a slight limp and has a heavily bandaged arm, both the result of injuries he sustained during the evacuation.

Sergeant Cragknuckle speaks Gnomish, Terran, and Undercommon, but not Common. If asked for advice on the mission, the sergeant offers the following information and guidance:

Friendly Advice. The sergeant urges the characters to move quickly and quietly through the town, doing their best to avoid Tockworth's automatons.

Avoid Cavemouth. The sergeant suggests the characters avoid the Cavemouth district due to the likely presence of monsters there. (Normally kept at bay by the clockwork automatons, monsters are likely to have ventured from their hidey-holes and into the streets. Gricks are a particular nuisance.)

Healing Aids. The sergeant recalls that *potions of healing* and healer's kits can be found in the city infirmary in Turbine Heights.

Additionally, if the characters show Sergeant Cragknuckle the map of Little Lockford provided by Mayor Broadfoot, the sergeant points out that the map flip-flops the locations of the infirmary (area L4) and the jail (area L5).

LITTLE LOCKFORD OVERVIEW

Due to its strategic location and proximity to valuable resources, Little Lockford has been a consistent target of attack. As a result, the deep gnomes have fortified the town, which is described in greater detail below.

GENERAL FEATURES

The town is situated in a vast cavern tinged red by the magma that flows through the channels that separate the various districts. By and large, the town is well maintained, with streets and buildings composed of gray stone bricks. Other noteworthy features are summarized in the sections that follow.

BRIDGES

Bridges made of wood and metal span the magma lake at various points, connecting the town's various districts to one another. Consoles in the power station (area L6) and the security center (area L12) enable these bridges to be raised or lowered, much like a modern-day drawbridge that spans a waterway.

To control the flow of traffic through town, Tockworth has raised the following bridges: the Old Lockford–Cavemouth bridge, the Cavemouth–Smoldertown bridge, one of the two Smoldertown–Turbine Heights bridges, and the two bridges leading to the Overlook from Old Lockford and Turbine Heights.

BUILDINGS

Most of Little Lockford's buildings are single-story stone structures (about 12 feet high) with stone doors that are 5 feet high and 3 feet wide. Building interiors tend to be unlit (which is of little concern to deep gnomes, who have darkvision), and they contain furnishings sized for gnomes.

Little Lockford contains many buildings not described in the adventure. If the characters investigate one of these buildings, roll on the Buildings of Little Lockford table to determine what kind of building it is. Each building's occupants took everything of value before fleeing Little Lockford, leaving nothing of value for characters to find.

BUILDINGS OF LITTLE LOCKFORD

d100	Building Type
01–25	Residence, squalid (quarters for 4d6 gnomes)
26–40	Residence, modest (quarters for 2d6 gnomes)
41–50	Residence, wealthy (quarters for 1d6 gnomes)
51–53	Alchemist's workshop
54–56	Bakery
57–58	Bathhouse
59–62	Brewery
63–64	Cartographer's workshop
65–66	Cobbler's workshop
67–69	Empty building (with a for-sale sign on the door)
70–72	Fungi restaurant (with a menu by the door)
73–76	Gemcutter's workshop
77–78	Haberdashery
79–82	Jeweler's shop
83–84	Scribe's workshop
85–88	Smithy
89–92	Tavern
93–96	Tinker's workshop
97–00	Wizard's domicile

DISTRICT ELEVATIONS

While most districts sit 150 feet above the magma lake, two do not. The Overlook, built into a rock formation at the center of the cavern, sits 170 feet above the magma. Cavemouth is 120 feet above the magma.

EXTERIOR LIGHTING

The roof and walls of Little Lockford are bathed in a fiery hue, thanks to the magma that fills the lake and heats the town. The town's power station (area L6) generates electricity that powers streetlamps in every district, although the streetlamps have gone out in Cavemouth. These lights can be switched on or off from control consoles in the power station and the security center (area L12).

MAGMA

Any creature that falls into Little Lockford's magma lake is likely to be killed instantly unless that creature is immune to fire damage. Any creature that enters the magma for the first time on a turn or starts its turn there takes 55 (10d10) fire damage.

SLAGLINE

Suspended above the magma lake is a carousel-like chain of dangling steel buckets called the Slagline. The buckets are spaced 15 feet apart. Roughly half of them contain ore and uncut gems from the mines; the rest are empty and big enough to carry five Small creatures or two Medium creatures each.

The Slagline is automated so that the buckets move counterclockwise around the town. (Normally, ore and gems from the Cavemouth district are received at the foundry in the Smoldertown district for smelting and refining. The processed materials are then transported past Turbine Heights to Old Lockford, where they are sold by merchants and guild artisans.) The Slagline alternates between running for 1 minute and then pausing for 1 minute to allow time to load and unload its buckets. Whenever the Slagline stops, the buckets suspended above the magma bob and sway slightly—not so much that they spill their contents, however.

Creatures can safely climb into buckets at one of four loading stations (two in Cavemouth, one in Smoldertown, and one in Old Lockford) and ride the Slagline from one district to another.

SECURITY FORCES

Tockworth created two primary types of automatons to protect Little Lockford:

Clockwork Defenders. Little Lockford has twenty **clockwork defenders** (see their description and stat block at the end of the adventure), not including ones that were destroyed during the town's evacuation or the damaged one in area L6.

Clockwork Observers. Little Lockford has eight **clockwork observers** (see their description and stat block at the end of the adventure). The observers are tasked with monitoring the streets to ensure nothing has penetrated the city's defenses. If an observer detects intruders, it contacts Tockworth telepathically, letting her know where the intruders are. Tockworth then orders the observer to use its next action to emit a piercing shriek, which is loud enough to summon 1d4 **clockwork defenders** (see their description and stat block at the end of the adventure). These reinforcements arrive 2 rounds later. If the number of clockwork defenders summoned is greater than the number left in Little Lockford, adjust the number of reinforcements accordingly.

Other Constructs under Tockworth's control include two suits of **animated armor** (see area L9a) and a **shield guardian** that lost its master and its control amulet. The shield guardian stands guard outside Tockworth's workshop (area L9).

WANDERING MONSTERS

Each time one or more visible characters exit a building or enter a new district, roll a d6. On a roll of 1 or 2 (or just 1 if the characters are trying to be stealthy), they attract the attention of one or more wandering monsters determined by rolling another d6 and consulting the Wandering Monsters table. See "Security Forces" above for more information about how many clockwork defenders and clockwork observers are present in Little Lockford.

In the Cavemouth district, the monsters encountered have all crawled from the mines. The characters encounter Tockworth's automatons elsewhere.

WANDERING MONSTERS

d6	Encounter in Cavemouth	Encounter Elsewhere
1	2 darkmantles following 1 grick	3 clockwork defenders
2–3	2 gricks	2 clockwork defenders
4–6	1 shambling mound made of fungi	1 clockwork observer

LITTLE LOCKFORD LOCATIONS

The following locations are marked on map 5.2.

OLD LOCKFORD (AREAS L1–L2)

Old Lockford is the oldest part of the town. The cobblestones here have been worn smooth over the centuries, and the streetlamps are wrought in a more ornate style than those in the rest of Little Lockford. A few dead deep gnomes lie in the streets; most wear the weapons and armor of the militia.

L1: ENTRANCE AND GATEHOUSE

When the characters are ready to enter the town, read or paraphrase the following:

> Sergeant Cragknuckle leads you to a bulwark hastily erected outside Little Lockford's impressive gates. The bulwark is defended by weary-looking members of the town militia, who salute the sergeant as he limps past them.
>
> Standing watch by the gates are two dour gnomes in black robes. On Cragknuckle's signal, each of these gnomes casts a spell that causes the gates to swing open before you. A wave of heat washes through the bulwark as the gates part, revealing a grim town bathed in hellish light and periodically brightened by flashes of lightning.

The outer gates lock automatically when they close. The two gnome mages on duty have prepared *knock* spells, which they use to circumvent the gates' complex locking mechanisms. It takes two *knock* spells to open the gates.

Sergeant Cragknuckle goes no farther. In Gnomish, he wishes the characters good luck, instructs them to knock on the gates seven times to signal that they're ready to exit, and assures them he will be here waiting for them. (If the characters don't speak his language, the sergeant raps his knuckles on the outer gates seven times to explain what they must do to signal for the gates to be opened.)

As soon as the characters enter the town, the gates lock behind them. True to his word, Sergeant Cragknuckle instructs the mages to open the gates if he hears someone on the other side knock on the gates seven times.

Gatehouse. A modest gatehouse stands inside the gates. Map 5.2 includes an inset map that shows the interior of the gatehouse, which the characters can use as a place to rest or regroup. The gatehouse contains sleeping quarters and an armory that was cleaned out during the evacuation.

L2: TOWN HALL

> The bodies of three dead gnomes clad in the armor of the town militia splay on the front steps of the town hall, the doors to which are wide open.

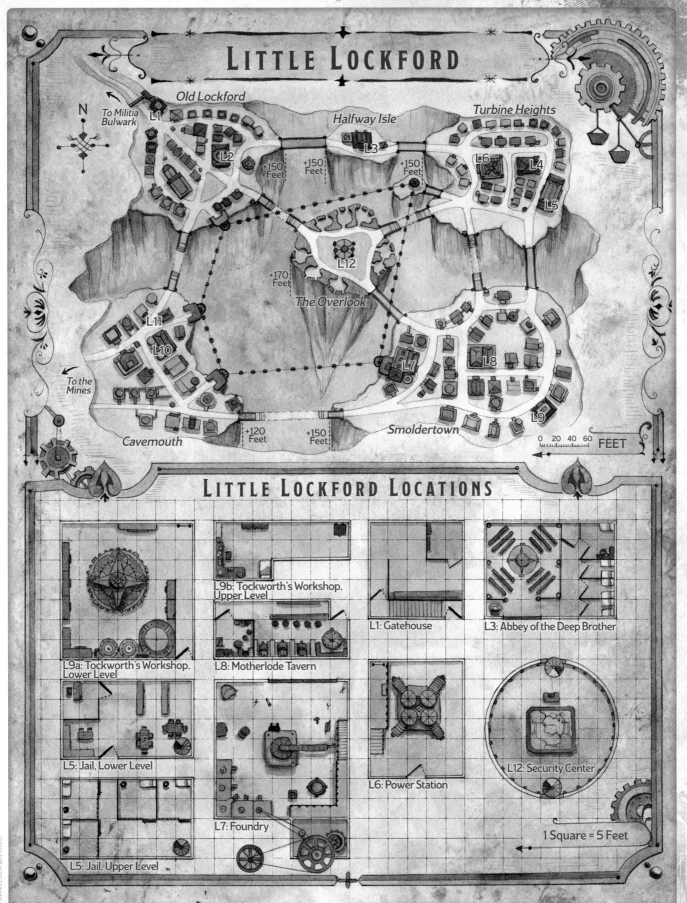

LITTLE LOCKFORD

N

To Militia
Bulwark

Old Lockford

L1

L2

Halfway Isle

L3

+150
Feet

+150
Feet

+150
Feet

Turbine Heights

L6

L4

L5

L12

+170
Feet

The Overlook

L11

L10

L7

L8

L9

To the
Mines

+120
Feet

+150
Feet

Smoldertown

Cavemouth

0 20 40 60
FEET

LITTLE LOCKFORD LOCATIONS

L9b: Tockworth's Workshop,
Upper Level

L1: Gatehouse

L3: Abbey of the Deep Brother

L9a: Tockworth's Workshop,
Lower Level

L8: Motherlode Tavern

L5: Jail, Lower Level

L6: Power Station

L12: Security Center

L7: Foundry

1 Square = 5 Feet

L5: Jail, Upper Level

FRANCESCA BAERALD

The town hall features a spacious chamber for large gatherings and has three small offices at the back.

Treasure. From Mayor Broadfoot's office, characters can retrieve four *potions of healing*, two flasks of alchemist's fire, and one use of *dust of disappearance* in a small packet. These items are kept in an unlocked footlocker under the mayor's desk. On the desk is a calligraphy set.

HALFWAY ISLE (AREA L3)

Halfway Isle used to be a giant stalagmite until the gnomes sheared off the top of it to create a plateau, atop which they built the Abbey of the Deep Brother (area L3). Bridges connect Halfway Isle to the neighboring districts of Old Lockford and Turbine Heights.

L3. ABBEY OF THE DEEP BROTHER

> Next to the road stands a squat stone building capped with a stone dome. The building's entrance is a double door carved to resemble interlocking hands, and centered above the doorway is a golden pick with a short handle.

Map 5.2 includes an inset map that shows the interior of this building.

A character who examines the golden pick and succeeds on a DC 13 Intelligence (Religion) check recognizes it as the symbol of the Deep Brother, Callarduran Smoothhands, a god worshiped by svirfneblin (particularly miners and stone carvers).

Abbey Interior. A 4-foot-tall statue of Callarduran, his face and figure hidden under a cowled robe, stands in an alcove just inside the entrance. The statue's right hand is held out, displaying stone-carved rings on every stubby finger.

The largest room in the abbey, directly across from the entrance, serves as a place of worship. Low benches face the middle of the domed chamber, where every word spoken—even a whisper—can be heard throughout the space. Skulking in the dark corners of this room are two prisoners who escaped the custody of their guards as they were being led from the jail (area L5) during the evacuation of Little Lockford. The two prisoners—a **goblin boss** named Slonk and a **bugbear** named Yuzzik—have manacles on their wrists and carry no weapons. Slonk was the leader of a gang of goblin brigands that preyed on travelers in the tunnels near Little Lockford. Yuzzik is Slonk's sole surviving bodyguard. Both are unscrupulous and will do almost anything to survive, short of betraying each other.

Other rooms in the abbey include sleeping quarters for svirfneblin monks, a private chamber for the abbot, and a privy. A search of these areas yields nothing of value.

Abbot Kavoda. The abbot Kavoda tried to flee Little Lockford with his fellow monks, but he didn't get far before one of Tockworth's automatons chased him back to the abbey. Minutes after Kavoda returned to the abbey, Slonk and Yuzzik showed up. Kavoda avoided them by casting *meld into stone*. He has been using *meld into stone* spells to hide ever since. As the characters explore the abbey, Kavoda hears one of them and emerges from a nearby wall when he thinks it's safe to do so.

Kavoda is a chaotic good **deep gnome** who speaks Common, Gnomish, Terran, and Undercommon. His Innate Spellcasting trait includes the ability to cast *meld into stone* three times per day. He wears a gray robe instead of armor (AC 12) and carries a *spell scroll* of *magic weapon* and a *potion of giant strength* (hill).

Kavoda doesn't want to stay in Little Lockford any longer. Desperate and hungry, he begs the characters to escort him safely to Little Lockford's outer gates (area L1), offering his magic items if they accept the quest. He insists they deliver him to the gates by the most direct route without delay, and he protests loudly if they dawdle or deviate from this course of action. If he is separated from the characters or wounded, Kavoda runs back to the abbey, crying "Callarduran, protect me!" all the way.

TURBINE HEIGHTS (AREAS L4–L6)

Turbine Heights is where members of the militia and their families lived. This district also contains a power station and an infirmary.

When the characters first arrive at Turbine Heights, read the following text:

> The streets of this district are filled with steam. Through the haze, you can see bright streetlamps and abandoned buildings. Every fifteen seconds, a bolt of electricity arcs from a metal tower in the middle of the district to similar towers in other districts.

The electrically charged metal tower is attached to the roof of the power station (area L6). Due to a backup at the station, steam has overflowed into the streets of Turbine Heights. Consequently, the district is lightly obscured, as if by fog. A *gust of wind* spell rids a street of steam for 1 minute.

L4. Infirmary

> A stone sign depicting a crutch hangs above the entrance to this one-story building. The double door below the sign is ajar, revealing a hallway beyond.

Beyond the double door is a long, dark hallway with three small examination rooms on one side of it and three small storage rooms on the opposite side (see "Treasure" below). At the far end of the hall, behind another double door, is an operating room. Characters who search the infirmary thoroughly can find crutches and wheelchairs sized for gnomes, as well as bandages and other mundane medical supplies.

Treasure. Characters who loot the storage rooms find six healer's kits and six *potions of healing*.

L5: Jail

> This fortified, two-story stone edifice has a heavy iron door that hangs open. In front of the building, four dead gnomes in armor lie amid the fragments of a doglike automaton.

The dead gnomes lying in the street are prison guards who were killed by Tockworth's automatons. The guards managed to destroy one of the clockwork defenders that attacked them, but the prisoners they were escorting slipped away (and ended up in area L3). Characters who search the corpses find a small ring of keys. These keys unlock all the cells in the jail.

Building Interior. Map 5.2 includes inset maps that show both floors of this two-story building. The lower floor contains a kitchen and mess hall for the jailers and an office reserved for the head jailer. A spiral staircase connects to the upper level, which contains prison cells.

L6: Power Station

> A thirty-foot-tall metal tower extends from the rooftop of this blocky, one-story stone building. The tower crackles with electricity and spews clouds of steam. Every fifteen seconds, it discharges an arc of lightning that leaps to a tower in another district.

The power station generates electricity that powers the bridges, the Slagline (see "General Features" earlier in the adventure), and various workshops scattered throughout the town. The electricity is transmitted through arc towers like the one rising from the power station's roof.

Building Interior. Map 5.2 includes an inset map that shows the power station's interior, which you can describe as follows:

> The interior of the power station is one big room filled with billowing clouds of steam. Four howling turbines take up most of the floorspace. Iron steps lead to a six-foot-high iron balcony on the west side of the room. At the north end of the balcony is an iron ladder that climbs to a trapdoor in the roof. The balcony also supports a metal console.

Damaged Turbine. A power station worker was cornered by a clockwork defender at the north end of the balcony and shoved the automaton off the balcony into the northwest turbine. One of the clockwork defender's hind legs became stuck in the turbine, causing the turbine to malfunction. Characters within 10 feet of the northwest turbine can see the damaged **clockwork defender**, which has 24 hit points remaining. This defender is restrained and unable to free itself, but it can attack creatures that come within reach of it.

Once the clockwork defender is defeated, a character can use an action to try to dislodge it from the turbine, doing so with a successful DC 17 Strength (Athletics) or Dexterity (Sleight of Hand) check. Removing the clockwork defender's mangled leg from the turbine's machinery causes the power station to stop spewing steam, with the steam throughout Turbine Heights dissipating 1d10 minutes later.

Control Console. The metal console overlooking the turbines is inscribed with a map of the town. Next to this map are several switches: one for every bridge and district, one for the Slagline (see "General Features"), and one for the power station. All are described below:

Bridge Switches. There's one switch for each of Little Lockford's nine bridges. A bridge can be raised by turning its switch to the left or lowered by turning its switch to the right.

District Switches. There's one switch for each of Little Lockford's six districts (Cavemouth, Halfway Isle, Old Lockford, the Overlook, Smoldertown, and Turbine Heights). The streetlamps in a district can be shut off by turning that district's switch to the left or switched on by turning its switch to the right.

Slagline Switch. There's one switch for the Slagline. Turning it to the left shuts off the bucket chain. Turning it to the right switches the bucket chain on.

Station Shutdown Switch. Turning this switch to the left shuts down the turbines in the power station, causing the streetlamps to turn off throughout town, shutting down the Slagline, and preventing the town's bridges from being raised or lowered. Turning it to the right switches the power back on.

Smoldertown (Areas L7–L9)

When the characters first enter this district, describe it as follows:

> The acrid stench of hot metal hangs over this district. Buildings here have no decoration, and nearly every surface is caked in decades of grime and soot. A few more gnome bodies lie face-down in the grit.

Smoldertown, with its many workshops and smithies, is the industrial heart of Little Lockford. Tockworth's workshop (area L9) is located here, but Tockworth herself is taking a break at the Motherlode Tavern (area L8).

L7: Foundry

> The soot-stained foundry stands at the edge of this district, overlooking the magma lake far below. Its huge sliding doors stand open, revealing dark furnaces and silent machinery. A raised loading dock allows access to the dangling buckets of the Slagline, which deliver unrefined ore to the foundry.

Map 5.2 includes an inset map that shows the foundry's interior, which is one large, open space. The building has no ceiling, allowing heat and smoke to escape. Ore from the Slagline's buckets can be dumped via chute into any of the foundry's five large furnaces.

Treasure. Characters who loot the foundry find three sets of smith's tools and two sets of tinker's tools.

L8: Motherlode Tavern

> Hanging above the entrance of this grimy stone building is a painted wooden sign that depicts gemstones pouring from a flagon. A minor magical effect causes the gemstones to glitter invitingly.

Map 5.2 includes an inset map that shows the tavern's interior, which consists of a cellar and a taproom.

Cellar. The cellar contains crates of worthless supplies, several kegs of a locally brewed mushroom beer called Rubbleclub Classic (named for its brewer, the svirfneblin Glyphy Rubbleclub), and several more kegs of an oaky whiskey called Oofenklanger's Finest (named after the family that originally distilled it).

Taproom. The taproom contains seating areas, including a row of stools next to a low bar made of carved basalt. Hanging above the bar are two soot-stained lanterns with *continual flame* spells cast inside them. Half-drunk flagons of flat mushroom beer rest on the bar and on the tables, abandoned by patrons in their haste to evacuate Little Lockford.

Tixie Tockworth. Unless she was defeated elsewhere, **Tixie Tockworth** (see her description and stat block at the end of the adventure) sits on the barstool farthest from the entrance, cradling an empty flagon while mumbling to herself.

The presence of intruders confuses, disturbs, and annoys Tockworth. If she is confronted by the characters here or if the *alarm* spell triggers on the safe in area L9b, she casts *dimension door* and steps through the spell's magical doorway into area L9b. As she leaves, she says, "Break time's over, Poots!" (The characters have no way to know this, but Poots is the name of an imaginary friend Tockworth invented in her childhood. This long-lost imaginary friend has resurfaced recently in response to Tockworth's mounting loneliness.)

L9: Tockworth's Workshop

> This windowless, two-story structure has a single door tucked near a corner on the ground floor. Standing in front of the door is an eight-foot-tall, bipedal construct made of chipped stone, rusty metal, and green copper. Its heavy iron gauntlets are clenched into fists, and the ominous helm that forms its head turns slowly from side to side.

Shield Guardian. The construct blocking passage into Tockworth's workshop is a **shield guardian** that lacks the Spell Storing trait. Its creator and control amulet were destroyed long ago. Tockworth found a way to reanimate the shield guardian without having to create a new amulet, rendering the shield guardian autonomous. The shield guardian has been loyal to Tockworth ever since. It defends itself if attacked and attacks anyone who tries to slip past it. It is too big to fit through the workshop's front door.

Workshop Interior. Map 5.2 includes inset maps that show both floors of Tockworth's workshop, which are described in areas L9a and L9b.

L9a: Workshop, Lower Floor

The ground floor is one big work area containing a smelter, drums filled with clockwork parts, and a dizzying array of tools. Mounted on one wall is an iron ladder that ends before a trapdoor in the ceiling.

Inscribed on the floor is a complex geometric design that pulsates with light. In the middle of this design, embedded in the floor, is a one-foot-square metal box with a keyhole in the top of it.

This workshop is where Tockworth creates her clockwork automatons. Two suits of **animated armor** named Rack and Pinion serve as her assistants and perform most of the hands-on work. These Constructs attack intruders on sight.

The workshop contains a smelter used to fabricate parts and tools. There are enough tools here to assemble one set of smith's tools and one set of tinker's tools.

The trapdoor in the ceiling opens into area L9b.

Geometric Design. A *detect magic* spell reveals an aura of abjuration magic around the complex geometric symbol inscribed on the floor. When a creature other than Tockworth enters the space above the symbol for the first time on a turn or starts its turn there, that creature becomes the target of a *crown of madness* spell (save DC 15) that has a duration of 1 minute.

Fail-Safe Device. If Tockworth's security key is inserted into the metal box embedded in the floor and turned counterclockwise, Little Lockford's clockwork defenders and clockwork observers are rendered unconscious indefinitely. Turning the key clockwise deactivates the magic of the geometric design on the floor and ends any ongoing effects of its magic. The security key is kept in Tockworth's safe (in area L9b).

L9b: Workshop, Upper Floor

The workshop's upper floor consists of a sparse room furnished with a simple cot and worktables covered in schematics. An iron safe, five feet on a side, stands against one wall, its thick metal door fitted with a combination lock and a handle.

Safe. The safe can't be moved, and a *detect magic* spell reveals an aura of abjuration magic around it.

A character equipped with thieves' tools can spend 1 minute trying to crack open the safe door, doing so with a successful DC 20 Dexterity check. Alternatively, a character can spend 1 minute pressing their ear to the safe's door while trying to delicately pick its combination lock, opening the door with a successful DC 16 Dexterity (Sleight of Hand) or Wisdom (Perception) check. The safe door also opens when the proper command word ("Poots") is spoken within 5 feet of it. A *knock* spell or similar magic also opens the safe.

Tixie Tockworth. If the safe door is opened by any means other than speaking the proper command word, a mental *alarm* spell alerts **Tixie Tockworth** (see her description and stat block at the end of the adventure). Unless she was defeated in area L8, Tockworth uses a *dimension door* spell to appear in the middle of the room and attacks any burglars she sees.

If Tockworth is reduced to 40 hit points or fewer, she uses her next action to cast *dimension door* again, then steps through the doorway into area L12.

Treasure. The safe contains an onyx-studded jewelry box worth 250 gp. The box is unlocked and holds the following items:

- Zircon ring (60 gp)
- Three amethysts (100 gp each)
- The security key to the fail-safe device in area L9a (the key is 8 inches long, made of brass, and decorated with clockwork designs)

CAVEMOUTH (AREAS L10–L11)

When the characters first enter Cavemouth, read the following text:

> Mining equipment lies abandoned in the alleys and stalagmite-lined streets of this gloomy district.

The Cavemouth district is where most of Little Lockford's miners live and work. Two roads lead to the mines, which are not shown on map 5.2.

The bridges to Cavemouth have been raised, and the streetlamps throughout the district have been shut off. The characters can lower the bridges and turn on the streetlamps using a control console in area L6 or area L12.

Mines. The mine entrances, once protected by Tockworth's automatons, are now unguarded. The mines are beyond the scope of the adventure. If the characters insist on exploring them, they eventually attract the attention of a wandering **cloaker** that tries to frighten them away with haunting moans.

L10: MINERS' GUILDHALL

> Hanging above the open doorway of this large, gem-studded building is a stone sign depicting a pick and a hammer.

The miners' guildhall has offices for senior guild members, stout metal lockers where miners can store their gear, and functional showers. Most of the building's former occupants vacated in a hurry, leaving sundry equipment scattered about.

Guildmaster Deepdelve. A thorough search of the building reveals the corpse of a robed deep gnome named Schnella Deepdelve, the master of the town's miners' guild. Schnella refused to leave and died fending off Tockworth's clockwork defenders. Her restless soul lurks in this building, manifesting as a troublesome **specter** known as a poltergeist (see the "Variant: Poltergeist" sidebar in the "Specter" entry of the *Monster Manual*).

Characters who disturb the body or spend more than 1 minute in the guildhall anger the poltergeist, which hurls picks and iron spikes at them until they leave or until the poltergeist is destroyed. The poltergeist is invisible and can't speak.

L11: WAREHOUSE 6

> Bright light seeps through cracks around the sliding metal doors of this otherwise nondescript warehouse.

If the characters slide open the doors, read:

> The interior of the warehouse is an open space roughly twenty feet wide and thirty feet long. Parked in the middle of the warehouse is a strange metal vehicle with treads. Quartz gemstones embedded in the hull shine light in all directions. Mounted to the front of this contraption is a large, cone-shaped drill. At the rear of the contraption is a closed, three-foot-square steel hatch. Two dead gnomes in armor lie on the floor next to the vehicle and a puddle of oil.

The dead gnomes are two **mimics** that attack anyone who touches or otherwise disturbs them. The mimics are working with a psychic **gray ooze** (see the "Variant: Psychic Gray Ooze" sidebar in the "Oozes" entry of the *Monster Manual*)—the "puddle of oil" mentioned above. The gray ooze and the mimics recently crept into the warehouse and are waiting for food to come to them.

Contraption. The vehicle in the warehouse is a Large, magical drilling machine used by the miners of Little Lockford to burrow new tunnels. The vehicle has the properties of an *apparatus of Kwalish*, with these changes:

Treads. Instead of legs and a tail, it has treads that give it a walking speed of 30 feet.

Burrowing Speed. Instead of a swimming speed, it has a burrowing speed of 10 feet. Using its drill, it can burrow through solid rock, leaving a 10-foot-wide, 10-foot-high tunnel behind it.

Lever 1. Moving lever 1 to the up position starts the drill. Moving the same lever to the down position shuts off the drill.

Lever 9. Moving lever 9 to the up position causes the contraption to move backward at its walking speed. Moving the same lever to the down position stops its backward movement.

Ignus Flint. An inventor named Ignus Flint (lawful neutral, deep gnome **mage** who speaks Common, Gnomish, Terran, and Undercommon) built the contraption and recently locked himself inside it with enough food and water to keep himself alive for 1 week. A metal hatch at the back of the vehicle is the only entrance, and Ignus used a *spell scroll* of *arcane lock* to seal it. A character can use an action to try to pull open the magically sealed hatch, doing so with a successful DC 25 Strength (Athletics) check. If the characters knock on the contraption, they hear Ignus's muffled voice shout, "Go away!" in Gnomish. Ignus attacks anyone who breaks into his contraption but surrenders if reduced to 10 hit points or fewer.

Ignus and Tockworth are rivals, and Ignus long suspected Tockworth's experiments would prove troublesome for Little Lockford. His public warnings about Tockworth went ignored, however. A character can use an action to try to convince Ignus to help them, first by impressing on him the importance of freeing Little Lockford from Tockworth's control and then by succeeding on a DC 14 Charisma (Persuasion) check. Once coaxed into helping the characters, Ignus pilots his contraption anywhere they need him to go. The vehicle has enough space inside for Ignus plus one other passenger. If a character asks Ignus to allow the party to drive the contraption, he adamantly refuses to part with his prized invention.

Questioning Ignus. Ignus knows the following useful information about Tockworth and her workshop, which he shares with characters who befriend him:

Animated Armor. Two suits of animated armor help Tockworth assemble her other contraptions.

Safe. Tockworth has an iron safe on the upper floor of her workshop.

Shield Guardian. Tockworth found a way to animate a derelict shield guardian and now uses it to guard the front door to her workshop. The guardian is too big to fit through the door. (Ignus covets the shield guardian and wishes he had one of his own.)

Who Is Poots? When Tockworth is upset, she speaks to an imaginary friend named Poots—as if Poots were standing right next to her. (Ignus doesn't know that "Poots" is also the command word to bypass the *alarm* spell on Tockworth's safe.)

THE OVERLOOK (AREA L12)

When the characters are close enough to see the Overlook, describe it as follows:

> The central feature of Little Lockford is an enormous, hollowed-out stalactite with luminous clock faces built into it.

The Overlook's clocks are mechanical wonders illuminated by magic. They keep perfect time.

A hollowed-out central chamber in the Overlook contains Little Lockford's security center (area L12). This facility is surrounded by rough-hewn chambers containing magnificent fungi gardens and open windows overlooking the town. Residents of Little Lockford used to come here to wander the gardens, pick mushrooms, and enjoy the views.

Characters can use the control consoles in areas L6 and L12 to raise and lower the bridges that connect the Overlook to the districts of Old Lockford, Smoldertown, and Turbine Heights.

L12: SECURITY CENTER

> A large, rough-hewn cavern in the heart of the Overlook has a floor that rises toward the middle. Scores of lizards—a few of them big enough to ride as mounts—sleep and crawl on the slopes of this natural rise. Perched atop the rocky mound is a squat stone building topped with a crystal dome. Multicolored light gleams within the dome.

The cavern is home to six **giant lizards** and hundreds of ordinary **lizards**, all of which are docile but skittish. The giant ones are trained to serve the svirfneblin as pack animals. A character who approaches a giant lizard can use an action to try to keep it from running away, doing so with a successful DC 13 Wisdom (Animal Handling) check. A giant lizard that doesn't run away can be used by that character as a mount.

Domed Building. Map 5.2 provides an inset map of the security center. Spiral staircases on the north and south sides of the building climb 15 feet to a circular chamber, which you can describe to the players as follows:

> Beneath a fifteen-foot-high crystal dome is a chamber containing a ten-foot-square, three-dimensional projection of Little Lockford. Rising from the floor near the projection is a metal console with numerous switches on it.

Control Console. The console functions like the one in the power station (area L6).

Magical Projection. The projection of Little Lockford is a harmless illusion that changes to match the current state of things in town; for example, if a bridge is lowered in Little Lockford, the projection's version of the bridge lowers as well. The projection has no substance, allowing creatures to pass right through it.

Tixie Tockworth. If she fled to this chamber using *dimension door*, **Tixie Tockworth** (see her description and stat block at the end of the adventure) is next to the console. She has attached an experimental jet pack to her body, giving her a flying speed of 30 feet and the ability to hover. She accuses the characters of being pawns and mocks their heroics. She occasionally speaks to an imaginary friend named Poots, saying things like, "We'll show them, Poots!" and "No one can stop us!"

If Tockworth is reduced to 0 hit points, her jet pack explodes in a 20-foot-radius sphere, blowing Tockworth to smithereens. Every other creature within that sphere must succeed on a DC 15 Dexterity saving throw or take 16 (3d10) piercing damage from flying shrapnel. If the explosion occurs under the crystal dome, the dome shatters, showering creatures in the room with harmless, confetti-sized quartz particles.

CONCLUSION

Once the characters use the security key to activate the fail-safe device and shut down Tockworth's automatons, the major threat to the city is ended.

Little Lockford's residents feel a mixture of grief and relief when they return to the town. They are grateful to the characters for saving the town and raise statues in the characters' honor. Furthermore, Mayor Broadfoot gives the characters their promised rewards (see "Rewards" earlier in the adventure), and invites the characters to stay in Little Lockford as long as they wish and return as often as they can.

FOR THE GOLDEN VAULT

If the characters are working for the Golden Vault, the organization's representative is waiting with Mayor Broadfoot to confirm the automatons were shut down. Once the representative confirms the characters' success, the organization rewards them with a rare magic item of their choice (subject to your approval) as payment. The item is delivered to the characters the next day. This reward is in addition to the treasures promised by Mayor Broadfoot.

STAT BLOCKS

This section provides stat blocks for new creatures encountered in this adventure.

CLOCKWORK DEFENDER

A clockwork defender is a mechanical quadruped that vaguely resembles a hound. Its eyes glow and can project intense but harmless beams of light. It tirelessly protects whatever its creator wants, and it can be programmed by its creator not to attack certain kinds of creatures.

CLOCKWORK OBSERVER

A clockwork observer serves as an aerial spy for its creator. It looks like a mechanical, grapefruit-sized orb suspended under softly humming propeller blades. Embedded in the orb are keenly perceptive crystal eyes that enable the observer to see in multiple directions at once. When it perceives something troubling, the observer sounds the alarm by emitting a shriek that can be heard within a range of 300 feet. The observer can also telepathically relay what it has discovered to its creator, provided the two are within 1 mile of each other.

TIXIE TOCKWORTH

Using magic and mechanical know-how, Tixie Tockworth has transformed most of herself into a machine. What was once her torso is now a steel carapace that can discharge jets of scalding steam. Her left arm ends in a humming blade. Her right arm ends in a metal shield. Her eyes are shiny, metallic red orbs that can see through illusions.

In her current form, Tockworth ruthlessly seeks to destroy anyone and anything that stands in the way of her ultimate goal, which is to become a Construct. If she's allowed to continue her work, she will achieve this apotheosis in a matter of weeks, after which her creature type changes to Construct. She also gains immunity to poison damage, as well as immunity to the paralyzed, petrified, and poisoned conditions. Her statistics are otherwise unchanged.

CLOCKWORK DEFENDER

Medium Construct, Unaligned

Armor Class 17 (natural armor)
Hit Points 42 (5d8 + 20)
Speed 30 ft.

STR	DEX	CON	INT	WIS	CHA
16 (+3)	15 (+2)	18 (+4)	3 (−4)	14 (+2)	1 (−5)

Skills Perception +6, Stealth +4
Damage Immunities poison
Condition Immunities charmed, exhaustion, frightened, paralyzed, petrified, poisoned
Senses passive Perception 16
Languages understands the languages of its creator but can't speak
Challenge 1 (200 XP)   **Proficiency Bonus** +2

Unusual Nature. The defender doesn't need air, food, drink, or sleep.

ACTIONS

Electrified Bite. *Melee Weapon Attack:* +5 to hit, reach 5 ft., one target. *Hit:* 7 (1d8 + 3) piercing damage plus 7 (2d6) lightning damage. If the target is a creature, it must succeed on a DC 13 Strength saving throw or be grappled (escape DC 13). A creature grappled by the defender takes the damage again at the start of each of the defender's turns. The defender can have only one creature grappled in this way at a time, and the defender can't make Electrified Bite attacks while grappling.

BONUS ACTIONS

Light Beam. The defender emits bright light from its eyes in a 60-foot cone, or it shuts off this light.

CLOCKWORK OBSERVER

Tiny Construct, Unaligned

Armor Class 14 (natural armor)
Hit Points 7 (2d4 + 2)
Speed 0 ft., fly 30 ft. (hover)

STR	DEX	CON	INT	WIS	CHA
1 (−5)	16 (+3)	13 (+1)	3 (−4)	15 (+2)	1 (−5)

Skills Perception +6
Damage Immunities poison
Condition Immunities charmed, exhaustion, frightened, paralyzed, petrified, poisoned
Senses darkvision 60 ft., passive Perception 16
Languages understands the languages of its creator but can't speak
Challenge 0 (0 XP)   **Proficiency Bonus** +2

Flyby. The observer doesn't provoke opportunity attacks when it flies out of an enemy's reach.

Telepathic Bond. While the observer is within 1 mile of its creator, it can magically convey what it sees to its creator, and the two can communicate telepathically.

Unusual Nature. The observer doesn't need air, food, drink, or sleep.

ACTIONS

Shriek. The observer emits a mechanical shriek until the start of its next turn or until it drops to 0 hit points. This shriek can be heard within a range of 300 feet.

TIXIE TOCKWORTH

Small Humanoid (Gnome), Chaotic Evil

Armor Class 17 (natural armor, shield)
Hit Points 75 (10d6 + 40)
Speed 30 ft.

STR	DEX	CON	INT	WIS	CHA
16 (+3)	13 (+1)	18 (+4)	17 (+3)	9 (−1)	10 (+0)

Saving Throws Int +6, Wis +2
Skills Arcana +9, Perception +2
Senses truesight 60 ft., passive Perception 12
Languages Common, Gnomish, Terran, Undercommon
Challenge 7 (2,900 XP)   **Proficiency Bonus** +3

Force Field. Tockworth generates a magical force field around herself. This force field has 15 hit points and regains all its hit points at the start of each of Tockworth's turns, but it ceases to function if Tockworth drops to 0 hit points. Any damage Tockworth takes is subtracted from the force field's hit points first. Each time the force field regains hit points, the following conditions end on Tockworth: grappled, restrained, and stunned.

ACTIONS

Multiattack. Tockworth makes three Shortsword or Lightning Discharge attacks.

Shortsword. *Melee Weapon Attack:* +6 to hit, reach 5 ft., one target. *Hit:* 6 (1d6 + 3) piercing damage plus 10 (3d6) force damage.

Lightning Discharge. *Ranged Spell Attack:* +6 to hit, range 60 ft., one creature. *Hit:* 16 (3d10) lightning damage.

Spellcasting. Tockworth casts one of the following spells, requiring no material components and using Intelligence as the spellcasting ability (spell save DC 14):

At will: *nondetection* (self only)
2/day: *dimension door*
1/day each: *blindness/deafness*, *blur*

BONUS ACTIONS

Scalding Steam (Recharge 5–6). Tockworth emits a jet of piping-hot steam in a 15-foot cone. Each creature in that cone must make a DC 15 Dexterity saving throw, taking 10 (3d6) fire damage on a failed save, or half as much damage on a successful one.

TWO ADVENTURERS HIDE FROM A GUARD OUTSIDE
THE GUILDHOUSE OF THE AGILE HAND.

MASTERPIECE IMBROGLIO

A GROUP OF SCHOLARS AND SAGES KNOWN as the Cognoscenti Esoterica recently purchased a painting of Constantori, a famous courtier rumored to once have been the most beautiful man alive. The portrait supposedly has occult properties, but before the sages could study it, the painting was stolen by the Agile Hand, a thieves' guild. In this adventure, the characters must retrieve the portrait of Constantori from the Agile Hand's guildhouse and return it to Adrisa Carimorte, a member of the Cognoscenti Esoterica.

ADVENTURE BACKGROUND

The Cognoscenti Esoterica collects obscure objects of curious origin and historical significance. The group's interests focus on items owned by powerful and popular individuals speculated to maintain covert ties with occult or nefarious organizations. Serious academics often write off the Cognoscenti Esoterica as charlatans or pranksters, and with good reason: the Cognoscenti rarely collect enough evidence to support their outlandish claims. Still, the organization occasionally stumbles upon something of true significance.

Recently the group acquired a magical painting known as *Constantori's Portrait*, a work reputed to depict one of the most beautiful men who ever lived. The group spent a small fortune acquiring the painting and prepared to host a debate over its cultural significance, the aesthetics of masculine beauty, and its influence on society. They also planned to research the portrait's magical properties (see the end of this adventure for a description of the painting's properties).

The day after the debate was announced, a small team of Agile Hand thieves raided the Cognoscenti's vaults. The thieves slew three guards during the

theft, then fled with the painting. Word has spread that the Agile Hand plans to fence the portrait in the next three days.

During the robbery, Cognoscenti guards captured a lookout working with the thieves. This captive is willing to trade information for his freedom.

The Cognoscenti Esoterica distrusts the authorities and doesn't wish to report the theft. Instead, the organization seeks skilled adventurers to recover the painting.

ADVENTURE HOOKS

If you're not using the Golden Vault as a patron (see "Using the Golden Vault" below), you can use any of the following hooks to help motivate the characters:

A Favor Owed. The characters either owe someone in the Cognoscenti Esoterica a favor or seek the counsel of one of its members. Upon arrival, this individual might request that the characters retrieve *Constantori's Portrait* to repay the individual's patronage or for mutual benefit.

Knowledge Sought. The characters have prior reason to find the portrait or seek knowledge they believe someone in the Cognoscenti Esoterica possesses. However, the knowledge actually resides in *Constantori's Portrait*.

Strike a Blow. One or more characters have clashed with the Agile Hand in the past and want to strike a blow against the troublesome thieves' guild.

USING THE GOLDEN VAULT

If you're using the Golden Vault as a patron, a golden key is delivered to the characters in whatever manner you deem fit. When the characters use this key to open their music box, the lid pops open and a soothing voice says the following:

"Greetings, operatives. A valuable painting has been stolen from a member of the Cognoscenti Esoterica, an organization with connections to the Golden Vault. The Cognoscenti Esoterica specializes in the study of rare objects of historical significance. We suspect that the stolen painting, Constantori's Portrait, has magical properties and ties to the occult.

"This quest, should you choose to undertake it, requires you to infiltrate the guildhouse of the Agile Hand, a dangerous thieves' guild. Find where the painting is kept, recover it, and return it to Adrisa Carimorte of the Cognoscenti Esoterica. A preliminary meeting with Adrisa has already been arranged, and a coach will arrive shortly to deliver you safely to her location. Good luck, operatives."

Closing the music box causes the golden key to vanish.

A coach pulled by two black horses arrives not long after the key vanishes. The coach driver, a cheerful woman, invites the characters to climb aboard and delivers them safely to Adrisa if they accept the ride.

BARN VISIT

Read or paraphrase the following if the characters choose to meet with Adrisa Carimorte:

Rain begins to fall as your coach pulls up beside an open barn surrounded by fields of dead corn. A tall, well-dressed human woman emerges from the barn as you exit the coach. "Thank you for coming," she says with a smile. "I'm Adrisa Carimorte. My organization would like to hire you to retrieve a painting that was stolen from us by a thieves' guild. For the painting's safe return, I'm prepared to pay you two thousand gold pieces. Let's go inside to escape the rain, shall we? There's someone else I'd like you to meet."

Adrisa Carimorte (neutral, human **mage**) is an influential member of the Cognoscenti Esoterica. If the characters turn down the offer, Adrisa has the coach driver return them whence they came. If the characters express interest in the job, Adrisa escorts them into the barn, which the Cognoscenti Esoterica sometimes uses as a warehouse and secret meeting place. The barn has magical wards that thwart all attempts to magically scry on its interior, as well as other wards Adrisa temporarily deactivated.

Adrisa leads the characters up a ladder to the barn's loft. Once everyone is in the loft, read or paraphrase the following:

In the middle of the loft, tied to a wooden chair, is a scrawny human man with patchy facial hair. He is sweating profusely and chewing nervously on a cloth gag.

The man tied to the chair is Grinky Brithwort (neutral evil, human **bandit**). He was captured during the theft of Constantori's Portrait and has useful information about the Agile Hand and its headquarters—information the characters can use to help plan their heist.

GRINKY'S DEAL

Grinky has been associated with the Agile Hand for years. During the theft of Constantori's Portrait, Grinky's job was to watch for guards. He was caught and given to Adrisa for questioning. Adrisa has offered to release Grinky in exchange for his help.

WHAT GRINKY KNOWS

Adrisa gives the characters a chance to question Grinky. During this conversation, Grinky shares the following true information:

Guildmaster Dusk. "Guildmaster Dusk leads the Agile Hand. She's a trained assassin with powerful political connections."

Getting Inside. "The windows of the guildhouse are boarded up, and its doors are usually locked. At least three guild members have master keys to the doors: Guildmaster Dusk; Elix the Saint, one of Dusk's lieutenants; and Jaymont the Sinner, the guild's resident spy. The master of ravens, Gwish, might have a key as well. If you want to get your hands on a master key, your best bet is to snatch it from Elix the Saint, who frequents a seedy tavern called the Tipsy Tankard."

Guildhouse Guards. "By late evening, most guild members have gone to sleep. Senior guild members bully lower-ranking guild members into taking the late-night shifts."

Guild Membership. "Dusk isn't accepting new guild members right now. I've been working for the guild since I was a kid, and I'm still not a ranking member."

Portrait's Location. "I don't know where the portrait is, but I'm guessing it's either in Guildmaster Dusk's quarters, which are on the second floor of the guildhouse's tower, or hidden in the basement, where new guild members are trained."

Supply Deliveries. "Supplies are sometimes delivered to the guildhouse by riders on horseback or by mule-drawn cart. All supplies are received and inspected by Laris Drot, the stablemaster, at the livery stables."

What Adrisa Knows

After the characters question Grinky, they can ask Adrisa questions about the Agile Hand or *Constantori's Portrait*. She knows the following:

Guildmaster Dusk. "Everyone seems to ignore the activities of Dusk and her guild. Larceny is the Agile Hand's specialty, but Dusk uses blackmail, extortion, threats of violence, and whatever else it takes to keep her enemies at bay."

Portrait Lore. "The portrait is the work of famed artist Dkesii Kwan and was commissioned by the late Daiyani Grysthorn, a grand dame in the criminal underworld. The painting is sentient and was made to eavesdrop on conversations and pass along secrets to its owner. Like its beautiful subject, the painting is notoriously vain."

Sense of Urgency. "It's likely that the Agile Hand has a buyer for the painting. Therefore, it's vital you recover it as quickly as possible before it ends up in an even more secure location."

Planning the Heist

The characters' goals are simple: locate the portrait and return it safely to the Cognoscenti Esoterica.

Grinky's Map

Grinky furnished Adrisa with a sketched map of the Agile Hand's guildhouse (see map 6.1). Adrisa gives Grinky's map to the characters.

Grinky is neither well informed nor a high-ranking member of the Agile Hand. Consequently, his map contains inaccuracies, such as the following:

- Grinky's guesses as to where Dusk stored the painting are wrong.
- Grinky's map is missing the topmost level of the tower, where the painting is kept (area G27 on map 6.2).

Elix the Saint

Characters can obtain one of the guildhouse's master keys from Elix the Saint (lawful evil, human **bandit captain**), a high-ranking member of the Agile Hand and one of Guildmaster Dusk's more capable lieutenants. After questioning Grinky, the characters should know that Elix the Saint frequents a tavern called the Tipsy Tankard, which is about a 45-minute walk from the guildhouse. He travels there alone because he likes to flirt with a bartender named Karyssa (neutral, human **commoner**).

Elix usually leaves the guildhouse at sundown and returns by midnight. Characters can approach him during this interval and take his master key by force or snatch it from him without his knowledge. As an action, a character within reach of Elix can try to snatch the key from his pocket, doing so with a successful DC 10 Dexterity (Sleight of Hand) check. If the attempt is made in a crowded place where others might notice the theft, increase the DC by 5.

Elix would sooner die than betray Guildmaster Dusk, although a *suggestion* spell or other coercive magic can wring information from him. For example, he knows where *Constantori's Portrait* is being kept (on the tower's third floor, above Guildmaster Dusk's private quarters).

Clever characters can steal Elix's identity as well as his key. If Elix is either detained or disposed of, a character can use magic (for example, *alter self* or *disguise self*) to mimic his appearance. A disguise kit can also help perpetrate such a ruse. In this form, a character can search most of the guildhouse without inviting altercations.

If Elix the Saint doesn't return to the guildhouse by midnight, the lookouts on watch assume he had too much to drink and either passed out in a field or got thrown in jail for brawling. His failure to return won't cause alarm.

Magical Surveillance

Characters can use *invisibility* spells to approach and observe the guildhouse without being seen. They can also use a *locate object* spell to pinpoint the painting's location (area G27 on map 6.2). If they don't have access to such magic, they can request Adrisa's help. Within a day, she can obtain a *spell scroll* of *locate object* for them.

The characters might have access to other magic that can help with surveillance, such as the *clairvoyance* spell. A wizard's familiar can slip inside the guildhouse without attracting too much attention, as can a druid using Wild Shape to assume the form of a stray cat or some other common animal.

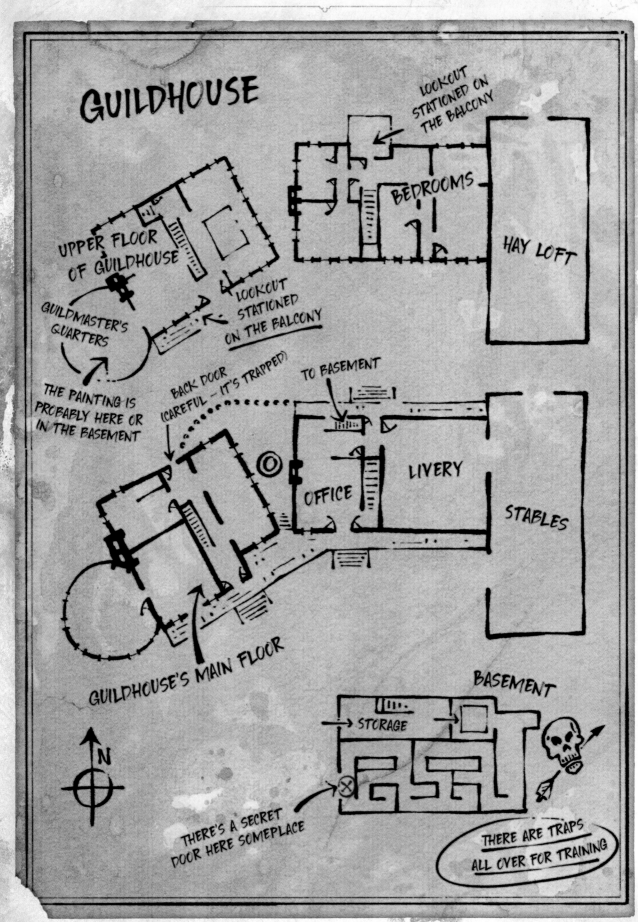

GUILDHOUSE

LOOKOUT STATIONED ON THE BALCONY

UPPER FLOOR OF GUILDHOUSE

GUILDMASTER'S QUARTERS

LOOKOUT STATIONED ON THE BALCONY

THE PAINTING IS PROBABLY HERE OR IN THE BASEMENT

BACK DOOR (CAREFUL – IT'S TRAPPED)

TO BASEMENT

BEDROOMS

HAY LOFT

OFFICE

LIVERY

STABLES

GUILDHOUSE'S MAIN FLOOR

N

BASEMENT

STORAGE

THERE'S A SECRET DOOR HERE SOMEPLACE

THERE ARE TRAPS ALL OVER FOR TRAINING

MIKE SCHLEY

Agile Hand Guildhouse

The Agile Hand's guildhouse is situated at the end of a winding, cobbled street that runs parallel to a small river. The back of the stables faces a grassy embankment scattered with mulberry trees.

The guildhouse is a wooden complex consisting of a main building with an adjoining tower and basement, as well as a livery area that includes stables, an office, and quarters for paying visitors.

General Features

Recurring features of the guildhouse are described in the following sections.

Doors

Doors in the guildhouse complex are locked unless otherwise noted. Some individuals have keys to specific areas, as noted in their descriptions. Others possess a master key that opens all locked doors in the complex.

As an action, a character can use thieves' tools to try to open a locked door, doing so with a successful DC 15 Dexterity check, or force open the door with a successful DC 15 Strength (Athletics) check. Each door has AC 15, 18 hit points, and immunity to poison and psychic damage.

Secret Doors. A secret door blends in perfectly with the wall that surrounds it. A character who uses an action to examine a stretch of wall can make a DC 15 Wisdom (Perception) check, finding any secret door hidden there on a success. The guildhouse complex's secret doors have well-oiled hinges, allowing them to be opened and closed quietly.

Floors

The upper floors, stable loft, and porches are un-lacquered hardwood planks. Rough, splintery, and slightly warped with age, these floors creak when walked on. Characters make any ability checks to move stealthily on the upper floors at disadvantage. The ground floor is paved with slate tiles, except the stable, which is hard-packed dirt. The basement is cobblestone.

Light

The stables are unlit. During the day, light filters in from the entrances and through cracks in the plank walls, filling the area with dim light.

The rest of the guildhouse complex is filled with bright light during the day, either from lanterns or the sun. At night, rooms and hallways are dimly lit by low-burning lanterns.

Guild members carry light sources with them when they descend into the basement, which is unlit.

Walls

The exterior walls are made of wood. The interior walls are plastered lath, making them relatively soundproof. The basement walls are made of clay bricks braced at regular intervals by thick, rough-cut wooden beams.

Windows

Most of the guildhouse complex's windows are boarded up (except the ones in area G21), but tiny cracks between the boards allow creatures to peer through. Prying away the boards is relatively easy, but doing so quietly requires a successful DC 13 Dexterity (Stealth) check.

Guild Member Names

If you need a name for a low- or mid-ranked member of the Agile Hand, pick one from the following list:

Brick Face	Night Lily
Deadly Nell	Ookie the Cheat
Evil Marvus	Pistachio
Farrow the Filcher	Stickyfingers
Greedy Pete	Vaelin Shadowblade
Grimbeard	Zeke the Sneak

High Alert

If a situation arises that puts the guildhouse on high alert, a task force assembles to deal with the threat. This force is summarized in the Guild Task Force table. Subtract any individuals who have already been neutralized.

Guild Task Force

Creature	Location
Guildmaster Dusk (**assassin**)	G26
Gwish (**oni**)	G21
Jaymont the Sinner (**doppelganger**)	G3
Elix the Saint (**bandit captain**)	G23
3 **bandits**	One each from G19, G22, and G24
3 **thugs**	One from G13 and two from G25

Guildhouse Locations

The following locations are keyed to map 6.2.

G1: Front Porch

> Nailed to this lengthy porch are short planks that bear the words "Private Property. No Trespassing!" in Common. A lookout is stationed on a second-floor balcony above the western end of the porch.

Any character who approaches the porch in plain view is spotted by the **bandit** on the south balcony (area G22), who calls out, "Hey, you, get lost! Can't you read the signs?" If this warning is ignored, the lookout shouts the same thing again, putting the guildhouse on high alert, then shoots a crossbow bolt into the ground near the character's feet as a final warning.

Drop Box. The staircase in front of the double door to area G10 has a loose plank near the top. This plank conceals a drop box where visitors stash black-market goods, fenced items, and guild tributes. Any character who lifts the plank sees a dusty satchel in the drop box. The satchel contains 25 sp and a piece of parchment that transfers ownership of two horses to Guildmaster Dusk.

G2A: LIVERY STABLES

> Ten horse stables and a hayloft line the walls of this barn, which has an open doorway at each end. Flies swarm around a full dung cart that exudes a horrible stench.

The stalls contain ten **riding horses**.

Cart. The dung-filled cart is a fire hazard. If the cart is pushed against a wall and set ablaze, the fire quickly spreads to the loft and ignites the hay there. After 1 minute, the smoke and panic of the horses put the guildhouse on high alert.

Fire. The Agile Hand isn't equipped to stop a fire that starts in the barn. Such a fire takes 1 minute to spread throughout the structure. After that, the fire moves 5 feet westward each minute until the whole east building is engulfed. After 5 minutes, the building collapses, and the stairs to the basement are buried in flaming debris. The west building is spared.

Ladders. A wooden ladder in each corner stall ascends to a trapdoor that leads to the hayloft (area G2b). The trapdoors are unlocked.

G2B: HAYLOFT

The hayloft is 10 feet above the stables and consists of a 5-foot-wide wooden walkway that runs the perimeter of the building. Broad, square loading doors open in the north and south walls, each fitted with block-and-tackle rigs for hoisting hay bales and other supplies into the loft. Hay bales and burlap sacks stuffed with feed grains take up most of the space. A few pitchforks, ropes, and feed buckets lie scattered about the bales.

Stable Hand. A young stable hand named Needly Pitts (neutral, human **commoner**) lazes in the loft, supposedly guarding against horse thieves. He has nodded off but wakes if characters disturb the horses, make too much noise in the barn, or start a fire. In the event of trouble, Needly bangs a metal pail and yells for the stablemaster (see area G16), who takes 1 minute to arrive.

G3: STAIRCASE

> Halfway up this flight of stairs is a sleeping figure wrapped in a wool blanket. A door is situated at the top of the stairs.

The door at the top of the stairs is unlocked and opens into area G14.

Jaymont the Sinner. The figure on the steps is Jaymont the Sinner, a **doppelganger** disguised as a drunken guest. Only Guildmaster Dusk knows Jaymont's true nature. The doppelganger pretends to be asleep, but a character can discern that it's awake with a successful DC 15 Wisdom (Insight) check. Jaymont doesn't start fights it knows it can't win and allows intruders to pass by. When the intruders are gone, Jaymont taps three times on the staircase wall to alert Gwish in area G21, then slinks away to alert Guildmaster Dusk in area G26.

Master Key. Jaymont carries a master key that unlocks all doors in the guildhouse complex.

G4: CARTWRIGHT'S WORKSHOP

> Three carts occupy this room. Pegs and hooks on the inner walls bear ropes, tackle, leather harnesses, wheels, and leatherworking tools. Shoved into a corner is a crate filled with horseshoes. Nearby, shelves hold smaller boxes filled with buckles, nails, cotter pins, and miscellaneous hardware.

The shop has two access points: the stables to the east and a door to the west that leads to area G7.

Treasure. Characters can assemble one set of leatherworker's tools from the tools stored here.

G5: LIVERY OFFICE

> A wooden countertop divides the room. Signboards display services and fees for stabling and room rentals. Two keys hang from hooks on the east wall above the counter. A third hook is bare.

When the office is staffed, a visitor can secure an upstairs bed for 5 cp per night (5 sp for a private room). Accommodations can also be made in the stables for a traveler's mount at a cost of 1 sp per night.

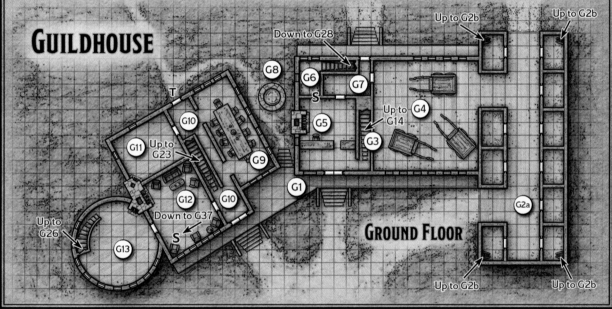

UPPER FLOORS

G27

Down to G26

Down to G13

G25

G23

Down to G10

G24

G26

Up to G27

G19

G20

G14

G15

G17

Down to G2a

Down to G2a

G21

G16

G18

Down to G3

G2b

Down to G2a

Down to G2a

GUILDHOUSE

Down to G28

Up to G2b

Up to G2b

G8

G6

G7

T

S

G5

Up to G14

G4

G10

G11

Up to G23

G3

G9

G1

G12

G10

Down to G37

S

Up to G26

G13

GROUND FLOOR

G2a

Up to G2b

Up to G2b

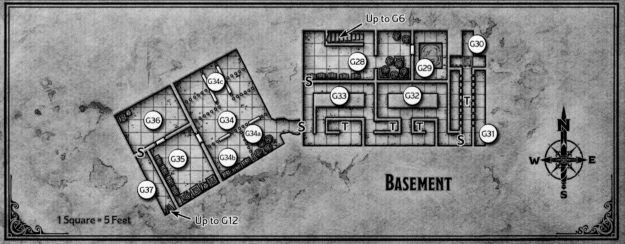

Up to G6

G30

G28

G29

G34c

G33

G32

S

G36

G34

T

G34a

T

T

T

S

G31

G35

G34b

S

G37

BASEMENT

N

W E

S

1 Square = 5 Feet

Up to G12

MIKE SCHLEY

Coin Box. Tucked behind the counter is a wooden coin box with a copper clasp. A character who inspects the coin box before opening it notices a row of tiny pinholes in the lid. The coin box contains 15 cp and 11 sp, as well as a **spider**.

Keys. The two keys hanging on the wall unlock the doors to areas G17 and G18, respectively.

Secret Door. A secret door in the office's back wall leads to area G6.

G6: Basement Staircase

> A wooden staircase in the northeast corner of this empty, boarded-up room leads to the basement.

The stairs descend 15 feet to area G28.

G7: Service Entrance

> Hanging on the walls of this small, muddy room are several riding cloaks, bits and harnesses, oil lanterns, and coils of rope.

Guild members store their riding gear here. A search of the room yields nothing of great value.

G8: Courtyard

> A cobblestone courtyard is wedged between the two main buildings of the guildhouse. Situated in the middle of the yard is a stone well rigged with a simple bucket winch.

The well is 30 feet deep and has fresh water filling its bottom 5 feet. The well's winch and rope are sturdy enough to bear 250 pounds of weight.

G9: Conference Room

> This room contains several unmatched chairs situated around a long oak table scarred with knife marks. On the table sits a half-eaten cheese wheel, four clay wine jugs, and some wine-stained flagons.

Guildmaster Dusk holds meetings here.

G10: Main Hall

Visitors who try to enter this hall through the north door must contend with a trap.

Back-Door Trap. The northernmost door has a "No Trespassers!" sign hanging on the outside of it and is nailed shut on the inside (a fact not discernible from the outside). As an action, a character can try to force open the door using brute strength, doing so with a successful DC 13 Strength (Athletics) check. Breaking down the door puts the guildhouse on high alert unless a *silence* spell or similar magic is used to muffle the noise.

A character who searches the door for traps can make a DC 12 Wisdom (Perception) check. If the check is successful, the character notices that the doorknob is loose and attached to a vial of poison gas hidden in the door itself. As an action, a character can try to disable the trap using thieves' tools, doing so with a successful DC 15 Dexterity check.

Unless the trap is disabled, tugging or turning the knob causes the vial in the door to break, releasing a cloud of poisonous gas that fills a 10-foot-radius sphere centered on the door. The trap also triggers if the door is forced open. Each creature in the trap's area must make a DC 14 Constitution saving throw. On a failed save, the creature takes 16 (3d10) poison damage and is poisoned for 1 minute; on a successful save, the creature takes half as much damage and isn't poisoned. The trap can be triggered only once.

Entering the Hall. Use the following boxed text to describe the hallway:

> A long, well-trafficked hall runs the width of the house. A staircase along the west wall leads to the second floor.

The stairs climb 15 feet to area G23.

G11: Kitchen

> A cooking hearth occupies one corner of this kitchen, and nets holding dried sausages, cheese, peppers, and garlic hang from the rafters. Other items found here include a butcher's block, a table for preparing meals, a pail of potatoes, a few cast-iron pots, a sack of flour, a tin filled with cooking utensils, a block of salt, and a knife with a cutting board.

The kitchen contains nothing of great value.

G12: Parlor

> This room contains a fireplace, a tattered couch, and several upholstered chairs, one of which is bright blue. Playing cards and coins lie scattered across a table. Slumped around the table are four drunken guild members clutching empty mugs and reeking of ale.

The four guild members have been drinking and playing card games. The motley crew consists of three **thugs** and one **gladiator**. The thugs are poisoned and unconscious, while the gladiator is merely poisoned and spoiling for a fight. The unconscious condition ends on a thug who is wounded, knocked out of their chair, or splashed with a pint or more of liquid.

Blue Chair. The blue chair in the south corner covers a secret trapdoor in the stone floor. A character who examines the floor near the chair can make a DC 10 Wisdom (Perception) check, finding the trapdoor on a success. Pulling open the trapdoor reveals a wooden ladder that descends 15 feet to area G37.

Treasure. The coins on the table amount to 65 cp, 35 sp, and 11 gp.

G13: TOWER ROTUNDA

> A lit fireplace warms this mostly empty tower chamber. A wooden staircase hugs the west wall.

A **thug** sits near the bottom of the stairs, engrossed in a saucy novella. If this guard detects intruders, he tries to run up the stairs to wake Guildmaster Dusk in area G26.

G14: UPSTAIRS FOYER

> This rectangular room has a door on every wall. A plaque on the west door says, "Private Rooms."

The north door leading to area G19 is locked; the other doors are unlocked.

G15: L-SHAPED HALL

> Wooden doors line the walls of this L-shaped hallway.

Closets. The two small rooms to the north are closets behind unlocked doors. One stores a mop and broom, a few buckets, and a stack of copper chamber pots. The other has shelves holding linens, blankets, soap, and candles.

G16: STABLEMASTER'S QUARTERS

This room belongs to the stablemaster, Laris Drot (neutral, human **commoner**), who is a stout woman in her fifties. Laris carries two keys on her person: one unlocks the door to this room, and the other unlocks the doors to area G7.

A wooden trunk at the foot of Laris's bed contains folded clothing and personal effects.

Treasure. On a nightstand, next to a set of keys to the stables, is a coin pouch containing 5 gp, 13 sp, and 25 cp.

Development. If Laris is here when the stable hand in area G2b bangs his pail, Laris heads to the stables to find out what's going on. It takes her 1 minute to get there.

G17: SMALL COMMON ROOM

This room stinks of horse manure due to its proximity to the stables. It contains two neatly made beds, two empty footlockers, and a nightstand with an oil-filled lantern hanging above it. Beneath each bed is a copper chamber pot.

G18: LARGE COMMON ROOM

This room stinks of horse manure due to its proximity to the stables. It contains four neatly made beds, each with its own nightstand and empty footlocker. An oil-filled lantern rests atop each nightstand. Beneath each bed is a copper chamber pot.

Treasure. One of the lanterns is a *lantern of revealing*. No one in the guild is aware the lantern is magical.

G19. NORTH BALCONY

> A wooden railing encloses this balcony. Mounted on one corner of the railing is a copper spyglass.

A **bandit** stationed atop this balcony watches for trouble coming from the north and west. If she sees anything suspicious or threatening, she shouts loud enough to put the rest of the guildhouse on high alert. This bandit carries a key that unlocks the door to area G14.

Spyglass. The spyglass attached to the balcony is missing one of its lenses and is nonfunctional.

G20: PRIVATE ROOM

> This private room contains a bed, a nightstand, a footlocker, and a small fireplace. A small oil lamp, a pewter water pitcher, and two mugs rest on the nightstand. Sitting on the edge of the bed is a heavy man in a nightgown.

A traveling merchant named Thyval Horne (neutral, human **commoner**) rents this room. On the nightstand rests a key that unlocks the door to this room. Beneath the bed is a copper chamber pot.

Roleplaying Thyval. The merchant hasn't had a good night's sleep in days and quickly angers if disturbed. Characters who threaten Thyval or use magic to coerce him can pry the following information out of him:

- Guildmaster Dusk is hosting an unscrupulous, well-connected noble named Dartinal Livereth. (Thyval suspects the two are lovers.)
- Jaymont the Sinner, the guild's resident spy, is a master of disguise.
- Thyval can't sleep because of the squawking birds in the room next door (area G21).

G21: Gwish's Room

The room contains a large bed, a sturdy trunk, a wooden nightstand, and a darkened fireplace. The windows here aren't boarded, and the window in the west wall is open slightly. In the middle of the room, an old man in an oversized black robe carefully removes a strip of parchment coiled around the leg of a raven while muttering kind words to the bird. Two more ravens watch from the rafters.

The man is an **oni** named Gwish. Guildmaster Dusk is the only other guild member who knows Gwish's true nature.

Gwish is reclusive and rarely interacts with the other guild members. The oni has three **ravens** that act as messengers, and it uses a *ring of animal influence* to speak with them. These ravens deliver secret messages to the guildmaster's spies abroad and receive similar messages from those spies.

If one or more characters interrupt the oni, it politely asks them to leave. If they refuse, it shoos away the ravens and attacks the characters. The oni's glaive leans in the northeast corner behind the door.

Gwish's Trunk. When the oni is hungry, it sneaks from the guildhouse and invisibly preys on the city, feeding primarily on anyone sleeping outside. The trunk at the foot of Gwish's bed is filled with gnawed bones mixed with small bundles of torn clothing.

Master Key. One of the deep pockets on Gwish's robe contains a master key that unlocks all doors in the guildhouse.

Raven's Note. Gwish has received a note from one of Guildmaster Dusk's spies. The note is written in code on a slip of parchment, and only Guildmaster Dusk is authorized to read it. Gwish plans to deliver the message to Dusk once her guest leaves (see area G26).

A *comprehend languages* spell can decipher the note, as can a character who succeeds on a DC 20 Intelligence (Investigation) check after studying the note for 1 minute. It reads, "Constantori in danger. Cognoscenti retaliation imminent. Be on high alert."

G22: South Balcony

A wooden railing encloses this balcony. Mounted on one corner of the railing is a copper spyglass.

A **bandit** stationed atop this balcony watches for trouble coming from the south and east. If she sees anything suspicious or threatening, she shouts loud enough to put the rest of the guildhouse on high alert. This bandit carries keys that unlock the doors to areas G23, G24, and G25.

Spyglass. The spyglass, which is damaged but functional, is worth 250 gp.

G23: Stolen Goods

Deep scrapes crisscross the floor of this spacious room, and wood shavings scatter the perimeter. A string of oil lanterns dangles from the ceiling, suspended on block and tackle above several containers—mostly small casks and crates, although there's an earth-encrusted coffin here as well.

Elix the Saint (lawful evil, human **bandit captain**; see the "Elix the Saint" section earlier in the adventure) works here during the day. Armed with a crowbar, he examines containers stolen by the Agile Hand. He then records their contents (and the estimated value of those contents) in a leather-bound ledger.

Master Key. Elix carries a master key that unlocks all doors in the guildhouse complex.

Treasure. The following stolen goods are stored here:

- Six casks of exquisite elven wine (250 gp each)
- Wooden chest containing six poisoner's kits
- Wooden crate containing eight sets of thieves' tools
- Wooden crate containing two spyglasses (1,000 gp each) packed in beds of straw
- Dirty wooden coffin containing the moldy corpse of a human priest wearing a copper holy symbol shaped like the sun (25 gp), a sun-shaped death mask made of gold (250 gp), and a *necklace of prayer beads*

G24: Elix's Office

This office contains a plain wooden desk, a simple chair, and a fireplace. A door in the south corner sports a plaque that says, "Private! Enter at your own risk."

A stealthy rogue tries to sneak upstairs without disturbing Guildmaster Dusk and her lover.

A **bandit** stands guard outside the door to Guildmaster Dusk's quarters (area G26). The bandit's job is to shout at the first sign of trouble, thus alerting the guildmaster.

Desk. If the characters search the desk at night, they find a leather-bound ledger in an unlocked drawer, along with a writing quill and a jar of ink. The ledger provides an account of stolen goods acquired by the Agile Hand, but *Constantori's Portrait* is not among the items listed.

G25: Shared Bedroom

Guild members take turns resting here. The room contains two beds, two nightstands, and two trunks (each one packed with linens). Tucked beneath each bed is a copper chamber pot. A hearth in the south corner keeps the room warm.

Sleeping Guards. Two **thugs** sleep in the beds. They wake if disturbed and spend their first action scrambling for their weapons.

G26: Dusk's Quarters

This circular room contains a canopied bed with a leather trunk at the foot of it and a fireplace. Wooden staircases hug the walls—one leading up, the other down. The scent of tobacco hangs in the air.

Unless she has been lured elsewhere, Guildmaster Dusk (lawful evil, half-elf **assassin**) is asleep in bed with her lover, a politically influential noble named Dartinal Livereth (lawful evil, human **noble**). Neither is wearing armor, but they keep their weapons within reach.

If the guildhouse is on high alert, Dusk leaves the room to find out what's happening. Meanwhile, Dartinal smokes a pipe in bed and waits for Dusk to return.

Fireplace. Resting on the fireplace mantel are a wedge of soap, a brush, a clay pipe, and an ivory tobacco jar carved in the shape of a skull. Buried in the ashes of the hearth is a spare shortsword covered with soot.

Leather Trunk. This trunk holds a spare, loaded light crossbow under some linens, bedding, and neatly folded outfits.

Master Key. Guildmaster Dusk keeps a master key on a nightstand next to her bed, and she takes it with her when she leaves the room. The key unlocks all doors in the guildhouse complex.

G27: Tower Peak

This room is situated at the top of the tower and is off limits to everyone except Guildmaster Dusk, who comes here to reflect, doodle in her diary, and gaze upon her latest acquisition: *Constantori's Portrait*.

AMONG THE CLUTTER ON THE GUILDMASTER'S DESK IS A DIARY THAT MIGHT CONTAIN A SECRET OR TWO.

Trap. Canisters of poisonous gas are hidden in the wall behind the painting. Removing the painting from its hooks without first disabling the trap causes the gas to spew from tiny holes previously concealed by the painting. Each creature in the room when the gas is released must make a DC 14 Constitution saving throw, taking 36 (8d8) poison damage on a failed save, or half as much damage on a successful one.

A character who searches the alcove for traps spots the holes behind the painting with a successful DC 12 Wisdom (Perception) check. This check is made with advantage if the character saw the trap's sketch in Dusk's diary. Once the trap is detected, a character can spend 1 minute trying to disable it, either by plugging the holes or by placing counterweights on the hooks as someone else carefully lifts the painting. The character trying to disable the trap must make a DC 15 Dexterity (Sleight of Hand) check, disabling the trap on a success and triggering the trap on a failure.

G28: CELLAR

This room lies at the bottom of a wooden staircase that climbs 15 feet to area G6. The cellar is unlit.

> This dank cellar reeks of soured wine. Wooden trunks line the south wall, and a chamber to the east contains stacks of barrels and crates.

The crates, barrels, and trunks are all empty.

Secret Door. A secret door in the south wall can't be opened from this side without magic (see area G33 for details). It leads to area G33.

Thieves' Test. The door leading to area G29 is unlocked and has the following note (handwritten in Common) tacked to it:

> Here are the rules. Look for keys and keyholes. Watch out for my pets. Follow the arrows, but don't let them hit you. Trust your ears, and remember: a little pressure can be a good thing. Get out alive. Remember, you wanted this. Good luck, grunt.—Dusk

Areas G29–G33 contain challenges that are meant to test thieves who want to join the guild. The note is meant for those applicants, but characters would be wise to heed its advice:

- "Look for keys and keyholes" and "Watch out for my pets" refer to challenges in area G29.
- "Follow the arrows, but don't let them hit you" refers to the set-up in area G31.
- "Trust your ears" and "A little pressure can be a good thing" speak to areas G32 and G33.

> This tower chamber is lit by a pewter chandelier suspended from beams that support a conical roof. A cluttered writing desk and a padded chair are positioned opposite the descending staircase. A gold-framed painting of a beautiful, well-dressed man hangs in a shallow alcove near the top of the stairs.

Characters who search the guildmaster's cluttered desk find sketches and descriptions of deadly mechanical traps, including a rough sketch of the trap in this room (see "Trap" below).

Constantori's Portrait. The painting that hangs in the alcove is *Constantori's Portrait* (described at the end of the adventure). Guildmaster Dusk is attuned to the painting and has commanded it to defend itself against all creatures except her. As an action, a character can throw a sheet over the painting, making it unable to cast spells.

The Cognoscenti Esoterica was wrong about one thing: Guildmaster Dusk has no intention of selling the painting. By learning its secrets, she hopes to become as notorious and wealthy as the late Daiyani Grysthorn, the crime lord who commissioned the painting in the first place.

G29: Murky Pool

> A ten-foot-square pool of murky water occupies most of this unlit room. A narrow ledge surrounds the pool, and a chalk-drawn arrow on the east wall points down.

The pool is 10 feet deep, and the murky water reduces underwater visibility to 0 feet. Characters can find the way to area G30 by exploring the pool:

Pool Floor. A nonmagical silver key rests on the floor of the pool. A character submerged in the pool can take an action to feel around its floor, finding the key with a successful DC 15 Intelligence (Investigation) check.

Pool Walls. The east wall of the pool has a tiny keyhole in the middle of it. A character submerged in the pool can take an action to search the pool's walls, finding the keyhole with a successful DC 15 Intelligence (Investigation) check.

Secret Exit. If the pool's silver key is inserted into the pool's keyhole, a section of the pool's east wall retracts, revealing a 4-foot-high, 4-foot-wide, flooded tunnel containing a **swarm of quippers**. The swarm attacks the nearest prey. A character who swims to the far end of the tunnel and feels around for an exit finds an unlocked trapdoor in the ceiling that pops open to reveal a dry, T-shaped chamber (area G30) and a passageway leading south (area G31).

Light Sources. Characters who don't have darkvision must find a way to keep their light sources dry, or else they could end up fumbling in the dark until their light sources dry out.

G30: Trapdoor

This unlit, T-shaped area is empty except for a wooden trapdoor in the floor. A tunnel (area G31) leads south from here.

Trapdoor. Below the trapdoor is a 4-foot-wide, 4-foot-high tunnel filled with murky water and a hungry **swarm of quippers** (see area G29 for details). Characters who follow this tunnel west come to a dead end unless they previously opened that end of tunnel in area G29.

G31: Follow the Arrows

Characters who have darkvision or a light source can see the following:

> Chalk arrows drawn on the floor point toward the south end of this narrow corridor. Arrow slits are evenly spaced along the walls.

The arrow slits are too narrow for a Small or larger character to squeeze or crawl through. Behind the arrow slits are two closed-off chambers—one to the west and one to the east. A character who has darkvision or a light source can peer through nearby arrow slits to see what each closed-off area contains: five freestanding human skeletons draped in cobwebs and clutching shortbows. Most of these skeletons are inanimate, propped-up dummies made to look threatening. Each one is a Medium object with AC 15, 4 hit points, and immunity to poison and psychic damage.

Only two **skeletons** are animated, and they guard the hallway's midpoint. When a character enters the square marked T on map 6.2, one animated skeleton uses its reaction (if available) to make a Shortbow attack, targeting that character. The character can make a DC 15 Dexterity (Acrobatics) check to tumble out of the way; if the check is successful, the skeleton has disadvantage on its attack roll.

If a character somehow gains access to one of the closed-off chambers, perhaps by shrinking to Tiny size or by assuming a gaseous form, the animated skeleton in that area stops guarding the hallway and instead attacks that character.

Secret Door. A secret door at the south end of the hallway is unlocked and can be pushed open to reveal a tunnel leading to area G32.

G32: Eastern Maze

Characters who have darkvision or a light source can see the following:

> Branches in the tunnel ahead suggest you're entering some sort of maze. You hear the sounds of heavy breathing coming from somewhere ahead.

Permanent *minor illusion* spells create the sounds of heavy breathing. These sounds originate in the two spaces marked T on map 6.2. Any character who succeeds on a DC 10 Wisdom (Perception) check can track the sounds to their points of origin. A character who enters one of these squares steps on a pressure plate that sinks 1 inch into the floor and remains in that position for 1 minute before resetting itself. A character who searches that section of floor before stepping on it must make a DC 13 Wisdom (Perception) check. If the check is successful, the character spots the pressure plate and can avoid it. If the characters depress the two pressure plates here along with the one in G33, the north secret door in area G33 swings open.

G33: Western Maze

This maze is like the one in area G32, right down to the heavy breathing. The square marked T on map

6.2 contains a hidden pressure plate on the floor identical to the ones in area G32.

Secret Doors. This maze contains two secret doors, one to the north and the other to the west:

North Secret Door. This secret door has three separate locks built into it. If all three pressure plates in the maze (the one in this area and the two in area G32) are in their sunken positions, the door unlocks and swings open on its own, revealing area G28 beyond. Otherwise, each of the door's three locks requires a separate *knock* spell or similar magic to bypass. The locks are hidden and can't be picked.

West Secret Door. This secret door is unlocked and pushes open to reveal area G34 beyond.

G34: Cell Block

Characters who have darkvision or a light source can see the following:

> Vertical iron bars stretch from floor to ceiling, dividing this room into six cells. The two southernmost cells have wooden barrels and trunks in them, while the cell in the northern corner contains a scruffy-looking prisoner.

All the cell doors are locked, and a secret door connects the cell block to area G33.

G34a: Smugglers' Barrels. This cell contains four wooden barrels that have padded interiors and air tubes for breathing. The thieves use these barrels for smuggling people.

G34b: Smugglers' Trunks. Three iron-bound trunks rest against the back wall of this cell. The chests have padded interiors and air tubes for breathing. Like the barrels in the adjoining cell, these trunks are used for smuggling people.

G34c: Prison Cells. Each of these cells contains a wooden bench and a small drain hole in the floor.

Imprisoned in the northernmost cell is a thief named Dury Sneeth (neutral evil, human **spy**), who was caught taking a bribe from a member of the Velvet Glove, a rival thieves' guild. After he was rightly accused of spying for the Velvet Glove, Dury was locked up and interrogated. He found a dagger hidden behind one of the bricks in the wall of his cell, and he keeps it hidden on his person. He has no other weapons.

Guildmaster Dusk is satisfied that Dury is guilty of betraying the Agile Hand, but she hasn't gotten around to punishing him yet and has, in fact, told Dury that she's willing to give him a second chance if he behaves himself from now on. Dury is not convinced Dusk has his best interests at heart and pleads for release.

G35: Storage Room

> Lining two walls of this room are four wooden crates and four wooden chests.

The crates contain stolen weapons and ammunition: ten scimitars, twelve light crossbows, five heavy crossbows, and hundreds of crossbow bolts. The chests are filled with ordinary cutlery, candlesticks, plates, pitchers, and mugs.

Treasure. One of the chests has a secret compartment, which a character searching the chest can find with a successful DC 13 Wisdom (Perception) check. The secret compartment contains six pieces of costume jewelry (5 gp each), a gold necklace with a black pearl pendant (750 gp), and a *necklace of fireballs*.

G36: Storage Room

> This room is mostly empty except for a small wooden crate shoved in a corner next to a paper-wrapped block of butter.

The crate is a **mimic** that loves the taste of salted butter. To keep the mimic on friendly terms, Guildmaster Dusk brings it a fresh block of salted butter every few days. The mimic attacks any character who tries to steal the block of butter but otherwise prefers to be left alone. The mimic can carry on conversations in Common.

Secret Door. Hidden in the room's south corner is a secret door that swings open into area G37.

G37: Secret Tunnel

This tunnel has a secret door at one end and a 15-foot-tall ladder at the opposite end. The ladder climbs to a stone trapdoor in the ceiling that leads to area G12. A character at the top of the ladder can try to push open the trapdoor, doing so with a DC 15 Strength (Athletics) check; the check is made with disadvantage if the blue chair in area G12 is weighing down the trapdoor.

Conclusion

If the characters return *Constantori's Portrait* to Adrisa Carimorte, she gives them their promised reward. If they also present Elix the Saint's leather-bound ledger (see areas G23 and G24), Adrisa offers to buy it for 500 gp.

If the characters deciphered the coded message delivered by Gwish's raven (see area G21) and share the message with Adrisa, she suspects one of Guildmaster Dusk's spies has infiltrated the Cognoscenti

Esoterica. She thanks the characters for the information and gives them a pair of *sending stones* as an added reward. Identifying the spy is beyond the scope of this adventure but a good hook for a future one.

FOR THE GOLDEN VAULT

If the characters are working for the Golden Vault, Adrisa Carimorte arranges to give the characters a rare magic item of their choice (subject to your approval) as payment for delivering the painting to her. The item is delivered to the characters the next day.

MAGIC ITEM

This section presents *Constantori's Portrait* as a magic item. In your campaign, the artist might have painted other magical portraits of Constantori, perhaps with slight differences to distinguish them.

CONSTANTORI'S PORTRAIT
Wondrous Item, Very Rare (Requires Attunement)

This painting by famed artist Dkesii Kwan depicts Constantori, a beautiful courtier, who was paid a staggering sum to be Dkesii's model. Whether Constantori's actual appearance matches the painting remains a subject of debate. The portrait is one of several paintings commissioned by the late Daiyani Grysthorn, a crime lord who frequently gave magical paintings as gifts to her most esteemed associates.

Sentience. *Constantori's Portrait* is a sentient, lawful evil item with an Intelligence score of 14, a Wisdom score of 12, and a Charisma score of 8. It can hear within a range of 120 feet and has darkvision within a range of 60 feet, but it can't see anything behind itself.

The painting can converse in Common, Draconic, and Elvish as if it were a living person, though Constantori's mouth doesn't move. Whenever conversation occurs within the portrait's auditory range, the painting eagerly gathers secrets, the names of secret tellers, significant events, or any political conversations.

Personality. *Constantori's Portrait* is demanding, condescending, and vain. It doesn't like being covered or placed out of sight, and it loudly condemns anyone who tries to remove it from its gold-leaf frame.

Wealth of Information. The painting's primary purpose is to observe and recall conversations. Over the past few decades, *Constantori's Portrait* has quietly observed countless conversations and now possesses an unquantifiable amount of lore—everything from criminal conspiracies to secret passwords. The DM decides what the painting knows and what it doesn't.

While attuned to the painting, you can take an action to telepathically contact it over any distance, provided you and the painting are on the same plane of existence. The painting can't telepathically contact you, however. Maintaining telepathic contact with the painting requires your concentration (as if concentrating on a spell).

Guardian Portrait. While you are attuned to the painting, you can command it to guard its location against one or more creatures you identify as the painting's enemies. The painting performs this function until you command it to stop or until your attunement to the painting ends.

The painting has 3 charges. When a creature the painting identifies as its enemy starts its turn in a space the painting can see, the painting expends 1 of its charges to cast *magic missile* (3 missiles), targeting that creature. The painting regains all expended charges daily at dawn.

The painting is a Small object with AC 12, 20 hit points, and immunity to poison damage. In its gold-leaf frame, the painting weighs 15 pounds. If the painting has at least 1 hit point and is targeted by a *mending* spell, it regains 2d6 hit points.

CONSTANTORI'S PORTRAIT

NIKKI DAWES

A CHASME DEMON AIMS TO THWART A
BARD'S BOLD ESCAPE FROM SKALDERANG
CONSERVATORY.

AXE FROM THE GRAVE

FAMED BARD FRODERIC DARTWILD IS DEAD, and his beautiful mandolin, called Golden Axe, has been stolen from his grave. Even worse, Froderic has risen as a zombie, terrifying the hamlet of Toadhop. In this heist, the characters must track down Golden Axe from the music school owner who stole it and return it to Froderic so the bard can rest peacefully in death once again.

ADVENTURE BACKGROUND

Froderic Dartwild—Frody to those who knew him well—was a gifted human bard born and raised in the hamlet of Toadhop. He could play the mandolin by age three and performed regularly at Toadhop's local tavern until his eighteenth year, when he left this bucolic backwater and became an adventurer. But his adventuring exploits paled in comparison to his reputation as a performer. So gifted a musician was he that an admiring wizard gave Frody an *instrument of the bards*—a famous Canaith mandolin called Golden Axe. The mandolin's magic served Frody well during his many adventures but wasn't enough to save his life. On a crisp autumn day, Frody and his companions were beset by manticores on a lonely stretch of road, and Frody was killed by a manticore's tail spike.

Frody's body was returned to Toadhop and laid to rest in the earth next to his mother, Veena, and his sister, Marigold. Golden Axe was buried with him. Shortly after Frody was interred, a tiefling named Sythian Skalderang, who lived many miles away, learned of the famous bard's untimely death.

Sythian had inherited his parents' estate and debts, but a mysterious poison killed off the family's olive orchard, leaving him with nothing but the mansion and its furnishings. Those furnishings included a multitude of musical instruments Sythian's

parents had bought in the hopes of making him a musical prodigy. While he excelled at none of the instruments, he realized he could pay off his family's debts by turning his home into a conservatory for young musicians from wealthy families. One of his current students, Wylie van Timmel, shows great promise. Sythian hatched a plan to snatch Golden Axe from Frody's grave and give it to Wylie as a present, hoping to earn the favor and long-term financial support of her wealthy family.

Sythian hired a pair of halflings named Mackerel Mudbottom and Trout Bonanza to dig up Frody's remains and pry the Canaith mandolin from his hands. They did just that, leaving behind an open grave. After the halflings fled with the mandolin, Frody awakened, crawled from his coffin, shambled to his mother's old cabin, and knocked on the door. The young family living there fled in terror at the sight of him and took shelter in a neighbor's barn. The good folks of Toadhop have been on edge ever since.

The characters arrive in Toadhop and quickly discover that someone has disturbed the grave of a famous bard named Froderic Dartwild and that Frody's corpse is "none too happy about it." Locals ask the characters to speak with Frody, who is holed up in a cabin on the outskirts of the hamlet. From Frody's zombified corpse, the characters learn that the stolen mandolin is called Golden Axe. They also learn the identities of the grave robbers who stole the mandolin, as Frody's restless spirit heard the halflings refer to each other by name before they inadvertently animated his corpse. Frody refuses to return to his grave until the mandolin is returned to him.

If the characters agree to retrieve the mandolin, they find Mackerel and Trout at their riverside abode, five miles from Toadhop. The two halflings reveal that their employer, Sythian Skalderang, has Golden Axe in his possession and plans to give it to one of his students. Stealing Golden Axe from Skalderang Conservatory forms the crux of this adventure. Ideally, at least one character in the party should be a bard.

The hamlet of Toadhop can be situated in any countryside. Skalderang Conservatory stands in the middle of a dead olive orchard on the outskirts of a city that's about two days' travel from Toadhop on horseback.

Using the Golden Vault

If you're using the Golden Vault as a patron, a golden key is delivered to the characters in whatever manner you deem fit. When the characters use this key to open their music box, the lid pops open and a soothing voice says the following:

> "Greetings, operatives. A Canaith mandolin has been stolen from the grave of a famous bard, whose spirit remains restless from the injustice. The Golden Vault wants the instrument returned to its proper owner. This quest, should you choose to undertake it, requires you to travel to the village of Toadhop. Details will reveal themselves to you shortly after your arrival. Good luck, operatives."

Closing the music box causes the golden key to vanish.

Toadhop

The rustic hamlet of Toadhop boasts a population of thirty—all hardworking folk. Two local establishments cater to visitors: a ramshackle inn called Misty's Bunks and a quaint tavern called My Left Boot. Toadhop's honorary mayor, a brown sow named Jenna Bean, pays visits to the tavern to greet strangers. To dispel any doubts concerning Jenna Bean's role in Toadhop, the hamlet's cheery tavernkeeper, Huberta Hadley, uses white paint to write the word "Mayor" on the friendly sow's flanks.

Frody Dartwild

Read or paraphrase the following boxed text to begin the adventure:

> Froderic Dartwild, a famous bard born and raised in Toadhop, is all anyone in the hamlet can talk about. You've already met Toadhop's honorary mayor: a friendly sow named Jenna Bean. You've also seen the frightened, troubled looks on the faces of the simple, hard-working folk who inhabit this rustic thorp.
>
> You see, Frody died almost a month ago. Everyone in town attended his funeral. Now, he's crawled from his grave and returned to the cabin where he was born and where he spent his childhood. The family that owns the cabin now is out of sorts, to say the least. The family that lives there—a father, a mother, and their three daughters—is staying with neighbors until this grave matter is resolved.
>
> The good folk of Toadhop would like it very much if you, being adventurers, could pay a visit to the old Dartwild cabin and find out why Toadhop's most famous bard has returned from the dead. The sooner he stops stinking up the place, the sooner he can be laid to rest—again.

If the characters wish to help Frody and the people of Toadhop, they can get directions to the old Dartwild cabin and check it out. Four unkempt youths led by a rabblerouser named Ebbin Fulchre spot the characters as they make their way to the Dartwild cabin and follow them, curious to see what happens next.

The Old Dartwild Cabin

As the characters approach the cabin, read the following text:

> The front door of the cabin is wide open, and a rotten stench emanates from it. A noise behind you signals the arrival of four clumsy local youths, who keep their distance from the cabin once they catch a whiff of something unnatural.
>
> "Dang if they ain't goin' inside!" exclaims one youth.
> "Shut up, or Frody might hear you!" hisses another.

Ebbin Fulchre and his three companions are unarmed **commoners** who refuse to enter the cabin, even on a dare. Morbid curiosity brought them here, but they're nothing more than harmless spectators.

When the characters enter the cabin, read the following text:

> The cabin is full of buzzing flies. Seated in a dark corner behind a rickety kitchen table is what's attracting the flies: a putrid human corpse with yellow eyes. In a raspy voice, the creature says, "Well met. My name is Froderic Dartwild. My friends call me Frody."

Frody Dartwild is neutral good, speaks Common, and has an Intelligence score of 10; he otherwise uses the **zombie** stat block.

Bard's Quest

Frody didn't intend to frighten away the cabin's proper owners, but his appearance can't be helped, and he has nowhere else to go. Toadhop's inhabitants are too frightened to speak to him, so Frody has been waiting for braver souls to arrive so he can explain his plight to them. Given the chance, he imparts the following information:

Grave Theft. Two halflings dug up his grave in the dead of night and stole his Canaith mandolin (an *instrument of the bards*). Frody wants it back. ("It was a gift," he says.) The mandolin has a name: Golden Axe.

Halfling Robbers. The grave robbers' names were Mackerel and Trout. Frody's waking spirit could hear the halflings talking to each other as they broke into his coffin. However, Frody could do nothing to stop the theft of his mandolin, and the halflings were long gone by the time he figured out how to animate his own corpse.

Halflings' Whereabouts. The two halflings had local accents. Someone in Toadhop might know where to find them.

Frody agrees to return peacefully to his grave if the characters find and retrieve his stolen mandolin. If the characters slay Frody instead, he reappears 24 hours later as a neutral good **ghost** and haunts Toadhop until his spirit finds rest—which happens only when Golden Axe is returned to Frody's grave.

Mackerel and Trout

Characters who share what they learned with the living residents of Toadhop discover that Mackerel Mudbottom and Trout Bonanza are well known in these parts. The two halflings live about five miles away, in a hut on stilts next to a river. The halflings catch crayfish and frogs and sell them in Toadhop occasionally.

If the characters pay Mackerel and Trout a visit, read the following text:

> A lopsided wooden hut squats on four wooden stilts next to the sandy shore of a shallow river.
>
> You see two halflings in overalls, both enjoying the day. One is next to the hut, feeding a carrot to a mule, while the other stands in the middle of the river, futzing with a broken crayfish trap.

Mackerel and Trout are unarmed **commoners**. The characters can approach the halflings openly or attempt to sneak up on them. The **mule**, which the halflings have named Lucky Me, doesn't startle easily.

The mule doesn't belong to the halflings; they found it tied to a tree by a road and took it, probably while its owner was answering the call of nature. The halflings feed the mule wild carrots and turnips that grow in a tiny garden under their hut.

Questioning the Halflings

Mackerel and Trout used to pick olives in the Skalderang orchard until all its trees died suddenly. They suspect the orchard was poisoned (by whom, they don't know). Now they catch and sell crayfish and frogs, supplementing their meager income by performing occasional chores for Sythian Skalderang.

Mackerel and Trout were paid to steal the Canaith mandolin. Characters who search the halflings' cramped hut find a small purse containing 20 gp. The halflings have yet to decide what to buy with their ill-gotten gold. They reckon they might get a nice dragonchess set, although neither of them knows how to play the game.

The halflings have no idea their foray into grave robbing has awakened an undead creature; the thought of Froderic Dartwild exacting revenge from beyond the grave is enough to make them confess everything. In fact, any serious questioning or threat of harm earns the pair's cooperation. The halflings readily share the following information:

Sythian. Sythian Skalderang has Golden Axe.

Sythian's Debts. Sythian is plagued by debt collectors. To help pay off debts, Sythian turned his mansion into a conservatory where young musicians from wealthy families can hone their craft. Sythian is a musician himself, though neither Mackerel nor Trout has heard Sythian perform or is familiar with his work.

Van Timmels. Sythian plans to give Golden Axe to Wylie van Timmel, one of his pupils. The van Timmels are filthy rich, and Sythian believes their financial support is worth more than the mandolin itself.

SKALDERANG
CONSERVATORY

Front

Back

Halfling Sandcastle

Mackerel and Trout don't have a map of Skalderang Conservatory, but they know it well enough to make a miniature version from sand. Building the sandcastle takes them about 20 minutes.

When the halflings' sandcastle is complete, show players the accompanying Skalderang Conservatory sandcastle illustration (map 7.1), which depicts the location from two points of view. The characters can use the sandcastle to help plan their heist.

Planning the Heist

The rest of the adventure revolves around the theft of Golden Axe from Skalderang Conservatory. Whether the characters return the mandolin to its proper owner, keep it for themselves, or do something else with it is for them to decide.

In addition to providing a sandcastle model of Skalderang Conservatory, Mackerel and Trout furnish the characters with the following information, which is framed as boxed text that you can read or paraphrase to the players.

About the Conservatory

> "The conservatory has four floors, counting the roof. The outer doors—that's a double door in front and a back door leading to the kitchen—they're good, sturdy oak and barred shut at night. And all the windows are latched shut from the inside. We maybe checked.
>
> "From the skylights on the roof, you can see the third-floor room that holds Sythian's fancy instruments. Sythian's quarters are somewhere on the third floor, too. He let most of the staff go, excepting the cook and housekeeper. They sleep next to the kitchen on the ground floor. The students live on the second floor—they each get a room, but they take their vittles in the dining hall on the first floor.
>
> "There are staircases between all the floors in the towers, and an elevator powered by magic that runs between the dining hall and the second and third floors."

About Sythian Skalderang

> "Sythian is a tiefling with blue skin and black horns. He's not the most likable person. He rains on everyone's parade. His folks must've never taught him how to be nice, so when he tries, he mucks it up. He's always unhappy and never has anything nice to say.

> I got no idea what a rich guy like that's got to be unhappy about.
>
> "Sythian wears a master key around his neck that unlocks doors inside the conservatory. Vordell, the housekeeper, has another master key.
>
> "One more thing. Sythian is terrified of frogs and toads—has been ever since he was swallowed by a giant toad as a young boy. He'd kill us for telling you that."

Mackerel and Trout know that frogs commonly huddle near the river. A character who spends at least 15 minutes walking along the shoreline can make a DC 13 Wisdom (Survival) check, locating 1d4 **frogs** on a success. Catching a frog requires a successful DC 10 Dexterity (Acrobatics) check.

About Joster Mareet

Sythian Skalderang has an **incubus** acquaintance who goes by the name Joster Mareet. This servant of the demon lord Graz'zt usually takes the form of a tall, beautiful, male tiefling. The incubus has telepathy out to a range of 60 feet, enabling the fiend to have telepathic conversations with Sythian even when they're not in the same room.

Joster came knocking shortly after Sythian inherited the Skalderang estate. Unknown to Sythian, Joster was responsible for poisoning the Skalderang olive orchard. Joster was following instructions from Graz'zt, with the goal of making Sythian stop growing olives. Joster wants Sythian to use connections gained through the students' elite families to earn their patronage. With that newfound wealth and influence, Sythian could ruin lives and lead a decadent cult worthy of Graz'zt.

Sythian knows Joster is an incubus but is under the false impression that Joster cares for his well-being.

Mackerel and Trout know the following information about Joster:

> "One of Sythian's friends is staying at the castle—a tall, handsome tiefling chap named Joster Mareet. He has red skin, yellow horns, and a smoky voice. Joster doesn't do much except hang around the estate, although sometimes he paints portraits of the students.
>
> "Joster showed up shortly after the Skalderang orchard died and encouraged Sythian to open his home to gifted musicians. We caught Joster chatting with a little green-skinned demon, which turned invisible the instant it saw us. Joster pretended like the demon wasn't there, but we saw it, all right."

ABOUT THE STUDENTS

> "Sythian has four students currently. They all reside at the conservatory, but their families have grand estates in the nearby city.
>
> "Wylie plays strings and has a beautiful singing voice. She is attending her father's birthday party and won't be back for a couple of days. That leaves Embry, a talented composer and horn player; Mazia, who plays the flute; and Mytchyl, who plays the drums and the harpsichord.
>
> "All the students are good-natured and kind."

A TYPICAL DAY

If the characters request information about how the conservatory's occupants spend a typical day, Mackerel and Trout share the information in the Conservatory Schedule table.

CONSERVATORY SCHEDULE

Start Time	Activity
8 a.m.	Breakfast is served in the dining hall (area C1) on level 1.
9 a.m.	Sythian supervises rehearsals in the music hall (area C11) on level 3 while the servants work and Joster lazes about.
Noon	Lunch is served in the dining hall (area C1).
1 p.m.	A courier drops off Sythian's mail, which he reads in his study (area C14) on level 3, with Joster present, while the students relax in the gallery (area C4) on level 1.
5 p.m.	Dinner is served in the dining hall (area C1).
6 p.m.	The students practice their music unsupervised, either in their quarters (area C7) on level 2 or in the music hall (area C11). Sythian writes letters in his study (area C14) or prays in the shrine (area C5) on level 1, usually with Joster present.
9 p.m.	Sythian, Joster, and the students gather in the dining hall (area C1) to tell stories, share city gossip, snack, and discuss music theory.
Midnight	Sythian, Joster, and the students retire to their quarters (Joster and the students in area C7 on level 2, Sythian in area C15 on level 3) while the servants tidy up.

SKALDERANG CONSERVATORY

When the characters are close enough to see the conservatory, describe the location as follows:

> You recognize Skalderang Conservatory at once: a brooding keep surrounded by rows of dead olive trees. A long, straight, cobblestone driveway in need of repair passes through the orchard on its way to the conservatory, forming a loop before the entrance. Where the driveway meets the main road, someone has posted a plain wooden sign that reads as follows:
>
> "Skalderang Conservatory—School for the Musically Gifted. No Tours! No Solicitors! No Amateurs!"

The earth throughout the orchard is saturated with demon ichor, which killed the olive trees. A character who takes a minute to examine the earth and succeeds on a DC 15 Intelligence (Nature) check can determine that the ground is saturated with a putrid, oily substance not found in nature. A character who gets a 20 or higher on the check identifies the substance as demon ichor.

If the characters tell Sythian that his orchard was poisoned with demon ichor, he concludes Joster Mareet is responsible but keeps his suspicions to himself. The revelation makes Sythian bitter toward the incubus and poisons their long-term relationship.

GENERAL FEATURES

Skalderang Conservatory has stone walls and a stone-tiled ground floor. The upper floors have polished mahogany floors and wainscoting. Other prevalent features are summarized in the sections that follow.

CHIMNEYS

The conservatory's chimneys haven't been cleaned in a long time. A Small character can try to squeeze up or down one, doing so with a successful DC 15 Dexterity (Acrobatics) check. A failed check indicates that the character makes no progress. To enter or exit a chimney from the top, one must first use an action to try to remove the chimney's stone cap, doing so with a successful DC 18 Strength (Athletics) check. A character in gaseous form can navigate a chimney without having to make these checks or remove the chimney cap.

DOORS

The conservatory's doors are made of thick, sturdy oak with iron fixtures. Locked doors are noted in their area's heading and require a master key to open. Sythian has one master key; Vordell, the

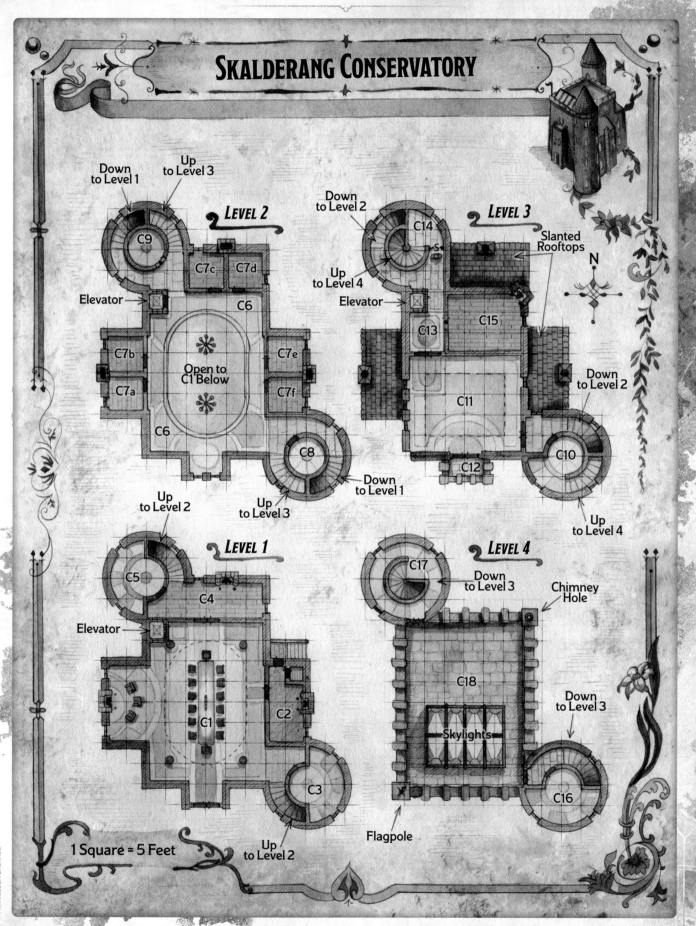

SKALDERANG CONSERVATORY

LEVEL 2

Down to Level 1

Up to Level 3

C9

C7c   C7d

Elevator

C6

C7b   C7e

Open to C1 Below

C7a   C7f

C6

C8

Up to Level 2

Up to Level 3

Down to Level 1

LEVEL 3

Down to Level 2

C14

S

Up to Level 4

Slanted Rooftops

Elevator

C13

C15

N

C11

Down to Level 2

C12

C10

Up to Level 4

LEVEL 1

Up to Level 2

C5

C4

Elevator

C1

C2

C3

Up to Level 2

LEVEL 4

C17

Down to Level 3

Chimney Hole

C18

Skylights

Down to Level 3

Flagpole

C16

1 Square = 5 Feet

FRANCESCA BAERALD

housekeeper, has another. A character can take an action to try to pick a lock using thieves' tools, doing so with a successful DC 18 Dexterity check.

ELEVATOR

A 5-foot-wide cage elevator fitted with stained-glass windows connects the dining hall on level 1 (area C1) to the mezzanine on level 2 (area C6) and the hallway on level 3 (area C13). The elevator is powered by magic. A creature in the elevator need only say "level 1," "level 2," or "level 3" in Common, and the elevator will ascend or descend to that floor, clattering noisily and taking about 6 seconds to move from one floor to the next. The elevator doesn't respond to commands while it is moving.

EXTERIOR LIGHTING

The conservatory's exterior walls are lit up at night by golden *continual flame* spells spaced evenly around the building's foundation. These spells are suppressed during daylight hours.

INTERIOR LIGHTING

Natural light illuminates most of the conservatory's interior spaces. Students and servants who lack darkvision use candles, lamps, or lit fireplaces to see at night.

WINDOWS

The conservatory's windows are 6 feet tall and 3 feet wide, their lead frames fitted with dozens of small, diamond-shaped panes of frosted glass. Each window has small hinges on one side of it, allowing it to be swung open like a door. All windows are latched shut from the inside except on hot days. As an action, a character can try to force open a latched window, doing so with a successful DC 15 Strength (Athletics) check, or use thieves' tools to unlatch a window from the outside, doing so with a successful DC 15 Dexterity check.

INHABITANTS

Sythian Skalderang is described at the end of the adventure. His muse, the **incubus** Joster Mareet, clings to him like a shadow and uses telepathy to communicate secretly with him. The conservatory's other regular inhabitants are described below.

DEMONS

Joster Mareet petitioned and received aid from Graz'zt in the form of one **chasme** and six **quasits**:

Chasme. This Large demon crawls around the outside of the conservatory and is usually encountered on the rooftop (area C18). It attacks enemies it detects in the air, on the ground, or on the third-floor balcony (area C12).

Quasits. These Tiny demons haunt the conservatory, where they remain invisible or take the forms of bats and giant centipedes.

Sythian and Joster are the only ones at the conservatory who are aware of the demons' presence, as the demons take care to hide themselves from students, servants, and most visitors. When a demon dies, it dissolves into a puddle of putrid ichor.

STUDENTS

Sythian has opened his home to four students:

Embry Hale (chaotic good) is a loud, 17-year-old human who plays a mean horn. He also composes his own songs and lyrics, recording them on scraps of parchment. He plans to become an adventuring bard but hasn't the courage to tell his parents, who would never tolerate such a pedestrian, dangerous life for their son.

Mazia Foulard (lawful good) is a 20-year-old tiefling who has taught the other students a sign language she and her deaf grandmother created together. Mazia can play several instruments, but her favorite is the flute. She doesn't think Sythian is a particularly good teacher but has great love and respect for her fellow students.

Mytchyl Dwyer (neutral good) is a 13-year-old human who was born without legs. He gets around in a gold-trimmed wheelchair. When it comes to music, his lack of discipline prompted his parents to send him to the Skalderang Conservatory. He was unhappy at first, but he warmed to the company of the other students and secretly idolizes Embry.

Wylie van Timmel (lawful good) is a 16-year-old human who comes from a loving home and enjoys a life of privilege. Great things are expected of her, and she intends to make a name for herself. She is absent when the characters arrive and won't return for a couple days.

Should their statistics become necessary, the students are unarmed and unarmored **nobles** with an extra skill: Performance +7. The students are friendly but scream loudly and try to hide if confronted by unidentified intruders. They refuse to cooperate with anyone opposed to Sythian until his true colors are revealed to them.

Embry, Mazia, and Mytchyl saw the halflings Mackerel and Trout deliver a mandolin to Sythian, and they know what Sythian plans to do with it. They assume he procured the instrument legally and are unaware that it was stolen from a grave. Should they learn about the grave robbery, the three students instruct the housekeeper to pack up their belongings, and they leave the conservatory at once.

Sythian can't afford to lose his students, so if the characters threaten to tell the students about his grave robbing or the fact that he consorts with demons, he surrenders the instrument to ensure the characters' silence.

SERVANTS

Sythian employs two full-time servants, both **commoners**:

Merle (lawful good) is an 83-year-old dwarf cook. He has a neatly trimmed beard and a cheerful disposition. He doesn't socialize with the students much except to crack jokes. Merle has been a fixture in Skalderang Conservatory since before Sythian was born and doesn't have an unkind word to say about anybody except for Joster Mareet, whom he suspects is up to no good.

Vordell (lawful neutral) is a dour, 50-year-old human housekeeper with a full head of salt-and-pepper hair pulled into a ponytail. He carries a master key that opens all locked doors in the conservatory. If he could find employment elsewhere, Vordell would abandon Sythian in a heartbeat. Vordell doesn't like that Sythian partakes in demon worship but keeps his misgivings to himself. Joster's invisible quasits torment Vordell by soiling or breaking things, which Vordell must then tidy up. Vordell doesn't know who or what to blame for these unexplained messes.

The servants are indifferent toward guests and hostile toward burglars. Duty and loyalty prevent them from cooperating with intruders willingly.

THE DIRECT APPROACH

Although he doesn't like unexpected guests, Sythian has enough grace to briefly entertain visitors who arrive at the conservatory without an appointment. Characters who knock on the front door or otherwise announce their presence are greeted by Vordell or one of the students and led by that individual into area C1, where the characters are expected to wait until Sythian and Joster arrive to question them. Should this encounter occur at night, Sythian is doubly annoyed by the disturbance, and Charisma checks made to influence him have disadvantage.

"ARE YOU ACCEPTING NEW STUDENTS?"
A character who is a bard (or pretends to be one) can petition Sythian to become a student at Skalderang Conservatory. The character must first prove they can afford Sythian's tutelage (by displaying treasure worth 250 gp or more), after which the character

> ### WHERE'S THE MANDOLIN?
> Golden Axe is in Sythian's quarters (area C15). If you're running this adventure for one or more players who have played through the adventure before, you might move the mandolin to a different location in the conservatory.

must impress Sythian by playing a musical instrument and succeeding on a DC 20 Charisma (Performance) check. On a failed check, Sythian delivers a scathing critique of the character's musical ability before sending the characters away empty-handed. Sythian changes his mind if the characters pay him a bribe of 500 gp or more. On a successful check or upon receiving such a bribe, Sythian allows the would-be student (and only that character) to stay overnight and orders Vordell to prepare a room for them (area C7d).

"SURRENDER THE MANDOLIN OR ELSE!"
If the characters use their audience with Sythian to demand that Golden Axe be handed over to them, Sythian lets out a haughty laugh and orders the characters to leave at once. If the characters refuse, Sythian and Joster flee to area C15, where Sythian equips himself with Golden Axe and tries to escape out the window using the mandolin's *fly* spell while Joster makes his own escape.

"WE'RE DEBT COLLECTORS."
Sythian owes money to various loan sharks and banks. Characters who claim to represent one of these individuals or institutions must succeed on a DC 15 Charisma (Deception) check to convince Sythian that they are who they say they are. If one or more characters fail this check, Sythian becomes suspicious (see "Sythian's Suspicion" below).

If the characters trick Sythian into believing they are debt collectors and demand a payment of no more than 200 gp, Sythian fetches the sum from his study (area C14) while Joster keeps a watchful eye on the characters. After making the payment, Sythian sends the characters on their way. If the characters demand more than 200 gp or anything other than coins, Sythian becomes suspicious (see below).

Sythian's Suspicion. If Sythian becomes suspicious of characters posing as debt collectors, he entertains them long enough for Joster to "fetch the payment." The incubus rounds up the demons in areas C4, C11, and C18 before returning to dispose of the visitors. When combat erupts, Sythian retreats to his bedroom (area C15) and grabs Golden Axe. If the characters catch up to him, he tries to escape out the window using the mandolin's *fly* spell.

Conservatory Locations

The following locations are keyed to Skalderang Conservatory as shown on map 7.2.

C1: Dining Hall

At night, the double door to the south is barred shut from the inside.

> A large dining table stands in the middle of this hall, surrounded by tall-backed wooden chairs. Suspended above the table are two chandeliers fitted with wax candles. Encircling the hall at a height of fifteen feet is a wooden mezzanine that can be reached by a cage elevator in one corner. West of the dining room is a cozy niche with a fireplace, three padded chairs, and a sideboard. Hanging above the mantelpiece is a framed portrait of two stern, well-dressed, middle-aged tieflings: a short, pudgy fellow and a tall, thin woman. The surrounding walls bear numerous smaller paintings, mostly of young people.

During the day, characters are most likely to encounter Vordell, the housekeeper (**commoner**), here, setting the table or returning clean dishes and cutlery to the sideboard. Depending on the time of day, the characters might find **Sythian Skalderang** (see the end of the adventure), Joster the **incubus** in tiefling form, and students here as well (see the Conservatory Schedule table).

Chandeliers. Simple rope-and-pulley mechanisms allow the chandeliers to be raised or lowered from the mezzanine (area C6).

Paintings. The painting above the mantelpiece depicts Sythian Skalderang's parents, Vexxis and Alyrria. The smaller portraits in the room were painted by Joster and depict Sythian's students, past and present.

C2: Kitchen and Pantry

> A large pot hangs in the fireplace of this cluttered kitchen, and stout worktables sized for a dwarf are covered with handy implements. A closet pantry stands in the corner next to a door that leads outside.

Merle, the dwarf cook (**commoner**), works here from 6 a.m. to midnight. When confronted with danger, he grabs a rolling pin (treat it as a club) and defends himself.

The door that leads outside is used mainly for food deliveries and is barred shut from the inside at night.

C3: Servants' Quarters

> This room contains three two-level bunk beds, one of which is currently in use. A washbasin stands in a nearby corner.

Merle, the cook, claims the lower bunk as his. Vordell, the housekeeper, sleeps in the bunk above him.

Treasure. Each servant has a footlocker that contains personal effects and earnings. Characters who empty the two footlockers find a total of 8 gp, 55 sp, and 62 cp. Merle's footlocker also contains an ivory smoking pipe (25 gp), an electrum-framed hand mirror (25 gp), and a small pair of silvered shears (10 gp) he uses to trim his beard.

C4: Gallery

> Several padded armchairs are arranged in this narrow chamber, the walls of which are festooned with hunting trophies and crossbows. Bare hooks and pale rectangles mark places on the walls where paintings once hung. Standing in the southwest corner near a single door is a stuffed wolf, its glassy gaze fixed on a stone staircase going up.

Between 1 p.m. and 5 p.m., Sythian's students relax here. Three **quasits** lurk by the stuffed wolf and use their Invisibility action to remain unseen. They attack characters who try to break into area C5.

The missing paintings were sold at auctions to pay off some of Sythian's debts. The remaining decor includes three light crossbows and three heavy crossbows (all of which are functional but missing ammunition) mounted on the walls, as well as a stag's head mounted above a fireplace.

C5: Shrine (Locked)

Students and guests are not allowed in this room, which is why Sythian locks the door.

Sythian's father, Vexxis, worshiped gods of the hunt and the harvest. When he died, this room fell into disuse until Joster Mareet showed up and convinced Sythian to empty it and repurpose the shrine for the worship of Graz'zt. Vordell, the housekeeper, is the only person besides Sythian and Joster who's allowed to enter this area.

> Dark curtains cover the windows of this room, which looks like it might have been a chapel, though most of the decor is gone, leaving empty niches and pedestals. A demonic stone hand rises from the floor and

JOSTER MAREET CONSPIRES WITH THREE QUASITS, INCLUDING
ONE IN CENTIPEDE FORM AND ONE IN BAT FORM.

clutches a three-foot-tall, three-foot-wide brazier. The
hand has five fingers instead of four.

The stone hand merges seamlessly with the stone
floor. Spilling a few drops of Humanoid blood into
the brazier causes the brazier's coals to produce
a hissing purple flame and oily, purplish smoke
that reeks of offal. When Sythian summons the
flame and speaks to it, the flame responds to him in
Graz'zt's whispered voice, but only when the demon
lord is in the mood to talk.

A character who examines the brazier and succeeds on a DC 17 Intelligence (Religion) check
realizes that it's used by worshipers of Graz'zt to
commune with the demon lord, who requires a
blood sacrifice. As an action, a character can spill
some of their own blood into the bowl and utter a
prayer to Graz'zt; doing so has a 10 percent chance
of annoying the demon lord, who causes four
shadow demons to appear in the room and attack.
These demons return to the Abyss after 10 minutes
and disappear instantly when slain. (Graz'zt speaks
only to those he considers worthy of his attention;
the characters don't qualify in this regard.)

C6: MEZZANINE

This wooden mezzanine encircles the dining hall at
a height of fifteen feet, and the ceiling is fifteen feet
higher still. Two chandeliers hang from ropes, the
ends of which are wrapped around hooks bolted to
the railing—one to the north, the other to the south.

The mezzanine creaks loudly when stepped on.
Dexterity (Stealth) checks made to cross the mezzanine quietly have disadvantage.

C7: STUDENTS' QUARTERS

Students sometimes practice music in their rooms
from 6 p.m. to 9 p.m. All students can be found in
their rooms from midnight until shortly before 8
a.m. (see the Conservatory Schedule table).

Each of these rooms contains a single bed, a
dresser, a washbasin, a chamber pot, and an iron
stove with clawed feet with a stovepipe that fun-
nels smoke into the nearby chimney. A mirror is
mounted on the inside of the door. Other features of
each room are summarized below:

C7a: Wylie's Room. Resting on the dresser is a
wooden case containing a beautifully crafted lyre
(250 gp) that belongs to Wylie van Timmel.

C7b: Joster's Room. Joster has claimed this vacant room for himself and uses it primarily as a studio to paint portraits of new students. (These paintings end up on the walls in area C1.) A wooden easel stands near the window, and a collection of paints and brushes rests on the windowsill. Leaning against the base of the easel are three blank canvases stretched over wooden frames.

C7c: Mytchyl's Room. When present, Mytchyl Dwyer lies on his bed with his wheelchair close by. Mounted on the wall above the headboard are three songbirds carved from driftwood.

C7d: Spare Room. No one uses this room currently.

C7e: Mazia's Room. Mazia Foulard keeps a diary and a small leather case tucked under her pillow. The case contains an exquisitely crafted silver flute (250 gp) that was given to Mazia by her grandmother.

C7f: Embry's Room. Odors waft into this room from the kitchen. Embry Hale has a framed painting on one wall that depicts the silhouette of a satyr playing a trumpet (25 gp). Tucked under Embry's mattress is a wooden smoking pipe and packet of pipe tobacco.

C8: Bathroom

> Dry towels are stacked on a shelf above a row of empty hooks by the door. Protruding from the far wall is a funnel-shaped shower head, below which is an iron knob.

The servants shower here every night after finishing their chores, while students shower here before breakfast each morning.

Turning the iron knob causes hot water to spring from the shower head. The water, which is produced magically, disappears through drains in the floor.

C9: Sythian's Bathroom (Locked)

Sythian showers here every morning before breakfast. This room is otherwise identical to area C8.

C10: Laundry Room

> The window of this room is opened a crack to let in fresh air. Damp towels and clothing hang on wooden racks, and a washtub with a scrubbing board rests under a spigot that protrudes from one wall, near a shelf lined with bars of soap.

Turning the spigot on the wall causes hot water, which is produced magically, to flow from a faucet and into the washtub, which has a drain plug in the bottom of it.

C11: Music Hall

> This spacious room contains several large instruments, including a harp, a harpsichord, a piano, a cello, and three kettle drums. More portable instruments—such as fiddles, ukuleles, accordions, bagpipes, lutes, lyres, oboes, brass horns, bongos, and violins—rest on padded chairs spaced evenly around the perimeter. Eight rectangular, stained-glass skylights give the chamber a cathedral-like aspect. The room's three double doors have built-in, hand-carved panels depicting scenes of dancing and merrymaking.

Sythian Skalderang (see the end of the adventure) is here with his students from 9 a.m. to noon. The students often return to this room between the hours of 6 p.m. and 9 p.m. to play music without supervision.

Three **quasits** lurk under chairs, using their Invisibility action to hide. They attack any intruder who picks up or plays one of the instruments.

Instruments. Sythian could pay off most of his debts by selling his impressive collection of musical instruments, but he refuses to do so.

C12: Outdoor Balcony

> A stone battlement encloses this balcony, which overlooks the main entrance.

The **chasme** on the rooftop (area C18) creeps down the exterior wall to attack characters on this balcony. It's a 30-foot drop from the balcony to the ground.

C13: Hallway

> Standing in an alcove at the north end of this hallway is an empty suit of armor, its vacant helm staring past the cage elevator toward the double door at the opposite end of the hall.

The elevator climbs no higher than this hallway.

Trapped Secret Door. A secret door disguised to look like a section of wood-paneled wall is hidden behind the suit of armor. A character can detect the secret door by searching the wall and succeeding on a DC 14 Intelligence (Investigation) check. A successful check also reveals a faint glyph on the secret door—the telltale sign of a *glyph of warding* spell. Only Sythian can open the door without triggering the glyph. When the glyph triggers, each creature in a 10-foot-radius sphere centered on the suit of armor suffers the effect of a *shatter* spell (save DC 14). The spell also causes the suit of armor to fall to pieces and alerts Sythian and Joster in area C15 if they are there. Once the spell goes off, the secret door is no longer trapped.

The secret door is unlocked and leads to area C14.

C14: SYTHIAN'S STUDY

> An unlocked rolltop desk is pushed against the west wall of this study. The desk's chair has a large *S* carved into its backrest. Near the desk, a wooden staircase spirals up.

Between the hours of 1 p.m. and 5 p.m., **Sythian Skalderang** (see the end of the adventure) is here, reading and writing letters, as well as reviewing applications from the families of young hopefuls who seek to benefit from his tutelage. While Sythian is here, Joster the **incubus** reverts to his true form and looms over Sythian's shoulder.

Treasure. The desk is stuffed with quills, ink jars, candles, wax seals, and sheets of parchment. A thorough search of the desk takes 1 minute and yields a small wooden coffer containing 270 gp, 165 sp, and 89 cp.

C15: SYTHIAN'S QUARTERS (LOCKED)

> This room contains a canopied bed and other furnishings, including a corner fireplace flanked by stone-carved hunting mastiffs. A large trunk rests at the foot of the bed.

Sythian Skalderang (see the end of the adventure) is here from midnight until 8 a.m.

Trapped Trunk. A character who examines the trunk and succeeds on a DC 14 Intelligence (Investigation) check detects a faint glyph on its lid—the telltale sign of a *glyph of warding* spell. The first time a creature other than Sythian opens the trunk, the spell goes off, targeting the creature that opened the trunk with a *suggestion* spell (save DC 14). On a successful saving throw, the creature resists the spell. On a failed saving throw, the creature is compelled to leave the room empty-handed and not return for 8 hours (the duration of the spell). Once the glyph is triggered, the trunk is safe to open.

Treasure. The trunk contains, among personal items and clothing of little value, the *instrument of the bards* (Canaith mandolin) stolen from Froderic Dartwild's grave.

CANAITH MANDOLIN

C16: ATTIC

> Gray sheets cover old furniture in this dusty attic.

Characters who spend at least 1 minute searching the attic find two life-sized wooden mannequins—one wearing a green wedding dress, the other a white funeral dress. Both dresses belonged to Sythian's mother. They also find a wooden chest that is padlocked; the key is lost, but a character can take an action to try to pick the lock using thieves' tools, doing so with a successful DC 17 Dexterity check.

Treasure. Inside the padlocked chest, wrapped in leather, is a flat wooden case whose lid is engraved with a pair of stags locking horns. The case contains six *+2 crossbow bolts*. Sythian is unaware of these items and won't miss them if someone takes them.

C17: LIBRARY (LOCKED)

> Empty bookshelves stand between the windows of this musty tower attic.

Sythian sold his family's collection of books to pay off debts. A locked door leads to the rooftop (area C18).

C18: Rooftop

> A three-foot-high stone battlement encloses this rooftop. Mounted on one corner of the battlement is a flagpole flying a black pennant emblazoned with a golden olive tree. A chimney pipe juts from the opposite corner, and an oak door leads to each tower.
>
> A five-foot-wide walkway wraps around a convex structure composed of eight large stained-glass windows in lead frames. Each skylight is a work of art, its panes shaped and colored to resemble a rising or setting sun.

It's a 45-foot drop from the rooftop to the ground.

Unless it has been fought and killed elsewhere, a **chasme** guards this area. At your discretion, the demon might be perched above a doorway, waiting to ambush intruders emerging from one of the towers.

Flagpole. The flagpole in the southwest corner is made of metal and is sturdy enough to bear the weight of characters who wish to lower themselves down a wall or through a skylight.

Skylights. There are eight skylights, each one a Large object with AC 13, 5 hit points, and immunity to poison and psychic damage. Rather than shattering an entire skylight, a character can take an action to break or pry out one of a skylight's panes, creating a hole big enough to slip through. It's a 15-foot drop from the skylights to the floor of area C11.

Leaving Post-Heist

If the characters leave the conservatory with Golden Axe and the **chasme** in area C18 is still alive, the demon swoops down and attacks the characters before they get too far. The demon's goal is to return the mandolin to the conservatory. The mandolin is, after all, Sythian's ticket to earning the patronage of Wylie van Timmel's family.

You can make this final encounter deadlier by adding either a second **chasme** or a **barlgura**.

Conclusion

Once Golden Axe is safely in their possession, the characters must decide whether to keep it for themselves (in which case the adventure ends here) or return it to its rightful owner (see "Buried Again" below).

Buried Again

If Golden Axe is returned to Frody Dartwild, read:

> Froderic Dartwild plucks the strings of the mandolin and plays a happy tune. Meanwhile, the news of your return spreads through Toadhop like wildfire. Everyone comes out to greet you, including Honorary Mayor Jenna Bean, who snorts contentedly. Frody apologizes to everyone for the trouble he has caused and says he looks forward to returning to his grave. His words bring tears as well as cheers.

A local carpenter named Lewth Fulchre (the father of local rabblerouser Ebbin Fulchre) offers to repair Frody's coffin, which shouldn't take more than a few hours. While Frody waits, he performs his favorite music to an enrapt crowd outside My Left Boot. If there's a bard or another musically inclined individual among the player characters, Frody suggests they perform together as a duet. If the character agrees, award them inspiration.

Everyone in Toadhop attends Frody's second funeral, which you can summarize as follows:

> After Frody is returned to the earth, Toadhop's residents stand around his grave wearing straw hats—a local custom, you reckon—to sing a somber hymn. A little girl lays a tiny flower on the dead bard's grave before returning to the arms of her weeping parents. As the crowd disperses, locals pat you on the back and shoulder and congratulate you on a quest well done.

For the Golden Vault

If the characters are working for the Golden Vault, a representative of the organization offers the characters a rare magic item of their choice (subject to your approval) as payment for returning the Canaith mandolin to Frody. The reward is delivered to the characters a day or two after Frody's reburial.

SYTHIAN SKALDERANG

Sythian Skalderang has been blessed by the demon lord Graz'zt. Graz'zt's gift to Sythian manifests in several ways, including Sythian's ability to conjure demonic whispers that can fray enemy minds.

When he was a young boy, Sythian went on a hunting trip with his father. A giant toad attacked them and swallowed Sythian. Although Sythian escaped after his father slew the monster, the attack left Sythian with an acute fear of frogs and toads.

Sythian's parents hoped his interest in music would lead Sythian to become an extraordinary musician; he became a mediocre one instead, despite the help of several renowned tutors. Years later, Sythian resents their efforts, as the money his parents lavished on his education left him with many unpaid debts. Now that his parents are dead, he is determined to hold on to his estate and will do whatever it takes to keep what he has left.

Sythian has attuned to Golden Axe so that he can learn and exercise the Canaith mandolin's properties. Although he hopes Golden Axe will earn him the good graces and financial support of the van Timmels, Sythian would sooner lose the instrument than see any harm befall his students, as his reputation and financial success hinge on their well-being. He gladly gives up the instrument to save himself.

Sythian is an impatient and demanding teacher who holds his students to a rigorous schedule. His bone conductor's wand doubles as a spellcasting focus.

SYTHIAN SKALDERANG
Medium Humanoid (Bard, Tiefling), Chaotic Evil

Armor Class 15 (Graz'zt's Gift)
Hit Points 99 (18d8 + 18)
Speed 30 ft.

STR	DEX	CON	INT	WIS	CHA
10 (+0)	15 (+2)	13 (+1)	14 (+2)	11 (+0)	16 (+3)

Saving Throws Dex +5, Wis +3
Skills Arcana +5, Deception +6, Performance +6
Damage Resistances fire
Senses darkvision 60 ft., passive Perception 10
Languages Abyssal, Common
Challenge 7 (2,900 XP)   **Proficiency Bonus** +3

Fear of Frogs and Toads. Sythian is frightened while he is within 20 feet of a frog or a toad (of any size) that he can see.

Graz'zt's Gift. Sythian's AC includes his Charisma modifier.

ACTIONS

Multiattack. Sythian makes two Poisoned Shortsword or Poisoned Dart attacks and uses Whispers of Azzagrat.

Poisoned Shortsword. *Melee Weapon Attack:* +5 to hit, reach 5 ft., one target. *Hit:* 5 (1d6 + 2) piercing damage plus 5 (1d10) poison damage.

Poisoned Dart. *Ranged Weapon Attack:* +5 to hit, range 20/60 ft., one target. *Hit:* 4 (1d4 + 2) piercing damage plus 5 (1d10) poison damage.

Spellcasting. Sythian casts one of the following spells, using Charisma as the spellcasting ability (spell save DC 14):

At will: *mage hand, prestidigitation*
1/day each: *charm person, faerie fire, unseen servant*

Whispers of Azzagrat. Each creature in a 15-foot cube originating from Sythian must make a DC 14 Wisdom saving throw. On a failed save, a creature takes 18 (4d8) psychic damage and is incapacitated until the end of its next turn. On a successful save, the creature takes half as much damage and isn't incapacitated.

REACTIONS

Fiendish Rebuke (3/Day). Immediately after a creature within 5 feet of Sythian hits him with an attack roll, Sythian forces that creature to make a DC 14 Constitution saving throw. The creature takes 14 (4d6) fire damage on a failed saving throw, or half as much damage on a successful one.

NIXYLANNA VIDORANT'S GUARDS ARE NOT YET
AWARE OF THE WOULD-BE THIEVES LURKING
BELOW THEM.

VIDORANT'S VAULT

O VER THE YEARS, THE NOTORIOUS ELF THIEF Nixylanna Vidorant has stolen many famed prizes and stored them in her vault. Her former partner believes one of these trophies—a ruby diadem—rightly belongs to him. He hires the characters to infiltrate Vidorant's vault, bypass its security features, and steal the diadem. In a twist, the characters come face-to-face with Vidorant, and she offers them a deal that's hard to refuse.

ADVENTURE BACKGROUND

The Silver Fingers Society is no mere guild of pickpockets and ruffians. The elite thieves of this multinational organization pull off impossible heists, targeting crown jewels, national secrets, and other heavily guarded prizes. Decades ago, the elf Nixylanna Vidorant joined the Silver Fingers, where she partnered with a dwarf named Samphith Goldenbeard. These friendly rivals made a good pair. Vidorant was skilled with picking locks and deftly getting into tough places, and Goldenbeard used his connections and quick thinking to research targets and talk the pair's way out of trouble.

As the years passed, the duo rose in the ranks of the Silver Fingers. But their partnership abruptly ended when they stole the Ruby Diadem, an heirloom once worn by Queen Erlynn Blessedore. Goldenbeard's family traces its lineage to the dwarven queen, who was captured in a battle centuries ago, and he desperately wanted to reclaim his family's diadem. The heist seemed like any other—until thirty guards suddenly surrounded the pair of thieves. Vidorant nimbly escaped via the roof with the diadem in hand, but Goldenbeard was caught. He avoided imprisonment by calling in favors with powerful friends, but when he tracked down Vidorant, she refused to hand over the diadem despite his family's claim to it.

Goldenbeard claimed Vidorant set him up and alerted the authorities. Meanwhile, Vidorant claimed innocence, insisting Goldenbeard was covering for his own inability to escape the situation. Whatever the truth, she kept the diadem, the once-friendly rivalry turned bitter, and the two have tried to outmaneuver each other ever since.

Recently, their uneasy relationship changed again with the death of the longtime leader of the Silver Fingers Society. Vidorant and Goldenbeard each competed to win leadership of the society, calling in favors from every ally they had in the organization. Unfortunately for Vidorant, Goldenbeard proved defter at internal politics, winning leadership of the society—and getting Vidorant expelled in the process. Goldenbeard promised harsh retaliation against anyone who helped Vidorant, ensuring none of her former allies would stand against him.

Weeks after his takeover of the Silver Fingers Society, Goldenbeard made an even bigger move against Vidorant. He promised a favor to any existing or aspiring Silver Finger who steals the Ruby Diadem of Erlynn Blessedore and delivers it to him. This challenge is the talk of scoundrel circles as everyone vies to steal the diadem from Vidorant. Doing so won't be easy, as Vidorant keeps her treasures in her secure vault on the outskirts of the city.

Using the Golden Vault

If you're using the Golden Vault as a patron, a golden key is delivered to the characters in whatever manner you deem fit. When the characters use this key to open their music box, the lid pops open and a soothing voice says the following:

> "Greetings, operatives. An heirloom diadem from a dwarven queen is in the possession of master thief Nixylanna Vidorant. The queen's descendant, Samphith Goldenbeard, would like the diadem returned, and the Golden Vault finds value in allying with his Silver Fingers Society. This quest, should you choose to undertake it, requires you to infiltrate Vidorant's vault and recover the diadem. Start by meeting with Goldenbeard. Good luck, operatives."

Closing the music box causes the golden key to vanish.

Steal the Diadem

To kick off this adventure, the characters receive an invitation to meet with the head of the Silver Fingers Society, Samphith Goldenbeard (lawful neutral, dwarf **noble**). A character who is a thief or has the criminal background is familiar with the Silver Fingers Society, an elite organization for exceptional thieves.

Alternatively, the characters could hear about Goldenbeard's challenge to bring him the diadem through the gossip of other thieves; in this case, skip to the "Preparation" section.

If the characters are too lawful or good to work with a thieves' guild, consider Goldenbeard approaching them simply as a descendant of Erlynn Blessedore, asking them to return the Ruby Diadem to its rightful heirs.

Mission from Goldenbeard

Goldenbeard asks the characters to meet with him in the back room of a restaurant, the Spoke and Wheel. When the party arrives, read the following:

> An elegantly dressed dwarf greets you in the back room of the Spoke and Wheel, a polite smile gracing his face. He introduces himself as Goldenbeard and offers you tea. After everyone is served, he casually dips a pinky into his own cup and tastes a drop before taking a larger sip.

Once the characters sit down near him, Goldenbeard addresses them:

> "It's a pleasure to meet you all. I'm sure you've heard of my organization, the Silver Fingers Society. Only the most elite thieves in the world qualify for membership.
>
> "You may have heard that Nixylanna Vidorant, my former partner, is no longer with the Silver Fingers. We've withdrawn all protection from her and her property, and we now have room in the society for new members.
>
> "As such, I present to you a challenge. Whoever brings me the Ruby Diadem of Erlynn Blessedore from Nixylanna's personal vault will become a member of the society. As my family is descended from Queen Erlynn, we've wanted the diadem returned to us for years.
>
> "You can keep a few things for yourself from her collection, but I'd advise against too much distraction. Nixylanna has been a problem for me for a long time because she is very good at what she does. And remember: you cannot trust her."

Goldenbeard relates the information from "Adventure Background"—though told from his perspective. He explains the diadem is of only moderate value and has no magical properties, but its connection to his family and his history with Vidorant make it valuable to him.

If the characters are uninterested in membership in the Silver Fingers, Goldenbeard offers a reward of 2,000 gp, though he grumbles the reward is far more than the diadem is worth.

Preparation

The party's preparation for the heist might include seeking information from Vidorant's former guards, surveilling Vidorant at her mansion, or staking out her vault. Though each approach can yield useful information, the characters shouldn't delay too much; other Silver Fingers may also be preparing to steal the diadem (at your discretion).

Gathering Intelligence

By combing through local pubs or asking around with their own informants, the characters can locate up to six guards (**veterans**) formerly employed by Vidorant. Use the Former Guards table to help you roleplay each guard.

FORMER GUARDS

d6	Ex-Guard
1	Turolga Flathelm (neutral dwarf), a gruff woman who has a soft spot for stray cats
2	Ballidyr Josephon (neutral human), a pompous man who refers to himself in the third person
3	Jeniana Damaritz (lawful neutral human), an aloof woman who talks to only the most well-dressed of the characters
4	Pelten Kiwaris (chaotic neutral human), a gregarious person who invites the characters to join them at a party
5	Kavton Bouldersight (neutral halfling), a jocular man who sells stolen goods
6	Breelen Fibblezot (chaotic neutral gnome), a cheerful woman who fidgets constantly

To convince a former guard to share information about the vault and its defenses, a character can make a DC 12 Charisma (Persuasion) check or another appropriate ability check, depending on their approach. A character who offers a bribe of 10 gp reduces the DC of this check by 5.

On a failed check, the former guard walks away, disinterested in further conversation. If other characters approach the guard later, the guard remains unwilling to share information about the vault.

On a successful check, the character convinces the former guard to reveal the basic layout of the vault's first floor, as shown on map 8.1. The guard also answers simple questions about Vidorant and her physical appearance, the guard uniforms, and other information every guard would know.

If the check succeeds by 5 or more, the character also learns one of the following pieces of information:

- The basic layout of the vault's second floor, as shown on map 8.1
- The location of the secret door between area T3 and the building's exterior
- The password to bypass the conjuration rune in area T9: "quixotic"
- The location of a switch to disable one trap (either the pit trap in area T3 or the statues in area T6)
- The guard rotation (detailed in "Vault Guards")

SURVEILLING THE TARGET

If the characters spy on Vidorant, they can find her at her mansion in a well-to-do neighborhood near the vault. This doesn't yield useful information about the vault, but the characters can get a good glimpse of Vidorant and several associates, which can aid the characters in creating disguises.

Vidorant is a tall elf woman with sleek black hair. She usually wears black clothes accented with tasteful but clearly valuable silver jewelry. She's brusque, authoritative, and direct, though she listens with remarkable patience and intensity whenever anyone addresses her directly.

While no one in the Silver Fingers Society would dare help Vidorant right now, she still has a few informants and cronies from outside the organization. If the characters watch her long enough, they see meetings with four people: a muscular half-orc woman in a fine suit and hat, a sneering human man carrying a large leather case, an unkempt halfling man with patched clothing, and a smiling elf woman who bears a striking resemblance to Vidorant but is noticeably younger. Learning the identities of these associates would take additional sleuthing.

CASING THE JOINT

If the characters scout the vault before the heist, read or paraphrase the following:

> The vault stands in a rundown neighborhood, but the street and alleyways around the vault are unobstructed. Small windows glint from high on the vault's stone walls. Two guards keep watch on the second-floor balcony, while another guard patrols around the structure at ground level.

Vidorant's vault is an unmarked building on the city outskirts in an area with moderate foot traffic. The neighboring buildings stand at least 20 feet from the vault and don't share walls with it. Nearby businesses include a jewelry store, a lumberyard, a brewery, and a forge. Several other nearby buildings are empty and are ideal locations for a stakeout.

If the characters observe the vault before the heist, they learn the general exterior layout, including the locations of the main door, balcony door, and windows. They also get a good look at the guard uniforms—dark blue with gold stitching—which can aid in creating disguises.

If the characters venture within 30 feet of the south side of the building, they hear animal noises coming from the zoo (area T8), and a character who succeeds on a DC 15 Intelligence (Investigation) or Wisdom (Perception) check finds the secret door leading from the exterior to the gem room (area T3).

If the characters observe the vault for at least 4 hours, they learn two guards are always on duty on the balcony, accessed via a rope ladder the guards leave hanging down to ground level. The characters also learn the basic exterior and interior guard rotation (detailed in "Vault Guards").

The Vault

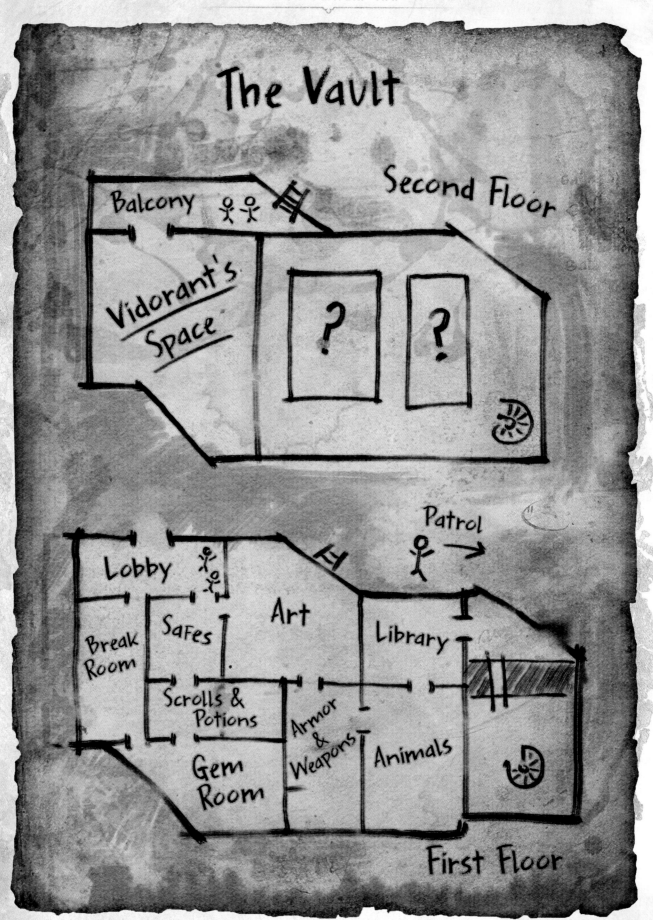

Second Floor

Balcony

Vidorant's Space

? ?

Patrol

Lobby

Break Room

Safes

Art

Library

Scrolls & Potions

Armor & Weapons

Gem Room

Animals

First Floor

The Vault

On the day (or night) of the heist, nothing notable has changed from the party's previous surveillance. If the characters didn't visit the vault earlier during their preparations, read the read-aloud text from "Casing the Joint" as they approach the vault.

Vault Features

Vidorant's vault has the following features.

Ceilings

Ceilings throughout the vault are 15 feet high.

Doors

Doors in the vault are made of wood, except for the inner vault's metal door.

Locked Doors. As an action, a character can try to unlock a locked door in the vault, doing so with a successful Dexterity check using thieves' tools, or force the door open with a successful Strength (Athletics) check. Either check's DC is 15 unless the text states otherwise.

Light

Unless otherwise noted, all areas are brightly lit by lamps imbued with *continual flame* spells.

Walls and Floors

The vault's walls and floors are made of thick stone. The characters can use the *stone shape* spell or similar magic to create a passage into the vault, though a guard patrol spots them if the characters spend more than a minute getting everyone inside. Each 10-foot section of wall has AC 15, 200 hit points, and immunity to poison and psychic damage. Damaging the wall catches the attention of the guards unless the characters take extraordinary measures.

Wards

The building is warded against teleportation and planar travel. Effects like the *dimension door* spell can't be used to enter, exit, or move within the building.

Windows

Areas T2, T3, T7, T8, and T9 have windows 10 feet above the ground, and area T13 has a window 20 feet above the ground. Each window is locked and can be unlocked easily from the inside. As an action, a character can use thieves' tools to try to unlock a window from the outside, doing so with a successful DC 16 Dexterity check.

Each window is warded with an abjuration rune that sounds an audible alarm if the window opens (see "Caught in the Act"). A character who searches a window for traps notices the rune with a successful DC 10 Wisdom (Perception) check and can use an action to try to disable it, doing so with a successful DC 14 Intelligence (Arcana) check or a *dispel magic* spell. A character who disables the alarm on one window can do the same on other vault windows without having to repeat the check.

The windows are too small for a Medium creature to climb through, but a Small creature can squeeze through one with a successful DC 20 Dexterity (Acrobatics) check.

Vault Guards

Vidorant employs a dozen guards (use the **veteran** stat block) to protect her treasures—three guards outside and nine inside the vault. Guards remain alert for noises elsewhere in the vault, and if the characters do something particularly loud, a guard might investigate at your discretion.

Exterior Security

Characters who learned the guard rotation in the "Preparation" section know two guards are posted on the balcony and one guard patrols around the outside of the building at ground level.

A character can avoid the notice of the exterior guards with a successful DC 12 Dexterity (Stealth) check. An effective distraction might lower the DC or even bypass this check entirely. At night, the DC of this check decreases to 9.

Interior Security

Characters who learned the guard rotation in the "Preparation" section know two guards are posted in the lobby, seven guards patrol the first floor of the vault, and no guards patrol upstairs.

Rather than requiring you to track each patrolling guard's location, this adventure represents the guards moving about the vault by having you roll to determine whether a guard is present in any given room. In areas specified as part of the guard rotation, roll a d4 to determine if a guard is present when the characters approach that room. On a 1, a guard is present in that room. If the characters learned the guard rotation in the "Preparation" section, roll a d6 instead of a d4, reflecting their increased ability to avoid the guards.

If the characters spend more than 10 minutes in any room that's part of the guard rotation, a guard interrupts them. Any character who has a passive Wisdom (Perception) score of 14 or higher hears the guard coming 2 rounds before the guard enters the room.

Evading Guards

When guards are present in an area, characters can resolve encounters without resorting to combat. Some examples are listed below, though the characters may come up with creative alternatives:

Bluffing. A character can lie their way past a guard with a successful DC 16 Charisma (Deception) check. If the party's preparations convincingly support their story—such as wearing guard uniforms while claiming they're new guards—the DC decreases to 12.

Bribing. A character can convince a guard to look the other way with a 50 gp bribe and a successful DC 10 Charisma (Persuasion) check.

Hiding. Before entering a room, a character can tell if a guard is present by listening at the door and succeeding on a DC 15 Wisdom (Perception) check. The party can make a DC 14 group Dexterity (Stealth) check to hide in their current room until the guards leave. On a successful check, the guard leaves without noticing the characters, allowing the party to enter the next room undetected. On a failed check, the guard discovers the characters, likely by entering the room the characters are in and spotting them.

Intimidation. A character can frighten a guard into letting them pass with a successful DC 17 Charisma (Intimidation) check.

If you wish, a character who succeeds on one of the above checks by 5 or more might also learn one piece of information from the "Gathering Intelligence" section, perhaps by overhearing a conversation or persuading a guard to share it.

Caught in the Act

If the characters are spotted by a guard and don't talk their way out of it, the guard yells loudly for backup and attempts to run away, taking the Dash action. The guard returns 3 rounds later with an additional 1d4 + 1 guards (unless there aren't that many guards left). The guards (use the **veteran** stat block) fight until reduced to 10 hit points, then flee.

If the characters set off any audible alarms in the building, a guard immediately investigates, arriving 3 rounds after the alarm sounds. The alarm also puts the guards on high alert throughout the vault. For 1 hour after an alarm sounds, when rolling to determine if a guard is present in a room, roll two dice instead of one; if either result is a 1, a guard is present. Additionally, the DC on checks made to nonviolently deal with guards increases by 2 (see "Evading Guards"), and the price to bribe a guard increases to 100 gp.

Changing of the Guard

If the characters neutralize all nine interior guards, the party has the run of the building until the next shift's guards show up. However, the three guards outside the building remain alert to loud noises inside the vault and enter the building to investigate suspicious sounds. A new shift starts every four hours, and six guards show up at each shift change.

Vault Locations

The following locations are keyed to map 8.2.

T1: Lobby

> This beautifully decorated lobby has stone floors polished to a mirror finish. To the west, a large statue depicts a human woman wielding a bow and arrow. To the east, two comfortable chairs accompany a small table. A double door leads outside to the north, and two doors on the south wall lead into the vault.

Guards. Two guards watch the unlocked front door while sitting in the lobby's chairs. Though suspicious of people trying to get in, they're accustomed to confused people occasionally entering the unmarked building.

Locked Door. The door to area T5 is locked.

T2: Break Room

> This break room smells faintly of sweat and greasy food. Scuffed wooden furniture and a large couch provide comfort for off-duty guards.

The room includes a table and chairs for eating, a couch and several chairs for lounging, and a privy. A trunk on the east wall contains a dozen spare guard uniforms.

Guards. Two off-duty guards are playing cards at the table. They aren't expecting to be interrupted, and each has a passive Wisdom (Perception) score of 7. If the characters try a nonviolent approach (as detailed in the "Evading Guards" section), the DC of those checks decreases by 2 against the off-duty guards.

Locked Door. The door to area T3 is locked. Each guard in the vault has a key that unlocks this door.

T3: Gem Room

> This room contains open crates of gems sorted by color and type. Most are neatly faceted, though a few remain uncut.

Guards. This room is part of the guard rotation. Roll to determine if a guard is present (as described in "Interior Security").

Locked Door. The door to area T2 is locked. Each guard in the vault has a key that unlocks this door.

Secret Door. The southwest wall of this room contains a secret door to the exterior. Vidorant uses this door often. A character who examines the wall

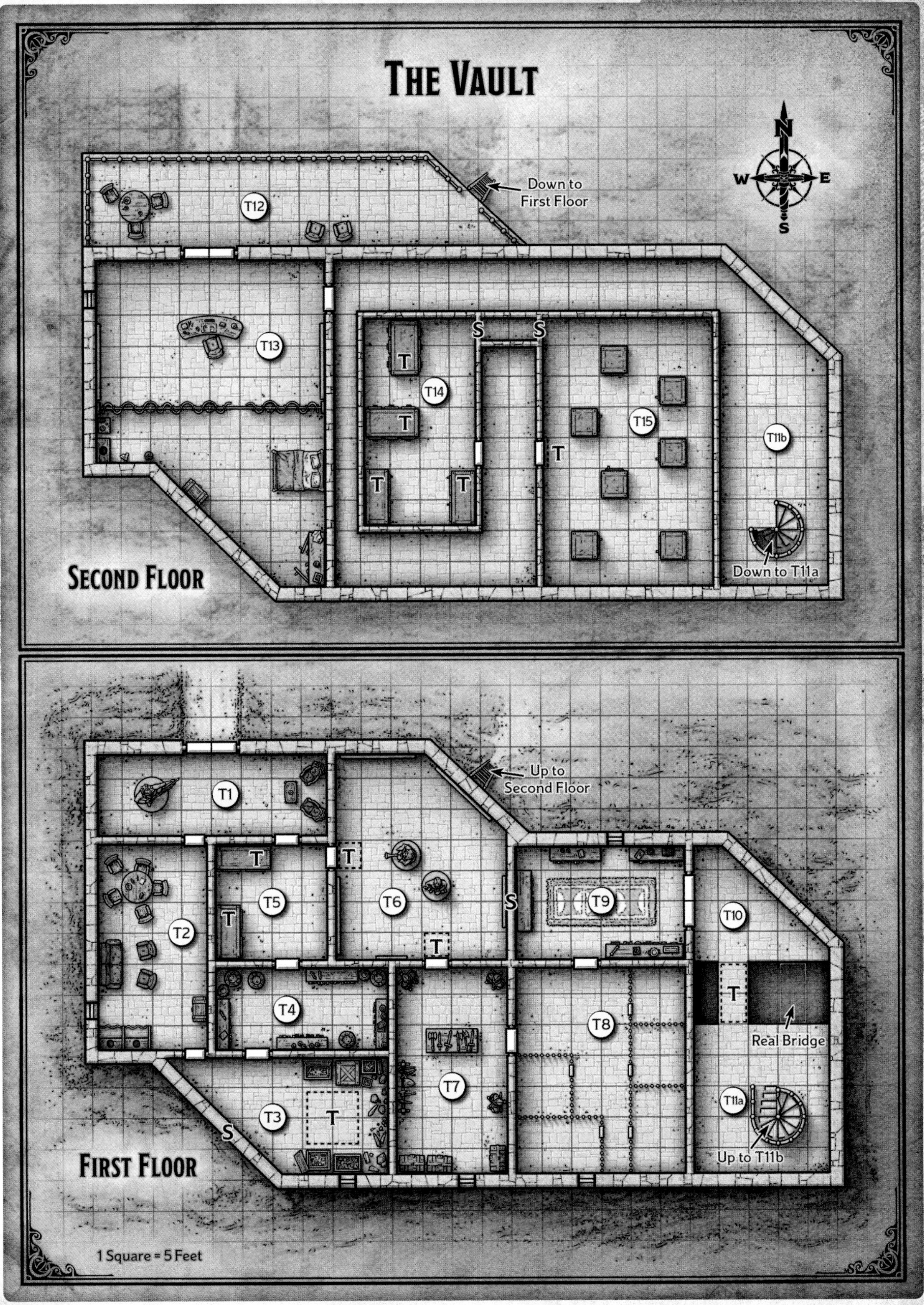
The Vault
N
W
E
S
Down to
First Floor
T12
T13
T14
T15
T11b
S
S
T
T
T
T
T
Down to T11a
Second Floor
Up to
Second Floor
T1
T2
T3
T4
T5
T6
T7
T8
T9
T10
T11a
T
T
T
T
T
S
S
Real Bridge
Up to T11b
First Floor
1 Square = 5 Feet

MIKE SCHLEY

and succeeds on a DC 15 Wisdom (Perception) check spots the door, which opens silently.

Trap. Any character who has a passive Wisdom (Perception) score of 15 or higher notices the floor is unusually clean in a 10-foot square in front of the gem crates. When a creature steps on this area, the floor collapses into a 10-foot-deep pit with poisoned spikes lining its floor. Any creature on the collapsing floor falls into the pit, taking 3 (1d6) bludgeoning damage and landing prone. In addition, the creature must succeed on a DC 14 Dexterity saving throw or be impaled by 1d3 spikes, each of which deals 3 (1d6) piercing damage plus 7 (2d6) poison damage.

A character who searches the floor for traps and succeeds on a DC 15 Wisdom (Perception) check detects the trap, which can be disabled by placing a strong object such as a pole or crowbar between the floor panels. If the check made to detect the trap succeeds by 5 or more, the character also spots a concealed switch on one wall that disables the trap.

Treasure. The crates hold 60 pounds of gemstones. The valuable gems include a large uncut diamond (1,000 gp), four small diamonds (100 gp each), a bag of diamond dust (300 gp), four flawed rubies (50 gp each), and four pearls (100 gp each). The remainder of the semiprecious stones in the crates are worth a total of 1,000 gp.

T4: SCROLLS AND POTIONS ROOM

> This room has four short bookshelves, each bearing eight glass vials of liquid. Several open barrels hold rolled-up sheets of parchment.

Guards. This room is part of the guard rotation. Roll to determine if a guard is present (as described in "Interior Security").

Shelves of Potions. The four shelves each hold eight potions in vials (see "Treasure" below). Any character who has a passive Wisdom (Perception) score of 18 or higher notices the shelves are precariously balanced. To safely remove a potion from a shelf, someone must steady the shelf with a successful DC 12 Dexterity (Sleight of Hand) check or the shelf collapses, shattering all the potion vials on it. Each creature within 5 feet of a collapsing shelf must make a DC 12 Dexterity saving throw, taking 17 (5d6) acid damage on a failed save, or half as much damage on a successful one. The noise alerts the guards in the lobby (area T1), who arrive 2 rounds later to investigate.

Treasure. The shelves contain twenty-six vials of acid, a *potion of animal friendship*, two *potions of healing* (greater), two *potions of resistance* (one fire, the other poison), and one *potion of water breathing*.

The sheets of parchment in the barrels include *spell scrolls* for each of the following spells: *charm person* (2 scrolls), *cure wounds* (1 scroll), *detect magic* (2 scrolls), *dispel magic* (1 scroll), *false life* (1 scroll), *identify* (4 scrolls), *invisibility* (1 scroll), *lesser restoration* (2 scrolls), and *nondetection* (1 scroll).

T5: DOCUMENTS ROOM

> This room holds two large iron safes.

Guards. This room is part of the guard rotation. Roll to determine if a guard is present (as described in "Interior Security").

Locked Door. The door to area T1 is locked. Each guard in the vault has a key that unlocks this door.

Trapped Safes. The two document safes in this room contain secret information about local nobles and government officials. Each safe is trapped with enchantment magic. If a creature attempts to open a safe without Vidorant's personal key, the safe's trap emits an audible alarm (see "Caught in the Act") and casts *hold person* (save DC 16) on the three creatures nearest the safe. A character who uses an action to search the safe for traps notices the trap's rune with a successful DC 15 Wisdom (Perception) check. Once the trap is detected, a character can use an action to try to disarm the trap, doing so with a successful DC 16 Intelligence (Arcana) check or a *dispel magic* spell.

A character using thieves' tools can try to unlock a safe, which takes 1 minute. At the end of that time, the character must succeed on a DC 17 Dexterity check, or the safe remains locked. The safes are full of documents. Every minute a character spends looking through the documents yields one of the following:

Bribe. A tattered parchment details how a prisoner, jailed for stealing racehorses, was freed after a noble bribed a local government official.

Disputed Will. A parchment bears the original will of a recently deceased local noble. As the noble's family members are currently fighting over the estate, this will would be of great value to the heirs named in it.

Goldenbeard's Secret. Small scraps of parchment hold notes from Goldenbeard. Though Vidorant's half of the correspondence is absent, the notes suggest Vidorant and Goldenbeard plotted a fake heist and used their "breathtaking success" to gain entrance to the Silver Fingers Society. Vidorant didn't use this information while vying for control of the Silver Fingers, as it implicated her too, but nothing would stop her from using it now.

Love Letters. Several perfumed envelopes hold romantic letters between a local noble and a government official. The affair would be a scandal if revealed.

None of the documents in the safe have intrinsic monetary value, though they could be used to gain money or influence through blackmail.

T6: Gallery

Landscape paintings cover the walls of this room. In the center of the floor stand two marble statues of a human man and woman, both holding musical instruments. One statue faces the door to the south, and the other faces the door to the west.

Fire-Breathing Statues. When a creature steps on a square marked T on map 8.2, the statue closest to that square breathes magical fire, which fills the two squares between the statue and the door nearest to it. Any creature in that area must make a DC 15 Dexterity saving throw, taking 22 (4d10) fire damage on a failed save, or half as much damage on a successful one.

As an action, a character can search a trapped area and make a DC 15 Intelligence (Investigation) check. If this check succeeds, the character finds a tiny switch on the wall next to the nearest door. Flipping the switch temporarily disables whichever statue breathes fire toward that door. The trap reactivates 1 minute later.

Guards. This room is part of the guard rotation. Roll to determine if a guard is present (as described in "Interior Security"). Guards enter the room only via its secret passage, and they leave through either of the main doors after flipping the switch to temporarily disable the traps.

Secret Door. A character who inspects the paintings and succeeds on a DC 15 Intelligence (Investigation) check discovers a large painting on the east wall pivots—along with the bookshelf on the other side of the wall—revealing a secret way to area T9.

Treasure. Four 12-foot-wide paintings (400 gp each) and a smaller 2-foot-wide painting (1,000 gp) are on display. A character who examines them and succeeds on a DC 15 Intelligence (History) check recognizes the small painting is by a famous artist and is significantly more valuable than the others.

T7: Armory

Three suits of armor stand against the walls with swords in hand, watching over this armory. Three large chests sit along the south wall.

The two easternmost suits of armor are **helmed horrors**. They attack creatures (other than Vidorant) that aren't wearing guard uniforms. They obey Vidorant's spoken commands. If she's not present, they obey anyone wearing a guard uniform, even if commanded to attack another guard. They don't leave this room, and they ignore orders that would cause them to do so.

Guards. This room is part of the guard rotation. Roll to determine if a guard is present (as described in "Interior Security").

Treasure. The chests hold more weapons. Most of the equipment in this room is nonmagical, but a character who is proficient with smith's tools or who succeeds on a DC 17 Intelligence (Arcana) check immediately spots the most finely crafted items: a *+1 battleaxe*, a *+1 shortsword*, and a suit of *+1 scale mail*.

T8: Zoo

This room contains five large cages holding unusual creatures. It smells of fur and feathers. Chirps, grunts, and howls fill the air.

Cages. Each cage has a door held shut by a rudimentary latch. One contains exotic birds. Another holds two **giant lizards** and six **flying snakes**. A third contains harmless mammals, including jerboas, chinchillas, and a capybara. The last two cages each hold one **displacer beast**. The giant lizards, flying snakes, and displacer beasts are aggressive but accustomed to being placated with food by Vidorant and the guards.

Guards. This room is part of the guard rotation. Roll to determine if a guard is present (as described in "Interior Security"). Any guard in this room carries food for the animals.

T9: Library

This room smells strongly of incense and paper. It has several bookshelves filled with antique books. A large, embroidered rug covers the floor.

A character who has a passive Wisdom (Perception) score of 18 or higher notices a conjuration rune peeking from under the rug. After discovering it, a character can use an action to try to disable the rune, doing so with a successful DC 18 Intelligence (Arcana) check or a *dispel magic* spell.

If a creature steps on the rug without saying the password, "quixotic," the rune summons an **invisible stalker**. The invisible stalker doesn't reveal its presence or attack immediately, waiting to do so until the characters either remove a book from the room or try to cross the spiked pit in area T10.

Guards. This room is part of the guard rotation. Roll to determine if a guard is present (as described in "Interior Security"). The guard uses the password if forced to step onto the rug.

Secret Door. A character who inspects the bookshelves and succeeds on a DC 15 Intelligence (Investigation) check discovers the bookshelf to the west pivots—along with the painting on the other side—revealing a secret way to the gallery (area T6).

Treasure. Most books in this room have no monetary value, but three of the oldest books are worth 500 gp each. A character can identify these valuable books if they spend 5 minutes examining them and succeed on a DC 14 Intelligence (History) check:

Adventures of the Mystique (first edition, mint condition) is a transcription of a first mate's logbook, which recounts several harrowing adventures aboard a galleon called the *Mystique*.

The Diabolical Codex (covered in spined devil hide), written by a tiefling named Nadir, provides tips and tricks for surviving bargains with devils.

Eight for Dinner (first edition, signed by the author) is a murder mystery in which an inquisitive mind flayer detective solves a murder aboard a planar locomotive called the Concordant Express.

T10: Pit

> A ten-foot-wide pit with spikes at the bottom divides this room from east to west. A sturdy-looking stone bridge spans the pit. The room is dimly lit by a flickering lamp on the north wall. Near it, a double door leads west. On the south side of the pit is a spiral metal staircase going up.

Guards don't patrol this room. If the invisible stalker was summoned in the library and hasn't attacked yet, it attempts to shove a character into the pit, then attacks the party.

Illusions. Two permanent *silent image* spells have been cast over the pit, one on the east side and another on the west. The illusion on the west side depicts a bridge spanning the pit. The illusion on the east side shows an open pit, hiding a real bridge that can be used to safely cross. Touching the fake bridge (which is shown on map 8.2) reveals that it has no substance. Similarly, feeling around the pit for the real bridge reveals it in short order. Casting *dispel magic* on either illusion ends it.

Spiked Pit. Any creature that falls into the pit is impaled by 1d3 spikes, each of which deals 3 (1d6) piercing damage plus 7 (2d6) poison damage.

T11A–B: Stairwell

> A spiral metal staircase ascends gracefully, connecting the first and second floors. A flickering lamp casts dim light on the stairs.

Guards don't patrol this area.

T12: Balcony

> On the second floor's large balcony, a table and chairs allow for dining while enjoying a lovely view of the city. The view is unimpeded by a low railing. To the east, a rope ladder hangs from the balcony to the ground fifteen feet below. A double door leads into the building.

A creature that falls off the balcony can catch the railing with a successful DC 16 Dexterity saving throw. On a failed save, the creature falls to the ground 15 feet below, taking 3 (1d6) bludgeoning damage from the fall.

Guards. Two guards are posted here. During shift changes, guards access the balcony via the rope ladder and never enter area T13. A guard who notices suspicious activity below uses an action to pull up the rope ladder.

Locked Door. The double door to area T13 is locked. The balcony guards have a key but use it only if they detect intruders inside.

Vidorant. If Vidorant teleports to the vault (see the "Vidorant Arrives" section later in the adventure), she arrives on the balcony, as the interior of the vault is warded against teleportation magic.

T13: Vidorant's Quarters

> The north half of these luxurious living quarters holds a study area with a fine desk and two beautiful paintings of night festivals. A delicate curtain opening to the south reveals a sleeping area. The bed is piled high with sumptuous linens. This area also holds a sturdy wooden wardrobe and a privy.

Guards don't patrol this room, the eastern door of which is unlocked. Though Vidorant lives in a mansion nearby, she sometimes sleeps here after working late in her vault. Her bedroom includes a wardrobe with several changes of clothes, which could be useful if a character wants to fashion a disguise.

Desk. Vidorant's desk drawer is locked. As an action, a character can use thieves' tools to try to unlock it, doing so with a successful DC 15 Dexterity check. The desk contains many documents.

DISGUISED AS A VAULT GUARD, AN ADVENTURER SETS HIS SIGHTS ON THE PRECIOUS RUBY DIADEM OF ERLYNN BLESSEDORE.

A character who examines them for 1 minute and succeeds on a DC 15 Intelligence (Investigation) check finds the plans for Vidorant's next heist, targeting a noble with close ties to Goldenbeard.

Locked Door. The door to area T12 is locked but easily unlocked from inside this room.

Treasure. The two paintings of night festivals are worth 250 gp each.

T14: STRONG ROOM

> This room contains four large metal cabinets.

Guards don't patrol this unlocked room.

Secret Passage. Any character who has a passive Wisdom (Perception) score of 18 or higher notices that the hallway between areas T14 and T15 doesn't extend as far north as this room does. A character who searches the northeast corner of the room can make a DC 15 Wisdom (Perception) check, finding a secret door on a success. Beyond it is a passage ending at another secret door. No ability check is required to spot the door from inside the passage. Characters can use this route to enter area T15 and avoid the trap there.

Trapped Cabinets. All four cabinets in this room are locked and trapped. A character who examines the cabinets for 1 minute can make a DC 15 Intelligence (Investigation) check, finding all four traps on a success. Inside each cabinet is a delicate glass vial containing poison gas. The vial breaks if the cabinet is opened by any means other than using the proper key (which is in Vidorant's possession). A character can use thieves' tools to try to disarm one of these traps, doing so with a successful DC 18 Dexterity check. Failing the check by 5 or more triggers the trap.

A character can use thieves' tools to try to unlock a cabinet, doing so with a successful DC 15 Dexterity check. However, if the trap hasn't been disarmed, the cabinet releases its poison gas. The gas from one vial is enough to fill the room but dissipates quickly. Each creature in the room when the gas is released must succeed on a DC 12 Constitution saving throw or take 11 (2d10) poison damage.

Treasure. Each cabinet holds 1,000 gp.

T15: INNER VAULT

This room's main door, situated in the middle of the west wall, is locked (DC 18 to open) and made of metal.

Trap. Just behind the door, inside the room, is an electrically charged metal wire resembling a trip wire. When the door opens, it makes contact with the wire. Any creature touching the door takes 22 (4d10) lightning damage from the shock. The wire then snaps, disabling the trap. The trap is easy to disarm from inside the room (no check required), but it can't be disarmed from outside the room.

Characters can avoid the trap by entering the room through a secret door in the northwest corner (see area T14).

> This room has marble flooring and ivory-colored wall-paper with silver accents. The room contains seven glass cases on pedestals, each enclosing a small item.

Display Cases. On each case, a notecard written in elegant handwriting bears the item's name and a brief description:

Jeweled Human Skull. The card reads, "Unclear if genuine skull or replica. Found in ancient tomb." This skull is coated with gold. Large diamonds are mounted in its eye sockets, and small rubies drip down its cheekbones like bloody tears. (The skull is worth 2,000 gp.)

Lost Map of Tishanos. The card reads, "Reportedly from Pirate Queen Shrixette Laderie. No other records of Tishanos found. Must mount expedition." This weathered map details an island that lies about a hundred miles from an unidentified coastline. (The map has no intrinsic monetary value but could lead to adventure.)

Royal Scepter. The card reads, "Used in the coronation of Queen Calinia. Possible gift from elven court." This golden scepter is intricately engraved and set with diamonds and sapphires. (The scepter is worth 2,000 gp.)

Ruby Diadem of Erlynn Blessedore. The card reads, "Owned by Queen Erlynn Blessedore, ancestor of Samphith." Each spire of the diadem is studded with rubies. (The diadem is worth 2,000 gp.)

Silvered Dagger. The card reads, "Used to assassinate Prince Angryn Sheselitte. Nonmagical." This dagger is unremarkable, though high quality. (The dagger is worth 1,000 gp as a collector's item.)

Snowy's Collar. The card reads, "Owned by legendary fortune-teller Gratchia Gartirio. Dog reportedly told the future." This fine silk collar, sized for a small dog, has a diamond-encrusted tag reading "Snowy." (The collar is worth 1,000 gp.)

Thesis of Mortinsor. The card reads, "Owned by Mortinsor, the famous necromancer. Possibly contains secrets of longevity, but difficult to decipher." This oversized tome is full of esoteric, archaic text that would require extensive research to decipher. A character who spends 12 weeks studying it and succeeds on a DC 22 Intelligence (Arcana) check finds a page that serves as a *spell scroll* of *sequester.* (The thesis is worth 500 gp.)

Each item is protected by two separate abjuration runes that trigger *alarm* spells. The first rune is on the display case, and it sounds an audible alarm when that display case is opened (see "Caught in the Act"). The second rune is on the item itself, and it silently alerts Vidorant when that item is removed from the room (see "Vidorant Arrives" below).

A character who examines the various treasures and succeeds on a DC 15 Wisdom (Perception) check notices the first set of runes on all the display cases. A character who succeeds on this check by 5 or more also notices the second set of runes on the items themselves.

A character can disable a particular rune (and its linked *alarm* spell) with the *dispel magic* spell or a successful DC 18 Intelligence (Arcana) check. A character who fails the check by 5 or more triggers the alarm. The first time a character successfully disables one of these runes, the DC to do so on the others decreases to 13. Alternatively, a character can slip an item out of its case without triggering the display case alarm by succeeding on a DC 18 Dexterity (Sleight of Hand) check. On a failed check, the audible alarm activates (see "Caught in the Act").

VIDORANT ARRIVES

Once the characters obtain the diadem, they must escape the vault to complete the heist.

If Vidorant (chaotic neutral, elf **assassin**) is alerted to the theft by an alarm in her inner vault (area T15), she uses a custom-made ring that functions as a *helm of teleportation* (to which only she can attune) to teleport to the balcony 5 rounds after the alarm is triggered. She heads toward the characters while calling loudly for the guards. The balcony guards follow her, and all other guards in the vault go on high alert (see "Caught in the Act").

VIDORANT'S OFFER

If Vidorant intercepts the characters, she makes a surprising offer:

> An elf woman with sleek black hair approaches you with a smile. "You've done well. Not just any thieves could make it to my personal vault. I congratulate you. I'm sure this means the Silver Fingers placed a bounty on that ruby diadem—Goldenbeard's been furious about that thing for years. But if you'll allow me a moment, perhaps I can make you a better offer?"

If the characters refuse to hear her deal, Vidorant attacks them. If they agree to listen to her deal, she continues speaking:

"I could try to dispatch you—and I might succeed—but more thieves will keep trying to interfere with my business. Instead, what if you went back and told everyone my vault was impenetrable and I thoroughly defeated you? It would head off a lot of trouble. In exchange, I'll give you this." She pulls a delicate ring from her finger. "It's worth more to you than the diadem—after all, it's part of how I've become such a famous thief. Goldenbeard is planning to take the diadem for himself, right? He's still mad about our heist all those years ago. But this ring you can keep. Tell whatever story you like about where you got it, as long as it's not from me. You get rich, I look strong, and no one's the wiser."

The ring is a *ring of evasion*. If the characters agree to Vidorant's terms or negotiate her into a reasonable compromise, she upholds her part of the deal.

If Vidorant knows the characters have taken items of significant value from her vault, she suggests an even better deal: if they return the most valuable items they stole, she'll also give them her *gloves of thievery*, which she's currently wearing invisibly on her hands.

If all parties agree, she hands over the ring (and possibly the gloves) in exchange for the diadem, then escorts the characters outside, loudly bragging about their defeat and threatening violence if she ever sees them again.

CONCLUSION

If the characters return the diadem to Goldenbeard, he offers them lifetime membership in the Silver Fingers Society. He also promises them a personal favor they can redeem next time they need help with a situation. If the party prefers a cash reward instead, he happily obliges and still promises a favor.

If the characters took Vidorant's deal or decided to keep the diadem for themselves, they must succeed on a DC 16 Charisma (Deception) check to convince Goldenbeard they were unable to retrieve the diadem. If Goldenbeard realizes they're lying to him, he grows very serious. He doesn't attack the party himself; instead, he uses the Silver Fingers Society to steal back the diadem or otherwise make the characters' lives difficult.

If the characters fool him or were simply unable to recover the diadem, Goldenbeard is disappointed, but he reassures the characters there will be other opportunities to work together in the future.

NIXYLANNA VIDORANT

BLACKMAILING GOLDENBEARD

If the characters found the blackmail material regarding Goldenbeard in Vidorant's safe and they bring it up with him, his face goes blank and he responds:

"I see. She couldn't reveal that without implicating herself, but you have no such hesitation. I have no comment on its truth—but it would be messy if revealed. I am willing to buy this from you."

He offers the characters 1,000 gp for the original copy of Vidorant's blackmail material. A character who succeeds on a DC 17 Charisma (Intimidation or Persuasion) check convinces him to increase his payment to 2,000 gp.

FOR THE GOLDEN VAULT

If the characters are working for the Golden Vault and they return the diadem to Goldenbeard, the organization offers the characters a rare magic item of their choice (subject to your approval) as payment. The item is delivered to the characters the next day.

AN UNEARTHED TOMB HOLDS THE KEY TO
SAVING A NEARBY TOWN, AS ADVENTURERS
ARE ABOUT TO DISCOVER.

AN ADVENTURE FOR 8TH-LEVEL CHARACTERS

SHARD OF THE ACCURSED

A MYSTERIOUS SHARD MADE OF OBSIDIAN places a curse on everyone who bears it. When the shard comes into the characters' possession, they must break its curse by returning the shard to the ancient tomb it came from. But a dangerous crime syndicate controls the tomb and its riches, and the criminals won't take kindly to the characters' intrusion.

This adventure isn't a typical heist; rather, it's a reverse heist. Instead of retrieving a valuable item, the characters are tasked with returning one to its proper place.

ADVENTURE BACKGROUND

Long ago, a giant named Xeluan was attacked by his ruthless kin and left to die. After a group of heroes found him and nursed him back to health, the grateful giant pledged his life in their service. Xeluan and his heroic friends went on to perform great deeds.

When earthquakes and volcanic eruptions threatened to destroy the heroes' homeland, Xeluan carved a citadel into a mountainside, creating a refuge for the heroes and their people. The giant harnessed earth magic to create a protective ward around the settlement, but the devastation proved unstoppable. As the mountain crumbled and volcanic rifts threatened to engulf those he loved, Xeluan lifted the sanctuary above his shoulders and made a final, desperate sacrifice. He wove his life energy into the magic protecting the citadel, allowing it to withstand the onslaught. In doing so, Xeluan sacrificed his life to save thousands.

After the calamity, the heroes looked for the giant amid the changed landscape. They found his petrified body buried beneath the citadel, still holding it aloft. When all efforts to restore him failed, the heroes built a mausoleum around Xeluan's body to honor his sacrifice. The heroes lived prosperous lives, and afterward, their bodies were interred in Xeluan's tomb. When the last hero died, the tomb was sealed, and so it remained for centuries. Xeluan's sacrifice was lost to legend, and the heroes were remembered only as fables. As the citadel eroded to ruins, the tomb below it was all but forgotten.

About a century ago, a group of explorers found the ruins of the citadel, its protective wards still intact. Around the citadel, these explorers founded the settlement of Oztocan. The settlement grew into a thriving hub of commerce. Today, that prosperity is threatened by the machinations of a criminal organization known as the Onyx Scar. The criminals have unearthed Xeluan's tomb and are mining the giant's petrified corpse, selling his remains at local markets. Additionally, their delving has weakened the citadel's wards, causing earthquakes to plague the region.

THE ACCURSED SHARD

This adventure revolves around an obsidian shard imbued with powerful magic. In the course of the adventure, the characters discover that the shard is a fragment of Xeluan's petrified heart. Only by using the shard to mend Xeluan's broken heart can they stop the earthquakes that rock Oztocan.

SHARD OF XELUAN

SHARD RUMORS

Some of this adventure's impact relies on the mis-understood nature of the *shard of Xeluan*. No one remembers Xeluan's sacrifice or knows the shard is a fragment of his petrified heart. Moreover, the shard has gained an undeservedly sinister reputa-tion because of rumors surrounding it.

Use the Shard Rumors table to inspire stories the characters might hear about the item's his-tory. Whether a rumor is true or false is left to your judgment.

SHARD RUMORS

d4	Rumor
1	The shard comes from the Abyss. The misery it causes feeds a dying, long-forgotten demon.
2	A sage who tried to learn the magical properties of the shard dropped dead without warning, and her soul became trapped in the shard.
3	A group of bandits received the shard as ransom. That night, a sickly green light bathed their camp, and all but one bandit disappeared.
4	A knight tried to destroy the shard, but the shard's curse petrified her.

SHARD DESCRIPTION

The *shard of Xeluan* is described below. Characters don't become aware of the shard's curse until it comes into play.

SHARD OF XELUAN
Wondrous Item, Rare (Requires Attunement)

This 1-foot-long shard of obsidian has veins of silver and gold beneath its cold surface.

Empowered Magic. While holding the shard, you can use it as a spellcasting focus, and it gives you a +1 bonus to your spell attack rolls.

Enhanced Strength. Your Strength score increases by 4 while the shard is on your person. The shard can't raise your Strength score above 22.

Curse. Attuning to this item extends its curse to you. You remain cursed until you are targeted by a *remove curse* spell or similar magic, or until the shard is reattached to Xeluan's petrified heart.

The shard's curse causes misfortune to befall you. When you roll a 1 on an attack roll, an ability check, or a saving throw, roll on the Shard Misfortunes table to determine the misfortune. For as long as this misfortune lasts, no other shard misfortunes befall you.

SHARD MISFORTUNES

d6	Misfortune
1	You accidentally cut yourself with the shard and are poisoned until the next dawn.
2	You experience a vision of an ancient calamity—a beautiful city threatened by crumbling mountains and erupting volcanoes—and are stunned until the end of your next turn.
3	For a few seconds, the ground shakes under you. You and each creature within 10 feet of you must succeed on a DC 16 Dexterity saving throw or be knocked prone.
4	The shard releases three glowing darts of magical force that target one random creature within 30 feet of you. If no such target exists, you become the target. Each dart hits automatically and deals 3 (1d4 + 1) force damage to the target.
5	Until the next dawn, Beasts with an Intelligence score of 3 or lower are hostile to you.
6	Nothing seems to go your way. Until the next dawn, you have disadvantage on ability checks.

Adventure Hooks

Either the Golden Vault delivers the *shard of Xeluan* to the characters at the start of the adventure (see "Using the Golden Vault" below), or the characters come to possess the shard from one of the following individuals:

Jamishka Zaril. Oztocan is an important outpost for a flourishing trade organization called the Couatl Company. Its owner, Jamishka (lawful good, elf **veteran**), recently acquired the shard and has since learned that it must be returned to the tomb from which it was taken to stop the earthquakes that threaten Oztocan. Jamishka hires the characters to bring the shard to Leandro Sedhar, a playwright in Oztocan who can help them, and promises them a suit of *elven chain* (or some other rare magic item of your choice) as payment for stopping the earthquakes.

Yana Resendes. A kindly scholar named Yana (neutral good, hobgoblin **mage**) recently acquired the shard at a market. Her investigations revealed the shard comes from Oztocan, which is beset by earthquakes. In Yana's opinion, returning the cursed shard to the place from which it was taken is the best way to stop the earthquakes. If the characters vow to complete this quest, Yana gives them a *necklace of prayer beads* (or some other rare magic item of your choice) as a token of her thanks and instructs them to bring the shard to Leandro Sedhar, a playwright in Oztocan who can help them.

Using the Golden Vault

If you're using the Golden Vault as a patron, a golden key is delivered to the characters in whatever manner you deem fit. If the characters don't already have the *shard of Xeluan* in their possession, the golden key is tied to the shard, and both objects are delivered in a stoppered lead tube.

When the golden key is used to open the music box, the lid pops open and a soothing voice says the following:

> "Greetings, operatives. Earthquakes threaten the town of Oztocan, and the Golden Vault believes the enclosed shard is the heart of the problem.
>
> "This shard was taken from the tomb of a giant named Xeluan. A criminal organization called the Onyx Scar has been plundering Xeluan's tomb and selling off its treasures. The shard passed through many hands before the Golden Vault acquired it. Whoever attunes to the shard gains great strength and magical power but also suffers misfortune due to a curse.
>
> "This quest, should you choose to undertake it, requires you travel to Oztocan with the shard, descend into Xeluan's tomb, and return the shard to its rightful place. Once you reach Oztocan, contact a playwright named Leandro Sedhar. He knows vital information about Oztocan's history and can help you reach the tomb. Good luck, operatives."

Closing the music box causes the golden key to vanish. The *shard of Xeluan* and the lead tube remain.

What Really Happened

Two decades ago, an elf archivist named Rilago found crumbling journals and architectural plans in his family's ancestral library that mentioned a tomb beneath Oztocan. The town's mayor refused to allow Rilago to mount an excavation, but the mayor's daughter, Aminta, overheard their conversation and became obsessed with finding the tomb.

Years later, the mayor passed away and his son, Tavio, was elected to replace him. Aminta, who had become involved with the Onyx Scar crime syndicate, persuaded Rilago to join her search for the tomb and convinced Tavio to overlook their endeavor. Aminta and Rilago found the tomb and Xeluan's petrified remains, but no treasure. Disappointed, they tried to profit by shattering the giant's body, only to find it indestructible.

One day, as Rilago climbed on the scaffolding surrounding Xeluan, he punched the giant's stone chest in frustration. It unexpectedly cracked open, revealing a heart of obsidian. A single shard broke off from the heart, impaling and killing Rilago.

Unbeknownst to everyone involved, Rilago was descended from one of the ancient heroes Xeluan died to protect. One of Rilago's rings was a family heirloom from that ancestor. When he punched the giant with that ring, he literally and symbolically broke Xeluan's heart, weakening the magic that protects the giant's corpse.

The formerly indestructible giant began to deteriorate, allowing Aminta to collect broken-off pieces of Xeluan's body. This material, called "oztocanite," can be worked into precious gemstones or used to empower spells (see area X4). The sale of oztocanite has become a profitable enterprise for Aminta and has increased her status in the Onyx Scar.

TOWN OF OZTOCAN

Perched on a flat between two large mountains, the town of Oztocan is surrounded by deep canyons. The town shares the warm and dry climate of the region, which has sparse vegetation and rivers that run dry most of the year.

Magic radiating from Xeluan's tomb protects the town and the surrounding region from monster attacks and destructive natural occurrences, but the wards have weakened since Xeluan's heart cracked. Earthquakes that would normally be suppressed by the magic are now being felt, raising concerns that Oztocan is no longer safe.

ARRIVAL IN OZTOCAN

As the characters approach the town, read the following:

> Built on a large flat between two rocky mountains, the town of Oztocan is cradled by the crescent-shaped ruins of a massive stone citadel. Three guards stand at the point where the dusty road meets the town.

The three **guards** eye the characters warily, but they don't stop or interfere with the party in any way. If the characters ask about Leandro Sedhar, a guard directs them to a local inn called the Giant's Skull, where Leandro is known to spend much of his time.

TREMOR

As soon as the characters enter the town, whoever is carrying the *shard of Xeluan* feels it drawn downward, as if attracted to something underground. Simultaneously, a small tremor ripples through the town, shaking dust from buildings but otherwise causing no damage. The locals appear accustomed to the quake and continue their activities unfazed.

LEANDRO SEDHAR

Asking for Leandro around town leads the characters to the Giant's Skull, a welcoming inn made of wood and adobe. Leandro has been staying here for the past few weeks.

Leandro (chaotic good **noble**) is a tabaxi—a Humanoid with feline features, including claws and a tail. He's short and stout, with lush, sand-colored fur and thin whiskers. Tiny square glasses frame his

amber eyes. He was born in a distant land but has been traveling abroad for nearly twenty years. He arrived in Oztocan a few months ago and is working on a play inspired by the town's local legends. As a playwright, he often draws inspiration from history.

WHAT LEANDRO KNOWS

Leandro welcomes the characters and takes an interest in the *shard of Xeluan* if they show it to him. He asks to see it more closely but refuses to touch it.

In the course of a conversation, Leandro shares the following information with the characters:

Earthquakes. "Oztocan hasn't felt earthquakes in years, but quakes have become common in recent weeks. No damage has been done yet, but the quakes are getting worse. It's only a matter of time before someone gets hurt."

Rilago. "Years ago, an elf archivist named Rilago claimed to have proof of a giant's tomb beneath Oztocan. Rilago tried to mount a full-scale excavation, but the mayor wouldn't allow it. Rilago stayed in Oztocan until his disappearance a few weeks ago—around the time the earthquakes began."

Tavio. "I recently spoke to the Tavio Solana, the mayor. He grew uncomfortable when I mentioned Rilago. It was Tavio's father, the previous mayor, who refused to allow the excavation of Xeluan's tomb. I don't believe Tavio had anything to do with Rilago's disappearance, but I can't help but think Tavio knows something about it."

Aminta. "Tavio's sister, Aminta, commands the town guard. Rumor has it she was involved with Rilago romantically."

LEANDRO'S SECRET

Leandro knows that Aminta is a member of the Onyx Scar, a criminal syndicate with operatives scattered throughout Oztocan. Leandro is fond of Tavio, the mayor, and doesn't want him to suffer blame for Oztocan's troubles or Aminta's criminal pursuits, so he keeps these facts to himself.

Leandro recently confronted Tavio, who admitted he has been covering up Aminta's criminal activities and her excavation of Xeluan's tomb. Guilt-ridden over the earthquakes, Tavio stole a map of Xeluan's tomb from Aminta's quarters and gave it to Leandro for safekeeping.

> ### PLACING OZTOCAN
> Oztocan is situated amid the One Flint Sierras mountain range south of San Citlán, an industrial city-state that first appeared in the adventure anthology *Journeys through the Radiant Citadel*. If your campaign takes place elsewhere in the D&D multiverse, you can insert Oztocan into any mountainous location.

LEANDRO'S MAP

If the characters seem interested in stopping the earthquakes and solving the mystery of Rilago's disappearance, Leandro shows them the map Tavio gave him. (Give the players a copy of map 9.1 now.) The map is pieced together from several torn scraps and shows most of Xeluan's tomb, minus locations that hadn't been uncovered at the time the map was drawn. Leandro informs the characters that the handwriting on the map is Rilago's.

If the characters draw Leandro's attention to the words "Heroes Rest Here" on the map's upper level, Leandro shares an Oztocan fable about a band of heroes who defended their homeland with the help of a giant. When the giant died, the heroes honored their mighty companion by building a tomb around his petrified body. Leandro doesn't know what became of the heroes, nor does history remember their names, but the giant's name was Xeluan.

CASA SOLANA

Tavio and Aminta Solana are the children of the town's previous mayor, the late Nadario Solana. Oztocan has no aristocracy, but the Solana family is the next closest thing.

If the characters want to question Tavio Solana, Leandro informs them the mayor lives in a large two-story house with his sister. Well-tended gardens surround the house, which has six guards (**veterans**). Two guards stand outside the front entrance, two stand outside the back entrance, and two are inside the house within earshot of the mayor.

Tavio Solana

Tavio Solana (neutral, human **noble**) is the amiable and easily manipulated mayor of Oztocan. In his forties, Tavio has brown skin and sports short black hair, a scruffy beard, and simple clothes. Although he is smart, he has an aversion to conflict and is filled with self-doubt.

When the characters first arrive at the Solana residence, Aminta is not present, but Tavio is in the gardens.

Approaching the Mayor. If the characters approach Tavio and politely request his help, he hesitates before telling them that he wants his sister to stop despoiling the tomb, as he believes her actions endanger the town. If the characters press him for information, Tavio laments that most of the town guard is under the sway of the Onyx Scar, except for two guards who have been with his family for years. Tavio then reveals the following information in the course of a whispered conversation:

Aminta's Whereabouts. "It grieves me to say that my sister is obsessed with plundering the tomb under Oztocan. Of late, she talks of nothing else.

She doesn't trust anyone, which is why she is overseeing the operation personally."

Cause of the Earthquakes. "Unearthing the tomb has angered the gods, who send earthquakes as warnings. If we don't heed these warnings, Oztocan will be destroyed."

Rilago's Fate. "Rilago? He was so keen to explore the tomb—he and my sister, both. Aminta told me a trap killed him—an obsidian splinter through the heart. Poor man."

Workers Needed. "Aminta needs more workers to help remove precious stones from the tomb. I'm supposed to help her find workers who know how to keep their mouths shut."

Secret Entrance. "Workers are led to and from the tomb through a guarded passage in the ruined citadel around which the town is built."

If the characters show Tavio the *shard of Xeluan*, he tells them the following:

> "That's the splinter that killed Rilago! Aminta showed it to me after pulling it from his body. She told me it's from the heart of a giant statue. How did you come to acquire it?"

Regardless of what the characters tell him, Tavio urges them to return the shard to its proper place in the tomb. He also asks them to beware his sister, whose allegiance to the Onyx Scar is absolute.

INFILTRATION PLANS

The characters have several options for infiltrating the tomb.

Infiltrating as Workers

Tavio believes the characters could most easily infiltrate Aminta's operation by posing as workers, but he warns they'll be searched on the way in. His two trustworthy guards can hide the characters' gear in a chest near the workers' quarters. If the characters agree to this, Tavio concocts an excuse to visit Aminta at the tomb. He and his guards leave the party's equipment in area X9.

Tavio directs the characters to a spot near the citadel where workers wait to be escorted to the tomb (see "Ruined Citadel").

Rilago's Notes

Other than the citadel's main entrance (on the lower level of map 9.1), Rilago's notes point to three other possible means of entry: two ventilation shafts exiting to the hills outside Oztocan (see "Ventilation Shafts") and a fountain connected to a nearby grotto (see "Ironbed Grotto").

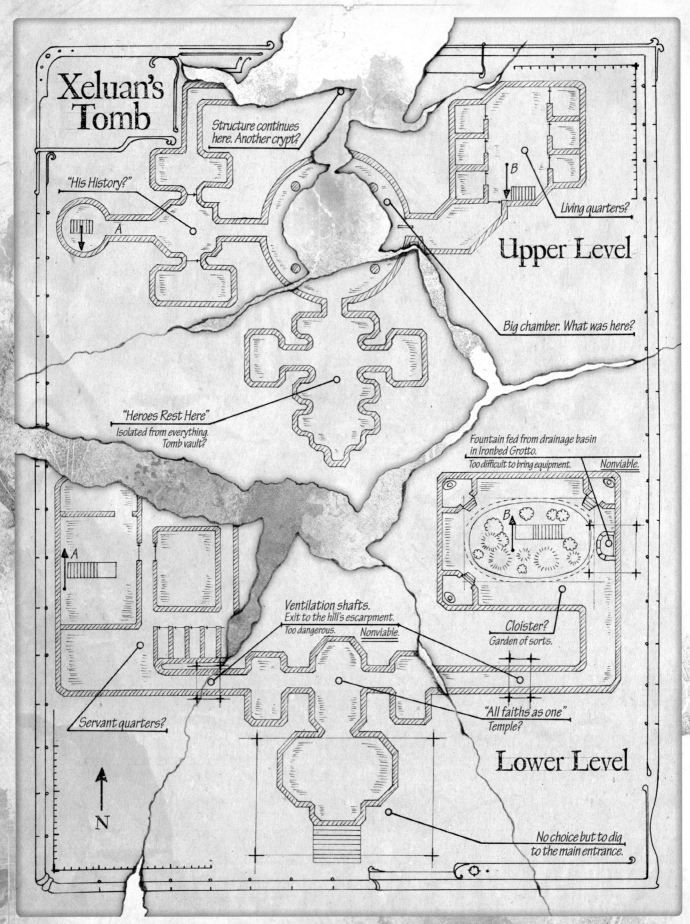

Xeluan's Tomb

Structure continues here. Another crypt?

"His History?"

A

Upper Level

B

Living quarters?

Big chamber. What was here?

"Heroes Rest Here"
Isolated from everything.
Tomb vault?

Fountain fed from drainage basin in Ironbed Grotto.
Too difficult to bring equipment. — **Nonviable.**

B

A

Ventilation shafts.
Exit to the hill's escarpment.
Too dangerous. — **Nonviable.**

Cloister?
Garden of sorts.

Servant quarters?

"All faiths as one"
Temple?

N

Lower Level

No choice but to dig to the main entrance.

Reaching the Tomb

The following locations provide different ways to access Xeluan's tomb.

Ruined Citadel

Oztocan's most prominent landmark is the ruined citadel around which the town was built. A recently excavated tunnel leads to Xeluan's tomb and is guarded at all times, as described below:

> Ten members of the town guard stand watch atop giant blocks of stone that were once part of a great citadel, now a tumbled-down ruin. A tunnel has been opened at the base of the ruined citadel. Crude, torch-lit steps descend into the earth.

The ten **veterans** guarding the tunnel entrance are loyal to Aminta and attack anyone who tries to enter the tunnel without an escort. If the characters come here in the guise of workers, five of the guards lead them to area X1 at the start of the next shift change, which occurs whenever you deem appropriate.

Ventilation Shafts

Ventilation shafts connect Xeluan's tomb to two caves: one to the east, the other to the west. Oztocan's residents are familiar with the caves but avoid them because they're hard to reach.

The characters must climb or fly 200 feet to reach either cave, which is situated in the middle of a hillside escarpment. Any such climb requires pitons, rope, and a successful DC 15 Strength (Athletics) check for every 100 feet climbed. On a failed check, a character falls 50 feet before they're caught by their climbing rope, taking 17 (5d6) bludgeoning damage from the fall.

Each cave is empty except for a ventilation shaft in its back wall. Both shafts are 20 feet wide, 20 feet tall, and made of smooth limestone. The east ventilation shaft leads to a corridor between areas X6 and X7. The west ventilation shaft leads to a corridor between areas X12 and X13.

Each ventilation shaft ends at a grate made of corroded, vertical iron bars, which the characters must bypass to enter the corridor beyond. As an action, a character can try to bend or break the rusty bars, doing so with a successful DC 17 Strength (Athletics) check and creating an opening big enough for Medium or smaller creatures to pass through.

Ironbed Grotto

Rilago's map mentions Ironbed Grotto—a name Leandro and Tavio recognize as a cavern network east of town. Near Ironbed Grotto's easily found entrance, an underground river winds through the caverns, eventually feeding the fountain in area X6. The cave network is devoid of town guards, but monsters might dwell here at your discretion.

Once the characters near the fountain, the caverns narrow into a small underwater channel the characters must swim through, as detailed in area X6. If the characters use this route, they enter the tomb soaking wet.

Xeluan's Tomb

Xeluan's brave companions built a tomb around the giant's remains so everyone who wanted to honor him could do so. One of these heroes—an elf monk named Itze—founded the Order of Xeluan, a sect of monks dedicated to preserving the tomb.

As the years passed, the tomb came to house the remains of Itze's other companions, who wished to join Xeluan in eternal rest. Finally, only Itze remained. In the final years of her life, she prepared to be buried with her companions. When Itze died, her remains were placed in the tomb, and the Order of Xeluan sealed the tomb and disbanded.

Tomb Features

Xeluan's tomb has the following features:

Ceilings. Ceilings are 15 feet high, with the exception of the 40-foot-high Great Chamber (area X4).

Doors. Unless otherwise specified, doors are made of iron-reinforced wood and are kept locked, requiring a successful DC 17 Dexterity check using thieves' tools or DC 17 Strength (Athletics) check to open. Guards carry keys to each door on their level unless otherwise noted.

Light. Areas X2, X3, X4, and X21 are brightly lit by torches imbued with *continual flame* spells. The rest of the tomb is dark. Members of the Onyx Scar use oil lamps to light their surroundings. Area descriptions assume the characters have a light source or other means of seeing in the dark.

Walls and Floors. The tomb is carved from limestone. The walls on the upper level are engraved with scenes depicting Xeluan's life, though they've eroded considerably after years of neglect.

Tomb Locations

The following locations in Xeluan's tomb are keyed to map 9.2.

X1: Main Entrance

A 200-foot-long, excavated tunnel connects the citadel ruins to a natural cavern under Oztocan. Torches light the tunnel at 10-foot intervals. When the characters reach the cavern, read the following:

> Dampness hangs in the air, and fungus clings to the walls of this limestone cavern. At the far end, worn steps lead up to a pair of massive doors. Each door is made of black iron and shaped like half of a giant face, cast with an expression of deep pain.

If the characters arrive here under the pretext of pretending to be workers, their armed escort (five **veterans**) leads them through the iron doors into area X2.

Iron Doors. The doors are held shut by two iron bars that can be removed only by creatures in area X2. If the party approaches the doors with an armed escort, one of the guards knocks on the doors six times, which signals the guards in area X2 to lift the bars and open the doors. The guards in area X2 won't open the doors unless they hear a sequence of six knocks—no more, no less. The doors have AC 17, 80 hit points, a damage threshold of 10, and immunity to poison and psychic damage.

The noise of breaking down the doors can be heard by all creatures on the tomb's lower level. These creatures remain in their respective locations but are alert for the next hour, during which time they can't be surprised.

X2: Vestibule

The following boxed text assumes the characters enter from the south. If they enter from the north, they can't see the carvings on the granite slab, the furniture behind it, or the guards:

> Torches mounted to four pillars light this ancient room. In the center of the room, a table and several chairs are situated in front of a vertical slab of granite measuring ten feet high and thirty feet wide. This slab bears carvings of people carrying offerings to a citadel nestled between two mountains.
>
> Four battle-ready members of the town guard stand next to the pillars.

This antechamber once welcomed pilgrims wishing to pay their respects to Xeluan, but the Onyx Scar has converted it into a guard post. The guards stationed here are four **veterans**.

If the characters are pretending to be workers, the guards search them for concealed armor and weapons before leading them to area X4. A character can try to smuggle a light weapon or smaller object past the guards. Doing so requires a successful DC 15 Dexterity (Sleight of Hand) check. If the check fails, the guards spot the prohibited item and try to confiscate it; the character must either talk their way out of trouble with a successful DC 18 Charisma (Deception or Persuasion) check or be attacked.

Barred Door. Two iron bars seal the double door to the south. Removing an iron bar takes an action.

X3: Arrow Slit Hallway

> A narrow hallway lined with arrow slits stretches north and south, opening into brightly lit chambers at each end.

This area once contained shrines to various gods, but the Onyx Scar renovated it, creating a hallway with arrow slits on both sides.

Arrow Slits. Four Onyx Scar **thugs** stand behind the western arrow slits, ready to shoot their crossbows at intruders who traverse the hallway without an Onyx Scar escort. The arrow slits give the thugs three-quarters cover.

No guards are stationed behind the eastern arrow slits.

X4: Great Chamber

> Encircling this domed chamber is a fifteen-foot-high mezzanine supported by four limestone pillars. In the room's center, a thirty-foot-tall statue made of lustrous black rock reflects the torchlight. The statue depicts a giant, his face frozen in determination and his arms bracing the ceiling. A hole in the statue's chest exposes an obsidian heart with glittering veins of silver and gold.
>
> Scaffolding around the statue provides easy access to the mezzanine. Standing on and around the scaffolding are several workers. Some are using pickaxes to chip away at the statue, while others are gathering chunks of the statue into crates.
>
> Passages here lead northwest, northeast, and south.

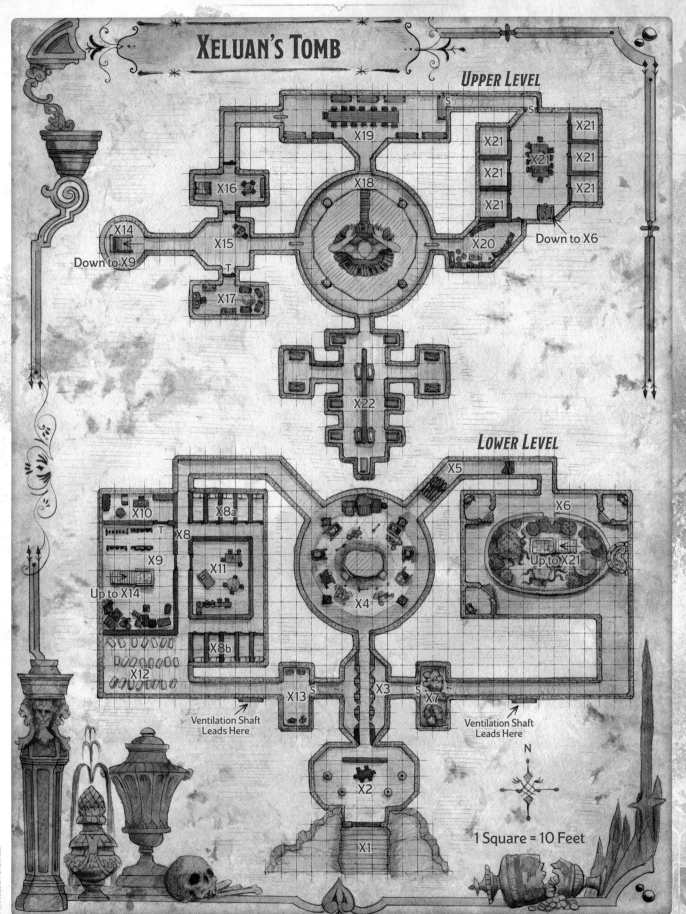

XELUAN'S TOMB

UPPER LEVEL

X19

X16

X21

X21

X21

X21

X21

X21

X21

X21

X18

X14

Down to X9

X15

Down to X6

X20

X17

X22

LOWER LEVEL

X5

X10

X8a

X6

X8

X9

Up to X14

X11

Up to X21

X8b

X12

X13

X3

X7

Ventilation Shaft Leads Here

Ventilation Shaft Leads Here

X4

N

X2

1 Square = 10 Feet

X1

FRANCESCA BAERALD

Tremor. The first time the characters bring the *shard of Xeluan* into this room or onto the mezzanine (area X18), the ground shakes and rubble falls from the ceiling. Each creature in these areas must succeed on a DC 12 Dexterity saving throw or take 3 (1d6) bludgeoning damage from falling debris.

Workers. Roll 1d6 + 3 to determine how many workers (**commoners**) are here when the characters arrive. One of the workers acts as an overseer. If the characters are pretending to be workers, the overseer gives them tasks as the other workers retire to area X12 for some much-needed rest.

The Onyx Scar pays the workers to keep their mouths shut. Any character who questions the workers can pry the following information from them with a successful DC 10 Charisma (Intimidation) check:

Aminta. Aminta was last seen on the upper level.
Edino's Research. An elf mage named Edino is conducting experiments on the giant's remains. Edino's study (area X10) lies west of here.
Trouble to the East. The Onyx Scar has sealed off the area to the east due to a "fungal infestation." That area contains a garden, a fountain, and a secret exit from the tomb. (The workers overheard two members of the Onyx Scar talking about area X6 but don't know any more details.)

Raw Oztocanite. Chunks of oztocanite (the giant's magic-imbued remains) are gathered into crates around the room. A fist-sized chunk of oztocanite can be used as a spellcasting focus that grants a +1 bonus to spell attack rolls. However, if its wielder rolls a 1 on a spell attack roll while using it as a focus, the chunk shatters and the creature takes 10 (3d6) thunder damage.

Giant's Heart. The first character to inspect Xeluan's body notices a large sliver is missing from his heart—the *shard of Xeluan* would easily fit into it. However, the characters can't mend Xeluan's heart without the help of Rilago's ghost in area X22.

If the characters attempt to place the *shard of Xeluan* in the heart without Rilago, the shard falls out again and nothing happens. A character who observes this and succeeds on a DC 14 Intelligence (Arcana) check realizes a mystical force shattered the giant's heart and that this same force might be able to mend it.

X5: Barricaded Corridor

The Onyx Scar barricaded this corridor after the myconids in area X6 began to attack anyone who got close to them. The hall contains two barricades, each one a floor-to-ceiling stack of wooden logs. A single character can remove a barricade in 30 minutes. Multiple characters working together can reduce this time proportionally.

X6: Forgotten Garden

> A haze of spores fills this large room, three corners of which contain walled-in shrines with steps leading up to them. Tangled mushrooms and roots have extended beyond a central garden to cover every visible surface.
>
> Rising from the garden is a staircase that connects to a wooden trapdoor in the ceiling. A burbling fountain protrudes from the wall east of the garden.
>
> A narrow hallway leads north, and from the southeast corner of the room, a wider hallway leads south.

The room is lightly obscured by clouds of spores. The Order of Xeluan used to harvest mushrooms from the garden, which is now the home of two **myconid sovereigns**, four **myconid adults**, and a **shambling mound**. These creatures lurk amid the garden's vegetation. Characters who have a passive Wisdom (Perception) score of 16 or higher see the creatures.

A recent effort by the Onyx Scar to clear the room for storage led to hostilities with the resident Plant creatures. The myconids and the shambling mound attack anyone who approaches the garden or emerges from the fountain (see "Fountain" below). If one or more myconids are killed, the surviving myconids use their Rapport Spores to signal their surrender. The shambling mound, however, fights until destroyed.

Fountain. A narrow underground river feeds the fountain and connects to the caverns of Ironbed Grotto (see "Reaching the Tomb"). Characters who enter the tomb via Ironbed Grotto emerge from the fountain's waterspout, which has an opening big enough for Medium or smaller creatures to crawl through.

Shrines. The shrines in the northwest, northeast, and southwest corners of the room contain statues representing gods of nature and protection.

South Corridor. The south corridor leads to area X7. Halfway down the east-to-west section of the corridor, a rusty iron grate in the south wall blocks access to a ventilation shaft (see "Reaching the Tomb").

Stairs. The stairs in the garden ascend to a trapdoor that Edino (see area X10) has sealed with an *arcane lock* spell. As an action, a character can use thieves' tools to try to bypass the magical lock, doing so with a successful DC 25 Dexterity check, or the character can try to force open the trapdoor, doing so with a successful DC 25 Strength (Athletics) check. A *knock* spell or similar magic also opens the trapdoor, which swings upward into area X21.

X7: RUINED SHRINES

> Crumbling altars, ruined statues, and idols of forgotten gods litter the floor of this small chamber.

This chamber once housed shrines to the gods of ancient local religions, but they have all been smashed and ruined.

Secret Door. Any character who examines the west wall and succeeds on a DC 16 Wisdom (Perception) check discovers a secret door in the middle of it. A character with the Stonecunning trait or proficiency with mason's tools has advantage on this check. The stone door is unlocked and can be pushed aside to access the eastern section of area X3.

X8: LIVING QUARTERS

> This area of the tomb has thick timber walls lined with wooden doors. The stone floor is strewn with dirt and covered with fresh bootprints.

Long ago, this area served as living quarters for the monks of the Order of Xeluan. Now it has been overtaken by the Onyx Scar for the same purpose.

X8a. North Quarters. Five Onyx Scar **thugs** sleep in these rooms, one per room. Each room contains a cot with an oil lamp hanging above it.

X8b. South Quarters. Each of these rooms contains a cot with an oil lamp hanging above it. All five rooms are currently unoccupied.

X9: STORAGE

> This room contains weapon racks, stacks of wooden crates, and doors leading to the north and east. In the center of the room, a staircase rises to the upper level.

If the characters were brought in as workers, Tavio's personal guards left a wooden chest in this area that contains any equipment the characters arranged for Tavio to smuggle in.

Stairs. The stairs ascend to area X14.

Warded Door. The door to area X10 is warded by an *alarm* spell that mentally alerts Edino if anyone touches it.

X10: Edino's Study

> A hulking figure made of clay stands on the other side of the door, its thick arms ending in balled fists, its head a featureless lump. Behind it is a room containing two bookshelves, a bed, a table, and a desk.

The hulking figure is a **clay golem** that doesn't wait for characters to enter the room before attacking them. It fights until destroyed.

A lawful evil, elf **mage** named Edino lurks in the room. Edino is the Onyx Scar's resident spellcaster and has cast *greater invisibility* on himself. If the characters defeat the golem, Edino hides until he can sneak to area X19 and alert Aminta.

Edino's Experiments. Edino experiments with oztocanite in this room. As part of his experiments, Edino has bound the souls of Xeluan's companions (from area X22) to four fist-sized pieces of oztocanite. One of these soul fragments sits on Edino's desk. The other three fragments are in a desk drawer. Any character who examines a fragment and succeeds on a DC 15 Intelligence (Arcana) check senses there's a life force trapped inside it but has no clue how to release it (see area X22).

Treasure. A spellbook on the western bookshelf contains the spells Edino has prepared plus *alarm*, *arcane lock*, *detect thoughts*, *dimension door*, and *glyph of warding*. The other books in Edino's collection aren't valuable and cover such topics as geology, gemology, and mining.

X11: Mess Hall

Loud voices and laughter can be heard through the door to this room.

> This room contains three mismatched tables at odd angles, each one littered with food scraps and empty mugs. A makeshift bar has been constructed along the south wall. Four ruffians in leather armor play cards at one table, while two town guards eat at the bar and chat with the dwarf bartender. All eyes turn to you as the door opens.

This area is used as a mess hall for workers and low-ranking Onyx Scar members. Four **thugs** sit at one table, while two **veterans** eat snacks at the bar. As soon as they detect intruders, the thugs and veterans draw their weapons and attack.

Brego, the dwarf bartender (lawful evil **spy**), is a longtime friend of Aminta's and a member of the Onyx Scar. He stands on a small crate to reach the bar's countertop. If a fight erupts, Brego ducks behind the bar and hurls flaming bottles of alcohol at intruders (treat each bottle as a flask of alchemist's fire) unless he is stopped. The bar gives Brego three-quarters cover.

X12: Worker Rest Area

> Nearly two dozen bedrolls are scattered across the floor of this dusty stone room. Some of the bedrolls have workers resting on them.

Four workers (**commoners**) rest in the room, along with any workers who left area X4. These workers aren't interested in helping the characters or in making an enemy of the Onyx Scar. If the characters attempt to persuade, deceive, or otherwise recruit the workers to aid them, they can make a relevant DC 15 ability check. On a successful check, the workers won't endanger themselves, but they might share helpful intelligence or agree to stay out of the party's way.

Southeast Corridor. The southeast corridor leads to area X13. A little more than halfway down the corridor, a rusty iron grate in the south wall blocks access to a ventilation shaft (see "Reaching the Tomb").

X13: Reconstructed Shrine

> This room contains four dilapidated altars—two against the north wall and two against the south wall.

Unlike the tomb's other shrines, which the Onyx Scar destroyed, the shrines in this room were repurposed so laborers could worship their gods and feel at peace while working underground.

Altar Deities. The deities represented on the altars are left to your judgment. Gods of work, industry, protection, and luck are particularly appropriate. If you're setting this adventure in the San Citlán region, La Catrina is the patron deity. She is a jovial death goddess represented as a skeleton dressed in expensive finery.

Secret Door. Any character who examines the east wall and succeeds on a DC 16 Wisdom (Perception) check discovers a secret door in the middle of it. A character with the Stonecunning trait or proficiency with mason's tools has advantage on this check. The stone door is unlocked and can be pushed aside to access the western section of area X3. If the guards in that area haven't been dealt with already, they attack the characters on sight.

X14: History Room

> The stone walls of this circular room are engraved with murals depicting a giant at various stages of his life. A hallway leads east, and in the center of the room, stairs descend to the lower level.

The murals in this room depict Xeluan's legend (see the "Adventure Background" section). If the characters already saw Xeluan in area X4, they recognize him in the etchings.

X15: Upper West Antechamber

> Reliefs on this room's walls depict people bowing in gratitude to a smiling giant. Hallways lead east and west, and doors lead north and south. Seated at a table in the northeast corner are two identical human women playing cards.

The women playing cards are two **doppelgangers** that look exactly like Aminta. If they see three or more intruders, the doppelgangers retreat to area X19; otherwise, they stand and fight.

Door to Area X17. Only the real Aminta has a key to area X17. The lock on the door is trapped with a capsule that contains poisonous gas. The capsule can be found with a successful DC 20 Intelligence (Investigation) check. A character who opens the door with Aminta's key safely disarms the capsule, as does a character who picks the lock and succeeds on their check by 5 or more. Otherwise, the capsule breaks when the door is opened, releasing a cloud of poisonous gas that fills a 10-foot-radius sphere centered on the door. Each creature in the area must succeed on a DC 16 Constitution saving throw or be poisoned for 2d4 hours. A poisoned creature falls unconscious but wakes up if it takes damage. The cloud disperses a few seconds after the trap triggers.

X16: Aminta's Quarters

> A large, neatly made bed occupies the west half of this room. Hanging from hooks on the walls are several dresses and cloaks, with pairs of boots and sandals placed neatly below them.
>
> On the east side of the room, dinnerware is stacked atop a low wooden table, and a fully stocked wine rack stands against the wall.

Treasure. A small coffer under Aminta's bed holds six zircons (50 gp each). Characters who search the wine rack find two bottles of exquisite wine (100 gp each) and three bottles of fine wine (10 gp each). The remaining bottles hold common wine.

X17: Treasury

> This room is lit by oil lamps resting atop two narrow tables. Other furnishings include a desk to the west and four wooden chests to the east.

The desk has a single drawer, inside which is a leather-bound ledger detailing how much money the Onyx Scar has invested in the tomb excavation thus far (nearly 15,000 gp).

Treasure. The four chests are unlocked, and each one contains 2,500 gp. Aminta needs this money to pay workers, bribe town guards, and keep the operation running.

X18: Mezzanine

This 15-foot-high mezzanine encircles the Great Chamber (area X4). A walkway made of wooden planks connects the mezzanine with the scaffolding that surrounds the petrified remains of Xeluan.

Revolving Stone Doors. Set into the mezzanine's walls are four heavy stone doors, each of which revolves on a vertical axis. The west and east doors are open, while the north and south doors are shut. These doors aren't locked but grind loudly when opened or closed, attracting the attention of anyone on the upper level or in area X4.

X19: War Room

> The air in this wide room is thick with the smell of dusty tomes. Eight bookshelves stand against the walls. Half of them have collapsed on themselves, while the remaining four bookshelves are packed with crumbling scrolls and books.
>
> The room's centerpiece is a long wooden table with an ornate, throne-like chair at one end and smaller chairs along both sides. Seated in the big chair is a human woman clad in leather armor, and she's not alone.

This room was once a library chronicling the history of Xeluan and his heroic companions. The Onyx Scar now uses it for leadership meetings. Aminta Solana (neutral evil, human **assassin**) claims the seat at the head of the table.

Aminta is a human in her late thirties. She has brown skin and long dark hair streaked with gray.

She is charming, confident, intelligent, and ruthless. In her pocket is a key to area X17.

Aminta is meeting with two of her distribution generals (**veterans**). Edino (the elf **mage** from area X10) and the two **doppelgangers** from area X15 might be here as well.

If the characters show up pretending to be workers, Aminta yells at them to leave and warns that another intrusion will result in their deaths. If the characters pose an obvious threat, she calls for the doppelgangers in area X15.

Aminta fights until reduced to 10 hit points or fewer, then attempts to flee. Edino behaves similarly. The doppelgangers look and act like the real Aminta, and they do their best to cover Aminta's escape. The two veterans are confident in their combat prowess and fight to the death.

Revolving Stone Door. Set into the west wall is a heavy stone door that revolves on a vertical axis. The door is currently open and grinds loudly when opened or closed. West of the door is an L-shaped hallway leading to area X16.

Secret Door. Characters who examine the bookshelf in the northeast corner see scratch marks on the floor that suggest the bookshelf has been pulled away from the wall more than once. Behind this bookshelf is a secret door that leads to area X21. The secret door can be found by any character who examines the wall behind the bookshelf and succeeds on a DC 11 Wisdom (Perception) check. A character with the Stonecunning trait or proficiency with mason's tools has advantage on this check.

The secret door opens to reveal a dusty tunnel with another secret door at the far end. Characters inside the tunnel can find either secret door without needing to make an ability check.

X20: Food Storage

> Containers of dried vegetables, breads, and cheeses are stacked against the walls of this room, and cured meats hang from hooks. A massive stone door to the west stands open, and a wooden door leads north. A gentle breeze causes the dust on the floor to stir.

This room contains enough food and refreshment to supply the Onyx Scar and its workers for weeks. The stone door west of this room is described in area X18. The north door leads to area X21.

An **invisible stalker** floats near the ceiling and is the source of the breeze. If one or more characters disturb the supplies, the stalker attacks them. The stalker doesn't attack if the supplies are left alone.

X21: Guest Hall

> This torchlit room contains a large table with several chairs. The ceiling is hung with black-and-green tapestries. Six doors are spaced evenly along the east and west walls. A seventh door stands in the southwest corner.
>
> Against the south wall, set into the floor, is a wooden trapdoor with iron hinges and a pull ring.

This room serves as a guest hall for prominent members of the Onyx Scar and others who come to do business with Aminta. The adjoining guest rooms, which are unlocked, are outfitted with beds and basic amenities.

Secret Door. On the north wall, an unlocked secret door leads to area X19. The secret door can be found by any character who examines the wall and succeeds on a DC 16 Wisdom (Perception) check. A character with the Stonecunning trait or proficiency with mason's tools has advantage on this check.

The secret door opens to reveal a dusty tunnel with another secret door at the far end of it. Characters inside the tunnel can find either secret door without needing to make an ability check.

Trapdoor. The trapdoor leading to area X6 is secured with an *arcane lock* spell. As an action, a character can use thieves' tools to try to bypass the magical lock, doing so with a successful DC 25 Dexterity check, or the character can try to wrench open the trapdoor, doing so with a successful DC 25 Strength (Athletics) check. A *knock* spell or similar magic also opens the trapdoor.

X22: Crypt of the Watched

> A large burial chamber opens before you, divided in two by a central wall running north to south. Engraved stone caskets displayed throughout the crypt are draped in cobwebs.
>
> A weak voice breaks the silence. "Hush. Come no closer, or you'll wake the angry spirits."

The stone caskets contain the earthly remains (dust and bones) of Xeluan's four companions and their loved ones.

Angry Wraiths. If the characters ignore the warning and enter the crypt, four **wraiths** emerge from the caskets that line the central wall. The wraiths don't respond to verbal entreaties and can't leave the crypt, but they attack anyone who sets foot inside.

Rilago's Ghost. The voice belongs to the **ghost** of Rilago. If the characters heed its warning and don't advance into the crypt, Rilago materializes in front of them and strikes up a conversation:

> "My name is Rilago, and I am responsible for the unrest that besets Oztocan. My foolishness broke Xeluan's heart. I come to you eager to make amends. Together, we can save Oztocan from destruction."

Rilago's ghost knows that only it can mend Xeluan's broken heart. If the characters present the *shard of Xeluan*, Rilago thanks the characters for returning the shard to Xeluan's tomb.

The ghost describes the events chronicled in the "What Really Happened" section, then asks the characters to release the spirits of Xeluan's heroic companions. Edino trapped their spirits in chunks of oztocanite (see area X10), and Rilago knows how to release them: each oztocanite fragment must be brought in physical contact with the giant's petrified remains (in area X4). Physical contact with Xeluan reduces each oztocanite fragment to dust and frees the spirit trapped inside it. Freed spirits manifest as motes of spectral light that the petrified giant seems to absorb.

Mending Xeluan's Broken Heart. Once the spirits of Xeluan's four companions are released from their oztocanite prisons, the characters can safely enter this crypt (the wraiths don't arise from their caskets) and reconvene with Rilago's ghost. The ghost reveals that it can mend Xeluan's heart only by possessing the body of a hero and using its host to place the *shard of Xeluan* where it belongs: with the rest of Xeluan's heart. The ghost then asks permission to possess one of the characters, leaving it up to the characters to decide which of them should become Rilago's temporary host.

Rilago's offer to mend the giant's heart is genuine. If the characters allow it, Rilago's ghost uses Possession against a willing character, who forgoes the saving throw to resist the effect. Only then can the ghost leave the crypt and return the *shard of Xeluan* to its rightful place. When Rilago's host touches the shard to the giant's heart, they bind as one. As the giant's heart is made whole again, Rilago's spirit is laid to rest, and the character ceases to be possessed.

CONCLUSION

The story might conclude in one of the following ways, though other outcomes are possible:

Xeluan's Heart Is Mended. If Xeluan's heart is mended, the earthquakes stop. Peace returns to Oztocan. Rilago's redemption and the characters'

RILAGO'S GHOST

heroism have strengthened the protective wards around Xeluan, rendering the giant impervious to further harm. No longer able to mine oztocanite from the giant, the Onyx Scar terminates its mining operation.

Xeluan's Heart Is Not Mended. If the characters fail to mend Xeluan's heart, the earthquakes worsen, forcing citizens of Oztocan to evacuate the town.

FOR THE GOLDEN VAULT

If the characters are working for the Golden Vault, the organization rewards the characters once the *shard of Xeluan* is returned to its rightful place. They receive a rare magic item of their choice (subject to your approval) as payment. The item is delivered to the characters the next day.

WHAT'S NEXT?

The characters' adventures in Oztocan can continue long after Xeluan's heart is mended. The Onyx Scar might send assassins after the characters, or the syndicate's leaders might continue searching for other secrets hidden in Xeluan's tomb.

THE CITY OF GHALASINE LIES IN RUINS, BUT
IT'S NOT TOO LATE TO UNDO THE DAMAGE
AND SET THINGS RIGHT.

HEART OF ASHES

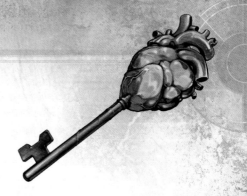

G HALASINE IS UNDER A TERRIBLE CURSE. An evil spellcaster has enacted a ritual to siphon life from the city's people and reduce the city itself to ash. Powering the ritual is the heart of Ghalasine's vanquished leader, King Jhaeros Astolko. In this adventure, the characters must infiltrate Castle Cinis and recover the king's heart to end the ritual, thereby saving Ghalasine.

ADVENTURE BACKGROUND

Known for its exquisite glasswork, Ghalasine was a prosperous city ruled by King Jhaeros Astolko. Governing from Castle Cinis, Jhaeros was advised by two councilors, Regine LaVerne and Charmayne Daymore, and a guard captain named Naevys Tharesso. Jhaeros's rule was compassionate, just, and kind. Over the last year, however, Naevys watched with growing concern as Jhaeros became more withdrawn and secretive, closing Ghalasine to trade and failing to honor his alliances.

A powerful spellcaster, Charmayne had become jealous of the king's passion and warmth. Longing to possess those qualities, she painstakingly created rituals to drain Jhaeros's vitality and charm, and to funnel these qualities into herself. However, the magic only enhanced her greed and jealousy; the more she took from Jhaeros, the hungrier for power Charmayne became, going so far as to murder her fellow councilor, Regine, while she slept.

Unaware of Charmayne's magical hold over the king but afraid for his well-being, Naevys sought the counsel of a mage's guild in a neighboring city. With the help of *scrying* spells, the mages gleaned the truth and revealed Charmayne's treachery to Naevys. The loyal captain returned to Ghalasine at once but found herself unable to enter the city. Charmayne had anticipated Naevys's return and prepared accordingly by invoking a powerful ward that prevents anyone born in Ghalasine from entering or leaving the city.

As she came to realize the people of Ghalasine didn't love her as they did the king, Charmayne became filled with rage. She used magic to tear out Jhaeros's heart while keeping it alive. She then used the still-beating heart as the focus of a ritual to destroy Ghalasine. A spherical void appeared in the sky above Castle Cinis, causing the city to slowly turn to ash and drawing the souls of the dead into it. The longer the void persists, the more quickly the city deteriorates.

Jhaeros has been transformed into a heartless puppet under Charmayne's command. It's up to the characters to steal the king's heart, thereby ending Charmayne's ritual. If the characters are successful, all the damage wrought by Charmayne's magic will be undone, restoring Ghalasine and its king to their former glory. If they fail, the city will be destroyed, and Charmayne's treason will be complete.

> ### ASHEN CREATURES
>
> Many of the creatures that haunt Ghalasine and guard Castle Cinis are ashen effigies of their former selves. These ashen creatures use their normal statistics, except they are lawful evil Elementals that have immunity to fire damage.
>
> When an ashen creature drops to 0 hit points, it is reduced to a pile of ash, and any equipment it was wearing or carrying falls to the ground.

Using the Golden Vault

If you're using the Golden Vault as a patron, a golden key is delivered to the characters in whatever manner you deem fit. When the characters use this key to open their music box, the lid pops open and a soothing voice says the following:

> "Greetings, operatives. The city of Ghalasine is under a terrible curse, and the Golden Vault has learned that the evil spellcaster Charmayne Daymore is behind it. Charmayne was once an adviser to King Jhaeros, but she used the king's heart to power a ritual that is devastating the city and killing its people. Our sources say that stopping the ritual will restore the city and its people. This quest, should you choose to undertake it, requires you to retrieve the king's still-beating heart and remove it from the city to stop the ritual. Start by meeting with the elf Naevys, guard captain for King Jhaeros. Good luck, operatives."

Closing the music box causes the golden key to vanish.

Heart of the Matter

Naevys (lawful good, elf **knight** equipped with a *flame tongue* longsword) approaches the characters with important business from Ghalasine. Her bronze-and-red armor gleams in tones that reflect her braided red-brown hair, and her skin is freckled. She is friendly toward the characters and asks to speak with them privately:

> "My city is in trouble," Naevys says. "It deteriorates with every passing second, and my king is part of it. Or rather, his stolen heart is.
>
> "Ghalasine is slowly being reduced to ash, and its people are dying and can't escape. King Jhaeros would do everything in his power to stop it if he could. I've served Jhaeros since I was a young squire. His father denied me knighthood—our family was poor, and I had no formal training—but Jhaeros made me his personal knight. That was the start of our friendship. He isn't just kind; he's warm and passionate, ever invested in the people of the city.
>
> "A mages' guild in a neighboring city used scrying spells to confirm my suspicion that one of the king's closest advisers—Charmayne Daymore—is behind this. She has stolen the king's heart and is using it to power a ritual. Jhaeros is now her obedient puppet."

Naevys assures the characters that Charmayne's ritual affects only people from Ghalasine; outsiders can safely enter the city. She asks the characters to steal Jhaeros's heart and deliver it to her outside the city, thereby thwarting Charmayne's ritual.

Naevys provides the following additional information, which she learned with the help of mages in a nearby city:

Ashen Defenders. Castle Cinis is guarded by ashen creatures that used to be the king's guards. The king's dogs, Cinnabar and Sol, have become hell hounds that wander the castle's interior.

Charmayne's Location. Charmayne spends most of her time in the mage tower (area S14).

Consuming Void. A spherical void has formed high above the castle. The souls of the dead and the ashes of the city are being drawn into it. Most people in the city have already died.

Regine LaVerne. Naevys doesn't know what happened to the king's other councilor, Regine.

Reversing the Ritual. According to the mages with whom Naevys consulted, Charmayne's ritual can be reversed and Ghalasine restored to its former glory by removing Jhaeros's still-beating heart from the city. This might be the only way to repair the damage Charmayne has wrought and restore the lives of those who died because of the ritual.

Saving the King's Heart. Simply destroying Jhaeros's heart would end the ritual without reversing the damage it has caused or undoing the terrible loss of life. Moreover, Naevys believes Jhaeros will almost certainly die if his heart stops beating.

Naevys is loath to discuss rewards until Ghalasine is either saved or lost, but if the characters press her for a reward, she promises to "drown them in gold coins" if they are successful. (In fact, the possible rewards are much greater than that, as discussed in the adventure's conclusion.)

Planning the Heist

Naevys has sketched a rough map of Castle Cinis for the characters. Give players a copy of map 10.1 for reference. Naevys believes Jhaeros's heart is in a secret room on the second floor that can be accessed from the king's bedroom, and she is correct, but she doesn't know that the magic of Charmayne's ritual has altered the castle's layout.

Getting Inside

If the characters ask Naevys for advice on how to enter the castle, she suggests the following:

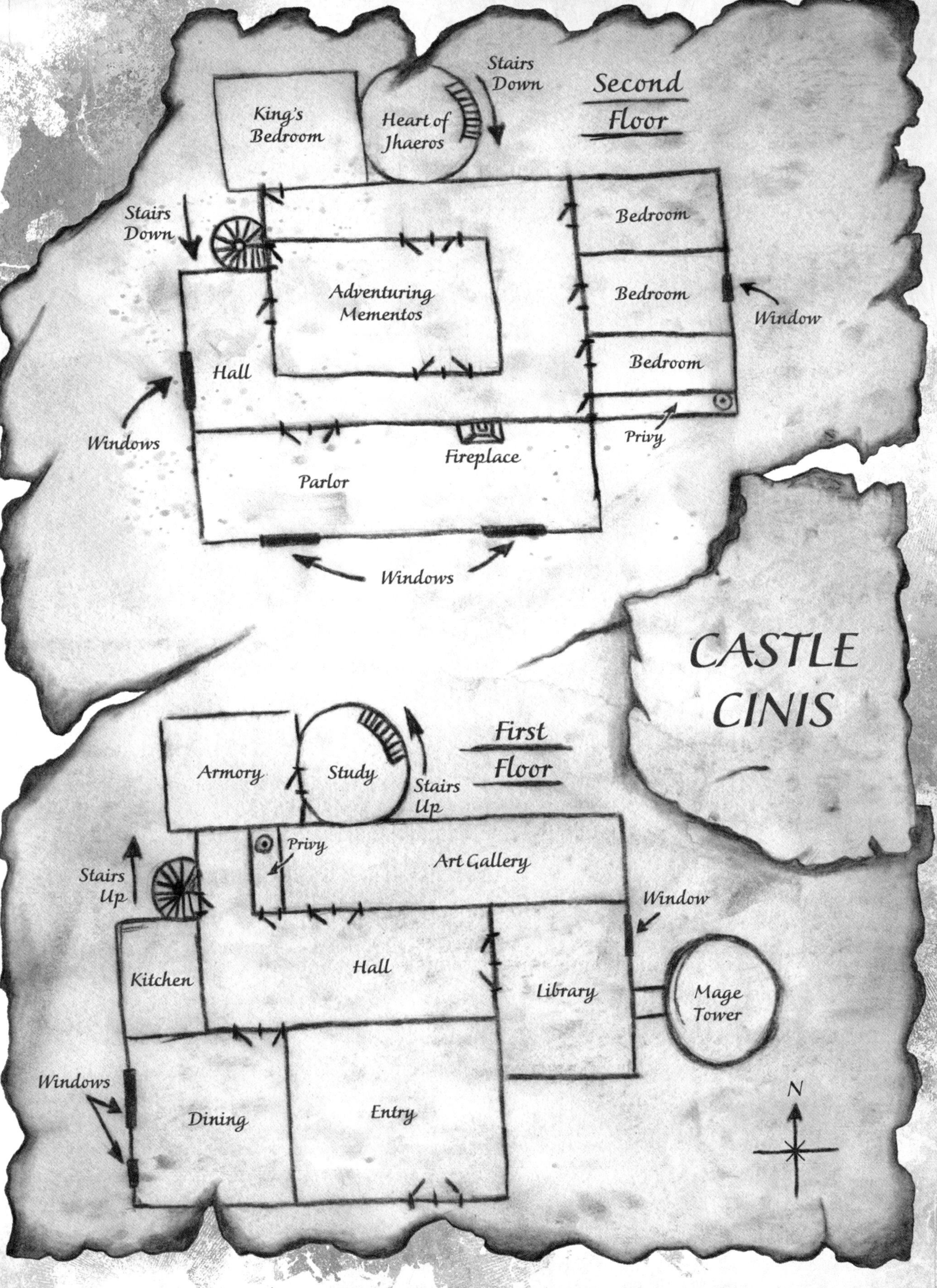
Stairs Down
Second Floor
King's Bedroom
Heart of Jhaeros
Stairs Down
Bedroom
Adventuring Mementos
Bedroom
Window
Hall
Bedroom
Windows
Privy
Fireplace
Parlor
Windows
CASTLE CINIS
First Floor
Armory
Study
Stairs Up
Privy
Art Gallery
Stairs Up
Window
Hall
Kitchen
Library
Mage Tower
Windows
Dining
Entry
N

FRANCESCA BAERALD

> "You can expect guards outside the main entrance as well as patrols circling the castle grounds. You could try to slip past the patrols and enter through a dining room window on the west side of the ground floor, out of sight of the main entrance, but close to the staircase that climbs to the second floor."

CHARCOAL FIGURINES

With the help of scrying magic, the mages with whom Naevys consulted obtained the following additional information, which Naevys passes along to the characters just before they set out for Castle Cinis:

> "Once you're inside the castle, keep an eye out for a set of charcoal figurines. Charmayne created the figurines herself, and I'm told she uses them to store her victims' psychic trauma. A clever spellcaster can turn the power of these figurines against her. I don't really understand how, but the mages with whom I consulted assured me of this fact."

See area S6 for more information about the charcoal figurines.

CASTLE CINIS

Starting at the edge of the city, it takes the characters 1 hour on foot to reach Castle Cinis. The city around them is grim and desolate. Its buildings are slowly turning to cinders, with clouds of ash rising toward the black, spherical void that looms above Castle Cinis.

The characters have no encounters on their way to the castle. When they arrive at the castle, read or paraphrase the following:

> Castle Cinis has deteriorated to the extent that sections of it now float in the air. Ash and detritus rise toward the spherical black void that hovers high above the castle. The void itself seems to be pulling the castle apart. The castle groans in protest as stone grates against stone.
>
> Two guards, their bodies made of ash, flank the castle's entrance. More ashen guards circle the castle in patrols of four guards each.

The characters can count a total of ten guards, all of whom are ashen **veterans** (see the "Ashen Creatures" sidebar). Two guards flank the door to area S1, and the remaining eight guards patrol the grounds in two groups of four.

Characters who spend a few minutes studying the guards' movements gain advantage on Dexterity (Stealth) checks made to approach the castle unseen.

If the guards at the entrance or the guards on patrol spot the characters, one of them blows a horn to summon the other guards, who arrive 1d4 rounds later.

CASTLE FEATURES

Castle Cinis has the following features:

Ceilings. Ceilings in the castle are 20 feet high and covered with ash (see "Tug of the Void" below).

Light. Each room in Castle Cinis is brightly lit by one or more torches, or by sunlight during the day if the room lacks a ceiling.

Tug of the Void. Objects in the castle that weigh 10 pounds or less and aren't being worn, carried, or held in place tend to drift in the direction of the void at a rate of about 1 foot per minute. (For more information about the void, see "The Void" section later in the adventure.)

Weakened Floors and Walls. The walls and floors on the second floor (areas S8–S13) and the floating areas (areas S14–S17) have been weakened by magic, such that each 5-foot-square section of floor or wall in these areas has AC 13 and 4 hit points. Reducing any such area to 0 hit points causes it to crumble away.

Windows. Unless the text states otherwise, all windows are latched shut from the inside. As an action, a character can use thieves' tools to try to unlatch a window from the outside, doing so with a successful DC 17 Dexterity check. Shattering a window is easy enough, but unless the sound is silenced by magic, all guards within 60 feet of the breaking window investigate.

CASTLE CINIS LOCATIONS

The following locations are keyed to map 10.2.

S1: ENTRY HALL

> Lining the west wall of this once grand hall are six hollow suits of crimson armor. Each one holds an ornate shield and an intricate glass lance, which is topped with a glowing glass sculpture that resembles a flickering torch.

Characters can cross this hall safely if they are wearing the uniforms of castle guards. Otherwise, any attempt by them to cross the hall causes magical flames to fill three of the suits of armor,

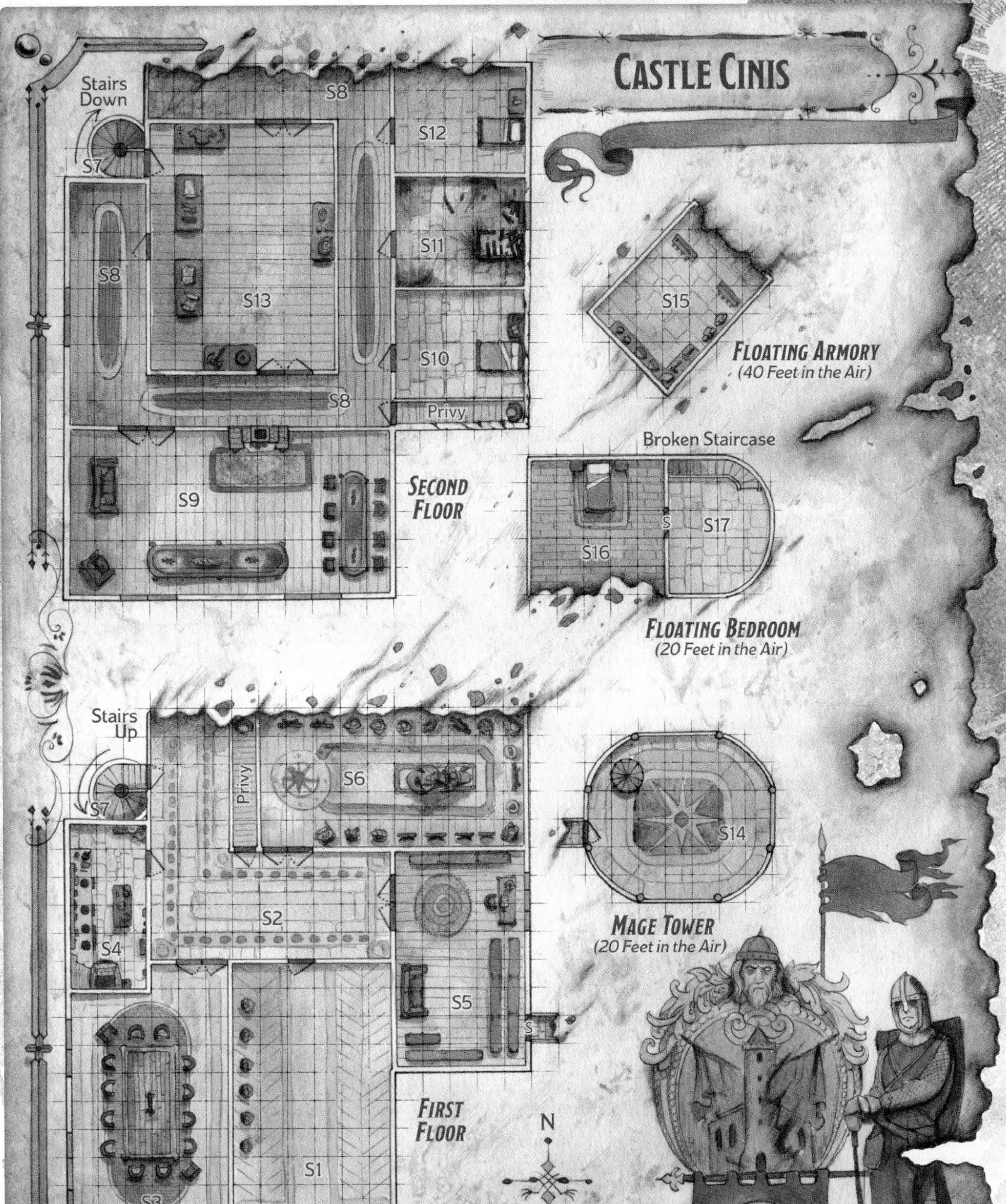

CASTLE CINIS

Stairs
Down

S7

S8

S12

S11

S10

Privy

S8

S13

S8

S9

SECOND FLOOR

FLOATING ARMORY
(40 Feet in the Air)

S15

Broken Staircase

S16

S

S17

FLOATING BEDROOM
(20 Feet in the Air)

Stairs
Up

S7

Privy

S6

S4

S2

S14

S5

S

MAGE TOWER
(20 Feet in the Air)

S1

S3

FIRST FLOOR

N

1 Square = 5 Feet

which spring to life as three **helmed horrors**. These helmed horrors also animate if anyone touches one of the suits of armor. The helmed horrors' Spell Immunity trait grants them immunity to *burning hands*, *fireball*, and *scorching ray* spells.

As a bonus action on its first turn in combat, each helmed horror drops its glass lance (which shatters on the floor) and conjures a longsword-sized blade of fire, which appears in its free hand. The helmed horror deals fire damage instead of slashing damage with its fiery sword, which disappears in a cloud of smoke when the helmed horror drops to 0 hit points.

S2: Hallway

The northernmost wall of this L-shaped hallway turned to ash as the armory (area S15) tore itself free of the castle, leaving a gaping hole.

Guards. Three ashen **veterans** (see the "Ashen Creatures" sidebar) guard this hall and are hostile toward interlopers. They are positioned as follows:

- One guard stands in front of the doors to area S5.
- One guard stands in front of the doors to area S6.
- One guard stands next to the door to area S7.

S3: Dining Hall

Large windows on the west wall of this opulent dining hall look toward the ashen city. Fourteen plush chairs surround a dark walnut table. Three seats at the head of the table face ornate place settings: fine goblets, plates, silverware, and a half-empty bottle of wine.

The goblets still have trace amounts of wine in them, and a few breadcrumbs and greasy streaks dirty the plates.

S4: Kitchen

The door to the kitchen hangs open.

Two hounds with smoldering black fur feed on a pair of charred human corpses in the middle of this kitchen.

The hounds were once Jhaeros's beloved dogs, Cinnabar and Sol, now transformed into **hell hounds**. The hounds' names are written on their collars in Common. They obey only King Jhaeros, and they transform back into friendly mastiffs if the effects of Charmayne's ritual are undone.

If the characters stay out of the kitchen and leave the hounds alone, Cinnabar and Sol ignore them and continue feeding on the cook and dishwasher they incinerated with their breath weapons.

The hounds attack characters who approach or harm them.

Eating the Food. Characters who search the kitchen can find plenty of food, all of which tastes like ash until the effects of Charmayne's ritual are undone.

S5: Library

The library might once have been cozy with its large desk, padded couch, spacious bookshelves, and rich woods. Now, the books are ash, and the furnishings are beginning to deteriorate similarly. Flakes of ash cloud the air.

All the library's books have been destroyed.

Secret Door and Bridge. A secret door is hidden in the east wall behind a bookshelf, and any character who searches the wall for secret doors finds it automatically. The secret door can be pulled open to reveal part of a stone bridge that used to connect to the mage tower (area S14). The bridge ends abruptly after 5 feet, as the tower has since risen 20 feet into the air and is now at the same level as the castle's second floor.

S6: Art Gallery

This gallery is missing its entire north wall, and what little remains turns to ashes before your eyes. Through the hole, you see two detached sections of the castle floating in the air.

The gallery itself contains beautiful glass sculptures attached to stone pedestals. The sculptures include a red glass dragon unfurling its wings, blue glass waves crashing against a lighthouse, a delicate teal dryad laughing, and more.

A narrow table toward the back looks out of place. Six charcoal figurines float above it.

Through the hole in the north wall, the characters can see area S15 (elevated 40 feet in the air) and areas S16–S17 (elevated 20 feet in the air). Both structures used to be attached to the gallery's north wall, but they have drifted outward about 10 feet as well as upward.

Charcoal Figurines. The six figurines are floating because they are subject to the tug of the void (see "Castle Features"). The figurines are shaped like tiny humans but lack fine features to distinguish them from one another. A *detect magic* spell reveals a dim aura of necromantic magic around each one. Each figurine represents someone who was killed by Charmayne. Five of the victims were guards or nobles who tried to defend Jhaeros and Regine; the sixth was Regine herself.

A character who holds a figurine experiences a flash of emotion like that felt by the victim in their final moments and, in a couple cases, a vision of Charmayne as seen by the victim:

Figurine 1 is full of terror. A momentary vision shows Charmayne (an auburn-haired woman in a scarlet robe) casting a fiery spell.

Figurine 2 holds the dying fear of someone fixated on a person they're leaving behind.

Figurine 3 seethes with anger and a craving for justice. A momentary vision shows Charmayne using magic to engulf the victim in fire.

Figurine 4 is sorrowful and filled with regret from a life that ended too soon.

Figurine 5 is full of undying loyalty to the king.

Figurine 6 exudes denial and refuses to accept what is happening.

After holding a figurine and experiencing the emotion bound within it, a character can make a DC 14 Intelligence (Arcana) check. On a successful check, the character realizes that the psychic power contained in each figurine can be turned against Charmayne. Specifically, each figurine can be used as a spellcasting focus once before it turns to ash. When used as the focus for a spell that targets Charmayne and requires a saving throw, Charmayne not only has disadvantage on her save but also takes 16 (3d10) psychic damage on a failed save, or half as much damage on a successful one.

S7: Stone Staircase

This 40-foot-high, spiral staircase connects area S2 on the first floor and area S13 on the second floor.

The stone tower that contains the staircase no longer has a roof over it; the conical rooftop turned to ash and was sucked into the void above the castle, leaving the top of the staircase open to the sky.

S8: Upper Hallway

This wide hallway wraps around area S13. The northernmost stretch of the hallway is missing an entire wall, which turned to ash and was sucked into the void above the castle.

Guards. Four ashen **veterans** (see the "Ashen Creatures" sidebar) guard the hall and are hostile toward interlopers. They are positioned as follows:

- Three guards stand outside the doors to area S13—one to the north, one to the west, and one to the south.
- One guard stands next to the door leading to area S12.

S9: Parlor

> This extravagant parlor holds a dining table, a fireplace, and cushioned couches. Windows along the south wall afford a spectacularly grim view of what has become of Ghalasine.
>
> A scratchy voice from the fireplace calls out, "Visitors? Visitors! Please, over here!"

Charmayne trapped a drow diplomat named Jalynvyr Nir'Thinn in the fireplace, from which he can't escape until Charmayne's ritual is undone. While trapped in the fireplace, Jalynvyr manifests as a **smoke mephit** that speaks Common and Elvish instead of Auran and Ignan. The mephit is restrained, and this condition can't be ended on it so long as Jalynvyr remains trapped. If the mephit is reduced to 0 hit points, Jalynvyr dies as the mephit's smoky form disperses.

Jalynvyr was a guest at the castle, learned of Charmayne's plans, and threatened to tell King Jhaeros. Charmayne lured him here under false pretenses so she could trap him in the fireplace. He's willing to share what he knows with anyone who vows to unravel Charmayne's evil plans:

Gift for the King. "I delivered a *flame tongue* longsword to King Jhaeros, who then bequeathed it to his most loyal captain, Naevys, as thanks for her years of faithful service. Charmayne was furious that Jhaeros wasted coin on a sword for Naevys, but then, she was always distracted by one petty jealousy or another."

Heart of Ghalasine. "After trapping me in the fireplace, Charmayne bragged that Jhaeros himself would destroy Ghalasine. 'The heart of Ghalasine has always been its king,' she told me, 'so it's fitting that the heart of the king is the key to Ghalasine's demise.'"

If King Jhaeros's heart is taken from the city of Ghalasine or if Charmayne is killed, Jalynvyr reverts to his true form (that of a lawful neutral, drow **mage**) and is no longer restrained by the fireplace. The next time he encounters the characters, he gives them one or more potions or *spell scrolls* as gifts for saving his life.

S10: Naevys's Bedroom

> The walls of this room are adorned with crossed swords and shields. Furnishings include a bed, a wardrobe, and a glass statuette on a nightstand.

The wardrobe holds spare uniforms and outfits.

Treasure. The statuette on the nightstand depicts a pillar of flame, weighs 12 pounds, and is worth 250 gp. Naevys would not approve of its theft.

S11: Regine's Bedroom

> This room has been torched. Soot blackens every surface, including a window on the east wall, and the chamber's furnishings have been reduced to charred flinders. The stench of burnt cloth, wood, and flesh hangs in the air.

Charmayne used magic to kill Regine while she was asleep in her bed, though no evidence of Regine can be found here.

Window. The window on the east wall is covered with soot on the inside but still intact. It's a 10-foot leap from the windowsill to the floating mage tower (area S14).

S12: Charmayne's Bedroom

> A pungent odor fills this room, which is cluttered with arcane materials and eerie trinkets. Much of the decor is slowly turning to ash and floating in the air.

Two elementals made of swirling ash and smoke (use the **air elemental** stat block) materialize and attack characters who enter this room. The elementals use their Whirlwind action to hurl characters through the castle's weakened walls (see "General Features" earlier in the adventure). It's a 20-foot drop to the ground from there.

The Match Thief. Resting on a nightstand next to Charmayne's bed is a thin, illustrated fairytale book titled *The Match Thief*, which is written in verse:

Striking a match against the rock in the hill,
Whit enveloped himself in the thrill.
As fire and smoke and passion did whisper
Of fluttering and risk the first time you kiss her.
The match held elation and a breath on the edge,
The trust strong between you as you lean in and pledge
To throw yourself into the wind with abandon,
A thrill unmatched and she takes your cold hand, and—
Ach! The emotion was gone, snuffed out by a breeze,
And Whit gripped the tinder, loathing the ease
With which mortals could carry this fervor and fire
Without burning inside out from their pyre.
Three matches to go, the impish fey thought,
The next one would give him all that he sought.
The next match would give him a soul bright and stark,
Three matches to go, while the world faded dark.

Charmayne drew upon this tale for inspiration while plotting the downfall of Ghalasine. The poem tells of a mischievous fey, Whit, who captures human emotions and traps them in matches. He experiences each emotion when he strikes a match. He lives a vibrant life, but the world around him grows dull and gray as he traps more and more of it. Soon he has a single match: one filled with sorrow. Whit must choose whether to return the emotion to a dull and empty world or to feel one last thing.

S13: Royal Gallery

> Glass cases on tables arranged about this room contain dragon scales, manticore tails, and other hunting trophies, as well as weapons, regal gifts, and royal trinkets—all important to King Jhaeros, no doubt. The glass cases are only just beginning to turn to ash.

This gallery is filled with objects King Jhaeros acquired throughout his youth and adult life. The four guards stationed in area S8 investigate any loud noises here.

Treasure. Among the many items on display is a *+1 battleaxe* Jhaeros wielded in his youth.

S14: Mage Tower

This tower used to be connected to the library (area S5) by a slender stone bridge. It now floats 20 feet off the ground, 10 feet from the window of area S11.

When the characters enter the tower, read or paraphrase the following:

> In the middle of this tower chamber, an ashen figure cackles with glee. Her scarlet gown billows and flaps as trails of ash swirl around her.
>
> "So bright with emotion!" she yells. "Give me rage, terror, righteous fury! Snarl at me so that I may savor it! Sustain me until the city is no more!" She then affixes her raging gaze upon you. "I can smell your soul-fires! They will be mine soon enough!"

Charmayne Daymore (see her stat block at the end of the adventure) is beyond redemption and doesn't shy away from a fight. When she drops to 0 hit points, she dies as her body crumbles to ash. She leaves behind her scarlet gown and a *potion of clairvoyance*.

The soul of any character killed by Charmayne becomes trapped in the void that hovers over Castle Cinis (see "The Void" later in the adventure).

S15: KING'S ARMORY

The first-floor armory is suspended 40 feet in the air, with nothing but the ground below it. The characters need magic or climbing gear to reach it. The northeast wall of the armory is gone, creating an opening through which the characters may enter.

> The armor and weapons found here are displayed on deteriorating tables, counters, and racks.

As soon as one or more characters set foot in the armory, two suits of armor come to life as ashen suits of **animated armor**, and four swords transform into ashen **flying swords** (see the "Ashen Creatures" sidebar). These creatures fight until destroyed.

   Treasure. Characters who search the armory find a *+1 shield*, eight *+1 arrows*, and two vials that each contain one use of *oil of sharpness*. All other equipment in the armory turns to ash when handled.

S16: KING'S BEDROOM

This location floats 20 feet in the air, with nothing but the ground below it. The characters need magic or climbing gear to reach it. Most of the room's south wall is gone, leaving a wide gap through which characters can enter.

> The king's bedroom is deteriorating to the extent that you can see furnishings being reduced to ash before your eyes. Mounted on the north wall above the king's bed is a painting of a regal man with kind eyes. The image is fleeting as you watch the painting dissolve into a cloud of ashes.

   Secret Door. Any character who searches the east wall for a secret door finds one that leads to area S17.

S17: HEART OF JHAEROS

This location is open to the sky. This room used to have a study below it, with a staircase connecting them. The study is gone, but the upper half of the staircase remains.

   The following description assumes the characters enter through the secret door in the west wall:

> This chamber holds the king in his new, terrible form: a hulking, ashen brute with his ribcage torn open, revealing an empty cavity where his heart used to be. You see no sign of the king's heart.

KING JHAEROS

Any character who touches the heart must make on a DC 15 Constitution saving throw, taking 22 (4d10) necrotic damage on a failed save, or half as much damage on a successful one. After taking this damage, the character can handle the heart safely.

The heart is twice the size of an adult human's heart. It is a Tiny object with AC 10, 5 hit points, and immunity to psychic damage. If the heart is reduced to 0 hit points, the following things happen:

The Heart Dies. The heart stops beating and dies.
Jhaeros Dies. Jhaeros in his golem-like form loses 20 hit points at the start of each of his turns.
The Void Collapses. The void above Castle Cinis collapses, freeing all the souls trapped within it. These souls then travel to the afterlife.
The Castle Falls. One minute after the heart dies and the void collapses, the floating pieces of Castle Cinis (areas S14–S17) fall to the ground and are destroyed. Creatures inside or underneath these areas when they fall take 55 (10d10) bludgeoning damage and are knocked prone.

FLEEING WITH THE HEART

If the characters had a relatively easy time getting their hands on Jhaeros's heart, use the following encounter to complicate their escape.

Two ashen **knights** mounted on ashen **warhorses** (see the "Ashen Creatures" sidebar) catch up to the characters as they make their way through the dead city of Ghalasine toward their rendezvous with Naevys. While the characters battle the knights, two ashen **shambling mounds** take shape and join the fray against the heroes.

Once these forces are defeated, the characters can conclude their business with Naevys.

THE VOID

The void above Castle Cinis is slowly consuming Ghalasine. If a creature dies in Ghalasine, the creature's soul (if it has one) becomes trapped in the void until the void collapses or the creature is raised from the dead by magic. The void already contains the souls of all those Charmayne killed, including King Jhaeros.

Characters would be wise to keep their distance from the void. Any creature that enters the void or starts its turn there takes 70 (20d6) necrotic damage. If this damage reduces the creature to 0 hit points, the creature, along with any nonmagical equipment it is wearing or carrying, turns to ash, and its soul becomes trapped in the void. Magic items that end up in the void remain trapped in it until the void is destroyed (see "Conclusion").

King Jhaeros is hostile and uses the **clay golem** stat block, with these changes:

- Replace the Acid Absorption trait with Fire Absorption. (All mentions of acid damage change to fire damage.)
- In this form, Jhaeros has Intelligence, Wisdom, and Charisma scores of 10.
- When Jhaeros drops to 0 hit points, he explodes in a harmless cloud of ashes, leaving nothing else behind.

Jhaeros won't leave this room except to chase after a character who has his heart (see below). Even then, he can't leave Ghalasine.

Heart of the King. King Jhaeros guards his heart, which is hidden in a cavity under the floor. The cavity, which is just big enough to contain the heart, is covered by a 2-foot-square stone tile. Characters within 5 feet of the tile can hear the heart beating.

As an action, a character in the middle of the room can try to lift the stone tile, doing so with a successful DC 10 Strength (Athletics) check. The check is made with advantage if the character uses a crowbar or similar tool. The heart can then be removed from the cavity under the tile.

CONCLUSION

If Jhaeros's still-beating heart is delivered to Naevys outside the city, it disappears in her hands. When the heart vanishes, the following things happen:

Charmayne Dies. Charmayne collapses, dies, and turns to ash.

The Void Collapses. The void above Castle Cinis collapses, freeing all the souls trapped within it. Everyone whose soul was trapped inside the void is restored to life with all their hit points, materializing in unoccupied spaces within the city. Characters whose souls are released from the void are deposited in area S9, as is King Jhaeros (lawful good, human **archmage**) and Councilor Regine LaVerne (lawful neutral, tiefling **noble**).

Ghalasine Is Restored. The damage to Ghalasine is undone, and the city is made resplendent once more, as though no calamity ever threatened it. Gray ash is swept away as the structures of the city are magically rebuilt before the eyes of weeping onlookers. Castle Cinis is made whole again.

Jalynvyr Is Set Free. Jalynvyr is released from captivity in area S9 and is restored to his true form at full health.

The Hounds Are Restored. The hell hounds Cinnabar and Sol transform back into friendly **mastiffs**.

If Jhaeros's heart dies or if things otherwise go wrong, Ghalasine is reduced to ashes. Her victory complete, Charmayne abandons the ruined city. The characters might encounter her again after she finds some other city to torment.

REWARDS

After delivering King Jhaeros's heart to Naevys, characters are eligible to receive one or more of the following rewards at the end of the adventure:

Naevys's Gifts. If Charmayne's ritual is reversed and Ghalasine is restored, Naevys gives the characters a *flame tongue* longsword, a *necklace of fireballs*, and a suit of *dragon scale mail* from Ghalasine's treasury. She also gives the characters 2,000 gp each from her personal savings. If the characters end the ritual but fail the undo the damage it caused, Naevys awards them the money but not the magic items.

Jhaeros's Favor. If King Jhaeros survives and Ghalasine is restored, the king gives the characters a tract of land, perhaps even a keep and titles. The estate's exact location is up to you.

FOR THE GOLDEN VAULT

If the characters are working for the Golden Vault, the organization rewards the characters with a rare magic item of their choice (subject to your approval) as payment for delivering Jhaeros's still-beating heart to Naevys and saving Ghalasine. The item is delivered to the characters the next day.

CHARMAYNE DAYMORE
Medium Elemental (Wizard), Neutral Evil

Armor Class 12 (15 with *mage armor*)
Hit Points 123 (19d8 + 38)
Speed 30 ft., fly 30 ft. (hover)

STR	DEX	CON	INT	WIS	CHA
8 (−1)	14 (+2)	15 (+2)	20 (+5)	14 (+2)	16 (+3)

Saving Throws Int +9, Wis +6, Cha +7
Skills Arcana +9, Deception +7, Perception +6
Damage Immunities fire
Senses passive Perception 16
Languages Common, Draconic, Elvish, Ignan
Challenge 10 (5,900 XP)   **Proficiency Bonus** +4

Legendary Resistance (3/Day). If Charmayne fails a saving throw, she can choose to succeed instead.

ACTIONS

Multiattack. Charmayne makes three Ashen Burst attacks. She can replace one of these attacks with one use of Spellcasting.

Ashen Burst. *Melee or Ranged Spell Attack:* +9 to hit, reach 5 ft. or range 60 ft., one target. *Hit:* 17 (5d6) fire damage.

Cinder Spite (Recharge 5–6). Charmayne creates a magical explosion of fire centered on a point she can see within 120 feet of herself. Each creature in a 20-foot-radius sphere centered on that point must make a DC 17 Dexterity saving throw, taking 35 (10d6) fire damage on a failed save, or half as much damage on a successful one. A Humanoid reduced to 0 hit points by this damage dies and is transformed into a Tiny charcoal figurine.

Spellcasting. Charmayne casts one of the following spells, using Intelligence as the spellcasting ability (spell save DC 17):

At will: *dancing lights, mage hand*
3/day: *mage armor*
1/day each: *dispel magic, invisibility, polymorph*

REACTIONS

Charmayne can take up to three reactions per round but only one per turn.

Elemental Rebuke. In response to being hit by an attack, Charmayne utters a word in Ignan, dealing 10 (3d6) fire damage to the attacker. Charmayne then teleports, along with any equipment she is wearing or carrying, up to 30 feet to an unoccupied space she can see, leaving a harmless cloud of ash and embers in the space she just left.

Fiery Counterspell. Charmayne interrupts a creature she can see within 60 feet of herself that is casting a spell. If the spell is 4th level or lower, it fails and has no effect. If the spell is 5th level or higher, Charmayne makes an Intelligence check (DC 10 + the spell's level). On a success, the spell fails and has no effect. Whatever the spell's level, the caster takes 10 (3d6) fire damage if the spell fails.

THE CONCORDANT EXPRESS ROCKETS THROUGH
THE OUTLANDS ON ITS WAY TO MECHANUS.

AFFAIR ON THE CONCORDANT EXPRESS

WANTED FOR CRIMES ACROSS THE MULTI-verse, an outlaw known as the Stranger is currently a prisoner aboard the Concordant Express, an interplanar train destined for Mechanus, where the outlaw is set to stand trial. In this heist, the characters must obtain a list of names the Stranger has committed to memory. The names in question are the true names of several powerful demons, devils, and yugoloths.

ADVENTURE BACKGROUND

The interplanar outlaw known as the Stranger had humble origins. The Stranger was born into a slum and orphaned as an infant. Early on, they used their knack for magic to masquerade as a lost noble scion and earn patronage as a spellcasting student. Inevitably, the school the Stranger was attending discovered the ruse, but the Stranger always slipped away and reemerged at an even more prominent academy in another city with a new false identity.

The Stranger perpetrated many crimes, none greater than the attempted theft of a book that held the true names of many demons, devils, and yugoloths (see "True Names" below). When the Stranger tried to flee with the book, a fiendish ward caused the book to disappear. By then, the Stranger had already committed many of the true names to memory. The Stranger then set off across the multiverse, making deals with various Fiends in exchange for keeping their true names secret. The Stranger survived all these dealings unscathed for years, but their luck eventually ran out.

Fiendish foes set their sights on the Stranger, forcing the Stranger to flee to the Material Plane and take refuge in the city-state of Akharin Sangar, which is ruled by a powerful angelic being. (Akharin Sangar is detailed further in *Journeys through the Radiant Citadel*). But the Stranger underestimated the vigilance of Akharin Sangar's celestial host and was caught impersonating an angel. When the Stranger refused to divulge any information about themselves, a deva enforcer named Omid was tasked with delivering the Stranger to Mechanus to stand trial. The prisoner was clamped in *dimensional shackles* and taken aboard the Concordant Express for safe transport.

TRUE NAMES

Every Fiend has a true name that it tries to keep secret. One who knows a Fiend's true name can use this name to bind that Fiend to service. Other powerful creatures such as Celestials and Fey might have true names that function similarly.

True names aren't restricted to spoken language or script. A creature's true name could be a specific gesture, sound, or other type of expression, such as the tolling of an iron bell, a mathematical equation, or a sequence of notes played on a particular kind of instrument.

ADVENTURE HOOKS

If you're using the Golden Vault as the hook for the adventure, skip ahead to the "Using the Golden Vault" section. Otherwise, choose one of the following adventure hooks.

BLOOD WAR BALANCE

A planar faction known as the Fixers aims to restore balance to the Blood War (the eternal feud between demons and devils) by obtaining the true names of a pit fiend commonly known as Karnyros, a balor called Errtok, and a marilith known as Hexalanthe. A representative of the Fixers hires the characters to obtain these Fiends' true names from the Stranger.

FIENDISH EXTORTION

A high-ranking member of the Fated, a faction in Sigil, has been captured and is being ransomed by an ultroloth known as Zeevok. Faction leaders hire the characters to obtain Zeevok's true name so the Fated can force Zeevok to release his captive without collecting a ransom.

PERSONAL REASONS

The characters seek the true name of a Fiend that has bedeviled them in the past.

USING THE GOLDEN VAULT

If you're using the Golden Vault as a patron, a golden key is delivered to the characters in whatever manner you deem fit. When the characters use this key to open their music box, the lid pops open and a soothing voice says the following:

> "Greetings, operatives. The Golden Vault needs you to obtain the true names of three powerful denizens of the Lower Planes: the pit fiend Karnyros, the balor Errtok, and the marilith Hexalanthe. Their true names are known to an outlaw called the Stranger, who is being transported to Mechanus on an interplanar train called the Concordant Express. This quest, should you choose to undertake it, requires you board the train, locate the Stranger, and acquire the true names from them. Expect to be contacted shortly by a quadrone named Glitch, a former train operative who now works for us. Good luck, operatives."

Closing the music box causes the golden key to vanish.

GLITCH THE QUADRONE

Not long after agreeing to undertake the adventure, the characters encounter a friendly **quadrone** named Glitch. (When and where this happens is up to you.) The quadrone used to oversee hospitality on the Concordant Express. For this reason, it was imbued with the ability to speak Celestial, Common, and Infernal in addition to Modron.

Conflicting directives from two pentadrone superiors caused a glitch that prompted the confused quadrone to quit its job. Glitch has become a free-thinking being with no desire to reintegrate into the modron hierarchy.

Eager to help the characters, Glitch speaks to them in Common:

> "Ah, hello! Yes, good, finally—friends looking to catch the Stranger—the Stranger who has already been caught. Here, take this map. It shows the train cars. Here are your tickets and a pen to write down names. Not ordinary names—secret names! I am Glitch, by the way."

Glitch hands the characters an old blueprint of the Concordant Express (see map 11.1), one train ticket per character, and an ink pen. The tickets are made from paper-thin sheets of brass and grant passage to Mechanus aboard the Concordant Express. Each ticket is stamped with a boarding time, and the characters have 24 hours until the train departs.

Glitch takes the characters to the train when they're ready (see "Catching the Train" below) and stays with them in the interim. Glitch also shares the following information:

Configuration. Like most trains, the Concordant Express includes an Engine Car at the front and a Caboose at the back. The number of other train cars and their configuration can change, so Glitch can't say much more about the size of the train or the order in which the cars will be arranged. The configuration of the cars might be different than what's shown on the blueprint. (In fact, it is. See the "Train Configuration" section for details.)

Fuel. The train is fueled by treasure, which is kept in the Engine Car.

Location of the Stranger. The Stranger is likely being held in the Jail Car, which has a skylight.

Patrols. Modrons patrol the exterior of the train.

Teleportation Ward. Creatures can't teleport into or out of the train.

THE CONCORDANT EXPRESS

The Concordant Express is a clockwork locomotive that traverses the multiverse. Modrons constructed the train with mathematical precision, and they operate it in the same way. The train's conductor is its sapient Engine Car, which delivers passengers and cargo to their intended destinations on schedule.

No terrain is too rugged for the train. Like the landmasses that make up Mechanus, the wheels of the Concordant Express are a network of interlacing cogs. A series of mechanical arms rapidly places levitating tracks before the train, while a similar set of arms beneath the Caboose collects the trailing tracks and delivers them to the Engine Car. This system allows the train to traverse inhospitable environments and to adjust course as needed.

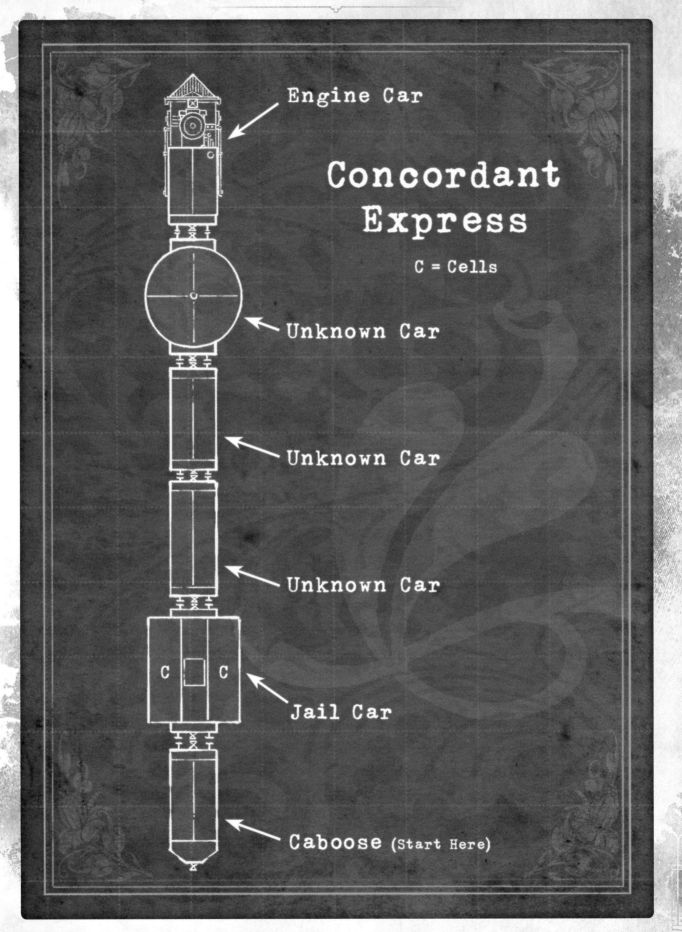

Engine Car

Concordant
Express

C = Cells

Unknown Car

Unknown Car

Unknown Car

C   C

Jail Car

Caboose (Start Here)

MIKE SCHLEY

TRAIN CONFIGURATION

The train has three mandatory cars and three optional cars, as described below.

MANDATORY CARS

In this adventure, the Concordant Express has one of each of the following cars:

- The Caboose (area E1) is the rearmost car.
- The Engine Car (area E9) is the frontmost car.
- The train has one Jail Car (area E8), which is adjacent to the Engine Car (not the Caboose, as shown on map 11.1).

OPTIONAL CARS

Map 11.2 includes maps for six additional cars: Abacus Car (area E2), Aquarium Car (area E3), Cargo Car (area E4), Planartarium Car (area E5), Passenger Car (area E6), and Temple Car (area E7).

Pick any three of these cars and add them to the train in whatever configuration suits you, provided the mandatory cars stay where they are. (You can choose a different set of optional cars each time you run the adventure.)

You can add more than three optional cars to the train, at the risk of increasing the heist's length and difficulty. Conversely, you may opt for fewer cars for a shorter, easier heist.

CATCHING THE TRAIN

Embedded in Glitch's body is an *amulet of the planes* that turns to dust (along with the rest of the quadrone) if Glitch is reduced to 0 hit points. Glitch uses this built-in amulet to cast *plane shift*, delivering itself and the characters to a field in the Outlands (see the *Dungeon Master's Guide* for more information about this plane of existence). There they must wait for the train to arrive.

As the train approaches the characters' location, read the following text:

> You pass the time on a grassy plain, waiting for the train to arrive. A few miles away, a colossal spire of rock rises into the sky, its peak lost in the clouds.
>
> Glitch grows fidgety and impatient. Suddenly, the distant blare of a horn draws Glitch's attention—and yours—to a column of smoke on the horizon. "Good," says Glitch. "Here it comes, right on time!"
>
> A locomotive hurtles across the sky toward you, laying down magical tracks before it. As it draws near, you can see clockwork limbs disassembling the tracks behind the train and passing them forward so the locomotive can lay down new tracks in front of itself.

> As the train descends to ground level, its horn blares once more. It swerves away from you, coming to a gradual stop until its caboose is a short distance away, pointing in your direction.
>
> "Got your tickets?" asks Glitch. "Excellent. Now go. Show your tickets to the modron in the caboose. This is where I leave you. Farewell, friends!"

Glitch exits the adventure at this point, using its *amulet of the planes* to return whence it came.

BOARDING THE TRAIN

The Caboose (area E1) doubles as a train station. Inside it is a booth containing a **duodrone** attendant with a built-in ticket puncher. All passengers must get their tickets punched by this duodrone before they're permitted to explore the rest of the train.

If one or more characters refuse to get their tickets punched, the duodrone whistles (no action required), causing four **tridrones** to emerge from hidden compartments in the walls and act as described in area E1. If the characters then comply to avoid an altercation, the tridrones return to their compartments.

CHOO, CHOO!

Once the characters' tickets are punched and the train is ready to go, read the following text:

> Machinery whirs and clicks as the train shudders and creeps forward, gradually picking up speed. Another horn blast signals that the Concordant Express is once again on the move.

GENERAL FEATURES

The Concordant Express has the following features:

Ceilings. Car ceilings are 15 feet high unless the text states otherwise.

Doors. At each end of every car is a sliding metal door. The doors to the Jail Car are locked (see area E8 for details); all others are unlocked.

Flight. The train has a flying speed of 60 feet and can't hover.

Lighting. All cars are brightly lit by magical orbs embedded in the ceilings.

Modrons. All modrons serving aboard the Concordant Express speak no languages other than Modron unless the text states otherwise.

Teleportation Ward. Creatures can't teleport into or out of the train, or to any space within 120 feet of it. Any attempt to do so is wasted.

Moving on the Train

To reach the Stranger, the characters must make their way from the Caboose (area E1) to the Jail Car (area E8).

Crossing between Cars

Creatures can safely move from one car to another by stepping across couplers situated between the cars' exterior platforms.

Falling off the Train

If an effect would result in a creature falling off the train, the creature must succeed on a DC 14 Dexterity saving throw. On a success, the creature instead falls prone in the nearest unoccupied space on the train. On a failure, the creature is sucked into the train's undercarriage, taking 33 (6d10) bludgeoning damage and landing prone in an unoccupied space at either end of the nearest train car.

If a character falls off the Caboose, the train's track-retrieval arms snatch up the character and deposit them into an empty cell in the Jail Car (area E8).

Guard Patrols

Hostile modrons patrol the rooftops of the cars, attacking anyone they see who isn't supposed to be there. Whenever one or more characters reach the midpoint of a rooftop on any car other than the Jail Car, roll a d6 and use the Guard Patrols table to determine if an encounter occurs. Assume the patrol begins the encounter on the rooftop of an adjoining car. All the modrons have truesight, and characters on the rooftop have nowhere to hide.

No random encounters occur on the roof of the Jail Car until after the squad of pentadrones stationed there is defeated (see area E8 for details).

Guard Patrols

d6	Encounter
1–3	No encounter
4–5	Three **tridrones** and one **quadrone** leader
6	Four **quadrones** and one **pentadrone** leader

Strong Winds

Creatures climbing on the outside the train or flying within 15 feet of it while it's in motion are subject to strong winds, the effects of which are as follows:

Difficult Terrain. The wind-whipped exterior of the train is difficult terrain.
Ranged Attacks. Ranged weapon attacks are made with disadvantage.

Planar Effects

The Concordant Express moves across the known planes of existence by passing through invisible portals only the train's sapient Engine Car can find. The train's next stop is Mechanus, but it will pass through several other Outer Planes on its way there. While the train shields passengers from the harmful planes through which it travels, creatures aboard the train aren't entirely immune to the planes' effects.

The Planar Effects table contains effects for various planes of existence on the train's current route. Unless otherwise noted, each effect lasts until the train leaves the plane. Some effects apply only to creatures outside the train.

The train enters a new plane whenever you like. Roll or choose from the options on the table to determine which plane the train is on and its accompanying effect. Once a train leaves a plane, it doesn't return to that plane for the rest of the adventure.

Planar Effects

d6	Plane and Effect
1	**Acheron.** The train flies over a vast battlefield where legions of devils clash with hordes of demons. Whenever one creature aboard the train deals damage to another creature aboard the train, both take 4 (1d8) psychic damage.
2	**Elysium.** All creatures aboard the train feel a sense of inner peace. No creature aboard the train can make an attack or cast a spell that deals damage.
3	**Mount Celestia.** Good-aligned creatures aboard the train gain a benefit of a *bless* spell that lasts until the train leaves Mount Celestia.
4	**The Nine Hells.** On one of the blisteringly cold layers of the Nine Hells (either Cania or Stygia), the train passes through a frigid gorge filled with whirlwinds of ice needles. Any creature outside the train takes 5 (2d4) cold damage plus 5 (2d4) piercing damage at the start of each of its turns. Modrons that normally patrol the outside of the train lock themselves in compartments for safety until the train leaves the plane.
5	**Pandemonium.** Howling darkness surrounds the train. Creatures outside the train are deafened. Outside the train, bright light becomes dim light, and dim light becomes darkness.
6	**Ysgard.** Silent, spectral warriors from Valhalla fly around the train on ghostly chariots pulled by ghostly steeds. Any creature aboard the train that would be reduced to 0 hit points drops to 1 hit point instead.

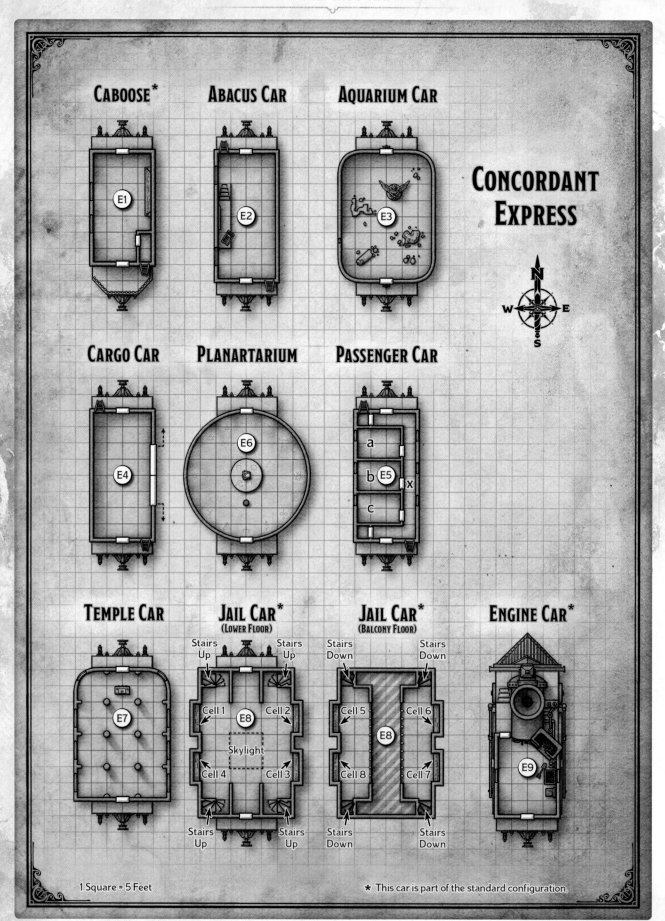

CABOOSE*

E1

ABACUS CAR

E2

AQUARIUM CAR

E3

CONCORDANT EXPRESS

N
W   E
S

CARGO CAR

E4

PLANARTARIUM

E6

PASSENGER CAR

a
b   E5   x
c

TEMPLE CAR

E7

JAIL CAR*
(LOWER FLOOR)

Stairs Up   Stairs Up

Cell 1   E8   Cell 2

Skylight

Cell 4   Cell 3

Stairs Up   Stairs Up

JAIL CAR*
(BALCONY FLOOR)

Stairs Down   Stairs Down

Cell 5   Cell 6

E8

Cell 8   Cell 7

Stairs Down   Stairs Down

ENGINE CAR*

E9

1 Square = 5 Feet

* This car is part of the standard configuration.

MIKE SCHLEY

Train Cars

The various train cars are shown on map 11.2. The earlier "Train Configuration" section explains how to choose and arrange the cars.

E1: Caboose

The characters are assumed to be in this car when the train gets underway. As the train begins to pick up speed and lifts into the air, a disembodied voice says, "Next stop: Mechanus!" in Common, Modron, Celestial, Infernal, Abyssal, and Primordial.

Modrons in the Caboose

The **duodrone** attendant who punched the characters' tickets has another function aboard the train: making minor repairs while the train is in motion. As the train gets underway, the duodrone dons gear from a nearby locker (see "Locker" below). It then departs to perform its duties, whistling as it marches to the next car.

Hidden in the walls of the Caboose are four **tridrones** that emerge from their compartments to attack passengers who refuse to get their tickets punched or who perform an unlawful act, such as threatening the duodrone or plundering the locker.

Locker

The locker contains a blue engineer's hat and a crew uniform consisting of a tool belt and a pair of grimy overalls labeled with a number.

Rear Platform

A railing on the car's rearmost platform prevents creatures from stumbling over the edge and into the dizzying blur of mechanical arms that retrieve the trailing railway tracks. A bronze ladder welded to the car provides access to its roof.

E2: Abacus Car

> Ten spherical modrons are lined up against the wall opposite a podium, behind which is a chalkboard covered with mathematical equations. Next to the podium stands a boxy modron wearing a wizard's cap. It taps the podium with a brass wand to get your attention. "Well met!" it says in Common. "I am the Math Wizard, Captain of Calculus, Admiral of Abaci, Unifier of Units! Welcome to my Sanctum Numerum, where any problem can be solved. I beseech thee, travelers, what numerical enigmas plague thee?"

The eleven modrons stationed here act as a mathematical calculator for passengers.

The self-proclaimed Math Wizard is a friendly **duodrone**. The Math Wizard speaks both Common and Modron.

The ten **monodrones** speak Modron only and are indifferent toward passengers. Each one holds a stack of ten placards numbered 0 through 9. When a creature inside the Abacus Car asks a mathematical question to which the answer is a number, the Math Wizard taps the podium with its wand and says, "Calculate!" In response, the monodrones select from their placards, shuffle around, and hold up their numerals to display the answer. The Math Wizard cheers "Huzzah!" after every successful calculation.

The monodrones do their best to calculate accurately, but sometimes they must estimate. Furthermore, if the ten monodrones are asked a question to which the answer exceeds 9,999,999,999 or the solution is uncountable, they scramble in circles while screaming in existential terror for a few moments before calmly returning to their positions.

Chalkboard

The chalkboard is covered with equations explaining, rather incomprehensibly, why the Great Modron March happens only once every 289 years. To anyone other than a modron, most of the equations are utter nonsense.

A character who studies the equations for at least 10 minutes can make a DC 25 Intelligence (Arcana) check at the end of that time. If the check fails, the character takes 3 (1d6) psychic damage and suffers a mild headache for the next hour. If the check succeeds, the character discovers a profound equation nestled among the others. Like a key, this equation unlocks something in the character's brain, with the effect determined by rolling on the Mysterious Equation table. A character who experiences this revelation gains no further benefit from studying the chalkboard equations. If any of the equations are erased, the modrons in the car turn hostile and attack, and no one can benefit from studying the equations.

Mysterious Equation

d8	Effect
1–3	You gain inspiration.
4–5	You gain proficiency in one tool of your choice.
6	You gain proficiency in one of the following skills of your choice: Deception, History, Insight, Investigation, Medicine, or Performance.
7	You learn a new language of your choice.
8	Your Intelligence score permanently increases by 2 (to a maximum of 20).

E3: Aquarium Car

> This car is filled with clear water that isn't displaced when the door opens. The car's interior space is a large aquarium, complete with a coral reef and algae-coated ruins. Tiny fish dart through the ruins and circle an alabaster statue carved in the likeness of an angel clutching a decanter. Nearby fish scatter at the sight of you.

This car is completely flooded, and magic keeps the water from being displaced when either door is opened. Creatures that can't breathe underwater must hold their breath in the aquarium. Magic instantly dries creatures as they exit the water.

The aquarium can be slowly drained by removing a fist-sized plug near the base of the car's portside wall. As an action, a character within reach of the plug can try to pull it out, doing so with a successful DC 17 Strength check. Once the plug is removed, the aquarium's water level decreases at a rate of 1 foot per minute. It takes 15 minutes for all the water to drain from the car. The car's fish can't survive more than a few minutes without water.

Angelic Statue

The alabaster statue is a petrified **deva** with a *decanter of endless water*. If any harm befalls the fish in the aquarium, the deva immediately reverts to flesh and chastises whoever is responsible. If the aquarium's plug was removed, the deva replaces it. If any water was drained from the car, the deva uses the decanter to replenish it. If any fish died, the deva uses *raise dead* spells to revive one fish per day for ten days. Once all is set right, the deva flies from the train and casts *plane shift* to return to Mount Celestia, taking the decanter with it.

E4: Cargo Car

> A battered war machine rests at one end of this spacious car. Acid drips from a hose-like weapon mounted on the front of the vehicle, leaving a sizzling hole in the train car's floor.

The war machine comes from the wastelands of Avernus, the first layer of the Nine Hells. The vehicle isn't operational, but its hose-like sprayer is. A creature standing within 5 feet of the nozzle can take an action to cause the weapon to spray acidic bile in a 30-foot cone. Each creature in the cone must make a DC 12 Dexterity saving throw, taking 40 (9d8) acid damage on a failed save, or half as much on a successful one. A creature reduced to 0 hit points by this damage is dissolved, leaving behind any objects it was carrying or wearing. Once used, the sprayer can't be used again.

A creature that interacts with the war machine spooks six invisible **imps** lurking in its bent chassis. The imps fly out and attack the source of their fright while yelling, "I can't go back to jail!" in Infernal. If the infernal war machine's acid sprayer hasn't already been used, one of the imps uses it.

A character who sits in the driver's seat notices a glowing *potion of resistance* (fire) jammed in a dirty glove compartment along with six unpaid infernal parking tickets.

E5: Planartarium Car

> Glowing symbols on the floor line the perimeter of this domed car. In the middle of the car is a mechanical model suspended over a dais that has more glowing symbols on it. The model resembles a large wheel with a tall spire protruding from the top. A tiny brass ring floats above the spire's peak.
>
> The spectral blue image of a modron materializes before the dais. It has a boxy shape and wears a pair of oversized glasses. The illusory modron adjusts its glasses and joyfully greets you in Common:
>
> "Hello, and welcome to the Planartarium. You can learn more about the planes of existence by donating to this car. All proceeds benefit the establishment of order across the multiverse." Before disappearing, the modron gestures toward a short tube protruding from the floor near the dais.

The sixteen glowing sigils on the floor represent each of the Outer Planes, while the raised dais in the center of the room bears symbols of the four elemental Inner Planes. The wheel-shaped model above the dais represents the Outlands and its sixteen gate-towns. The tiny ring at the top of the spire represents Sigil.

A magical mote of golden light denotes the train's location. Since the train's travels are usually limited to the Inner Planes, the Outer Planes, and the Outlands, this mote can be seen floating above one of the symbols or above the model wheel representing the Outlands. If the train is in some other location not represented in this car, no mote is visible.

Donation Tube

The short tube rising from the floor near the dais has a slot large enough to insert coins, gemstones, and other small valuables. Such valuables are then teleported to the cart in area E9.

Whenever a creature drops at least 10 gp worth of treasure into the tube, Cosmo, the illusory modron, reappears. It thanks the donor and asks which plane of existence they'd like to learn about.

Cosmo can give a brief lecture on any plane of existence described in the *Dungeon Master's Guide*. If a character asks about a plane on the train's route, Cosmo also alludes to noteworthy planar effects. For example, if asked about the Nine Hells, the spectral duodrone might say, "Rest assured, the Concordant Express is reinforced to withstand extreme heat and extreme cold." Cosmo lectures about one plane per donation and vanishes after each lecture.

If a character inserts something worthless into the donation slot or otherwise tries to fool it with counterfeits and the like, the tube disgorges poisonous gas that quickly fills the compartment. This gas duplicates the effect of a *stinking cloud* spell that lasts for 1 minute or until it is dispersed.

E6: PASSENGER CAR

A mind flayer in a beige coat kneels beside a body in the aisle of this passenger car. Three curious onlookers—a cambion, a drow, and bronze dwarf with flames for hair—poke their heads out of nearby cabins. "No one move a muscle!" warns the mind flayer. "This whole car just became a crime scene."

This car contains three cozy passenger cabins and two privies (one at each end of the car). Quintus Malvesh, an aasimar cartographer, lies dead in the aisle (in the square marked X on map 9.2), and a detective is already on the case.

ILLITHID DETECTIVE
The detective is a lawful neutral **mind flayer** named Ignatius Inkblot. Seeing the characters, Ignatius lights a pipe with a match it holds with one of its face tentacles. The pipe exudes a green vapor that smells of absinthe. Since the characters weren't on the car when the murder occurred, Ignatius doesn't regard them as suspects and is friendly toward them. Ignatius can speak Common but loathes doing so; the mind flayer prefers to converse telepathically. Its tone is strident, and it uses stereotypical detective phrases such as "The game is afoot!" and "The devil is in the details!"

Ignatius tries to enlist the characters in its investigation. If they agree to help, the mind flayer asks them to look for clues and question suspects. (In the meantime, the mind flayer quietly casts *detect thoughts*, focusing on every creature in the Passenger Car.) Ignatius asks that no one leave the car until the mystery is solved. If the characters leave anyway, Ignatius solves the case without their help.

What Ignatius Knows. Ignatius has already determined that Quintus was killed while walking to his cabin from one of the Passenger Car's two privies. The aasimar's body lies outside the door to the middle cabin, which Quintus and another passenger shared. Ignatius was using the other privy at the time of Quintus's death and heard the aasimar gasp before hitting the floor. Ignatius quickly reached the scene, but the killer was nowhere in sight.

MURDER SUSPECTS
The suspects aboard the Passenger Car are as follows:

Abernathy Vernus (lawful evil **cambion**) is a friendly, ingratiating fellow who claims to have won a free tour aboard the Concordant Express. He insists that others call him Vern. No other passengers occupy his cabin (the one marked "a" on map 9.2), which Vern shares with a **monodrone** valet that answers to the name Higglesworth.

Ethlynn Stalaczic (neutral, drow **mage**) is a friendly, somewhat gullible dragonologist on a planar quest to find a "time dragon" (which may or may not be a real thing). Until a few moments ago, Ethlynn and Quintus were cabin mates. Ethlynn currently shares her cabin (the one marked "b" on map 9.2) with a **monodrone** valet called Bot.

Meldar (lawful neutral **azer**) is indifferent toward others, speaks nothing but Ignan, and provides curt answers to questions put to them. The azer is returning to the City of Brass after attending a smiths' convention in Bytopia. Meldar shares a cabin (the one marked "c" on map 9.2) with Ignatius Inkblot and a monodrone valet known as Orb.

The monodrones never leave the train. Ignatius was already aboard when Meldar boarded the train a day ago in Bytopia. The other suspects boarded the train near Excelsior (a gate-town in the Outlands) shortly before the characters came aboard.

MURDER VICTIM
Characters can examine Quintus or cast spells on the corpse. The following information can be learned by doing so:

Examining the Corpse. A character who examines Quintus and succeeds on a DC 11 Intelligence (Arcana) or Wisdom (Medicine) check determines that the aasimar was killed by three bolts of magical force identical to those created by a *magic missile* spell. Given where the body fell, the direction Quintus was walking when he died, and where the wounds on the body are located, a character can deduce, with a successful DC 16 Intelligence

(Investigation) check, that the killer likely didn't come from Meldar's cabin.

Raising the Dead. A character who has the *raise dead* spell prepared can use it to restore Quintus to life. (The devas in areas E3 and E8 can also provide this service, if asked nicely.) Quintus is chaotic neutral and uses the **noble** stat block, although he is unarmored and carries no weapons. Alive, the aasimar is less cooperative than when he was dead, for reasons explained in the "Motive" section below. He offers no possible reasons for why someone would want to kill him.

Speaking with the Dead. If a *speak with dead* spell is cast on the corpse, the aasimar's spirit answers questions honestly. Quintus did not see his killer, but he knows one reason why every other passenger in this car (besides Ignatius) might want him dead. These reasons are summarized in the Murder Suspects table.

SEARCHING THE CABINS

Characters can search for clues in the passenger cabins and question the modron valet in each one:

Cabin A. This cabin holds Vern's battered suitcase, which contains two traveler's outfits, three odd-looking compasses, and a set of tinker's tools. If asked about the compasses, Vern says he builds and repairs them to pass the time on long trips.

Cabin B. Ethlynn shared this cabin with the murder victim and knows Quintus was a cartographer. Ethlynn confirms that Quintus left their cabin to use the privy at one end of the train car. Characters who search the cabin find Quintus's satchel, which contains two spare traveler's outfits, a set of cartographer's tools, and a map case containing what look like ancient treasure maps. A similar map, stolen by Ethlynn while Quintus was visiting the privy, is stuffed in her spidersilk handbag. (Ethlynn insists Quintus gave the map to her, which he never did. He did, however, tell her that the map shows the way to a time dragon's lair, which it does not.) A character who spends 1 minute examining any one of Quintus's maps can, with a successful DC 16 Intelligence (Investigation) check, cast serious doubt on the map's accuracy.

Cabin C. Meldar and Ignatius share this cabin, which contains nothing incriminating. Its occupants travel light.

Questioning the Modrons. Monodrone valets aboard the Concordant Express have built-in language interpreters instead of voice boxes; consequently, they can understand any spoken language but can't speak. Bot and Orb shrug their shoulders if questioned about the murder (of which they know nothing). Higglesworth simply points to itself if questioned about the murder.

Solving the Mystery

The monodrone Higglesworth killed Quintus using a *wand of magic missiles*, which is hidden in a secret compartment inside the monodrone's spherical body. The monodrone won't subject itself to inspection and attacks anyone who tries to search or dismantle it. Its impeccable valet programming prevents it from incriminating passengers or accusing them of any wrongdoing.

Higglesworth did not commit the crime willingly. The cambion Vern used his tinker's tools and magical know-how to reprogram the monodrone valet to murder Quintus using a wand Vern pilfered from a wizard's apprentice in Excelsior. Vern then used the modron's body to hide the murder weapon and instructed Higglesworth not to tolerate invasive scrutiny.

Murder Weapon. A character can use an action to search Higglesworth for a secret compartment, finding it with a successful DC 13 Wisdom (Perception) check, but this can be done only while the monodrone is incapacitated. The same is true for opening the compartment, which requires another action, thieves' tools or tinker's tools, and a successful DC 11 Dexterity check. Opening the compartment causes the wand to tumble out.

If Higglesworth is reduced to 0 hit points, its body disintegrates, but the *wand of magic missiles* hidden inside it remains.

One of the wand's charges has been expended—the same charge that killed Quintus.

Motive. Vern is a con artist who makes and sells "magic compasses" to gullible folk looking for an easy way to find that which their hearts desire. Quintus, also a con artist, made and sold bogus treasure maps. Vern and Quintus both identified Ethlynn as a likely mark, but Quintus got to her first by preying on her dream of finding a time dragon's lair. Vern decided to eliminate the competition while laying the blame on a malfunctioning modron that can't speak in its own defense.

J'Accuse! If the characters accuse Ethlynn or Meldar of murdering Quintus, Ignatius telepathically warns the characters that their investigation

has gone "off the rails." He then recommends they "look for clues within clues" and "try to understand the motive behind the killing." Gifted with the ability to cast *detect thoughts* at will, Ignatius has already identified Vern as the individual responsible for Quintus's death, but Ignatius wants the characters to see the truth for themselves—not simply take a mind flayer's word for it.

Case Closed. The mystery concludes with Ignatius confining Vern to his cabin until the authorities in Mechanus remove the cambion from the train. If the characters don't have the means to raise Quintus from the dead, Ignatius suggests they speak to the deva guarding the Jail Car and convince the angel to revive the dead aasimar. The characters are free to keep the *wand of magic missiles*, since Ignatius doesn't need it to make a case against Vern.

Ignatius won't press Ethlynn on the theft of Quintus's bogus map, but characters may do so. Ethlynn can be guilted into returning the map and apologizing for the theft. As for Quintus, the aasimar won't admit to any wrongdoing unless magic is used to coerce him.

E7: Temple Car

> Stained-glass windows decorate the walls of this car, while its floors are adorned with exquisitely patterned rugs. Several columns support a vaulted mosaic ceiling. Kneeling before an altar is a serene priest in sunny robes.

The priest is, in fact, a **gray slaad** using its Change Shape ability to fool the characters. The slaad was sent here to kill them, plain and simple. It killed the real priest, stole his robes, and threw his body and holy symbol off the train.

The slaad works for an evil, multiverse-spanning organization called the Syndicate of Terror, Extortion, Assassination, and Larceny (STEAL), which has been spying on the characters for some time and wants their mission aboard the Concordant Express to fail. (This is doubly true if the characters

Murder Suspects

Suspect	Possible Motive
Abernathy Vernus	The cambion seemed upset, maybe even jealous, that Ethlynn and Quintus were getting along so well. The cambion seemed to have his heart set on spending more time with Ethlynn, which necessitated getting rid of Quintus.
Ethlynn Stalaczic	Ethlynn was eyeballing Quintus's maps. Killing Quintus would allow her to steal the maps without anyone knowing.
Meldar	Quintus referred to Meldar as a "hothead" when he didn't think the azer was close enough to hear him. Killing Quintus could've been payback for the insult. (Since Meldar knows only one language—Ignan—and the insult wasn't spoken in that tongue, this motive evaporates quickly.)

are working for STEAL's rival, the Golden Vault.) If you're weaving multiple adventures from this anthology into your campaign, one or more villains from earlier adventures might have secret ties to this evil organization. Likely candidates (assuming they're still alive) include Quentin Togglepocket from "The Stygian Gambit," Guildmaster Dusk from "Masterpiece Imbroglio," and Nixylanna Vidorant from "Vidorant's Vault." If you're using the rivals described in this book's introduction, their patron might be a STEAL operative.

One of STEAL's operatives, having recently acquired the gray slaad's control gem, used the gem to command the slaad to slip aboard the Concordant Express and kill the characters on sight. The slaad loathes being surrounded by modrons on the train and fights to the death.

Scrying Sensor

The slaad's master watches the battle unfold through an invisible scrying sensor like the one created by a *scrying* spell. If the characters defeat the slaad, a magically altered voice issues from the invisible sensor and says in Common, "So much for that. Next time you won't be so lucky!" If the characters are working for the Golden Vault, the voice adds, "The Golden Vault won't be able to protect you from our wrath." The scrying sensor then disappears.

E8: Jail Car

This soundproof car is two stories tall (30 feet high) and encased in thick iron. Four **pentadrones** guard the rooftop. These guards are positioned near the corners of the roof, allowing them to spot trouble coming from the sides of the car.

The outer doors of the car are locked tight, as is the 10-foot-square skylight in the roof. As an action, a character with thieves' tools can try to open one of the doors or the skylight, doing so with a successful DC 17 Dexterity check. The skylight can also be shattered; it is made of thick glass and has AC 13, 27 hit points, and immunity to poison and psychic damage. Conversely, the doors are too strong to be forced open by anything other than *knock* spells or similar magic.

When the characters enter the car, read or paraphrase the following:

> Two iron balconies protrude from the side walls of this train car. Iron stairwells connect these balconies to the lower level. Lining the walls on both levels are cell doors made of riveted iron, each one fitted with a large, gear-shaped keyhole. Pale light shines through paper-thin gaps around the doors, but not the keyholes.
>
> A stocky angel with cerulean skin and a pointed helmet leans against the railing on one balcony, a radiant flanged mace at its hip and its fiery wings folded behind it.

Omid the Deva

The angel guarding the Jail Car is Omid, a **deva** with fiery instead of feathery wings. Omid has orders to deliver the Stranger safely to Mechanus, where judgment awaits.

The deva's glowing mace is reminiscent of a large key. The head of the mace lines up neatly with the gear-shaped keyhole on each of the car's eight cell doors. As an action, a character can use the mace-key to unlock any one of these doors, which can be opened no other way.

Omid remains in the Jail Car and can't be lured from it. When the deva encounters the characters, read the following:

> The angel unfurls its wings, releasing a flurry of glowing embers, and says, "Speak your business, trespassers, and speak it truthfully."

The characters need not resort to violence to obtain the deva's mace-key. Here are some alternate approaches:

Clever Deception. The characters can pose as emissaries of a jurisdiction with greater claim to the Stranger's custody. Convincing Omid to release the Stranger requires a successful DC 17 group Charisma (Deception) check. If the characters used a forgery kit to create documentation to support their claim, the group check is made with advantage.

Convincing Argument. Since Omid knows little about the Stranger, a character can convince the deva that the outlaw has been wrongly accused and should be released. Making the argument might take a minute or two, after which the character must succeed on a DC 17 Charisma (Persuasion) check to secure the Stranger's release.

Friendly Game. A character who has a gaming set can challenge the deva to a friendly game. Omid loves games and is too proud (and bored) not to accept. If the character wins the game, Omid allows the party to speak with the Stranger (but not set them free). Determine the game's outcome by having the deva's challenger make a DC 19 Intelligence check. Proficiency with the gaming set allows the character to add their proficiency bonus to their roll. If the check is successful, the character wins. On a failed check, the character can opt to cheat in the late stages of the game and make a DC 19 Charisma (Deception) check. A successful check overrides the earlier failure. If the character loses gracefully and didn't cheat, the deva (a gracious winner) still allows the party to speak with the Stranger.

CELLS

The door to each cell opens into a 10-foot-square extradimensional space brightly lit by magic. The cells and their contents are as follows:

Cell 1. This cell contains a hostile **nycaloth** known as Dardo (not its true name). If someone opens the door to its cell, Dardo tries to exit the cell on its next turn, attacking anyone who stands in its way. The nycaloth then tries to leave the train. The Stranger (see below) happens to know Dardo's true name: a simple math equation. The characters can use this knowledge to keep the nycaloth from attacking them, or to force it to work for them.

Cell 2. This cell is empty.

Cell 3. A bench against the far wall has a *+2 rod of the pact keeper* resting on it. The cell is otherwise empty.

Cell 4. This cell contains a friendly **erinyes** who recently helped an efreeti named Vrakir get his hands on the *Book of Vile Darkness*. Speaking with this prisoner might kick off "Fire and Darkness," another adventure in this book. The Stranger (see below) doesn't know this erinyes's true name.

Cell 5. This cell is empty.

Cell 6. This cell is empty.

Cell 7. A **monodrone** janitor accidentally locked itself in this cell.

Cell 8. This cell contains the Stranger (see below).

THE STRANGER

This individual looks like a human with a flat-brimmed leather hat and a tattered traveler's cloak. The Stranger's face is permanently obscured behind a shifting blur like that of a deep desert haze. The Stranger is chaotic neutral and uses the **archmage** stat block, though they abhor combat. The Stranger wears an invisible *ring of mind shielding* that thwarts magical attempts to read their thoughts. The Stranger also wears *dimensional shackles* but

THE STRANGER

is eager to be rid of them. One touch from Omid's mace-key causes the shackles to fall off, freeing the Stranger.

The Stranger is initially indifferent to the characters but becomes friendly if presented with the prospect of escape, at which point the Stranger replies in a gravelly voice:

> "Let me guess. You want a name. Maybe more than one. Got a pen?"

The Stranger promises to recite the true names the characters seek in exchange for freedom but warns them of the heavy toll such knowledge carries.

If the characters are after the true names of Karnyros, Errtok, and Hexalanthe, the Stranger reveals the following once free of the *dimensional shackles* and outside the cell:

- Karnyros's true name is a series of guttural growls and grimaces, followed by a sound like a popping balloon.
- Errtok's true name is Ar-lothe Gothu Ka.
- Hexalanthe's true name is a low-toned, rhythmic chant accompanied by a series of hand gestures, dance moves, and drumrolls.

OLIVIER BERNARD

A MONODRONE SHOVELS
TREASURE INTO THE
LOCOMOTIVE'S ENGINE.

dozens of mechanical arms lay railway tracks before the train.

Inside the car, two **monodrones** stoke the fire in the furnace by shoveling loot into it from a nearby cart (see "Treasure" below). A **shield guardian** stands next to the cart, guarding the treasure from thieves. Thanks to its Spell Storing trait, the guardian can cast *sleep* (4th-level version) once.

FURNACE

Any object not being worn or carried that is placed inside the blazing furnace is incinerated instantly. Even magic items succumb to the blazing furnace, though the flames aren't powerful enough to harm artifacts.

If the furnace isn't replenished every hour with at least 100 gp worth of treasure, the Engine Car sputters and the train comes to a halt, causing a guard patrol (see "Guard Patrols" earlier in the adventure) to investigate.

A creature that enters the furnace for the first time on a turn or starts its turn there takes 55 (10d10) fire damage. A creature reduced to 0 hit points by this damage dies and is reduced to a pile of ash.

The furnace door can be latched from the outside. A creature trapped inside the furnace can use an action to try to force open the door, doing so with a successful DC 20 Strength (Athletics) check.

TREASURE

The treasure cart contains 3,500 gp, 6,000 sp, and 1,200 cp. Scattered among the coins are the following items:

- Five amethysts (100 gp each)
- Gilded mind flayer skull (150 gp)
- *Horn of Valhalla* (silver)
- Suit of *mithral armor* (chainmail)
- *Potion of healing* (greater)
- Silvered *+3 greatsword* that once belonged to a githyanki knight

CONCLUSION

After imparting the true names, the freed Stranger tips their hat and leaps from the train. Once out of range of the train's teleportation ward, the Stranger casts *plane shift* and disappears. The characters can leave the Concordant Express in a similar fashion, or they can remain on the train until it arrives in Mechanus and secure safe passage home from there. Whether or not they helped solve the murder in the Passenger Car (area E7), characters who disembark in Mechanus see Ignatius Inkblot, the mind flayer detective, escorting the cambion Abernathy Vernus off the train and into the waiting arms of a group of modrons.

If the characters are after the true name of some other creature, perhaps a fiendish nemesis or tenuous planar ally, the Stranger might know that creature's true name as well and can reveal it to the characters. Even if the Stranger doesn't know a particular true name, they can give characters the true names of one or more Fiends who have the power to help the characters in some other way.

If you have trouble coming up with ideas for new true names, roll on the Random True Names table at the end of this adventure when you need one.

E9: ENGINE CAR

> A massive furnace dominates the interior of this noisy car. Two spherical modrons shovel coins into the roaring fire while a brawny, nine-foot-tall automaton guards a treasure-filled fuel cart nearby. "Faster!" bellows a deep, disembodied voice.

The sapient Engine Car is the source of the deep, booming voice. The car speaks Common and Modron. While it's moving and not talking, the Engine Car labors through an endless chain of short, forceful breaths timed with each rhythmic churn of its mechanisms. Its undercarriage chatters as

ALAYNA DANNER

For the Golden Vault

If the characters are working for the Golden Vault, the organization sends the group's contact to retrieve the true names the day after the characters record them. This operative offers the characters a rare magic item of their choice (subject to your approval) as payment, which is delivered to the characters the next day.

Other Rewards

If the characters helped solve the murder mystery aboard the Concordant Express, the mind flayer detective Ignatius Inkblot uses its *plane shift* spell to deliver a wrapped parcel to the characters several days later. The parcel contains a token of the illithid's esteem: a masterfully crafted magnifying glass worth 1,000 gp.

Characters can also leverage any true names they learn into further rewards, as discussed below:

Home Ownership. Knowing a creature's true name may entitle the characters to that creature's property, such as a parcel of land, lair, or stronghold.

Slayer's Weapon. A master smith might be able to work the true name of a creature into an *arrow of slaying* or other target-specific magic item.

Further Adventures

The characters might have made a number of planar enemies during this heist. Subsequent adventures could include the following:

STEAL. The rival organization STEAL (see area E7) might figure prominently in future adventures. At higher levels, run-ins with STEAL operatives or raids on STEAL vaults might place the characters in conflict with the syndicate's leaders, including arcanaloths and ultroloths with true names only the Stranger knows.

Trials and Tribulations. The characters might be forced to stand before a tribunal in Mechanus for aiding an interplanar fugitive or answer to a powerful Celestial for slaying an angel.

True Name Terror. Characters who learn the true names of powerful Fiends are marked for death by those Fiends, which send powerful underlings to slay the characters.

Random True Names

d100	True Name
01–03	Sequence of musical notes played on a lyre
04–05	"Zow Chokk Garthagua"
06–07	"Lureff Zadil"
08–09	Sound of a bucket dropped on the floor
10–11	"Batridd Morath"
12–13	"Agh Gizzirah Korondis"
14–15	Third line of an obscure Auran lullaby
16–17	"Naelurec" ("cerulean" backward)
18–19	"Si Uulth Uurek"
20–21	Sound of four eggs sizzling in a frying pan
22–23	"Lamoura"
24–25	"Haraknar Orvorag"
26–27	Nine-second hum of a tuning fork
28–29	"Kyrvaash Cesvyr"
30–31	"Tsul Vandar"
32–33	Sound of three pages tearing from a book
34–35	"Vrah Koruun"
36–37	"Jal-Shoth"
38–39	Seven tolls of an iron bell
40–41	"Barak-Shivad of the Night Realm"
42–43	"Winterglory"
44–45	Short whistle, followed by two long ones
46–47	"Kelefis the Thrice-Hated"
48–49	"Nefarion"
50–52	Three specific prime numbers strung together
53–54	"Zizz-Ganneth"
55–56	"Red Rust"
57–59	Sequence of red and blue lights flashing
60–61	"Xurgranach"
62–63	"Enchridus 3291"
64–65	Last spoken words of a long-dead hero
66–67	"Valmorag the White"
68–69	"Suzakiro Arzuun of the Rusty Blades"
70–71	Sound of fingers drumming on a table
72–73	"Myranna Vos Aeldar"
74–75	"Kzokzys"
76–77	Gasp of someone stabbed through the heart
78–79	"U'chud, the Eye of Zefir-Zaskos"
80–81	"Quas Quannok"
82–83	Sad mewling of a kitten
84–85	"Skuzrayle"
86–87	"Nebek Velflam Von Qwizzid"
88–89	Sound of a lute being smashed to pieces
90–91	"Old Sinisyphere"
92–93	"Ghax'ru the Abominable"
94–96	Sound of three acorns crunched between teeth
97–98	"Knob"
99–00	"The Nameless One"

A GALA AT PALISET HALL ATTRACTS NOT ONLY
GUESTS FROM THE MATERIAL PLANE BUT
ALSO GUESTS FROM THE FEYWILD.

PARTY AT PALISET HALL

EVERY YEAR DURING THE WINTER SOLSTICE, Zorhanna Adulare holds a grand gala in Paliset Hall, her palatial retreat in the Feywild. The characters are hired to infiltrate the gala and steal Zorhanna's *shard solitaire*, a magical diamond with peculiar properties. As the evening unfolds, they learn that nothing is quite what it seems.

ADVENTURE BACKGROUND

Lady Zorhanna Adulare is an elf and a retired adventurer. On one of her many adventures, she stole a diamond *shard solitaire* (a magic item described at the end of the adventure) from a trio of night hags known as the Crestfall Coven. Zorhanna later mounted the diamond into a glittering platinum necklace, which she often wears during special occasions. Trapped within the iridescent facets of the *shard solitaire* is an unstable extradimensional rift that gives the diamond its remarkable powers.

Every year during the winter solstice, Zorhanna and her husband, a werebear tinkerer named Eliphas, withdraw to their Feywild home of Paliset Hall to throw a lavish gala. Many guests from the Material Plane and the Feywild attend this pleasant gathering. This year, Zorhanna plans to show off her *shard solitaire* necklace once again, unaware that forces are conspiring to steal it from her.

FAR REALM INVADER

Some time ago, a malevolent entity from the Far Realm found a way into the *shard solitaire* through the extradimensional rift contained inside it. Since then, this bodiless entity has been trapped in the stone—but it won't be for much longer. The entity's presence is weakening the stone, and when the diamond finally cracks, the effects could be catastrophic.

A few days ago, unaware of the danger, Zorhanna donned the *shard solitaire* necklace to see how it looked with a new gown she planned to wear at the gala. Zorhanna's close contact with the necklace allowed the Far Realm entity to trap her inside the diamond. The entity then replaced Zorhanna with a simulacrum using one of the *shard solitaire*'s magical properties. Zorhanna's simulacrum now wanders Paliset Hall, preparing for the arrival of the gala's guests, while the real Zorhanna remains trapped inside the *shard solitaire*.

STEALING THE SHARD SOLITAIRE

The characters become embroiled in this story after Eliphas, suspicious of the simulacrum's behavior, sends a friendly satyr named Fifel to get help. Fifel gives the characters invitations to the gala and reads a letter from Eliphas, urging them to steal the *shard solitaire* necklace from Zorhanna and take it far from Paliset Hall.

An added complication occurs toward the end of the adventure, as the hags of the Crestfall Coven crash the gala and attempt to reclaim that which was stolen from them. The hags know nothing about the Far Realm entity or Zorhanna's simulacrum, but they have their own clever plan to steal the *shard solitaire*—a plan the characters can turn to their advantage, if all else fails.

Using the Golden Vault

If you're using the Golden Vault as a patron, a golden key is delivered to the characters in whatever manner you deem fit. When the characters use this key to open the music box, the lid pops open and a soothing voice says the following:

> "Greetings, operatives. A magical diamond called a shard solitaire is known to contain an unstable extradimensional rift. Its owner, Zorhanna Adulare, is a retired adventurer. Her husband, Eliphas, used to work for the Golden Vault. He suspects that an evil force has somehow entered the stone and is using it to control Zorhanna. He has asked the Golden Vault to steal the stone from Paliset Hall, where he and Zorhanna host their annual gala celebrating the winter solstice.
>
> "This quest, should you choose to undertake it, requires you to obtain the shard solitaire without harming Zorhanna, Eliphas, or their guests. You will be approached shortly by a messenger named Fifel, who has your invitations to the gala and directions to Paliset Hall, which is in the Feywild. Good luck, operatives."

Closing the music box causes the golden key to vanish.

Meeting Fifel

The adventure begins in earnest when the characters meet Fifel, a **satyr** who works for Eliphas Adulare. Where Fifel appears is up to you. You can use the following boxed text to describe what he looks like:

> Fifel is a lanky satyr with dark curly hair pulled into a small bun and golden eyes alight with excitement. He wears a maroon tunic, over which are slung various belts and bulging leather pouches. Rolled tubes of parchment jut from his haversack, and his pockets jingle and clank as he walks. "Salutations!" he says with a clumsy salute.

Fifel carries a *Heward's handy haversack*, in which he stores various documents. The satyr is a bit scatterbrained, but Eliphas trusts him to run errands and deliver important messages.

From his haversack, Fifel produces a handful of invitations and hands one to each character. Each invitation is contained in a pale-blue envelope that is cool to the touch and smells like a crisp winter morning. The invitations read as follows:

> Zorhanna and Eliphas Adulare request the pleasure of your company at Paliset Hall to celebrate the arrival of the winter solstice. Come to Loch Wynnis no earlier than three days before the winter solstice, then take the crossing there to the Feywild at sundown. The many splendors of Paliset Hall await you on the other side! Formal attire is expected but not required.

A *detect magic* spell reveals an invisible watermark on the back of each invitation, which is used to verify its authenticity.

Once the invitations are distributed, Fifel uncorks a scroll tube with his teeth, then flips the tube upside-down and shakes it vigorously until a rolled-up sheet of parchment falls out. He picks up the parchment, unrolls it, and reads what's written on it in Common:

> "I, Eliphas Adulare, have sent my esteemed messenger, Fifel Amberhoof, to lead you to the shores of Loch Wynnis, so that you may cross into the Feywild with great haste. The winter solstice is nearly upon us, and I fear evil forces are as well.
>
> "My wife, the archmage Zorhanna, has not been herself of late. I believe something or someone is controlling her through a magic diamond, which she acquired many years ago on one of her adventures. Zorhanna had it fitted into a necklace, which she wears on special occasions. A few days ago, she removed the necklace from our vault and wore it during a dress fitting. Since then, she has been uncharacteristically cruel to the household staff. When I confronted her, she dismissed me out of hand, clutched the necklace, and uttered something in a dreadful language I've never heard her speak before. All her warmth is gone. When I look into her eyes, I see a cold and spiteful woman staring back at me.
>
> "I want you to steal the necklace, which Zorhanna now refuses to remove. I can't safely do it myself. Fifel will give you invitations to our winter solstice gala at Paliset Hall. There will be other guests to distract Zorhanna while you figure out a way to remove the necklace.
>
> "Once we're rid of the necklace, Fifel will deliver your reward."

Fifel can tell the characters that Eliphas is offering the following items as payment for their help:

- Rust-colored *bag of tricks*
- *Figurine of wondrous power* (serpentine owl)
- *Gauntlets of ogre power* or *quiver of Ehlonna* (characters' choice)

These magic items are on display in Paliset Hall's art gallery (area P6).

If the characters accept the terms and agree to steal the necklace, Fifel leads them to Loch Wynnis, a lakeside hamlet with a fey crossing that serves as a gateway between the Material Plane and the Feywild (see the "Loch Wynnis" section for details). Fifel explains that the fey crossing works only seven days of the year: three days before the winter solstice, the day of the winter solstice, and three days after the winter solstice.

PLANNING THE HEIST

As they travel to Loch Wynnis in the company of Fifel, the characters can ask the satyr for information about the *shard solitaire*, the Adulares, the winter solstice gala, and Paliset Hall.

SHARD SOLITAIRE LORE

Fifel knows the following information about the *shard solitaire*:

Origin Story. Fifel thinks the *shard solitaire* formed when someone dropped a *Heward's handy haversack* full of jewels into a *bag of holding*, creating an explosive portal to the Astral Plane. One of the jewels absorbed some of the portal's volatile energy to become the *shard solitaire*. (See "Secrets of the Shard Solitaire" at the end of the adventure for what really happened.)

Previous Owners. When she was an adventurer many years ago, Zorhanna stole the *shard solitaire* from a trio of night hags known as the Crestfall Coven. She never encountered the hags again, to the best of Fifel's knowledge.

Safeguard. Zorhanna paid a master jeweler to craft a platinum necklace and attach the *shard solitaire* to it. If it is removed from Zorhanna's neck, the necklace automatically teleports to a secret vault in Paliset Hall. The vault is located somewhere in Zorhanna's bedchamber on the second floor. (Fifel is wrong about the vault's location.) The necklace doesn't teleport if it's removed from the vault, so stealing it requires that it be taken from that location.

THE ADULARES

Fifel knows the following information about Zorhanna and Eliphas Adulare:

Zorhanna's Past. Zorhanna had a long and successful adventuring career before she settled down and married Eliphas. During one of Zorhanna's adventures, she befriended an archfey who, years later, built Paliset Hall and bequeathed it to Zorhanna. Rumor has it the archfey was the Prince of Frost.

Eliphas's Past. Eliphas is a gentleman and a tinkerer. (Fifel doesn't reveal that Eliphas is a werebear.) For years, he offered his services to the Golden Vault, an organization dedicated to preserving historical relics and keeping powerful items out of evil hands. Eliphas designed the magical music boxes that the Golden Vault uses to communicate with its field operatives.

WINTER SOLSTICE GALA

Fifel knows the following information about the winter solstice gala hosted by Zorhanna and Eliphas:

Guests. The Adulares have invited guests from the Feywild and the Material Plane. Feywild guests don't need to use the fey crossing in Loch Wynnis; instead, coaches pulled by unicorns will deliver them to the palace.

Weapons and Armor. Guests may bring weapons and wear armor as fashion accessories.

MAP OF PALISET HALL

If the characters ask him questions about the layout of Paliset Hall, Fifel sketches a rough map of the manor and gives it to them (see map 12.1).

LOCH WYNNIS

Loch Wynnis is the name of both a deep lake and the hamlet next to it. The adventure assumes the characters arrive at Loch Wynnis shortly before sundown on the day of the winter solstice—just in time to attend the gala at Paliset Hall.

> Nestled in the highlands is a quaint hamlet, its cottages and shops idyllically situated between a thick, snow-dusted evergreen forest and a dark lake with icy shores. A wharf stands where the village meets the water.

For most of the year, the hamlet of Loch Wynnis has shuttered storefronts, too many empty tavern tables, and fewer than two dozen permanent residents. As midwinter approaches, the town's population balloons with seasonal merchants and visitors eager to glimpse Loch Wynnis's magical marvel: the opening of the fey crossing in the lake. The crossing opens briefly at sundown the day of the winter solstice, the three days before, and the three days after it.

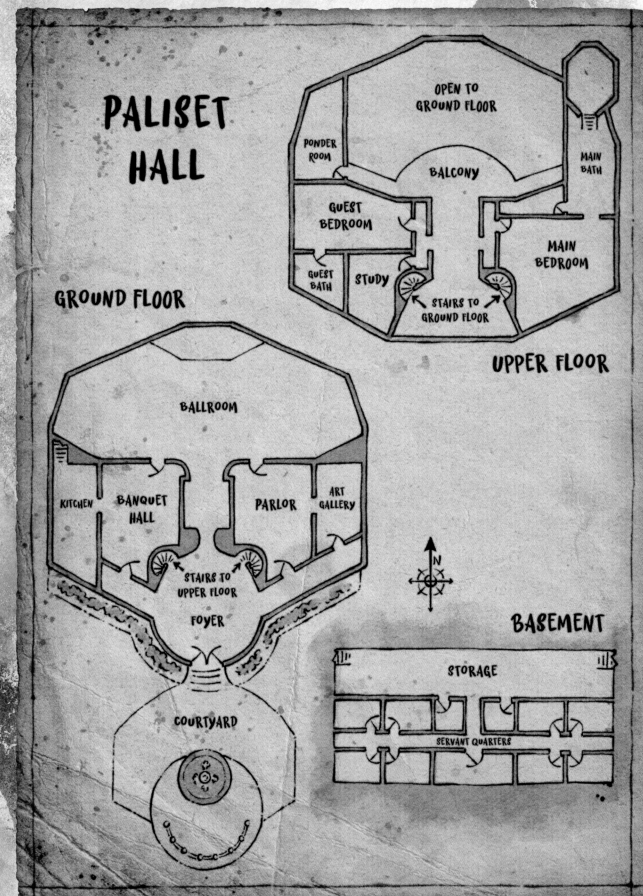

PALISET HALL

GROUND FLOOR

UPPER FLOOR

BASEMENT

OPEN TO GROUND FLOOR

PONDER ROOM

BALCONY

MAIN BATH

GUEST BEDROOM

MAIN BEDROOM

GUEST BATH

STUDY

STAIRS TO GROUND FLOOR

BALLROOM

KITCHEN

BANQUET HALL

PARLOR

ART GALLERY

STAIRS TO UPPER FLOOR

FOYER

N

STORAGE

SERVANT QUARTERS

COURTYARD

MIKE SCHLEY

PEOPLE OF LOCH WYNNIS

Residents of Loch Wynnis know of the winter solstice festivities that occur at Paliset Hall in the Feywild, even though few of these residents are invited to participate. Most are content to stay on the Material Plane side of the fey crossing, selling goods and services to passing tourists. The Adulares and their servants are known to the villagers, all of whom Fifel knows by name. Fifel encourages the characters to briefly tour the hamlet before heading to the lake by sundown.

OTHER GALA ATTENDEES

As the characters pass through the village, they may encounter other gala invitees waiting anxiously for the fey crossing to appear at sundown. You can use the Gala Guests table to generate random NPCs for the characters to meet. These NPCs don't wear armor or carry weapons, but every gala attendee has an invitation like the ones Fifel gave to the adventurers.

GALA GUESTS

d8	Guest
1	Kaden Lannis is a lonely human **noble** in his twenties. He hopes to find true love in the Feywild.
2	Verano Honeywell is a halfling **spy** employed by a big-city broadsheet to attend the gala and write a story about the goings-on in Paliset Hall.
3	Lycoris, a **dryad**, was Paliset Hall's head of staff until she retired six years ago. She comes to the gala every year to see her old friends, and she knows Paliset Hall's features and staff supremely well.
4	Berengar is a **werebear** and Eliphas Adulare's longtime friend. Eliphas is the only other person at the gala who knows Berengar is a werebear. Berengar likewise knows that Eliphas is a werebear.
5	Nix, a gnome **mage**, was Zorhanna's apprentice for several years. Nix has agreed to look after Paliset Hall once the gala ends and the Adulares return to the Material Plane. Nix plans to stay until the next winter solstice.
6	Eggsy, a gnome **bandit**, plans to pick some pockets at the gala. He attends under a false name ("Dworp Q. Guzzler, Esq., Gnome Adventurer") and has altered his appearance using a disguise kit. His disguise includes a curly wig, a more pronounced chin, copper-wired spectacles, and a fake beard. His invitation is a well-crafted forgery, including a fake invisible watermark on the back. Exposing it as a forgery requires a successful DC 17 Intelligence (Arcana or Investigation) check.

d8	Guest
7	Yalara is an elf **commoner** and singer whose music troupe was invited to perform at the gala. The other two members of her troupe were unable to make it to Loch Wynnis in time.
8	Mettle, an unarmed tiefling **scout** with horn-rimmed spectacles, pretends to be a noble named Adira and secretly works for the hags of the Crestfall Coven (see "The Crestfall Coven" later in the adventure). Upon arriving in the Feywild, Mettle slips a copper ring onto the third finger of her left hand. Affixed to the ring is a *hag eye*, a varnished eyeball that enables the hags to see what's happening at the gala (see the "Hag Covens" sidebar in the *Monster Manual* for details about this item).

LOCATIONS IN LOCH WYNNIS

The following locations are points of interest for characters who explore the hamlet of Loch Wynnis.

AUBERGE AURORE
Tavern and Inn

Wintertime visitors who don't have friends or family in the village stay in the Auberge Aurore while awaiting the solstice. When the characters arrive, the three-towered inn has two rooms available, each containing two beds. A bed costs 2 gp per night; a hot supper costs 1 sp.

The Auberge Aurore is owned and operated by Rei Paceran (neutral, elf **veteran**), who is also the village's sheriff. Stern and unflappable, Rei has no patience for any misconduct under her watch. Rei is wary of the Feywild and has no interest in going there.

KHORR'S KLOTHS
Tailor and Dress Shop

This small but vibrant fashion boutique is run by Khorr, a chaotic good **bugbear**. Born from Khorr's frustration at being unable to find clothes that fit his frame, Khorr's shop has since gained a reputation as a source of untraditional and striking outfits for Humanoids of all shapes and statures.

If the characters need outfits for the gala, Khorr is happy to oblige. An exquisite ensemble from Khorr costs 20 gp. Individuals can also come to the bugbear for tailoring services, which cost 5 gp.

LOCH WYNNIS DOCKS
Wharf

A few rowboats are tethered to these wooden docks. Visitors and residents who like to fish are free to use them. A thin layer of ice has formed around the boats, but the ice breaks apart easily.

Most of the docks are 10 feet long, but one particularly old and creaky dock is 50 feet long. This dock extends into the lake and allows easy access to Loch Wynnis's fey crossing (see "Sundown Crossing" below).

FIFEL TAKES HIS LEAVE

Eliphas gave Fifel strict orders not to return to Paliset Hall (for the satyr's safety) until the matter concerning the *shard solitaire* necklace is resolved. When the characters are ready to head to the lake, Fifel says the following:

> "My friends, here is where I take my leave. By my good lord's orders, I shall remain at the Auberge Aurore and await your return."

Fifel gives the characters a quick salute before skipping toward the tavern.

SUNDOWN CROSSING

Gala guests assemble at the docks shortly before sundown. As the sun sets, read or paraphrase the following text:

> When the last sliver of sun dips below the horizon, a silver glow emanates from deep within the water, and distant music and laughter drift through the air.
>
> Two wolves as big as horses materialize out of thin air at the end of the dock. They have snow-white fur and eyes as cold and blue as glacial ice. As they walk slowly down the dock, one of them says in Common, "Honored guests, the lady and lord of Paliset Hall eagerly await your presence. Once your invitation has been validated, please walk to the end of the dock and jump in the water."
>
> The other wolf reassures any first-time guests, "While Loch Wynnis's gateway is open, you will find the water neither cold nor wet."

The two **winter wolves** inspect every guest's invitation but are fooled by well-crafted forgeries. Each wolf can cast *see invisibility* on itself once per day, enabling it to see the invisible watermarks on the guests' invitations as well as to detect invisible party-crashers.

The wolves attack anyone caught trying to enter the Feywild without a validated invitation. When the last guest has crossed, the wolves return to Paliset Hall. If one or both wolves are killed, their failure to return is noticed by four more winter wolves on the Feywild side of the crossing (see area P1). These wolves recheck all invitations and attack anyone whose invitation fails a second inspection.

USING THE FEY CROSSING

Anyone who steps off the end of the dock and into the lake while the fey crossing is open appears in the courtyard of Paliset Hall (area P1), on their feet and completely dry. The fey crossing closes 10 minutes after sundown, although it can be reopened from the other side as described in area P1.

PALISET HALL

Paliset Hall is the winter palace of Zorhanna and Eliphas Adulare. It is situated in a peaceful meadow between snow-covered mountains and a mist-shrouded forest of evergreen trees. Winter's cool touch greets new arrivals, but there's no harsh wind.

Attempts by the Far Realm entity to escape from the *shard solitaire* have caused extraplanar energy to leak into Paliset Hall. This wayward energy has settled in the basement and is causing architectural anomalies to manifest briefly throughout the manor (see "General Features" below).

GENERAL FEATURES

Paliset Hall has the following features throughout:

Architectural Anomalies. Unstable energy leaking from the *shard solitaire* is affecting Paliset Hall, causing areas to warp in appearance momentarily. Whenever one or more characters enter a new area of the manor, roll a d6. If you roll an odd number, the characters notice iridescent cracks crawling up the walls, followed by a sudden shift in the architecture: a square window becomes circular, a wood panel turns to stone, and the like. Immediately after, the cracks vanish, and the architecture returns to normal.

Ceilings and Walls. The ceilings and walls of the manor are 20 feet high and carved from alabaster stone that's cold to the touch.

Decorations. Wintery decorations festoon many areas of the palace. Crystal snowflakes hang in the windows, illusory icicles dangle from the ceiling, frost fractals spreads across walls, and magically preserved ice sculptures perch atop similarly preserved ice pedestals. Some of the ice sculptures are, in fact, ice mephits assigned to guard an area (as noted in the area's description).

Doors. Unless otherwise stated, the doors of the manor are open and unlocked.

Lighting. The rooms of the manor are brightly lit with *continual flame* spells spaced evenly along the walls.

Music. Illusion magic creates jaunty music in the ballroom that can be heard throughout most of the palace—everywhere except the basement.

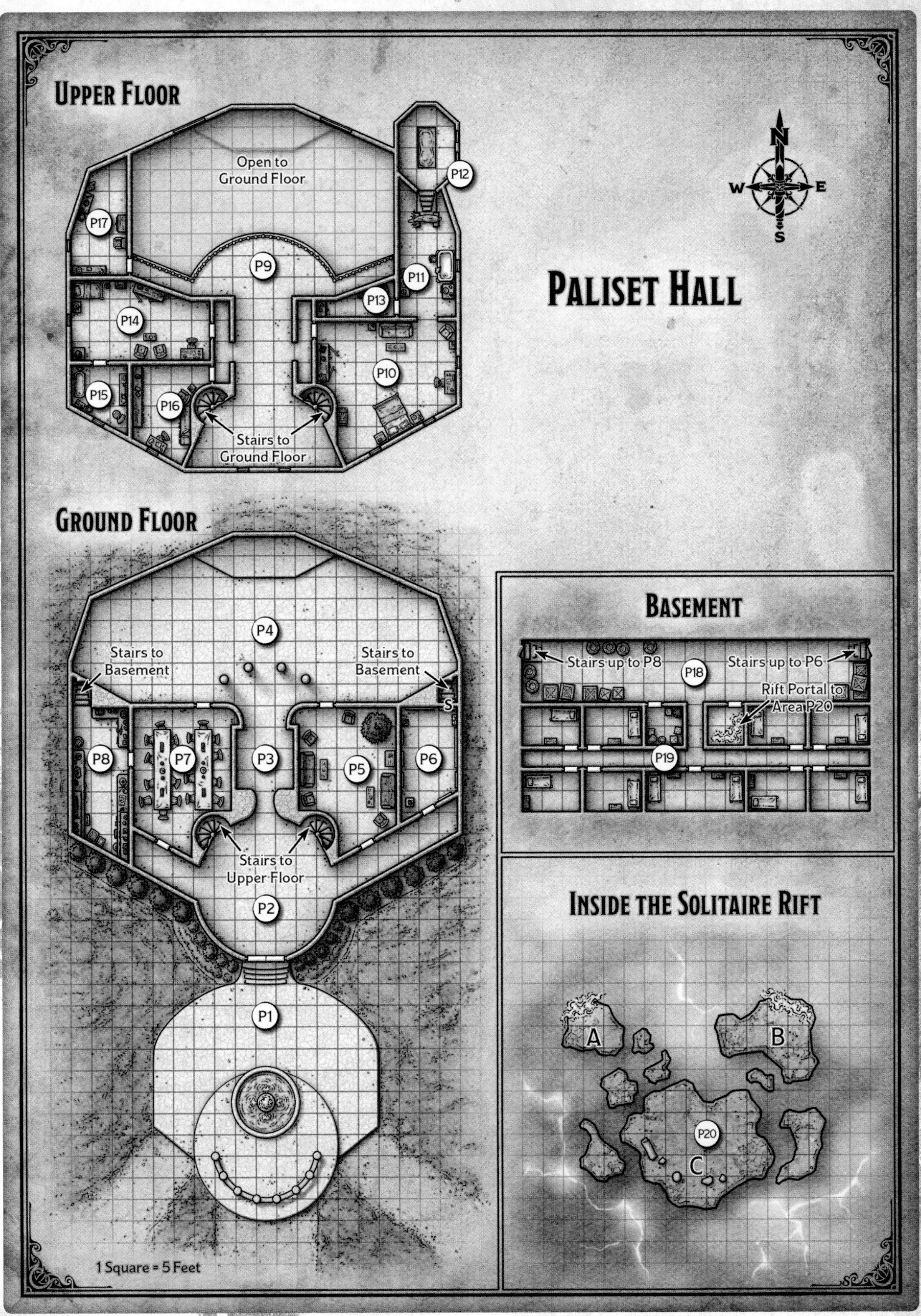

Upper Floor

Open to Ground Floor

P12

P17

P9

P11

P14

P13

P15

P16

P10

Stairs to Ground Floor

Paliset Hall

N
W E
S

Ground Floor

P4

Stairs to Basement

Stairs to Basement

S

P8

P7

P3

P5

P6

Stairs to Upper Floor

P2

P1

1 Square = 5 Feet

Basement

Stairs up to P8

Stairs up to P6

P18

Rift Portal to Area P20

P19

Inside the Solitaire Rift

A

B

P20

C

MIKE SCHLEY

ZORHANNA ADULARE

The real Zorhanna is trapped inside the *shard solitaire*, where she is under attack by the Far Realm entity trapped in there with her. Using the power of the *shard solitaire*, the Far Realm entity has created a simulacrum of Zorhanna.

ZORHANNA'S SIMULACRUM

Zorhanna Adulare's simulacrum appears identical to Zorhanna: a tall elf with purple skin and long, pale hair. The simulacrum wears a silvery gown embroidered with crystalline ferns and carnelian holly berries. It proudly shows off the *shard solitaire* it's wearing to guests. Any character who observes the simulacrum for 1 minute can discern its cold indifference with a successful DC 10 Wisdom (Insight) check.

Abilities such as truesight and magic that detects illusions reveal the true nature of the simulacrum: an elf made entirely of magical snow.

The simulacrum uses the **archmage** stat block, with these changes:

- The simulacrum is a neutral evil Construct.
- It speaks Common, Draconic, Elvish, Gnomish, or Sylvan while pretending to be Zorhanna, or Deep Speech when it is angry or frustrated.
- It can't regain expended spell slots or use the properties of the *shard solitaire* necklace. (The *shard solitaire* is currently attuned to the Far Realm entity trapped inside.)
- If the simulacrum drops to 0 hit points, it turns to snow and melts away, and the *shard solitaire* necklace teleports to the safe in Zorhanna's vault tower (area P12).

SIMULACRUM'S LOCATION

To determine the location of Zorhanna's simulacrum when the characters first arrive at Paliset Hall, or anytime the characters lose track of it and need to find it, roll a d4 and consult the Simulacrum's Location table, or choose an option you like.

SIMULACRUM'S LOCATION

d4	Location
1	Dancing in the ballroom (area P4)
2	Relaxing in the parlor (area P5)
3	Mingling in the banquet hall (area P7)
4	Observing from the balcony (area P9)

STEALING THE NECKLACE

As an action, a character can try to steal the *shard solitaire* necklace with a successful DC 20 Dexterity (Sleight of Hand) check, or a character can use a *suggestion* spell or similar magic to try to make the simulacrum relinquish the necklace. (Even though the simulacrum is a Construct, it can be charmed.) The simulacrum becomes hostile toward anyone who tries to take the *shard solitaire*. The simulacrum doesn't care about collateral damage to Paliset Hall, its staff, or its guests.

The instant the necklace becomes separated from the simulacrum, the necklace teleports to the hidden vault in area P12. Eliphas knows where this vault is located, but only Zorhanna and her simulacrum know the proper way to open it.

PALISET HALL LOCATIONS

The following locations are keyed to map 12.2.

P1: FOUNTAIN AND PATIO

The following description assumes the characters arrive here from Loch Wynnis via the fey crossing:

> You stand in a fountain of illusory water on a cobblestone patio. Colorful globes of light bob in the air, dancing in time with the stars that blink on the twilit horizon. The patio leads to a grand, two-story palace, its walls as white as fresh-fallen snow. The dark roof shimmers with the colors of an aurora. Crystal snowflakes decorate the windows, and music wafts through the palace's open doorway.
>
> Four winter wolves stand between you and Paliset Hall. After welcoming guests to the gala, the wolves insist on checking invitations once more before allowing anyone into the palace.

The four **winter wolves** are soon joined by the two **winter wolves** from Loch Wynnis. Each wolf can cast *see invisibility* on itself once per day, enabling it to see the invisible watermarks on the guests' invitations as well as detect invisible party-crashers. The wolves are forbidden from entering Paliset Hall without a command from Zorhanna or Eliphas. If someone tries to slip past the wolves, they alert the ice mephits in area P2, which attack the offender.

Fey Crossing. The fountain contains the fey crossing connected to Loch Wynnis. In addition to the few times when the fey crossing opens on its own, anyone can open the fey crossing from this side by reciting the rhyme, "Neither gleaming sword nor magic tome can soothe the soul like hearth and home." This rhyme is known to Zorhanna, Eliphas, the winter wolves, and Paliset Hall's staff. The fey crossing remains open for 10 minutes after the rhyme is recited.

Anyone who steps into the fountain while the fey crossing is open immediately appears, completely dry, on Loch Wynnis's longest dock at the end farthest from the shore.

Feywild Guests. The gala attracts not only folk from the Material Plane but guests from the Feywild as well. These guests (all of whom are dressed in fantastic, winter-themed outfits) arrive in coaches drawn by **unicorns** and driven by **satyrs**. Characters who linger on the patio might see one or more of these coaches arrive and deposit their guests.

P2: FOYER

> The front doors of the palace are made of stained glass with silvery fractal patterns. Garlands of frost wind around two spiral alabaster staircases in the grand foyer, and flakes of magical snow fall from the icicle-covered ceiling, disappearing as they touch the floor. Guests mill about, idly chatting.

Guests. At any given time during the gala, 1d6 **nobles** loiter in the foyer. You can add a named guest to the foyer by rolling once on the Gala Guests table.

Ice Mephits. Six **ice mephits** are disguised as ice decorations along the perimeter of the room. The mephits attack anyone who starts a fight in this area. Only Zorhanna, her simulacrum, and Eliphas can command the mephits to stop attacking and return to their posts.

Staircases. Spiral staircases in the northern corners of the room lead to the upper floor and balcony (area P9).

P3: COAT CHECK

Guests can entrust their coats to the manor's head of staff, a gray-haired, upbeat **satyr** named Oren. He carefully hangs the coats on hooks that line the west and east walls of this area between the foyer and the ballroom.

Oren is diplomatic and ingratiating without being obsequious. When confronted with turmoil, he does his best to maintain a calm facade.

Finding Zorhanna and Eliphas. Oren doesn't know where Zorhanna is, but characters who ask about Eliphas are told the following:

> "Lord Adulare wasn't feeling well and has withdrawn to the upstairs guest room for a trice. But pine not! I expect he'll rejoin us before long."

Oren senses trouble between Lord and Lady Adulare, but he won't pry into their affairs, and he gently discourages other staff from doing the same. He carries a key for the storage closets in the cellar (area P18) but doesn't recall anything important being stored in them.

A GNOME ADVENTURER ACQUIRES
THE *SHARD SOLITAIRE* NECKLACE AND A KEY
BELONGING TO PALISET HALL'S HEAD OF STAFF.

P4: BALLROOM

> A jaunty waltz draws you into this palatial ballroom. Above the dancing crowd spins a glittering chandelier that appears crafted from equal parts silver and frost. Icicles hang from the vaulted ceiling, sparkling in the light like jewels.

A 20-foot-high balcony (area P9) overlooks the ballroom floor.

Guests. At any given time during the gala, 2d6 × 2 **nobles** dance here. You can add a named guest to the ballroom by rolling once on the Gala Guests table.

Ice Mephits. Six **ice mephits** are disguised as ice decorations along the perimeter of the room. The mephits attack anyone who starts a fight in this area. Only Zorhanna, her simulacrum, and Eliphas can command the mephits to stop attacking and return to their posts.

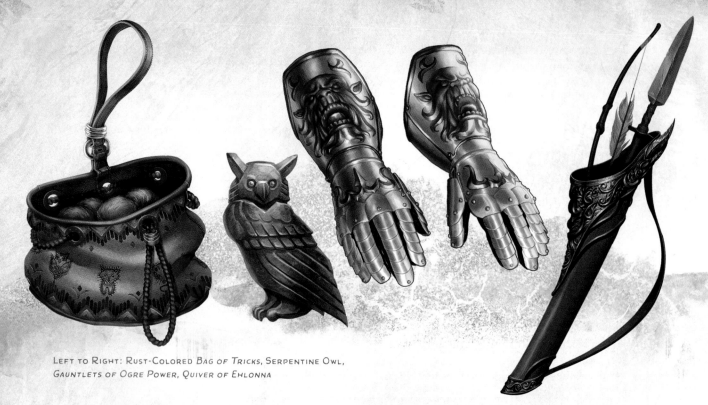

LEFT TO RIGHT: RUST-COLORED *BAG OF TRICKS*, SERPENTINE OWL, GAUNTLETS OF OGRE POWER, QUIVER OF EHLONNA

P5: PARLOR

> Gray chaise longues and sapphire-colored couches are arranged about this parlor, which is occupied by a handful of guests. A tall pine tree bedecked in tinsel and gilded baubles stands majestically in one corner.

Guests. At any given time during the gala, 1d8 **nobles** lounge in this room. You can add a named guest to the parlor by rolling once on the Gala Guests table.

P6: ART GALLERY

> Vibrant paintings and tapestries depicting the seasons hang in this grand room. Along the walls are displays of statuettes, crystal vases, and other art objects.

Secret Door. A secret door in the northeast corner of the room has a painting mounted to it. The painting depicts two tiefling children playing in the snow, and the painting's frame is made of gray wood carved with snowflakes. Pressing the snowflake in the bottom middle of the frame causes the secret door to swing outward on hidden hinges, revealing a staircase to the storage cellar (area P18). A character who examines the painting or searches the wall for secret doors and succeeds on a DC 17 Wisdom (Perception) check notices the sheen of frequent touches on the snowflake button.

Treasure. Four items on display are magical:

- Rust-colored *bag of tricks*
- *Figurine of wondrous power* (serpentine owl)
- *Gauntlets of ogre power*
- *Quiver of Ehlonna*

Some nonmagical treasures are displayed here as well, including three silk tapestries (250 gp each), eight paintings by famous artists (750 gp each), an onyx mountain goat statuette with garnets for eyes (250 gp), and a beautiful blue opal statuette depicting an archfey known as the Prince of Frost (5,000 gp).

P7: BANQUET HALL

> Two long, mahogany tables are piled high with sugared plums, decadent gingerbreads, and glazed meats. Two sprites flutter near them, encouraging guests to sample the food.

The two **sprites** are named Sysie and Val. Any character who converses with them and succeeds on a DC 10 Wisdom (Insight) check notices they are both uneasy. They sense something is amiss with Zorhanna, but neither sprite dares speak out for fear of inviting the Adulares' wrath or a stern lecture from Oren, the satyr head of staff. A character can convince either sprite to share their concerns by succeeding on a DC 13 Charisma (Persuasion) check, but this check is made with disadvantage if Zorhanna is within the sprite's line of sight.

Guests. At any given time during the gala, 1d6 + 2 **nobles** enjoy food and refreshments here. You can add a named guest by rolling once on the Gala Guests table.

P8: KITCHEN

> The scent of herbs and the clatter of pots fill this busy kitchen. Amid the satyr and pixie cooks stands a much taller figure with pale, knotted, bark-like skin. Her glassy black eyes survey the kitchen's staff with piercing sternness.

Two **satyrs** and three **pixies** busy themselves with cooking tasks. The dour **dryad** head chef, Anisetta, lords over the kitchen and barks out orders. Anisetta also carries a key for the storage closets in the cellar (area P18) but doesn't recall anything important being stored in them.

If Anisetta catches anyone who isn't staff in the kitchen, she sharply asks them to leave in Elvish. If that doesn't work, she tromps out of the kitchen to find Oren, the head of staff (see area P3), and demands he deal with the situation, which he tries to do diplomatically.

Staircase. A staircase leads to the storage cellar (area P18). This stairway is reserved for servants, but a character who succeeds on a DC 18 Charisma (Deception or Persuasion) check convinces Anisetta to let them access it.

P9: BALCONY

> This balcony, which overlooks the ballroom, is enclosed by an alabaster balustrade that has gold-leaf reindeer for balusters.

It's a 20-foot drop from the balcony to the ballroom floor.

Guests. At any given time during the gala, 1d6 **nobles** mingle here. You can add a named guest to the ballroom by rolling once on the Gala Guests table.

P10: MAIN BEDROOM

> Paintings in gilded frames hang on the walls of this spacious, lavishly decorated bedchamber.

Magic Painting. One of the paintings depicts a reindeer-shaped creature made of dark woven branches and emerald-green leaves. If a creature moves within 5 feet of the painting, the image animates, and the wooden reindeer-like creature

cheerfully introduces itself as Oak, personal assistant to Zorhanna and Eliphas.

Oak explains that his job is to keep track of Lord and Lady Adulare's schedule and remind them of any mundane tasks they might have forgotten. Oak doesn't normally share information with strangers, but Zorhanna and Eliphas have ignored the painting of late, and Oak is dying to talk to someone. Any character who asks Oak a question about Zorhanna, Eliphas, or the *shard solitaire* necklace can make a DC 12 Charisma (Persuasion) check. If the check is successful, Oak provides an answer other than, "Well, I can't really talk about that." Its answers are as follows:

Eliphas. "Eliphas has been staying in the guest room on the opposite side of Paliset Hall. If you see him, please remind him he has an appointment with that emissary from Prismeer in two days."

Zorhanna. "Zorhanna doesn't sleep, but she used to check in with me after finishing her trance. Lately, she won't even say hello. I don't know what I said to offend her."

Shard Solitaire Necklace. "That old thing? Zorhanna took it from the pool a few weeks ago for a dress fitting and hasn't taken it off since. Oh, dear, did I say pool? You know what? Forget I said anything."

The magic painting is a Small object with AC 11, 4 hit points, and immunity to poison or psychic damage. Reducing it to 0 hit points or removing it from the room renders it nonmagical. If a character threatens to destroy Oak, the painting reveals that Zorhanna's vault is "hidden in the tower pool beyond the bathroom," then nods toward area P11.

P11: MAIN BATHROOM

> A porcelain bathtub sits against one wall of this room, which also contains two tables stacked with clean towels, scented bars of soap, and bottles. At the back of the room, blocking a short staircase that climbs to a turret, is a ten-foot-tall marble statue of a reindeer.

The statue is a **stone golem** that guards the way to area P12. Zorhanna, her simulacrum, or someone disguised as Zorhanna can command the golem to move aside. Otherwise, the golem attacks if it takes damage or if someone tries to sneak past it into area P12. In combat, the golem uses Slow on its first turn. On subsequent turns, it makes Slam attacks with its hooves and antlers. If it is reduced to 0 hit points, the golem turns to dust, then re-forms and returns to its post 1d4 hours later. After it is destroyed three times, it doesn't re-form.

Treasure. Characters who search the room find a *potion of healing* (superior) and four bottles of scented bath oil (25 gp each) atop the table farthest from the bathtub.

P12: Vault Tower

> A rectangular pool is situated in the middle of this octagonal turret, which has tiled walls and a tiled floor. The turret's vaulted ceiling bears a painted mural of a fantastically beautiful fey creature who looks like winter incarnate. The pool's water is perfectly clear, revealing a tile mosaic at the bottom of it. In the center of the pool's mosaic are three concentric, gilded rings. The pool has no visible drain.

The painted mural on the ceiling depicts the Prince of Frost, an archfey of Zorhanna's acquaintance.

Pool. The pool is 10 feet long, 5 feet wide, 5 feet deep, and filled with frigid water. When a creature other than Zorhanna enters the water for the first time on a turn or starts its turn there, it must make a DC 17 Constitution saving throw, taking 14 (4d6) cold damage on a failed save, or half as much damage on a successful one.

No more than once per day, while Zorhanna is immersed in the pool, she can use it to contact the Prince of Frost and ask him up to three questions. He can choose not to answer a question or provide a truthful answer, but he can't lie. He can then ask Zorhanna three questions, each of which must be answered truthfully or not at all.

Rune Tile. The Elvish rune for "winter" is inscribed on the wall opposite the stairs. A character who examines that wall and succeeds on a DC 20 Wisdom (Perception) check spots the rune, which can also be found with a *detect magic* spell. Pressing the rune's tile opens hidden pipes at the bottom of the pool and drains it completely in 1 minute. The pool remains empty for 10 minutes, after which it automatically refills with frigid water.

Vault. The three concentric, gilded rings at the bottom of the pool are the locking mechanisms for a hidden safe. Each ring is flat and set in a shallow groove, such that it can be rotated. Once the water in the pool is drained, tiny Elvish runes representing the letters A through Z magically appear on the surface of each ring, with the letters spaced around the ring at equal intervals. Opening the safe requires that the three rings be turned in their grooves until their runes line up to form the word "OAK." Only Zorhanna and her simulacrum know the correct combination of letters (although "OAK" is a direct reference to the magic painting in area P10).

The safe has no mechanisms that a thief can exploit using thieves' tools, but a *knock* spell or similar magic can be used to open it.

When the rings are properly aligned or the safe is opened by other means, the circular area inside the innermost ring disappears, allowing access to a hidden compartment measuring 1 foot on each side. If the *shard solitaire* necklace was taken from Zorhanna's simulacrum, it rests in the compartment (the stone is still attuned to the Far Realm entity trapped inside it). Otherwise, the compartment is empty.

Seconds before the pool refills with water, the safe reseals itself and the runes vanish from the golden rings.

P13: Vanity

> Elegant dresses and blouses hang on racks along the walls of this narrow chamber. A white wooden dresser against the far wall has a circular mirror mounted above it.

The garments stored here are exquisite. The dresser's drawers contain enough materials (wigs, cosmetics, and whatnot) to assemble one disguise kit.

P14: Guest Bedroom

The door to this room is closed and unlocked.

> This bedroom is spacious and nicely appointed. A man wearing a rich-blue coat sits on the edge of a narrow bed. His trimmed white beard darkens at its roots, and kindly wrinkles frame his brow and eyes.
>
> "Looking to escape the crowds?" he asks with a thin smile. "I get that. You're welcome to hide in here with me for as long as you like."

Eliphas is a neutral good, human **werebear** who can adopt the form of a polar bear. He has an Intelligence score of 18 and the following additional action option:

Spellcasting (Humanoid or Hybrid Form Only). Eliphas casts one of the following spells, using Intelligence as the spellcasting ability (save DC 15):

At will: *light, minor illusion, prestidigitation*
2/day each: *detect magic, fog cloud*
1/day each: *phantasmal force, shatter*

If the characters reveal who they are and why they've come, a great weight seems to lift from Eliphas's shoulders as he thanks them for heeding his summons. "I knew Fifel wouldn't let me down!" he adds.

Eliphas knows the following pieces of information:

Zorhanna's Simulacrum. "I'm now convinced that my wife has been replaced by a simulacrum—a lookalike invested with her knowledge and spellcasting ability. I dimly recall Zorhanna mentioning that the *shard solitaire* has the power to create such a thing."

Secret Vault. "Zorhanna usually keeps her *shard solitaire* necklace in a vault hidden beneath a pool of frigid water in Paliset Hall's bathroom turret, which is guarded by a stone golem. Only Zorhanna can safely bypass the golem, and only Zorhanna knows the three-letter combination to the vault." (Eliphas can lead characters safely to area P11 if they ask to see the bathroom turret, and he will help them defeat the golem that guards it.)

Weird Anomalies. "Something strange is happening. I've seen walls, windows, and doors transform before my eyes, then suddenly everything is normal again. This only started a few hours ago, and it scares me. I just don't know what to do!"

If the characters tell Eliphas they've also seen weird anomalies, Eliphas begins to wonder if Zorhanna is causing the anomalies because she is trapped somewhere in Paliset Hall and trying to reach out to them. If a character suggests the anomalies are caused by the *shard solitaire* or something else trapped inside it, Eliphas urges the characters to search Paliset Hall until they discover the truth.

P15: Guest Bathroom

A porcelain tub rests against one wall of this bathroom. The mirror hanging above the vanity is cracked. If asked, Eliphas sheepishly explains that he cracked the mirror in a shaving accident.

P16: Private Study

An *arcane lock* spell has been cast on the door to this room. Zorhanna, her simulacrum, and Eliphas treat the door as though it were unlocked.

As an action, a character can try to open the magically locked door using thieves' tools, doing so with a successful DC 22 Dexterity check, or try to force it open, doing so with a successful DC 22 Strength (Athletics) check. A *knock* spell or similar magic also opens the door.

> The walls of this room are lined with tall shelves stuffed with leather-bound tomes. An elegant wooden desk is situated under a stained-glass window. Atop the desk is a thick book with a furry white cover and a crystal ball in a gilded stand.

The books on the shelves span many topics mostly related to nature, the planes, and the Feywild in particular.

Treasure. Any character who spends 1 hour examining the books on the shelves can, at the end of that hour, make a DC 20 Intelligence (Investigation) check. If the check is successful, the character finds a rare book worth 250 gp to a collector. Only four such books can be found here.

The fur-covered book on the desk is Zorhanna's spellbook, which contains the following spells: *arcane lock, banishment, cone of cold, counterspell, detect magic, detect thoughts, fire shield, fly, globe of invulnerability, ice storm, identify, knock, legend lore, lightning bolt, mage armor, magic missile, mind blank, mirror image, misty step, plane shift, polymorph, remove curse, scrying, sending, stoneskin, teleport, time stop, true seeing,* and *wall of force.*

The crystal ball on the desk is nonmagical but worth 1,000 gp. It can be used as a focus for the *scrying* spell.

Inside one of the desk drawers is a set of tinker's tools and a partially dismantled (and nonfunctional) music box similar in design to the ones used by the Golden Vault. Inside another desk drawer is a set of calligrapher's tools, three blank invitations to the winter solstice gala, some envelopes, a wax seal, and a silk pouch containing 50 pp.

P17: Powder and Fitting Room

> This room contains a wooden vanity with a circular mirror mounted to the wall above it. Other furnishings include a table, a padded chair, and a dresser.

The dresser contains folded garments, straight pins, scissors, wigs, and a cloth tape measure. The table bears an impressive selection of cosmetics.

P18: Cellar

> Wooden casks and crates line the walls of this cellar, which has an ascending staircase at each end. A pair of wooden doors flank a narrow passageway in the middle of one wall. Eerie, scintillating light streams around the edges of one of the doors.

The crates contain foodstuffs, and the casks contain wine. The staircases lead to areas P6 and P8, respectively.

Storage Closets. Both storage closets are locked. Oren (see area P3) and Anisetta (see area P8) carry keys to these closets. As an action, a character can use thieves' tools to try to open a locked door, doing so with a successful DC 11 Dexterity check, or try to

ADVENTURERS ARE TRAPPED IN THE *SHARD SOLITAIRE'S*
EXTRADIMENSIONAL SPACE WITH ZORHANNA ADULARE.

force open the door, doing so with a successful DC
15 Strength (Athletics) check. A *knock* spell or similar magic also opens the door.

The easternmost closet is the one emitting light.
When a character opens this closet for the first time,
read or paraphrase the following text:

> Floating in space is a pulsing rift of iridescent energy,
> like a jagged scar in the fabric of reality. The light dims
> for a second, revealing faint shadows shifting deep
> within the rift, before it flares once more.

Rift. The rift is a one-way portal to the extraplanar space inside the *shard solitaire*. A creature that
enters the rift's space immediately disappears, then
reappears in area P20 in a random unoccupied
space atop the rock marked A or B on map 12.2.
The rift can't be dispelled, but it disappears when
the *shard solitaire* ceases to be magical (see "The
Solitaire Cracks" later in the adventure).

P19: SERVANTS' QUARTERS
This hallway has numerous doors leading to simple
bedrooms for servants. All the bedroom doors can
be locked from the inside, but all are currently unlocked. No servants are here during the gala.

P20: INSIDE THE SOLITAIRE RIFT
Each character who enters the rift in area P18 is
deposited in the *shard solitaire's* extradimensional
space, appearing atop the rock marked A or B on
map 12.2. Divide the party as evenly as possible
among these two locations. To set the scene, read or
paraphrase the following:

> You appear on a smooth, flat-topped rock floating in
> the middle of a magically charged maelstrom filled
> with thunderous roars. Other rocks float nearby.
> Standing on the largest one is Zorhanna in her regalia.
> You also sense a terrible presence—something form-
> less and indescribable—lurking all around you.
>
>   Zorhanna points at you and laughs. "The shapeless
> evil finally appears! Whatever you are, you can't fool
> me! Prepare to face the wrath of Zorhanna Adulare!"

Zorhanna Adulare stands in the middle of the
largest floating rock (marked C on map 12.2). She
is a chaotic good, elf **archmage** who speaks Auran, Common, Draconic, Elvish, and Sylvan. She
has expended all her 6th-level and higher spell
slots trying to escape from the *shard solitaire's*
extradimensional space, to no avail.

Zorhanna's sense of reality has been warped by prolonged contact with the shapeless Far Realm entity that haunts the extradimensional space. She is convinced that the characters were conjured by this entity to harm her, so she attacks them. She casts *cone of cold* or *lightning bolt* every round on her turn for as long as she is able to do so. If one or more characters close to melee distance, she casts *shocking grasp* and *misty step* on her next turn, using the latter spell to teleport to another rock.

As an action, a character can make a DC 17 Charisma (Persuasion) check while trying to convince Zorhanna that the party is not her enemy. If the check is successful, Zorhanna does nothing on her next turn except mutter to herself as she ponders what the character said. If the check fails, Zorhanna continues her attack. Once three such checks succeed, Zorhanna concludes that the characters are not her enemies and calls for an end to hostilities. She then screams into the void, "You almost had me! Nice try, whatever you are!"

The characters can also convince Zorhanna to stop attacking them by returning her spellbook to her. The spellbook (found in area P16) excites her because it contains the *plane shift* spell—her ticket to freedom (see "Escaping the Rift" below).

Once Zorhanna is no longer hostile toward the characters, they can question her and learn the following information:

About the Shard Solitaire. "Years ago, I stole the *shard solitaire* from three hags who were trying to harness its extradimensional energy, which, as you can see, is highly unstable. I thought I could keep the diamond safe, but I couldn't resist showing it off from time to time. I let my vanity get the better of me."

The Entity. "Something alien and evil wormed its way into the *shard solitaire*'s extradimensional rift and became trapped here, just as we are. This entity has a mind, but no body or soul. I believe it comes from a dimension called the Far Realm. It is pure evil and can't be allowed to escape."

Extradimensional Rift. The rocks that float in the extradimensional rift are flat on top and suspended in the air at roughly the same elevation. A creature can leap from one rock to its closest neighbor without having to make an ability check.

Any creature that falls off a rock plunges into the rift. At the start of that creature's next turn, energy from the rift strikes the creature for 22 (4d10) force damage, then teleports the creature, along with anything it is wearing or carrying, to a random unoccupied space atop one of the larger rocks. Roll a d6 to determine which rock: 1–2, rock A; 3–4, rock B; or 5–6, rock C.

Far Realm Entity. The Far Realm entity can't be seen, heard, targeted, attacked, or harmed. Its presence can merely be felt. At the end of each hour spent in the extradimensional space with this entity, a creature must succeed on a DC 17 Charisma saving throw or take 7 (2d6) psychic damage.

If the characters crave more combat or if you think they've had too easy a time so far, the entity manifests three **invisible stalkers** that are hostile toward the characters. When a stalker drops to 0 hit points, it lets out a terrible howl as it disperses. Creating these stalkers takes energy the entity needs to free itself from the extradimensional rift, so it won't create more than three of them.

Escaping the Rift. A creature can't simply teleport from the *shard solitaire*'s extradimensional space. A *plane shift* spell or similar magic is required.

If Zorhanna obtains her spellbook, she can use it to prepare the *plane shift* spell, but only after finishing a 4-hour trance (the equivalent of a long rest for her). If the characters escape with Zorhanna before the *shard solitaire* cracks, she admits that the *shard solitaire* is too dangerous to keep in Paliset Hall and does everything in her power to make sure the characters leave with it. She also suggests the characters place it inside a *bag of holding* or some other item that contains extradimensional storage space, in case the *shard solitaire* explodes.

If Zorhanna and the characters have no means of escaping the extradimensional space on their own, they are released when the *shard solitaire* cracks (see "The Solitaire Cracks" below). Until then, they must try to resist the psychic damage caused by the Far Realm entity.

THE CRESTFALL COVEN

The hags of the Crestfall Coven have waited many years to steal back the *shard solitaire*. Until now, ill omens and vague auguries have stayed their hand, but the moment has finally come.

With the help of a tiefling **scout** named Mettle (see the Gala Guests table earlier in the adventure), the hags have been able to spy on the gala. Disguised as three elf nobles from the Feywild, the three **night hags** (whose names are Myrrel Malum, Esadora Crane, and Netheria Nightblossom) arrive at Paliset Hall in one of the Adulares's unicorn-drawn coaches. After exiting the coach, the hags present stolen invitations to the winter wolves standing guard outside, then waltz into Paliset Hall, cackling with delight at how well their plan is unfolding.

HUNT FOR THE SHARD SOLITAIRE

If all three members of the Crestfall Coven are within 30 feet of each other, they gain the benefit of the Shared Spellcasting trait described in the "Hag

Covens" sidebar in the *Monster Manual*. One of the three hags uses this trait to cast *locate object* to find the *shard solitaire*. If they find the *shard solitaire* in another creature's possession, the hags attack whoever has it. If the *shard solitaire* necklace teleported to Zorhanna's vault, the hags use Change Shape to assume Zorhanna's appearance and slip past the vault's stone golem guardian. One of the hags then casts *contact other plane* (which has a 1-minute casting time) to learn the three-letter combination needed to open the vault.

If the characters are trapped inside the *shard solitaire* or otherwise unable to thwart the Crestfall Coven, the hags snatch the necklace from the vault and use their *plane shift* spells to transport to Loch Wynnis, where they wait for Mettle.

Confronting the Hags

Characters in Paliset Hall might encounter the Crestfall Coven as the hags search for the *shard solitaire* necklace. The hags are willing to cut a deal with the characters, provided the coven gets to keep the *shard solitaire*. Clever characters might help the hags break into Zorhanna's vault, then betray the hags and claim the *shard solitaire* for themselves. Similarly, any character who took Mettle's *hag eye* can trade it for the *shard solitaire*, since the hags don't want to suffer the consequences of their *hag eye* being destroyed.

If a night hag is reduced to 50 hit points or fewer, it uses *plane shift* to flee. If two members of the coven are forced to flee in this manner, the third flees as well.

The Solitaire Cracks

At some point before the end of the adventure, the Far Realm entity finally breaks free of the *shard solitaire*, causing it to crack like a walnut. Here are some suggestions for when this event might occur:

- 1d8 hours after the characters return to the Material Plane with the *shard solitaire* in their possession
- If the characters are trapped in area P20 with the Far Realm entity and have no means of escape
- After the night hags obtain the *shard solitaire* but before they can use their *plane shift* spells to escape with it

The cracking of the *shard solitaire* is audible to anyone holding or wearing it. In that instant, the *shard solitaire* becomes a flawed, nonmagical diamond worth 500 gp, and all the creatures and extradimensional energy contained within it are released at once. If Zorhanna is alive, she materializes in an unoccupied space within 30 feet of the stone, as do any characters who were trapped in the stone with her.

The Far Realm entity is nowhere to be seen, and its presence can no longer be felt.

The extradimensional energy released from the stone has the same effect as a *staff of power*'s Retributive Strike property, centered on the stone itself. The explosion occurs a split second before creatures trapped inside the stone are released, sparing them from the effect.

If the characters placed the uncracked stone in the extradimensional space of a magic item such as a *bag of holding* or Fifel's haversack, the explosion is confined to that item's extradimensional space, doing no harm to the container; a split second later, creatures released from the stone appear in unoccupied spaces within 30 feet of that container, rather than inside its extradimensional space near the stone itself.

Conclusion

After the *shard solitaire* cracks, assuming they survive, the characters can take stock of their triumphs or failures.

Midwinter Miracles

If Zorhanna and Eliphas are reunited and the characters did their utmost to protect Paliset Hall and its guests, Eliphas sees that the characters receive their promised reward. If they already helped themselves to the magic items on display in the art gallery (area P6), Eliphas considers their reward paid in full.

If one or more characters died but Zorhanna survived, she makes arrangements with the Summer Queen, a powerful archfey, to have the characters brought back to life at no charge to the party, provided the characters didn't commit any despicable acts she's aware of. If Zorhanna perished but Eliphas survived, he calls in a few favors to raise characters from the dead.

Back in Loch Wynnis

When the characters return to Loch Wynnis, Fifel greets them and asks about their visit to the Feywild. If they need to borrow his *Heward's handy haversack* to safely contain and transport the *shard solitaire*, he empties it and hands it to them.

For the Golden Vault

If the characters are working for the Golden Vault, the organization rewards them only if Eliphas and Zorhanna both survived, no innocent lives were lost in Paliset Hall, and the *shard solitaire* didn't end up in the clutches of the Crestfall Coven. A Golden Vault operative offers the characters a rare magic item of their choice (subject to your approval) as a reward, which is delivered the next day.

It Came from the Far Realm

What happens to the Far Realm entity is for you to decide. As a thing of pure thought, it might corrupt creatures in its vicinity, transforming them into horrible Aberrations or zealous Far Realm cultists. Conversely, it might find solace in the body of some creature powerful enough to serve as its new host.

Secrets of the Shard Solitaire

Long ago, someone dropped a *bag of holding* full of jewels into a *portable hole*, creating an explosive portal to the Astral Plane. A 5,000 gp diamond contained within the bag absorbed some of the portal's volatile energy and became the *shard solitaire* featured in this adventure.

The same Far Realm entity that wormed its way into the *shard solitaire*'s extradimensional rift has also attuned to the stone. The entity can't do anything with the stone other than what it has already done to Zorhanna Adulare (as described in this adventure). When the entity escapes the rift, the stone cracks and becomes nonmagical.

Although the characters never get the chance to wield the power of Zorhanna's *shard solitaire*, other such items are scattered throughout the multiverse, waiting to be found.

Shard Solitaire

Wondrous Item, Legendary (Requires Attunement)

This gemstone contains an unstable extradimensional rift. Its facets are ribboned with iridescent veins that seem to move of their own accord. Five types of *shard solitaire* are known to exist, each one a different type of gemstone, as shown in the Shard Solitaire Types table.

Rift Step. As a bonus action, while wearing or holding the *shard solitaire*, you can teleport yourself, along with anything you're wearing or carrying, to an unoccupied space you can see within 30 feet of yourself.

When you use this property, you can tap into the unstable power of the stone's extradimensional rift to increase the teleport distance by up to 30 feet, but if you teleport more than 30 feet using Rift Step, you must succeed on a DC 16 Constitution saving throw or take 3d10 force damage immediately after you teleport.

Spellcasting. The stone has 6 charges and regains 1d6 expended charges daily at dawn. The Shard Solitaire Types table lists the spells common to all *shard solitaires*, as well as the spells specific to each kind of stone. As an action, you can cast one of the stone's spells by expending the requisite number of charges, requiring no material components (save DC 16).

ZORHANNA'S DIAMOND *SHARD SOLITAIRE*
DANGLES FROM A PLATINUM NECKLACE.

SHARD SOLITAIRE TYPES

Shard Solitaire	Spells
All	*Banishment* (3 charges; the target is banished to the stone's extradimensional space for the spell's duration), *mirror image* (1 charge)
Black sapphire	*Blight* (3 charges), *finger of death* (6 charges)
Diamond	*Ice storm* (3 charges), *simulacrum* (6 charges; the duplicate created by the spell has the same number of hit points as the creature it imitates)
Jacinth	*Fireball* (2 charges), *fire storm* (6 charges)
Rainbow pearl	*Prismatic spray* (6 charges), *water breathing* (2 charges)
Ruby	*Fly* (2 charges), *teleport* (6 charges)

AN EFREETI'S FORTRESS HOLDS THE *BOOK OF VILE DARKNESS*. GOOD LUCK STORMING THIS CASTLE.

FIRE AND DARKNESS

FOR CENTURIES, A POWERFUL EFREETI NAMED Vrakir sent his armies against numerous foes and burned countless cities to ash. Now, the tyrant has found an artifact of unimaginable evil: the *Book of Vile Darkness*.

In this heist, the heroes must infiltrate Brimstone Hold, the prison-fortress where Vrakir has locked away the *Book of Vile Darkness*, and escape with the efreeti's prize. The characters' contact is an arcanaloth named Nebukath, the hold's duplicitous administrator, who secretly covets the book and plans to betray the heroes as soon as the group recovers it.

ADVENTURE BACKGROUND

Vrakir obtained the *Book of Vile Darkness* by accident. The efreeti knew the red dragon Drendarylix laired only a few days' ride from Brimstone Hold, one of Vrakir's fortresses. Many adventurers over the years tried to slay the foul creature, which had attacked and looted nearby villages for decades. One day, word reached Vrakir that Drendarylix had been slain but that the dragon's vanquishers had also perished in the battle. Thinking the lair would be easy to plunder, Vrakir set off with a contingent of warriors to claim its riches.

When he arrived, however, Vrakir learned the truth: the adventurers who had supposedly slain Drendarylix were cultists who had arrived to worship the wicked beast. Worse, the cult was conducting a ritual to turn Drendarylix into a dracolich.

Displeased with the idea of a dracolich on his doorstep, Vrakir slew the cultists before they could finish the ritual, destroying Drendarylix in the process. Only once the dust settled did the efreeti learn what had given the cultists their power: the *Book of Vile Darkness*. Without hesitation, Vrakir claimed the artifact, taking it to Brimstone Hold to plot how best to use it to fuel his evil.

HOOKS AND REWARDS

If you're not using the Golden Vault as the characters' patron (see the "Using the Golden Vault" section), you can use one of the following hooks to get the characters involved in the adventure.

CLOSE TO HOME

Vrakir has set his mind to conquering the characters' homeland. The region's brave defenders have rebuffed his army's initial assaults, but they stand little chance of holding out once Vrakir unleashes the fell power of the *Book of Vile Darkness*.

Syr Isbeth, the human leader of the defense effort, received a missive from the arcanaloth Nebukath professing the arcanaloth's sympathies for her cause and providing information about the book's location. Syr Isbeth doesn't know whether Nebukath can be trusted, but stealing the book would stymie Vrakir's war effort—it's too good an opportunity to pass up. She asks the characters to undertake this perilous mission, promising them the title to a regional stronghold, along with its retinue of five **knights** and one hundred **guards**, if they bring her the book or proof of its destruction.

A Short Leash

The Fated (a faction based in Sigil) has interests throughout the multiverse, and many of them have been disrupted by Vrakir's conquests. The Fated has decided it is time to curtail Vrakir's power, so it contacted the opportunistic arcanaloth Nebukath for information about how to deprive the efreeti of his greatest weapon.

Farn Bindelbrot, a gnome operative for the Fated, identified the characters as having the skills needed for such a difficult task. Should the characters deliver the *Book of Vile Darkness* to Farn, he will reward them with an *amulet of the planes*. Farn promises the Fated will then safely secure the book.

Redemption

A halfling warlock named Remi Duskweather renounced her pact and dedicated herself to serving a holy order (potentially one connected with a cleric or paladin in the party). As her final test of faith, Remi has been tasked with using her connection to her former patron—the arcanaloth Nebukath—to help the holy order obtain and destroy the *Book of Vile Darkness*.

Remi has gotten the necessary information from Nebukath, but stealing the book is beyond her ability, so she recruits the characters to carry out this task for the order. Remi offers no reward, but if the characters bring the book or proof of its destruction to the order, each character receives a blessing of their choice, either from the gods they worship or from a god worshiped by Remi's holy order: a *blessing of health*, a *blessing of protection*, or a *blessing of understanding*, all of which are described in the *Dungeon Master's Guide*.

Using the Golden Vault

If you're using the Golden Vault as a patron, a golden key is delivered to the characters in whatever manner you deem fit, along with a hand-drawn map of Brimstone Fortress (see map 13.1).

When the characters use the golden key to open their music box, the lid pops open and a soothing voice says the following:

> "Greetings, operatives. The Golden Vault has learned that an efreeti named Vrakir has the Book of Vile Darkness. We need you to steal this evil artifact so we can destroy it. This quest, should you choose to undertake it, requires you to infiltrate the fortress of Brimstone Hold, where the book is kept.

> "We obtained a map of the fortress from an informant of ours, an arcanaloth named Nebukath, who works in Brimstone Hold. Nebukath is willing to provide further assistance, but we suspect the arcanaloth has reasons of their own to acquire the book, so be on your guard!

> "Nebukath is unsure how long Vrakir plans to keep the book in the fortress, meaning time is of the essence. Good luck, operatives."

Closing the music box causes the golden key to vanish.

Planning the Heist

Once the characters are ready to begin planning the heist, show the players map 13.1. The map arrives via whoever asks the characters to undertake this mission. Written on the backside of the map is the following note in Common:

> This is as detailed a map as I could find. The book's location is marked with an X. Please hurry, as Vrakir could move it at any time. I fear the chaos and destruction he will unleash once he has fully embraced the book's power.—N.

The following sections contain information that can help guide the characters as they form their plan. You can provide this information straightforwardly to the players, present it through conversations with the party's patron, or allow characters to use their skills and abilities to research and gather information.

Brimstone Hold's Inhabitants

Here's a summary of Brimstone Hold's inhabitants:

Efreet. Vrakir spends most of his time on the Elemental Plane of Fire, visiting Brimstone Hold only occasionally. In his absence, the hold is under the command of an efreeti named Jarazoun.

Nebukath the Arcanaloth. The characters' map was provided by an arcanaloth named Nebukath, who serves as Brimstone Hold's administrator and is working to undermine Vrakir. If the characters seek out Nebukath in the hold, the arcanaloth may help them.

Various Defenders. The hold is defended by erinyes devils (whose truesight allows them to see through most forms of magical concealment), duergar, and salamanders, as well as a young red dragon named Kalimrax and a beholder known as the Eye of the Efreet.

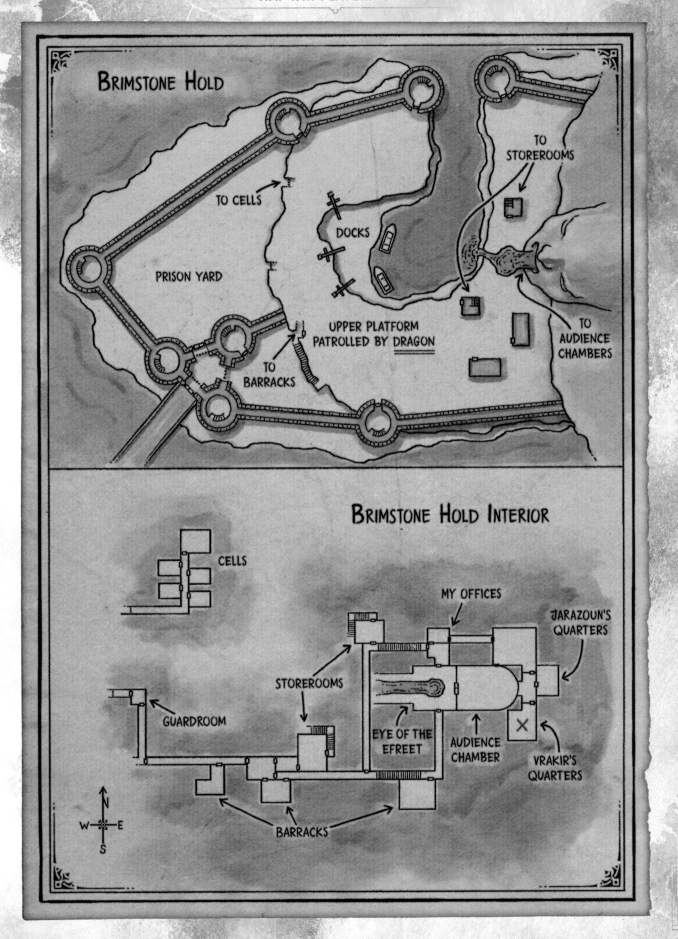

BRIMSTONE HOLD

TO CELLS

DOCKS

TO
STOREROOMS

PRISON YARD

UPPER PLATFORM
PATROLLED BY DRAGON

TO
AUDIENCE
CHAMBERS

TO
BARRACKS

BRIMSTONE HOLD INTERIOR

CELLS

MY OFFICES

JARAZOUN'S
QUARTERS

STOREROOMS

GUARDROOM

EYE OF THE
EFREET

AUDIENCE
CHAMBER

VRAKIR'S
QUARTERS

BARRACKS

W — E
N
S

Approaching Brimstone Hold

Possible ways to approach the fortress include the following:

Across Volcanic Terrain. The hold is built inside a rock wall at the foot of a volcano. Lava pours down the volcano's slopes on either side of the hold and forms a molten river that flows around the hold.

Main Entrance. A stone bridge spans the lava river and leads to the hold's main entrance. The bridge is mostly used by Vrakir's troops, who often return with prisoners in tow, and sometimes visitors who have business with Jarazoun approach this way.

The Harbor. A mile further down the lava river, a chaotic neutral cambion named Klax runs a trading depot that ships supplies to Brimstone Hold. Klax's fire-resistant boats dock at the hold's lava harbor once every ten days. The crews lay over in guest quarters at the hold before departing the following day. (If the characters embark on their mission while Klax's traders are at the hold, the cambion can be found in area B6.)

Additional Considerations

Here are some other things for characters to consider as they plan their heist:

Fire Protection. Many creatures and hazards in the hold deal fire damage.

Timing Arrival. The characters can time their arrival to coincide with the arrival of a prisoner escort or supply shipment. Timing their arrival to Vrakir's presence or absence is harder, since the efreeti travels to the fortress via the *plane shift* spell. Doing so might first require characters to spy on the hold's activities.

Avoiding Confrontation. Vrakir is a powerful adversary. The characters are best off avoiding a confrontation with him, at least until the *Book of Vile Darkness* is out of his grasp.

Brimstone Hold

Brimstone Hold is one of Vrakir's remote military outposts on the Material Plane. The adventure assumes the hold is built alongside an active volcano in the middle of a vast lava plain, but you can place the hold in any suitably fiery region in your game's setting.

Brimstone Hold is bordered on three sides by a river of lava. The hold is enclosed on its eastern edge by a rocky volcanic slope, and the hold's interior areas have been carved into the volcano. The main entrance into the interior has been carved to resemble a giant efreeti face, whose open mouth spews lava into the harbor below.

General Features

The following features are common throughout Brimstone Hold.

Ceilings

Interior areas have 15-foot-high ceilings, except in areas B22 and B25–B29, where the ceilings are 30 feet high.

Doors

All exterior doors are made of solid iron and are barred on the inside. As an action, a character can try to break down a barred door, doing so with a successful DC 25 Strength (Athletics) check.

Interior doors are made of iron and are unlocked unless the text states otherwise.

Secret Doors. Each secret door in the fortress is opened by stepping on a tiny pressure plate hidden in the floor nearby. As an action, a character can search the wall for secret doors and make a DC 15 Wisdom (Perception) check. If the check is successful, the character finds the secret door and the pressure plate used to open it.

Extreme Heat

Creatures that spend 1 hour or more anywhere in the hold, or sail on the river of lava, are subject to the effects of extreme heat as described in the *Dungeon Master's Guide*.

Illumination

Lava bathes the outer areas of the hold in dim light even on starless nights, while most of the hold's interior areas are dimly lit by braziers of glowing coals. Exceptions are noted in the text.

Lava

The lava around the hold and in the harbor is 10 feet deep, while the stream of lava pouring from area B22 is 2 feet deep. Any creature that enters lava for the first time on a turn or starts its turn there takes 55 (10d10) fire damage.

Outer Walls

The hold's 20-foot-thick curtain walls are faced with blocks of carved basalt and filled with a rubble core. The walls on the hold's lower level (bordering areas B4 and B5) stand 40 feet high, while those on the hold's upper level (bordering area B6) stand 20 feet high. Crenellations rise another 3 to 8 feet. Scaling a wall without magic or climbing gear requires a successful DC 20 Strength (Athletics) check.

Towers

Tower walls are 15 feet thick, made of carved basalt, and studded with arrow slits. The towers on the hold's lower level (areas B2a, B2b, and B3) stand 60 feet high, while those on the hold's upper level

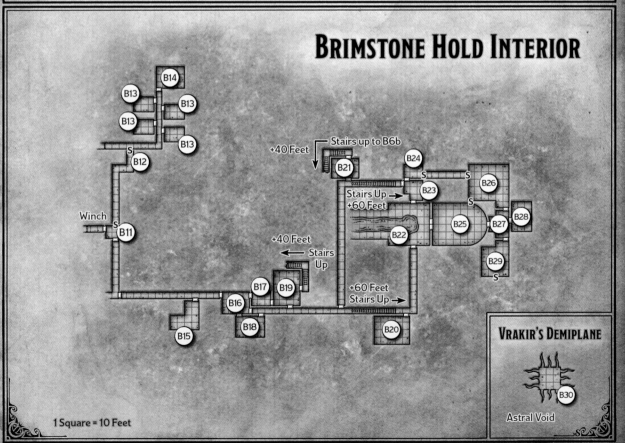

BRIMSTONE HOLD

Lava River

N
W · E
S

High Rock Platform

B9

B9

+40 Feet

Rock Wall

To B21

B6a

To B22

Lava
Falls

To B13

Winch

+40 Feet

Low Rock Platform

B3

B4

To B11

Cranes

B7

B10

To B19

+20 Feet

B6a

B2b

B2a

To B15

B6

B6b

B2

B5

+40 Feet

To B21

B6b

Rock Wall

Stone Bridge

B1

B2a

B8

Lava River

BRIMSTONE HOLD INTERIOR

B14

B13

B13

B13

B13

S

B12

Winch

S

B11

Stairs up to B6b

+40 Feet

B21

B24

S

B26

Stairs Up
+60 Feet

B23

S

B25

B27

B28

B22

+40 Feet

Stairs
Up

B29

S

B17

B19

B16

+60 Feet
Stairs Up

B18

B15

B20

VRAKIR'S DEMIPLANE

B30

Astral Void

1 Square = 10 Feet

MIKE SCHLEY

(areas B8 and B9) are 80 feet high. Towers have interior floors every 20 feet, with stone stairs along the inside walls leading between floors. Tower doors shown on the map allow access from ground level. All towers also have doors that open onto the walkways of adjoining curtain walls, as well as trapdoors that open onto the towers' roofs.

DENIZENS

The erinyes, duergar, and salamanders that defend the hold are united by their loyalty to Vrakir, but each group otherwise disdains the others. The defenders are slow to assist or seek assistance from members outside their own group.

Any fights or suspicious activities in the hold are reported to the **efreeti** Jarazoun, who places the defenders on high alert. Even if Vrakir is at the hold, the defenders bring their reports to Jarazoun first, allowing him to deal with any trouble himself rather than risk Vrakir's ire. While on high alert, the hold's inhabitants can't be surprised, and Jarazoun responds personally to any further reports of trouble, arriving after 1 minute with two **salamanders** from area B20. After 24 hours with no incidents, the hold goes off high alert.

VISITORS

Klax's traders and Vrakir himself are visitors rather than full-time occupants. You can determine whether Vrakir and the traders are present by rolling a d10 and a d20. A result of 1 or 2 on the d10 indicates that Vrakir is present. A result of 1 or 2 on the d20 indicates that Klax and her crew are present.

Alternatively, you can decide that Vrakir is either present or absent depending on how challenging you want the heist to be. The efreeti keeps his own schedule, and not even his most trusted servants know when or where he will appear next.

BRIMSTONE HOLD LOCATIONS

The following locations are keyed to map 13.2.

B1: BRIDGE

> A broad stone bridge spans the fiery river, its arches luridly lit from below. Three-foot-high barriers line the causeway's edges, funneling travelers toward the gatehouse of Vrakir's imposing fortress.

The bridge crosses the lava river at its narrowest point, spanning 300 feet and rising 30 feet above the river's surface. Constructed of heavy basalt blocks, the bridge's piers are plated with iron.

B2: GATEHOUSE

> Two mighty towers of black stone flank the fortress's iron gate, while a third tower looms behind it. Fiery orange banners hang from the towers' parapets, rippling in the plumes of heat that rise off the river of lava.

The banners are 20 feet long and emblazoned with Vrakir's symbol—a crown encircling the branches of a tree wreathed in flame—as well his motto, *atka ignari* (Ignan for "all shall burn").

Two **erinyes** are stationed on the rooftops of the towers closest to the bridge. If the characters approach the gatehouse and give a sound reason for being here, the erinyes open the way (see "Doors" and "Portcullises" below), escort the characters to area B10, and announce their presence to the salamanders in area B22 before returning to their posts.

When the hold is on high alert, a third **erinyes** from area B15 takes up position in the gatehouse's rear tower.

Doors. The entrances from areas B1 and B4 are each protected by an iron double door that stands 20 feet high. The doors are held shut with interlocking iron bars that can be levered up or down as an action from the first floors of the adjoining towers.

Lifting the bars from within the central yard of area B2 requires a successful DC 15 Strength (Athletics) check, while bursting the gates from area B1 or B4 requires a successful DC 25 Strength (Athletics) check. Any Medium or smaller creature attempting to force open one of these doors has disadvantage on its ability check to do so.

Portcullises. The gatehouse's portcullises are so large that they each require two winches to operate, one on the second floor of each adjoining tower, and the two winches must be operated simultaneously. For each winch, it takes 3 actions to raise a portcullis or 1 action to lower it.

As an action, a creature can try to lift a portcullis above its head, doing so with a successful a DC 25 Strength (Athletics) check. Any Medium or smaller creature attempting to do so has disadvantage on this check.

B3: PRISON TOWER

> A forbidding tower overlooks the yard below, its toothed parapets etched black against the sky's ruddy glow.

The **erinyes** stationed here carries a *rope of entanglement*, which it uses to ensnare any prisoner who tries to escape.

Gruk-Gruk. Tossed carelessly on the floor of the tower's lowest story is Gruk-Gruk, a rag doll the size of a halfling. It has a goblin's skull for a head. The doll belongs to Yug, the ogre in area B14. The erinyes stole the doll as an act of cruelty.

B4: Prison Yard

> Huge blocks of rough basalt lie scattered about the center of this spacious yard, where ten armored duergar oversee a large number of haggard prisoners. The prisoners are using chisels and mallets to turn the basalt blocks into smaller worked-stone blocks, which are then stacked in piles around the yard's perimeter. The yard's eastern wall is a natural stone cliff, with two entrances carved into the cliff face and secured with heavy iron portcullises.

Eighty prisoners (**commoners**) labor here under the watchful eyes of ten **duergar**.

The duergar pay little mind to anyone they believe to be on legitimate business in the hold. However, they don't allow anyone to communicate with the prisoners unless ordered to by one of the efreet. The duergar issue a stern warning the first time anyone makes unapproved contact with a prisoner, and they turn hostile after a second instance, attempting to subdue and capture the offender.

Most of the prisoners are too fearful to speak with visitors, but one prisoner named Venture (chaotic good, tiefling **gladiator**) tries to get the characters' attention, seeing the party's arrival as a golden opportunity to escape. If the characters smuggle her some weapons, rope, and a grappling hook, Venture agrees to start a prison riot (see "Prison Riot" below).

Portcullises. The passages into the hold's interior are blocked by portcullises. The winch to operate the northern portcullis is accessible from the yard. The winch to operate the southern portcullis is inside the passage leading to area B11. It takes 3 actions to raise a portcullis or 1 action to lower it using the winch. As an action, a creature can try to lift a portcullis above its head, doing so with a successful a DC 20 Strength (Athletics) check.

Prison Riot. If either Venture or the characters start a prison riot, all the duergar from areas B11 and B18 rush to area B4 to quell it. The erinyes in areas B2, B3, and B8 watch in amusement but don't intervene. If the characters aren't present, it takes the duergar 10 minutes to subdue the rioting prisoners.

If the characters return to the prison yard after obtaining the *Book of Vile Darkness*, the prisoners start another riot and overcome their captors.

Gruk-Gruk

B5: Inner Yard

> This empty yard is hemmed in by a rocky cliff on its eastern edge. A flight of stairs has been carved into the cliff face leading to the top, while a doorway at the base of the steps is set into the stone.

Behind the door at the base of the stairs is a long tunnel that leads to areas B11 and B15–B19.

B6: Upper Yard

> The large, horseshoe-shaped upper yard wraps around the harbor in its center. Sturdy wooden cranes to the west overlook the quay below, while the eastern side houses small outbuildings. Towering over the eastern edge of the yard is the volcano's ash-covered slope, featuring a giant efreeti face carved from the stone and spewing lava from its mouth.

The upper yard is patrolled by a **young red dragon** named Kalimrax. The dragon guards the fortress against aerial assault, but attacks from the air are few and far between. Kalimrax spends most of her time prowling about the harbor, idly threatening to devour any dockhands working there.

Kalimrax finds her task incredibly dull and looks to the hold's occasional visitors to provide some interest. The dragon interrogates newcomers, hoping to hear something other than the same tales of conquest Vrakir's armies always tell. A character who succeeds on a DC 15 Charisma (Performance) check can command Kalimrax's rapt attention for up to 1 hour. The dragon threatens to eat any character who fails to hold her interest.

Kalimrax attacks any character she sees trying to enter the hold by stealth or by force, but she doesn't pursue characters into the hold's interior. If reduced to 50 hit points or fewer, Kalimrax retreats to her lair in area B10.

Cranes. Three large, wooden cranes extend over the harbor. They are used to lift cargo unloaded from the boats in area B7 to the upper yard for transport to areas B19 and B21. The cranes' platforms also provide the only means for dockhands and traders to move between area B6 and area B7, 40 feet below. A creature can use an action to raise or lower the crane's platform 5 feet. Each crane can support up to 5,000 pounds.

Outbuildings. The yard's four outbuildings have 2-foot-thick walls of basalt blocks and 10-foot-high ceilings roofed with slate. The smaller buildings (area B6a) are littered with ropes and loading hooks and contain stairwells that lead to the hold's main storage rooms (areas B19 and B21). The larger buildings (area B6b) each contain a dozen cots and serve as quarters for the hold's visitors, most frequently Klax and her traders.

If the characters arrive at the hold while the traders are present, one of the larger buildings is inhabited by Klax (chaotic neutral **cambion**) and eight traders (**commoners**). The traders are indifferent to the characters, although Klax is protective of her business arrangement with Jarazoun and turns in the party to the hold's defenders if the characters seem likely to threaten that arrangement.

B7: Harbor

> At the stronghold's center is a harbor of lava connected by an inlet to the main river. A quay along the harbor's western edge is lined with iron mooring posts, while wooden cranes tower overhead. At the eastern edge, a stream of lava cascades into the harbor from the cliff above.

The harbor is primarily used by Klax's traders to make their regular supply runs. The traders unload their cargo onto the platforms suspended by the cranes, allowing for transport to the yard above.

Boats. If the characters arrive while the traders are at the hold, two boats are moored at the quay. The boats are 30 feet long and 10 feet wide, with wooden decks and iron-plated hulls fashioned to resemble dragon turtles. The boats are magically immune to fire damage and remain cool to the touch, even when floating in lava. Each boat has six flipper-shaped iron paddles protruding from its hull, which are controlled by levers on the boat's deck.

B8: Cliff Towers

These two towers stand at opposite ends of the fortress's high rock platform. Each one can be described as follows:

> This imposing tower is buttressed by the stone cliffs of the stronghold's upper level. Its battlements have a commanding view of the hold's upper and lower yards.

One **erinyes** is on guard in each of these towers, occasionally leaving the tower to walk the battlements of the adjoining curtain walls. Each erinyes is hostile to anyone attempting to climb the outer walls but is otherwise indifferent to the goings-on in the yards below.

B9: Harbor Towers

> Two mighty towers flank the entrance to the fortress's harbor. A great steel chain stretches between the towers, barring access from the lava river beyond.

Two **erinyes** guard access to the harbor, one in each tower. These guards are hostile to anyone attempting to enter or leave the hold via the river without Jarazoun's approval. The erinyes admit Klax and her traders after a cursory inspection of their cargo, although the erinyes become suspicious if the traders aren't following their usual schedule.

Each tower contains a large winch for raising and lowering the chain that controls access to the harbor. The chain is effective only if both sides are raised, and it takes 3 actions to fully raise or lower one end of the chain.

B10: Efreeti Face

> Carved into the slope of the volcano is the enormous visage of a scowling efreeti. A stream of lava issues from the efreeti's open mouth, falling to the yard below, where it pools before spilling into the harbor.

The efreeti's mouth is the main entrance to the hold's interior and is primarily used by Vrakir and Jarazoun, who can easily navigate its 20-foot elevation above the yard. A steel chain ladder coiled in a corner of the efreeti's mouth can be lowered to allow access for non-flying creatures.

Above the carved efreeti face, a fissure in the volcano's slope leads into a small cave not visible from the stronghold below. Kalimrax lairs here, returning for a few hours every evening to rest and check on her hoard, which consists of the plunder Vrakir allows her to take as payment for her service.

Treasure. Kalimrax's lair contains 14,213 sp, 7,029 gp, 923 pp, eighteen gemstones (500 gp each), a fan made of couatl feathers (1,250 gp), a *figurine of wondrous power* (bronze griffon), and a *mace of terror*.

B11: Guard Room

This small chamber is lit by a glowing brazier and furnished only with a pair of iron stools sitting next to a stone block that serves as a crude table.

Two **duergar** are always on guard here. They react with suspicion toward the characters, as visitors don't usually come through this area, and become hostile if the characters attempt to force their way to or from area B4.

Secret Door. A pressure plate in the corner of the floor behind the brazier opens a secret door leading to area B12.

B12: Secret Passage

This hidden corridor has a secret door at each end of it.

> The floor of this darkened corridor is coated with a fine layer of black dust, and the air is stale and hot.

The duergar created this passage to access the cells in case the prisoners ever managed to take control of the prison yard. The passage has never seen use, and Brimstone Hold's other defenders don't know it exists. The secret doors at each end are readily visible from inside the hallway and don't require an ability check to find.

B13: Prison Cells

> The door to this chamber bolts from the outside. Inside, bundles of rags have been gathered into squalid sleeping pallets.

At night, twenty prisoners (**commoners**) sleep in these cells. During the day, the cells are empty.

B14: Large Prison Cell

> The door to this chamber bolts from the outside. Inside, a pile of sackcloth and bones lies in one corner of the otherwise bare room, and the air is thick with the stench of filth. Sobbing on the filthy mound is an ogre wearing a loincloth.

A chaotic neutral **ogre** named Yug occupies this cell. For the past three days, Yug has been confined here for breaking a duergar's arm in anger over the theft of Gruk-Gruk, a crude rag doll.

Yug is initially wary of the characters but becomes talkative if they seem sympathetic to his plight. If the characters find and return Gruk-Gruk to Yug, the ogre happily aids them in any way he can.

B15: Erinyes Barracks

> The floor of this chamber is covered in smoldering cinders, heating the room like an oven. Several chain hammocks are slung from the walls.

Three **erinyes** lounge in their hammocks here, resting between shifts patrolling the walls. The erinyes are immediately suspicious of the characters, as visitors don't usually come here. Unless the characters provide a compelling reason for their intrusion and succeed on a DC 20 Charisma (Deception or Persuasion) check, the erinyes try to capture the characters for questioning.

B16: Common Room

> This room is furnished with two long trestle tables and several benches. Tin plates and cups are set on one of the tables next to several barrels with iron spigots jutting from their sides.

The duergar take their meals here. All but one of the barrels contain water. The last barrel holds dregs of sour beer.

B17: Kitchen

> A large iron stove occupies one side of this room, while a workbench stands against the opposite wall. Sacks of flour and baskets of tubers are piled in the corners. Two gray-skinned dwarves use iron spoons to sip from a stewpot, then begin arguing.

Two **duergar** are busily preparing the hold's next meal: tuber stew. They are arguing about how spicy the stew ought to be. If the duergar notice the party, they assume the characters are members of Klax's crew and start instructing them where to put the new supplies. Only if the characters ignore the cooks' instructions do the duergar become suspicious, attacking while shouting to the duergar in area B18 if the characters can't justify their presence.

Treasure. The duergar keep a vial of midnight tears poison (see the *Dungeon Master's Guide*) among the pots of seasoning on the table.

B18: Duergar Barracks

> This chamber is lined with stone bunks that protrude from the walls. Two iron chests stand in the back corners of the room.

Six **duergar** are sleeping here on the stone slabs that serve as their beds. They wear their armor and keep their weapons within arm's reach. The sound of normal movement doesn't wake them, but they are roused by the sounds of battle or other loud noises in areas B15–B19.

The duergar are alarmed if they wake to find the characters here and shout to the duergar in area B17. They demand the characters explain themselves and attack if the characters attempt to escape without giving an account of their presence.

Treasure. The iron chests are unlocked. Each chest contains ten spare sets of plain, dwarf-sized clothing. One chest also holds a small black pouch containing two eight-sided obsidian dice (50 gp) and a dagger with a malachite blade (250 gp). The other chest also contains a *potion of resistance* (fire) in a vial made from a hollowed-out dragon's fang.

B19: Storeroom

> Boxes, barrels, crates, and sacks are piled high in this chamber.

This is the fortress's primary storage area. Most of Klax's deliveries are carried here by the dockhands via the staircase from the outbuilding above (area B6a). The supplies primarily consist of food, water, timber, rope, and raw iron.

B20: Salamander Barracks

> The floor of this room is coated in solidified lava that resembles the undulations of waves on the sea. Lounging between the lava formations are two serpentine creatures with heat ripples and smoke rising from their bodies.

Two **salamanders** rest in these barracks, their bodies coiled to nestle into the depressions in the solidified lava. If the characters aren't escorted by other members of the hold, the salamanders assume the characters are a threat and attack immediately.

B21: Storeroom

> Boxes and crates are neatly stacked along one wall of this chamber, while iron braziers and spare furniture line the opposite wall.

This storage area contains supplies for the efreet's chambers. The items are delivered by Klax's crew via the staircase from the outbuilding above (area B6a).

Treasure. Among the supplies are twelve 20-pound crates of fine silk (1,000 gp each) and a small chest containing six blocks of rich incense (250 gp each).

B22: Antechamber

> A fountain of lava wells up from the floor of this antechamber, pooling in the room's center before running along a broad channel cut in the stone tile. A walkway along the pool's edge grants access to a grand set of brass doors behind the fountain, as well as to smaller iron doors along the side walls.
>
> Coiled before the brass doors are two serpentine creatures clutching spears. Floating ten feet above them is a spherical creature with a large central eye and ten eyestalks.

Two **salamanders** stand guard here along with a **beholder** known as the Eye of the Efreet. These creatures are hostile unless the characters arrive with an escort, in which case the characters are directed to area B23 to make an appointment to see Jarazoun. Once the characters proceed to area B25, the salamanders accompany them and remain there for the duration of their visit.

B23: Administrative Office

> The walls of this office are decorated with paintings depicting an array of otherworldly landscapes. At its center stands a heavy desk engraved with grotesque, fiendish figures, and seated at the desk is a slender, bipedal creature wearing a red robe, a sparkly ring, and a fez. The creature has the head and tawny fur of a fox.

JARAZOUN THE EFREETI

Nebukath the **arcanaloth** sees to the hold's administrative tasks. Nebukath is initially indifferent toward the characters and presumes they have come seeking an audience with Jarazoun. The arcanaloth languidly informs the characters that the efreeti is too busy to meet with them.

If the characters reveal their true purpose, Nebukath perks up and excitedly offers to aid them. The arcanaloth knows the routines of all the hold's inhabitants and can provide the characters with an alibi or escort if they need one. However, the terms of its magically binding employment contract prevent Nebukath from taking direct action against Vrakir, his forces, or his property (for example, by attacking the hold's defenders).

If Nebukath discovers the party's purpose, the arcanaloth follows them closely, waiting for the characters to steal the *Book of Vile Darkness*. Once the book is in the party's possession, the terms of Nebukath's contract no longer prevent the arcanaloth from seizing the artifact, and Nebukath attempts to steal the book from the characters.

Treasure. The office's three paintings are worth 100 gp each, or five times that to a collector of planar antiquities. Nebukath wears a *ring of telekinesis* and a platinum brooch set with tourmaline (1,000 gp).

B24: Nebukath's Chamber

> In this room, a bookshelf and armchair stand alongside a simple bed fitted with silken sheets.

When Nebukath isn't working in area B23, the arcanaloth rests here. A small brass bell attached to a rope in area B26 alerts Nebukath anytime they're needed by the efreet.

Secret Door. A creature can open the secret door leading to area B26 by pulling on a false book on the lowest rack of the bookshelf, which causes the adjoining section of wall to swing open (the door can be opened normally from the other side).

Treasure. Among the arcanaloth's library is a volume entitled *The Blood War*, which describes the unending conflict between devils of the Nine Hells and the demons of the Abyss. The tome is worth 500 gp to a collector. Scribbled in the margin of one page is the sequence for a teleportation circle that leads to Avernus, the first layer of the Nine Hells.

B25: Audience Chamber

> Pillars of writhing flame wrought in stone hold up the vaulted ceiling of this great hall. In the center, a magnificent, gilded throne gleams like the sun itself, reflecting the light of the roaring braziers at its foot.

If he hasn't been encountered and defeated elsewhere, the **efreeti** Jarazoun sits on the throne, acting as master of Brimstone Hold in Vrakir's absence. Jarazoun has little patience for the business of running a stronghold and leaves most of the decision-making to Nebukath. The stronghold's denizens see Jarazoun for the petty tyrant he is, but they obey him out of fear of his patron, Vrakir.

If the characters come before Jarazoun posing as visitors with legitimate business at the hold, the efreeti treats them with indifference. He enjoys lording his power over petitioners and denies any requests the characters make dismissively, relenting only if plied with substantial wealth or flattery—a very rare magic item, 10,000 gp worth of treasure, or a successful DC 25 Charisma (Persuasion) check suffices.

If the characters insult Jarazoun or reveal their true purpose, the efreeti becomes hostile and shouts for the salamanders in area B22 to apprehend the characters and imprison them in area B13. If the party resists, Jarazoun fights desperately, fearing Vrakir's wrath if the characters were to escape.

Secret Door. A secret door hidden in the north wall leads to area B26.

Treasure. Jarazoun wears a gold chain of office studded with fire opals (5,000 gp) and eight gold rings set with precious stones (250 gp each). He also carries the key to area B28.

B26: LOUNGE

> The walls of this chamber are draped with silk, and its floor is festooned with cushions. A fountain in the room's center burbles with ruby-red liquid, while an ornately wrought brazier stands in the corner.

Jarazoun entertains favored guests here. The ruby liquid is firewine imported from the City of Brass. Any creature that drinks the wine gains 15 temporary hit points. The creature must finish a long rest before it can gain this benefit again.

Secret Doors. A secret door in the west wall leads to area B24, and a secret door in one corner of the south wall leads to area B25.

Treasure. The brazier is a *brazier of commanding fire elementals*. Its command word, *ilkath keri* (Ignan for "blaze brightly"), is inscribed along the brazier's inside rim.

B27: VESTIBULE

> Woven carpets line this corridor, which has doors leading in all four directions. Two large statues of efreet warriors stand sentinel here, one at either end of the corridor.

The doors to areas B28 and B29 are both locked. Jarazoun carries the key to area B28, while Vrakir carries the key to area B29. As an action, a character can use thieves' tools to try to pick either lock, doing so with a successful DC 20 Dexterity check.

Statues. The statues are two **stone golems** that are normally quiescent and don't react to the characters' presence. However, the golems are magically attuned to the door to area B29 and become hostile if a creature attempts to open the door by any means other than using Vrakir's key. A character who succeeds on their ability check to pick the lock by 10 or more avoids triggering the golems. Entering area B29 by using magic (such as the *passwall* spell) to bypass the door entirely doesn't trigger the golems.

B28: JARAZOUN'S CHAMBER

> A large bed with brass posts and silk curtains dominates this chamber. In the corner, a lyre engraved with elaborate figures leans on the wall next to a cushioned stool.

Jarazoun is usually here when he isn't conducting business in area B25 or entertaining visitors in area B26.

Treasure. The lyre is an *instrument of the bards* (Cli lyre) decorated with carvings of phoenixes. Jarazoun fancies himself a musician but is unable to attune to the instrument.

B29: VRAKIR'S CHAMBER

> The luxurious appointments of this palatial bedchamber are at odds with its back wall. There, scorch marks and cracked masonry radiate from a grotesque face carved into the stone, its forehead set with a blood-red gem. Sitting on a desk off to one side is a black tome, its cover emblazoned with fell iconography.

The tome resembles the *Book of Vile Darkness* but is actually a trained **mimic**. Any character who examines the tome and succeeds on a DC 20 Intelligence (Arcana) check recognizes it as a fraud. The mimic attacks any creature that touches or attacks it.

The room's back wall appears solid but is the anchor for a magical doorway to area B30: the demiplane where Vrakir keeps the real *Book of Vile Darkness*. Anyone examining the wall using *detect magic* can see the outline of the door. The scorch marks and cracked masonry are due to the book's corrupting influence, which seeps out every time the doorway is opened.

The key to opening the door is the gemstone set in the wall carving. The gem is trapped with a 6th-level *glyph of warding* spell. The glyph casts *disintegrate* on any creature that touches the gem without speaking Vrakir's motto: *atka ignari*. While touching the gem, a creature can take an action to open the door to area B30 as if the creature had cast the *demiplane* spell; this causes the face in the wall to stretch its mouth wide as a shimmering gray portal appears within. Removing the gem from the wall causes the doorway to disappear, trapping anything in area B30 in the demiplane until the gem is replaced or someone else accesses the room with a *demiplane* spell.

Treasure. If removed from the wall, the gem continues to radiate magic but doesn't otherwise function. It is worth 5,000 gp.

B30: Vrakir's Demiplane

> On the floor of this otherwise empty room rests an open book, its ancient pages rustling ominously despite the lack of breeze. The flagstones around it are charred and cracked, and the room's walls are veined with narrow fissures that disappear into darkness.

If the characters had a relatively easy time getting here, add two invisible **nycaloths** as guards. The nycaloths are mercenaries hired by Vrakir to protect the *Book of Vile Darkness*, and their *invisibility* spells end when they attack.

Treasure. The *Book of Vile Darkness* is so blasphemous that its mere presence erodes the demiplane Vrakir made to contain it. Review the artifact's description in the *Dungeon Master's Guide*, then replace its Random Properties with the following preset ones:

Circle of Death. While attuned to the book, you can cast *circle of death* (save DC 20) from it as an action. After you cast the spell, roll a d6. On a roll of 1–5, you can't use this property again until the next dawn.

Condition Immunities. While attuned to the book, you can't be charmed or frightened.

Evil Presence. The book houses an evil spirit that is hostile toward you. When you become attuned to the book, the spirit tries to leave the book and enter your body. If you fail a DC 20 Charisma saving throw, it succeeds, and you become an NPC under the DM's control until the intruding spirit is banished using magic such as the *dispel evil and good* spell. The banished spirit returns to the book.

Conclusion

After the characters escape Brimstone Hold, they might find themselves pursued by Nebukath, Vrakir, or both. The former is focused solely on obtaining the *Book of Vile Darkness*, while the latter seeks vengeance against the characters regardless of

The *Book of Vile Darkness*

what happens to the artifact. Meanwhile, the book has its own designs, and it might subvert the aims of the party's patron or find its way back into the party's possession if it senses a character is ripe for corruption.

For the Golden Vault

If the characters are working for the Golden Vault, they must deliver the *Book of Vile Darkness* to their contact. Once they do, the organization rewards the characters with a very rare magic item of their choice (subject to your approval) as payment. The item is delivered to the characters the next day.

Further Adventures

Recovering the *Book of Vile Darkness* could be the first in a series of adventures revolving around the party's efforts to contain or destroy the artifact—efforts that might involve courting the aid of powerful celestials, unearthing ancient spells of binding, or undergoing trials of purification.

Meanwhile, even without the book, Vrakir and his armies remain a threat. The characters might have to fend off a reprisal by the efreeti's forces before traveling to the Elemental Plane of Fire to deal with Vrakir himself.

INDEX